Felix is a vampire—a fierce creature of the night who strikes ~~~~~~ the hearts of everyone unlucky enough to become his prey. Or at least, that's what he thought was true, until he met John. John is completely unimpressed with Felix, much to his dismay. Felix becomes fixated on proving his ferocity to John—and when that doesn't work, he strives to make any impression on him at all.

John is a witch, and as all witches know, vampires are notoriously stupid creatures who only have the power to hurt those who fear them. Besides, he's under a curse much more frightening than any vampire. Felix's desperate attempts to impress him annoy John at first, but gradually, they become sort of endearing. Because of his curse, John has pushed everyone in his life away. But Felix can't be hurt, so there's no harm in letting him hang around.

Felix is technically dead. John has nothing left to live for. But together, they might have a shot at life.

This dark and witty vampire romance for adults is complete at 100,000 words, with no cliffhanger. Despite some dark twists and turns, it ends with a solid HEA.

A NineStar Press Publication

Published by NineStar Press
P.O. Box 91792,
Albuquerque, New Mexico, 87199 USA.
www.ninestarpress.com

Curses, Foiled Again

ISBN: 978-1-947904-39-2

Printed in the USA
First Edition
November, 2017

Also available in eBook, ISBN: 978-1-947904-38-5

Warning: This book contains sexually explicit content, which may only be suitable for mature readers, blood play, and graphic depictions of violence and murder.

Curses, Foiled Again

Again

Sera Trevor

To my husband, Brian, who shares my heart, and to my writing partner Gillian, who shares my brain.

Acknowledgements

I would also like to give special thanks to my betas, Kevin and Susanna, who provided invaluable feedback. Thank you!

One: The Witch Boys of Sunset Boulevard

SOMEONE SMELLED DELICIOUS.

Felix really ought to have been sated. He had fed that night already, but in spite of his satiety, the new aroma tempted him like nothing before. It was the same dark tang that normally inspired his appetite, but with a sweet note buried in the scent—like an orange at the peak of its sweetness, right on the cusp of rotting. It didn't take him long to discover the source of the aroma; it was a young man in a hooded sweatshirt, making his way down Sunset Boulevard. He walked with remarkable confidence for being on his own at two o'clock in the morning. Felix grinned. He liked the confident ones; their shock when confronted with the likes of him was always amusing.

He raced ahead of the young man with superhuman swiftness, jumping in front of him with his fangs bared. Felix loved this part, right before the attack—the moment when human confusion and animal terror mixed together as his victim realized their fate. Any moment now, he would scream. Or at least, he would try to. By then it would be too late.

The young man jumped and inhaled sharply at Felix's sudden appearance. But once he'd given Felix a good once-over, he let out his breath in a relieved puff. There was no screaming, no futile attempt to flee or freezing in terror. In fact, it was Felix who froze in place, confused by the young man's strange reaction.

As Felix tried to gather his wits to think of what to do next, the young man brushed past him and continued on. Felix shook himself out of his muddle. He brought a hand up to his mouth, feeling to make sure his fangs were still bared. They were. Perhaps the young man hadn't seen him clearly; the lighting here was particularly poor, and mortal vision was not very good.

He zipped ahead of the young man and jumped out at him again, making sure he was directly under a streetlight. He raised his arms and hissed for good measure.

"You can stop doing that," the young man said. "I'm not afraid of you."

"Oh really?" Felix sneered, although in honesty he was taken aback. "We'll see if your bravery lasts when I sink my fangs into your yielding flesh!"

He attempted to pounce, but nothing happened. He tried again, but his limbs just wouldn't cooperate. As he stood there in confusion, the young man stepped around him and continued walking.

Once Felix had collected himself, he set out after the young man again, this time trotting beside him. The young man paid him no attention.

"Have you put a spell on me?"

"No."

"Then why can't I attack you?"

"Because I'm not afraid of you," he said. He wasn't even looking at Felix. "Vampires can only attack people who fear them."

Felix scoffed. "That can't be true."

"Think about it. Can you ever remember a time when a potential victim wasn't afraid of you?"

"Not that I recall."

"Then if you only ever confronted people who were afraid of you, how would you have found out you couldn't attack someone who wasn't?"

Felix turned that over in his mind. It *did* make a certain amount of sense.

They continued to walk together. Felix tried to startle him a few more times, hoping it would raise enough fear for Felix to strike, but it didn't work. The young man's face remained expressionless, as if Felix weren't even there. He was a remarkably good-looking fellow, with sandy-blond hair and blue eyes. He was so pleasant to look at that Felix eventually ceased his efforts to frighten him in favor of simply gazing at him. His sweatshirt was not zipped all the way, but the T-shirt underneath was too baggy to give even a suggestion of the body it concealed. He wished the young man would take it off, or at the very least remove the hood.

After some time, they came to an apartment building. The young man approached one of the doors on the first floor. "Well, I would say it was nice meeting you, but it wasn't, really," he said as he took out his keys. "Good night." He unlocked his door.

Felix blocked the door with his body, preventing the young man from entering. "You've led me straight to where you live," he said in his scariest voice. "I could strike when you least expect it, in your very home. Certainly that will frighten you enough for me to attack!"

"Vampires can't enter a home unless you invite them. Did you really think I wouldn't know that?"

Felix scowled. "How do you know all this?"

"None of your business. Now unless you want to stand around here until dawn, get your hand off my door and go away."

"Maybe I do want to stand around here," Felix said. "You can't make me leave."

The young man rolled his eyes. "Fine." He leaned on the wall a few steps away from the door and took a pack of cigarettes and a silver lighter out of the pocket of his hooded sweatshirt. He perched a cigarette between his pink lips and lit it.

Felix remained where he was. The young man didn't even spare him a glance as he smoked his cigarette, gazing instead at the smoke as it left his lips and dissipated into the night air. Felix felt annoyed; surely he was more interesting than a cloud of smoke!

"Why are you out alone so late?" Felix asked. "While you may not be afraid of vampires, you are still vulnerable to mortal attackers." An idea flashed through Felix's mind. "What if I got a gun? Would you be afraid of me then?"

The young man rolled his eyes again. "Why are you so intent on killing me?"

"I don't want to kill you. I want to drink your blood."

"And that's not the same thing?"

Felix had to think about it. "No, I don't think it is," he said. "It's true that my victims swoon, but I'm fairly certain they survive."

The young man raised an eyebrow. "You don't know for sure?"

"There isn't much reason for me to linger after I've fed, is there?"

"I guess not." He took another long drag of his cigarette. "So why do you want to drink my blood? You've already fed tonight."

Felix looked at him with surprise. "How did you know that?"

"You've got blood on your chin."

Felix wiped his face with the hand that wasn't holding the door shut. Sure enough, it came away red. "Doesn't that make you feel at least a little scared?" he asked plaintively.

The young man finished his cigarette with one final inhale, dropped the butt on the street, and then stubbed it out with his toe. "Sorry to say, but it takes a lot to make me feel anything at all." He pulled out his pack of cigarettes again and took another one. "Would you like one?"

The young man offered the pack and his lighter. Felix stared at the cigarettes and then back at his face. The young man put his hand forward farther. "Go on. Take one."

Felix frowned, wondering at the young man's sudden generosity. John stood just out of reach, so Felix had to step closer to him to accept the pack and the lighter. Felix's fingers brushed over the skin of the young man's hand. It was so warm.

"Thank you," Felix said, a little dazed.

"No problem." The young man's smile was dazzling.

Felix smiled back and turned his attention to the pack of cigarettes, pulling one out and readying the lighter—

—and then, quick as lightning, the young man slipped inside his apartment and slammed the door shut behind him.

"*Goddamnit!*" Felix shouted after him, pounding on the door. "Come back out here!"

There was no answer. Felix stomped around in a circle, cursing. Once he composed himself, he went back to the door. "Well, I'm keeping your cigarettes! And your lighter! And you'll never get them back!"

This also failed to get a response. Felix examined the lighter. On one side there was a figure etched into the metal: a dragon, or a demon. Some mythical creature, at any rate. On the other side, there was an engraving: *To John. Love, Rob.*

A gift, then. Perhaps he could use its sentimental nature to his advantage. "I really mean it!" he shouted. "I'll throw this lighter in the sewer!"

Still no response.

With a huff, he zipped away. His preternatural speed meant he only had to travel a few moments before he reached the estate in Beverly Hills where he resided with his sister, Cat, and her husband, Richard. The sprawling wrought iron gates were shut, but unlike the young man's closed door, the gates posed no barrier to him. He launched himself upward and over the curled letters that spelled out the name of the estate: HAPPY ENDINGS. Under it was the image of a boar, cast in iron.

The sign's rusted state made the promise of the words ring a bit false. Nevertheless, it was the only home he had, and he had no desire to meet the dawn.

THE MANSION WAS dark and silent when Felix entered. His footsteps echoed through the marble foyer as he made his way to the stairs. Normally, he would go straight to his room after such a feed, but the events of the night had him riled. He decided to seek out Cat, although she was in torpor the last time he checked. She might be cross with him for waking her up; Cat held no great love for the waking world. But he had something interesting to tell her, which was a rarity. Perhaps it would put her in a better humor.

He went into her room, which was decorated in bold Art Deco patterns of black and gold. There was a grand vanity in one corner of the room with an equally impressive bureau in the other. An enormous television took up most of the south wall. Most impressive was the four-poster bed, surrounded by thick black and gold curtains that were drawn.

As he made his way to the bed, he passed bookshelves and end tables that held remembrances from her days of movie stardom long past. There was the veil from her debut role in *The Deathly Lover*; a ruby encrusted dagger from *Hatshepsut: Queen of Egypt*; the famous mermaid photo spread promoting her movie *Mermaids of the Blue Lagoon*; and of course her crowning achievement: the Oscar, won for her role as Ophelia in 1948, which was her last role. Her husband hadn't been able to coax her into another role after that. It was a source of much contention between them. He'd attempted to recreate his past successes with other starlets, but his greatness as a producer declined, until they both deteriorated into mere memories of an age past.

Felix parted the curtains of the bed and climbed in. Cat lay there in her silk nightgown, with a frilly pink sleeping mask covering her eyes. Her dark hair was twisted up in curling papers.

"Cat," he whispered. She was usually rather cranky when she was woken, so he tried to be as gentle as possible. He gave her a little nudge. No response.

He lifted the mask and peeked at her face. Despite the fact that they'd been undead for over a century, it still bothered him to see her so pale and still. He wondered if she felt the same way when she saw him in torpor.

"Cat," he said a little more forcefully. When that still didn't get a response out of her, he grabbed her by the shoulders and shook her. "*Cat!*"

She shot up suddenly, letting out a screech. It startled Felix so badly that he fell off the bed. As he got to his feet, his sister threw the curtain open. She tried to remove her sleeping mask, but it got caught on her curlers.

"What's happened?" she asked, her voice panicked. "Are you all right?"

Felix sat down beside her and helped untangle the mask. "Nothing's happened. I'm all right."

She crossed her arms. "Then why have you awoken me?" The concern had left her voice, and now that she was unmasked, Felix was subjected to her formidable glare.

Felix rubbed his neck. "Well—I had a very curious encounter."

She gave him a look. "And?"

"And I'd like your opinion on the matter."

"Couldn't you have waited until I had woken up on my own?"

"How much rest do you need? You've been out for nearly three months!"

Cat blinked rapidly. "Three months?" She grabbed the remote control on her nightstand and turned the TV on, switching immediately to the DVR. Her mouth dropped into a silent O as she examined the screen. "I've missed half a season of the *Real Housewives of Beverly Hills*."

"Do you still want me to leave?"

Cat shook herself out of it and turned back to him. "No. You're right. I should get up. Fetch my dressing gown."

Felix went to the bureau and selected a leopard-print robe with large, feathery sleeves and brought it to her. They made their way to the vanity. Two things were unusual about it: the first was that there were two stools rather than one. The second was that there were no mirrors in the frames. While vampires could appear in photographs, they lacked reflections, so mirrors were pointless. They wouldn't have been visible anyway; there were stacks of beauty products piled all over the counter. Cat was a Home Shopping Network enthusiast.

Once she was seated, Cat reached for one of the papers on her head and began to undo it. Felix sat down beside her and reached for a curl as well. Soon her whole head was a mass of silky, dark springs. He'd always helped her with her hair. A long time ago, it had been down to her waist, but she'd cut it all off when she met Richard. It hadn't grown back since.

Cat sorted through the mess on the vanity until she found a brush. "So?" she asked as she brushed the curls. "Tell me about this 'curious encounter.'"

"I met a man I couldn't feed on. Every time I tried to attack him, I found myself frozen in place."

"Now that *is* strange," she said. She held out her hand. "Hair spray."

Felix shifted through the mess until he found a can and handed it to her. "I think he might be a witch."

Cat stopped midspritz. "A witch? Are you sure?"

"I don't know. I couldn't get a straight answer out of him."

"Are you saying you stayed to converse with him after your attack failed?"

"Yes. He told me vampires can't attack anyone who isn't afraid of them."

"Why wasn't he afraid of you? Did you jump out at him from the shadows, catching him completely by surprise?"

"Yes."

"Did you bare your fangs and hiss at him?"

"Of course I did!"

"That is indeed a puzzle." Cat shuffled through the clutter on her vanity. "Now where on earth is that blasted contraption?"

Felix slid the phone out of his pocket. "Here, allow me." He snapped a photo of her and then handed the phone to her.

She examined the picture. Her hair was the height of fashion, circa 1943.

"Satisfactory," she concluded. "Now help me put on my face."

Felix searched around for some foundation, combing through boxes of makeup, anti-aging creams, and blemish concealers, which were useless since she neither aged nor blemished. Why she kept buying them was an enduring mystery. At last he found her favorite foundation and some sponges, and then he set to work.

Felix had always done Cat's makeup. Since she didn't have a reflection, she couldn't do it herself, and any makeup artists would have been very startled at said lack of reflection. She had experimented with using the laptop computer when web cameras were invented, but found them cumbersome. Besides, it was the comfort of the ritual that was important. It wasn't as if she was going anywhere.

Felix did fine with the rouge but fumbled with the eyeliner, accidentally poking her in the eye. She jerked back with a cry. "Watch what you're doing!"

"Sorry."

Cat peered at him. "You're bothered by this mortal, aren't you?"

Felix scoffed. "No!"

Cat just gave him a look.

"All right, yes. He was just so unimpressed! Like I was a stray dog who followed him home."

"Why does it matter? It isn't as if you're starving—I can smell the blood in you."

"It's the principle of the thing. He ought to have been afraid."

"Well, if he is truly a witch, you should count yourself lucky that you escaped with no further rebuke than his disdain. Let it go. Nothing good can come of dealings with witches." She took the phone from his hand and snapped another picture. "I almost look alive, don't I?"

"Almost."

Cat gave him a look. She got up from her stool and glided over to the sofa without a backward glance. Felix sighed inwardly; she could be so sensitive. He joined her on the sofa. Cat turned on the television again and queued up her show. Angry orange women filled the screen. Cat poured them both a glass of wine from a dusty bottle that had been sitting on the coffee table.

"You know, I really don't understand the appeal of this," Felix said after they'd been watching for a while.

"I'm curious about mortal life nowadays," she said. "And this is reality television—not pretend like those other shows." She watched for another few moments. "They don't seem particularly happy, do they?"

"I suppose not."

Cat settled back on the couch and took a long sip of her wine. "That's what I thought."

They'd just finished their second bottle of wine when he felt it—the dawn. He and Cat shivered. Even in their shut-up old manor with dark curtains covering every window that wasn't bricked over, he could feel the sun creeping above the horizon.

He left Cat and went to his own suite, where he peeled off his bloodstained clothes before dropping them on the floor as he made his way to the shower. He laid his forehead against the tile as the warm water washed over him. Afterward, he dried himself, stumbled into bed, and drew the curtains behind him.

But he didn't fall asleep right away. The events of the evening nagged him. He got out of bed and found his discarded trousers, and then reached into the pocket and pulled out John's lighter. He crawled into bed, flicked it open, and lit it. He stared into the dancing flame for a long time as consciousness began to fade. There was something about the way it danced that made him reluctant to put it out. He succumbed to an impulse to wave his finger through the flame. He noticed with triumph it didn't hurt, but the second time he did it, it stung. Strangely, he didn't mind. It was a feeling, even if it was a bad one. It had been quite some time since he'd had a real feeling. He wasn't going to give up on this John yet, although what exactly he wanted and how he was going to get it remained a bit hazy.

He shut the lighter and stuck his smarting finger in his mouth. The lighter was still curled in his other hand as he drifted into darkness.

FELIX WOKE UP suddenly.

He always woke up suddenly, with a great gasp, even though he was long beyond the need to breathe. It was as if all at once, his body forgot it was dead and jolted back into animation, spurred by whatever dark magic made him possible in the first place.

His fist flexed around something in his hand—the lighter. It took him a moment to remember John and that strange night. He knew he hadn't dreamed it, because he didn't dream. Still, the memory felt hazy, as memories often did for him; he was nearly a century and a half old and events tended to blur together. He gripped the lighter firmly. He wouldn't forget this.

He left his room and went to his sister's. She was reclining on her sofa, watching television. In her hands, she held a candy dish full of pills. "Are you up already?" she asked without turning from the television.

Felix stretched. "How long has it been?"

"I don't know. A week or so."

Felix lay back on the sofa, putting his feet on his sister's lap. On the screen, a British man yelled at some people in a restaurant.

"Why is he so angry?" Felix asked.

"Oh, mortals are very particular about food nowadays," Cat said knowledgeably. "If they don't get it exactly right, everyone will be poisoned. He will summon the police if they continue to cook badly, although it hasn't come to that yet, thank goodness."

They watched the show in silence until the commercial break, although Felix didn't pay much attention. He couldn't stop brooding about John.

"Perhaps I simply did not try hard enough to scare him."

Cat turned from the television to look at him. "Who?"

"John. The witch boy."

Cat raised an eyebrow. "'John?' I hadn't realized you had made introductions."

"We didn't, exactly."

"Then how *did* it go, exactly?"

Felix avoided looking his sister in the eye. "It doesn't matter. By the end of this night, he will tremble before me!"

"You can't seriously be considering going after him again?" Cat asked with equal parts disbelief and disdain. "Do you have no sense? Leave him be!"

Felix scowled. "I am not entirely helpless. I am a fierce creature of the night! Besides, he lives in a hovel. If he's a witch of any real power, surely he would keep himself in better comfort."

"Perhaps his seeming poverty is a ruse," she said. "You can't trust witches."

Felix rolled his eyes. "And what, pray tell, do you imagine he'll do to me? If he were powerful enough to end me, I would not be standing here."

"He could ensnare you."

"Yes, well, he'd need my consent for that, wouldn't he? I'm not foolish enough to give it to him."

He regretted his words immediately. Cat always had a lost, wounded look about her, which grew even worse at his unkind words. He knelt in front of her and took her hand in his.

"Forgive me," he said.

She sighed. "For what? Speaking the truth?" She encouraged him to stand up. "If you are determined to be a fool, I suppose I cannot stop you. Just—be careful."

Felix kissed her hand. "I will."

He left her to her television program, retreating to his room to change into some suitably sinister yet also alluring clothing, and then he was off to John's place.

But when he got to John's apartment, he wasn't home. Should he come back later? After a moment's thought, he decided against it. He didn't want to miss any opportunity. He retreated to the bushes across from the building, waiting for his return. Several hours passed. He dozed a little. At last, around two in the morning, he spotted John walking down the street. Felix rubbed his hands together in glee; his campaign of terror could at last begin! Unfortunately, he hadn't thought of what exactly to do yet. Before he could think of anything, John had entered his apartment.

That was fine, though. He would make him feel unsafe in his own home. Felix racked his brain, trying to think of something unsettling. Perhaps he could rattle the windows and run away? He knew he himself would be unsettled by inexplicably rattling windows.

He tapped on the window and then hid in the shadows. A few minutes later, he did it again, and then once more. On his fourth trip, however, the window opened just as he was about to rattle it, and he came face-to-face with John. He froze under John's gaze, distracted for a moment by how very attractive he was. His hair shone like sand on the beach in the summer, and his eyes were dark blue, like stormy ocean waters.

"What are you doing?" John looked more annoyed than unnerved.

Felix felt somewhat deflated, but he soldiered on. "I am stalking you."

"Why?"

"Because I'm a fierce creature of the night."

"So you think you can annoy me into being frightened of you? Is that your plan?"

Felix didn't say anything; when he heard John say it out loud like that, it sounded stupid.

"You're wasting your time. I will never be afraid of you. You have a whole city full of people to terrify. Go bother them." He made to close the window.

"Wait!" Felix said as inspiration struck him. "I will kill your family! All of them!" He crossed his arms smugly. That would surely frighten him.

"I don't have any family."

"Oh." Felix thought for a moment. "What about your friends?"

"I don't have any of those, either."

"What about Rob?"

John did look surprised at that. "Rob? How do you know about—" He stopped. "The lighter. You still have it."

"Yes!" Felix said with a surge of triumph. "I will find and kill your Rob! What do you say to *that*?"

"Rob lives in Cincinnati."

Felix's face fell. He was all out of ideas.

John sighed. "Look, it's nothing personal. You're a scary guy. Really. But even if you did manage to scare me, you wouldn't be able to kill me."

That was a rather extraordinary thing to say. "How can you be so sure of that?"

"I just know."

Felix scoffed. "The arrogance of witches."

John once again looked taken aback. It wasn't the same satisfaction as having him trembling in terror, but Felix would take it. "And how did you know—" He cut off. "Never mind. I'm done with this conversation. Get out of here before I call the police."

Felix laughed. "The police? Do you really think they can stop me? I could kill them easily!"

"You could kill *one* easily, maybe," John said. "But there will probably be two of them, and while you're killing one, the other will shoot you."

"Mere bullets cannot kill me."

"Maybe not, but I bet they can knock you out if they put enough bullets in you. Then it's off to the morgue, where you'll be trapped. If you manage to escape, you'll be stuck in a hospital, and you'll eventually stumble into the sunlight, and then you'll be burned into ashes."

As Felix tried to think of a response to that, John shut the window. "I'm not leaving!" Felix shouted through the glass. "You shall know my wrath! Your life will become a living nightmare!"

He kept it up until he heard the sirens. He scowled; he was certain he could evade capture, but had to admit that the scenario John had laid out was not beyond the realm of possibility. Best to retreat for now.

Two: Half in Love with Easeful Death

THE VAMPIRE WAS still stalking him.

To his credit, he was subtle about it. John probably wouldn't have noticed if he hadn't taken the precaution of creating a warning crystal. He'd enchanted it to turn red in the vicinity of supernatural creatures, and it had glowed each and every night. He'd look casually over his shoulder and see an abnormal shadow out of the corner of his eye, which vanished as soon as he got it in sight.

John figured he'd get bored of it in a few days, but he didn't. By the tenth day, John started to get worried. He swapped shifts with one of the other waiters for a couple of days so he could work during daylight hours—maybe if the vampire never got a glimpse of him, he'd leave him alone. It didn't work. The crystal remained red. Despite himself, he was starting to feel unnerved, which in turn made him annoyed. As if he didn't have enough shit to deal with.

He entered his apartment and bolted the door. His cat, Astray, trotted up to meet him, rubbing against his legs.

"Just a minute," he told her. He went to his dresser and pulled out an old flannel shirt and then put it on. After he was properly dressed for a cuddle session, he sat down on his ratty armchair. The cat jumped up and settled on his shoulders, gnawing at the well-chewed collar as she purred in bliss. She'd been half-starved when he found her—he could have taken her to a shelter, but she was so sweet that he couldn't bring himself to do it. He hadn't meant to get a cat; the whole reason that he moved to LA was to sever connections, to make it easier for things to come. But Astray had wandered into his life and refused to leave, and he didn't have the strength to get rid of her.

"Can I ask you a personal question?" he asked the cat.

Astray ignored him, too lost in the delights of flannel gnawing.

John forged ahead anyway. "I assume that before you got this cushy gig with me, you had to hunt for your food sometimes. Tell me—did you ever develop an interest in one particular mouse?"

Astray ceased her chewing and jumped into his lap. She butted her head against his hand, encouraging him to pet her.

"I bet you didn't," he said as he stroked her. "I'm sure if one mouse got away, you went and found yourself another mouse. You didn't go looking for that same mouse ever again, right? I mean, that would just be crazy. Unprecedented, even."

Astray just closed her eyes in contentment.

John put the cat down for a moment so he could get one of his three-ring binders of spells and lore out of the closet. He returned to the chair, and Astray jumped back on his shoulder as he opened the binder. He flipped through the laminated pages until he found what he was looking for: the curses of vampirism.

Vampires was actually a term for several distinct varieties of undead creatures, each the victim of a different curse. There were the "low" vampires of the Old World. The curse that made them was fairly easy to cast, which meant the results weren't that impressive; they were little more than shambling corpses. The modern age had pretty much driven them to extinction.

Then there were "high" vampires, who were more like what people thought of nowadays, with deadly beauty and incredible power and a lot of existential angst. But they were rare; most of them were witches who cursed themselves into immortality back in the eighteenth century, thinking they'd found a clever way of beating death, only to discover that the side effects did not exactly make for easy living. Lots of them ended up killing themselves, and the ones who didn't tended to keep a low profile. That definitely didn't apply to the creature stalking him.

That left the variety in the middle, who existed because of a misguided curse laid out by the infamous Raimundus Waldram, otherwise known as Mundy the Mad. All powerful magic users tended to be on the eccentric side, but Mundy was out there even for them. Although undeniably powerful, he was also kind of stupid, in the way that power-mad people often are, and the vampiric curse was the crowning "achievement" of his career. It was a piece of magic both immensely powerful and incredibly shortsighted and was held up as an example of exactly what not to do when crafting a spell. For instance, the curse was twenty pages long. The best spells were concise; there was less room for error.

It also helped to have a clear aim in mind, since magic was the focusing of will. Whatever inspired Mundy to write this particular curse was anyone's guess, as was what exactly he hoped to achieve. It began "O Wretched World, the foul domain/Of the wicked and the vain/I would cleanse humanity/Of every villain that I see." It went on in that vein for another page or so; he seemed to have a special hatred for good-looking, wealthy people who, John inferred, did not invite him to their parties. He spent a lot of time insulting his enemies' intellect—a prime example of how loss of focus could have unintended consequences.

After airing his scattered grievances, he got around to the actual cursing, condemning the individuals he found most loathsome: "Living corpses, they will be/Their empty-headed vanity/Will curse them to ne'er know peace/Instead of food, on blood they'll feast." He set up some "torments" John was sure Mundy thought were cleverly ironic. For instance: "These vain monsters will ne'er more see their reflections/And the sun will burn their fair complexions."

He then seemed to have some second thoughts about releasing such monsters upon the public at large, because he added "Only the wicked need fear their bite/Those with conscience clear will escape this blight." The phrasing was obviously unclear—who qualified as "wicked?" Although vampires were often attracted to people with dark auras, there was nothing to really stop them from attacking anyone they wanted to. Because of the lack of clarity, the practical application of the curse worked in reverse—anyone who wasn't afraid was assumed to have a clear conscience, and thus immune to vampiric attack. That was good news for those who were already well informed, but not so good for innocent victims who didn't know any better.

He went on for several more pages, adding in not only some seemingly random weaknesses, such as an allergy to garlic, but also inadvertently gave them superpowers. Most of it was just sloppy wording; he emphasized their "flightiness," which accidentally gave them the powers of flight and speed. He also railed against their "bewitching charms," which gave them the ability to compel people into doing their bidding. Many savvy vampires had coaxed mortals into keeping them in style—that way they had not only a place to escape the sun, but also an unlimited food supply. Not that it would necessarily stop them from going on the prowl. Like house cats who still went after vermin, they couldn't help themselves. It was their nature.

What Mundy failed to realize was that his earlier rants against the subjects of his curse's intellect made it so that vampires were much too vapid to appreciate their supposedly cursed state. And his fixation on their "heartlessness" left them with no compassion for their victims, anyway. Mundy added the provision of immortality under the delusion that it would prolong their torments, but his curse had rendered them so heartless and callous that they were incapable of remorse.

It was all very interesting, but there was nothing in it that gave John any more insight to the strange vampire who had taken a liking to him.

"Is he looking for a new thrall?" he asked out loud. "He's got to realize that witches can't be enthralled." He gave Astray a scratch. "Besides, I'm done with taking in strays. No offense."

Astray did not look offended. She rubbed her head against the hard, pointy corner of the binder and started to chew on it. John took the binder back to the closet. After a moment's thought, he reached for a sketchbook and pencil. He didn't sketch as much as he used to; it was something he did back when he had feelings to work through, and he tried very hard not to have feelings anymore.

He sat back down on the bed and opened the sketchbook. Carefully, he brought his pencil up and began to draw. The vampire was tall—at least four inches taller than John, who was not *that* diminutive at five foot nine. John drew the figure looking down, his arms held up as if he were about to pounce. Dark hair framed his face, blocking everything but his sneering lips and protruding fangs. Oh yes, very scary. He was an A-plus loomer. He drew a pair of high heels on him, because it annoyed him when people were tall for no reason.

John turned the page and began drawing again, this time bringing his mind to when they'd been standing in front of his apartment. He drew the vampire in portrait now, with his shoulders slumped and his expression no longer drawn into a sneer, but instead slack with bafflement. John tried to remember the details of his face. Unnaturally smooth skin—no hint of a beard. High cheekbones, a long sloping nose. His lips formed a perfect cupid's bow when his fangs weren't out. His eyes were the stand-out, though—unusually round, almost childlike. He'd actually seemed—well, cute. And there was something about him that seemed vaguely familiar, although he couldn't quite put a finger on it.

With a sigh, he closed the book. That had been more confusing than enlightening. He put the book away and went to shower and change his clothes. He might as well switch back to the night shift. It suited him better, and it clearly wasn't helping with the vampire. He made sure Astray's food and water dishes were full.

"Sorry, kitty," he said. "I'm going out tonight. I'll be back in the morning. Well, maybe," he amended. "Unless I find my dream man tonight."

He had an understanding with his landlady that she would find a place for the cat if something bad ever happened to him. She'd been alarmed by that; hopefully she would keep her promise. After giving the cat another scratch behind the ears, he grabbed his smokes and a book and headed out.

He took a bus to Echo Park. After buying a hot dog from a stand, he sat on a bench to eat and read. He'd picked up a light book today—a book of funny essays—but it failed to cheer him up. In general, his despair ebbed and flowed, and it was flowing thick and heavy today. He gave up on the book eventually, placing it on the bench beside him. He reached for his cigarettes and began to smoke, cigarette after cigarette, watching people as they passed him by. He liked people watching—all the hustle and bustle of those who had lives to live. He often wondered how many of them thought about their impending demise.

An old woman with a tiny dog stopped in front of him. "Those things will kill you," she said as her dog stopped to take a shit.

John took a deep drag and let it out. "Unfortunately, they won't. But thanks for your concern."

The woman just shook her head, although John wasn't sure if it was pity or disgust. The dog finished its business, and the woman scooped it up in a plastic bag and hurried away. John stood and stretched. He slid his phone from his pocket. It would be another couple hours before the clubs opened. He lit another cigarette and wandered the park for a while, past the empty children's playground and the fountains, which were lit up in fantastic colors as the night fell.

He made his way to Whiplash, one of his regular clubs, just as the doors opened at eight. He got a drink at the bar and then another as people gradually arrived. When the dancing started in earnest, he slipped into the crowd. He didn't enjoy dancing, exactly, but he did like the way he could lose himself in the throbbing mob. Someone pressed up against his back, hands snaking around his waist. He ground his ass backward; he felt a kiss on his neck. He spun around, and the man smiled at him. John smiled back, but it wasn't the person he was looking for.

The man bought him a drink. They exchanged names, but John forgot it the moment he said it. It didn't matter. They went back to the dance floor. As the man ground against him, John searched the crowd, looking for *him,* the man of his dreams—or well, his nightmares, really. But it was hard to distinguish faces in the crowd.

Not that it mattered. *He* would find John, one way or the other—the man who was destined to kill him. John just wished it would be sooner rather than later. He was ready—more than ready.

His cousin Abigail had died in a nightclub. Some drug deal went wrong and the whole place was shot up. She hadn't even been the target; afterward, everyone said she had been in the wrong place at the wrong time. In actuality, she had been in the right place at the right time. She would have seen her killer's face, if only for a moment. That was the way the curse worked. Was it just moments before, or did she see him well before the shooting? Whichever it was, she didn't try to run. That was smart. Her death was instantaneous.

John danced some more. Things began to blur together—the music, the crowd, the lights in the dark. The man took him by the hand and escorted him out of the club. The two of them stumbled through the streets, stopping in the occasional dark alley to grope and kiss one another.

John's Aunt Mary had been killed in an alley. It was a mugger. John had a feeling the man of his dreams was also a criminal; he had a shifty look about him, a cruelty in his eyes. That's why John walked the streets alone at night, hoping to find him. Mary's death had been a good one, too. A single shot to the heart. No pain.

John's hookup for the night actually giggled as he fumbled with the keys to his apartment. He was cute, too—red hair, freckles, thick-framed glasses. Belatedly, John realized that he had chosen someone who looked a little like Rob. John was apparently as adept at torturing himself subconsciously as he was doing it on purpose. It was a lousy talent to have.

They stumbled inside. While his date went to pour them a couple of unnecessary drinks, John woozily took in the surroundings. The place was nice; whatever the guy did for a living paid well. There were pictures of his family on the walls. John imagined, very briefly, what being this man's boyfriend might be like. Meeting the parents. Getting together with friends for brunch. They'd probably get a dog, although Astray wouldn't like it.

His date returned. The drinks ended up on coasters on the coffee table, untouched, because John immediately pulled the man into the bedroom to do what they came here to do.

They fucked. Afterward, John grabbed his jeans from the floor.

"Where're you going?" his date slurred sleepily.

"Going for a smoke."

"You can do it here."

"It'll stink up your place."

"I don't mind."

John shrugged. If he wanted his bedroom to smell like an ashtray, that was his prerogative. He pulled his cigarettes and lighter out of his pocket and lit up.

His date got out of bed. "Don't go anywhere," he said. "I'll be right back."

He returned a few moments later with their forgotten drinks and a ramekin. "Voila," he said, handing the little dish to him. "Your ashtray."

"Thanks." He set it on the nightstand. His date seemed livelier than he'd been a minute ago, which was unfortunate. John just wanted to get some sleep. The man handed him his drink and got back into bed, his own drink in hand. John was a little ashamed of himself for being so antisocial with someone he'd just slept with, so he took a sip. It was whiskey. He hated whiskey.

His date just watched him smoke for a little while, sipping on his own drink. "If I tell you something, do you promise not to be weirded out?"

John repressed a sigh. "Sure."

"I've actually been watching you. Not like a stalker or anything," he added quickly. "I've just seen you at the club a lot."

John had absolutely no idea how to respond to that, so he went with a vague. "Oh yeah?"

"You're just so different. Like, everyone is having fun and you just look so miserable."

John gave him a look.

His date laughed. "Sorry, that came out wrong. You're just... everyone's looking to get laid and have fun, but there's something sad about you. Like you're a character in a Shakespearean tragedy."

"Is that supposed to be a compliment?"

He laughed again. "Yeah. Sorry, I'm drunk. I just mean, you're like *real*, you know? Like, deep. Most guys are so shallow. I've got this one friend who posts the most inane 'inspirational' shit on Facebook all the time; I know I should probably just filter him out, but it's actually kind of funny how dumb he is. I think people who are happy all the time are probably pretty stupid, don't you? Like when I was at the grocery store the other day, and this one lady..."

By the time he was finished talking, John had smoked three cigarettes and choked down the rest of the whiskey. He'd managed to tune him out after a while; listening to a long list of reasons why this dude was so much smarter than everyone around him, especially his ex, was not exactly the lullaby he'd been hoping for. But he couldn't go home in the dark since the vampire would be waiting for him, and he didn't feel like sleeping on a park bench somewhere.

The man ran out of steam eventually. He gave John a sloppy kiss before falling into the deep, snore-filled slumber of the self-satisfied. Rest didn't come so easy for John. He managed to doze for a little while. As the sun crawled over the horizon, he got up. He put his clothes on and sneaked out the door, leaving his companion still snoozing soundly.

It took a moment for John to figure out where he was. He found a bus stop; thirty minutes later, he was home. He checked the crystal; it was blood red. The vampire must have just left.

John went inside and collapsed facedown on the bed. Astray climbed on top of him, purring as she kneaded the blanket over John's butt. He shooed her off and tried to make himself comfortable. But even though he was bone-tired, sleep wouldn't come.

When it became clear he wasn't going to sleep, he flipped on the TV to the classic movie channel. *West Side Story* was on; Natalie Wood's beatific face filled the screen as she and Richard Beymer sang "One Hand, One Heart." Or well, as they appeared to sing it; Marni Nixon and Jimmy Bryant actually did the vocals. Not many people knew that. He shut it off after the song was done; he wasn't in the mood for love stories—particularly not doomed ones.

A sense of dread began to gnaw at him, like a dog on an old bone. His date's inane chatter bothered him more than it should. He'd called John deep. He said he was "real." But the truth was, John was nowhere near real. He barely even existed. There was only one place to go when he felt like this. He called Uber to arrange a ride—he was going to visit Forest Lawn.

THE UBER DRIVER was a young guy with dreadlocks and an open, honest face. He seemed like a talker, but fortunately he refrained from trying to engage John in conversation. Maybe he could sense that he needed some space. John told the driver his destination. With that done, he slumped in his seat, his head resting on the window. As the scenery rolled by, he began to relax. It was a nice day. It was always a nice day in southern California. That was part of the reason he'd moved here.

By the time they reached Forest Lawn Memorial Park, John was significantly calmer.

The driver gave a low whistle at the sight of the enormous iron gates. "Wow. Those are pretty impressive."

"They're the largest iron gates in the world, actually," John said. "Bigger than Buckingham Palace."

"I had no idea this park was here."

"It isn't a park, really. It's a cemetery."

"It's a pretty fancy cemetery."

"Probably the fanciest, but there are some other really good ones here. Hillside Memorial has this one really amazing tomb—it's black marble and has an enormous dome and six Roman columns. The best part is the six-story waterfall."

"Whose tomb is it?"

"Al Jolson."

"Who?"

"He starred in the first talking picture," John said. "All the great tombs are old Hollywood people. Over at Hollywood Memorial Cemetery, Douglas Fairbanks has this big sarcophagus surrounded with Roman columns and a portico. It's got a picture of him in bas-relief. I thought that was kind of genius; you can actually look at his face while you're looking at his grave."

"And who was he?"

"Silent film star. The King of Hollywood, actually." John paused. "It's funny how no one remembers them anymore. That's the way of things, I guess. Everyone's forgotten eventually."

"So are you just a cemetery enthusiast, or is someone you know buried here?"

"Yes," John said. "And not yet." He gestured forward. "Just follow the signs to the right; you can drop me off at the Great Mausoleum."

The car peeled away as soon as John stepped out of it. He took a moment to look at the fifty-foot Builder's Creed inscribed on one of the walls of the Great Mausoleum. The Creed was the testament of Dr. Hubert Eaton, who in 1917 had a vision for death that John found extraordinary. It was sentimental, grandiose, and a little naive, but it comforted John more than he cared to admit. He knew it by heart. Under the massive inscription were two marble statues of a little boy and girl, with a puppy on a wagon beside them. They were gazing at the creed with eternal fascination. John gave the kids a pat on the head before continuing onward.

Jane, a big friendly woman in her fifties, was on guide duty today. She greeted him with a smile. "Hey, John. How are you today?"

"I'm fine."

His answer must not have been convincing, because her smile faltered. "Well, you just let us know if there's anything we can do for you."

John took his time walking through the building, its grand architecture more in line with the great cathedrals of Europe than the modern architecture of Los Angeles. Replicas of famous old-world statues and paintings were everywhere. He had spent whole days at the park, walking through the three churches and the museum, admiring the beautiful stained-glass windows and statuary. There were over fifteen hundred statues scattered throughout the park. He'd seen them all. His favorite was the replica of the statue of Hans Christian Anderson's Little Mermaid. It probably compared poorly to the original, since it sat in a small artificial lake instead of perched grandly in a Danish harbor, but he still found it charming.

He made his way out of the mausoleum to the expansive grassy hills behind it. There were no looming tombstones; all the graves were marked with small, flat placards. He thought about the Builder's Creed as he made his way across the lawn: *I believe in a happy Eternal Life...*

The view of the city below was spectacular; it was a lot prettier than being in the city itself. He stayed to the path, careful not to tread on any of the graves. *I therefore know the cemeteries of today are wrong, because they depict an end, not a beginning...*

The park was huge: over a quarter of a million people were buried here. It was quite a ways to where he was headed, but he didn't mind the hike. *I shall endeavor to build Forest Lawn as different, as unlike other cemeteries as sunshine is to darkness, as eternal life is unlike death.*

The park was organized into sections: Eventide, Graceland, Inspiration Slope, Babyland (a heart-shaped plot for infants), Slumberland (for children and adolescents), Sweet Memories, Whispering Pines... He hiked until he reached Vesperland. Settling down on the grass, he took out a cigarette. You weren't supposed to smoke, but the staff never bothered him about it. They all thought he was dying, which wasn't a lie, exactly. *Everyone* was dying. He finished his cigarette, stubbed it out, and then tucked the butt into his pocket. He lay back with his fingers laced behind his head. The sky was so clear and so big; he imagined himself as a balloon, floating away.

His mother had been cremated in Cincinnati, a place she hated, and scattered halfheartedly over a lake she had never seen on a gray day in March that didn't seem to belong to any particular season. His grandmother had been tight-lipped and grim as the ashes were dumped. John was old enough that he was able to remain as stone-faced as she while he watched the last of his mother disappear. He didn't think he had any tears left in him, anyway. His grandmother had never forgiven his mother for trying to break the curse. Her gruesome end was her own fault. It could have been so much easier if she just let it happen.

When the curse took his grandmother, she was also burned and scattered with as little ceremony. The curse should have died with her. They had all assumed John was immune, since he was a boy. It turned out he wasn't. When he had his first vision, he picked up what little he had and moved to Los Angeles, spending the bulk of the inheritance his grandmother had left him to buy himself a plot at Forest Lawn.

Forest Lawn shall become a place where lovers new and old shall love to stroll and watch the sunset's glow, planning for the future or reminiscing of the past; a place where artists study and sketch; where school teachers bring happy children to see the things they read of in books...where memorialization of Loved Ones in sculpted marble and pictorial glass shall be encouraged...

It wasn't a bad place to spend eternity. He could think of worse places to end up.

Three: The Five Star Diner

FELIX BURST INTO the mansion, slamming the door behind him. The dawn had nearly caught him that time; he'd waited until the last moment before abandoning his post outside John's apartment.

He'd been unsuccessful yet again. John had failed to appear. He gave the door a fierce kick out of frustration. Unfortunately, he kicked a little too hard; the door burst off its hinges, forcing Felix to sprint away from the encroaching light.

He ended up in Cat's room. She was at her usual perch on the sofa. "Another unsuccessful night?"

"He has vanished!" Felix wailed. "I haven't seen a trace of him in weeks." He sat on the opposite end of the sofa, grabbing a throw blanket and wrapping himself in it. He hadn't fed in a while, so he was cold.

"Perhaps he no longer lives there."

"I don't know. I tried peeking in the windows, but the blinds were shut tight."

Cat sighed and put her show on mute. "This is getting ridiculous. Do you even know what you want from him?"

Felix shrugged. "I just want to talk to him again. I had this...I don't know. This feeling. It's been such a long time since I've had one of those." He paused. "I'm going to ask Richard to help me find him."

"Oh yes, because adding another witch to the situation is exactly what you need," Cat said with annoyance. "Give up this foolishness. Go find someone to eat, for God's sake. Maybe that will clear your head." She turned back to her show.

Felix left the room. The sun was well and truly up now. Although the windows were all safely covered, he could still feel the sunlight drawing at his energy, especially since it had been so long since he had fed. Cat was right. He should let this whole John business go. He took the lighter out of its usual place in his pocket. He wanted to chuck it out the window or something dramatic like that, but that was out of the question, what with the sun being out and all. A trash can would have to do. He tried to think of where the closest one would be.

As he wandered down the hall in search of a trash can, he passed the library. He stood in front of the two massive wooden doors, turning the lighter over and over in his hand. He could feel Richard in there, smell the sweet rot of him—human, but not. Alive, but not quite.

After a few moments, he worked up his nerve and creaked open one of the doors. He found Richard was sitting in his favorite armchair, reading. A cup of coffee sat on a table by his side. He wore a gold brocade dressing gown and velvet slippers. Felix began to approach him, but then stopped. He seemed rather engrossed with his book. Maybe this was a bad idea; he should leave. Before he'd made up his mind, Richard looked up from his book.

"Ah, Felix!" he said with a smile. He pulled his reading glasses up and perched them in his silver hair. "What a pleasant surprise. It's been ages since I've seen you."

"I suppose it has," Felix said as casually as possible.

Richard looked at him expectantly. Felix shuffled, fixing his gaze first on the ceiling and then on the floor—anywhere but on the powerful witch before him. He'd forgotten how unpleasant it was to be in Richard's presence. It brought up memories Felix did not care to recall.

"So have you just come to say 'hello' then?" When Felix didn't answer, Richard stood up and started to make his way toward him. It took a while; he didn't move as quickly as he used to. When he was finally at Felix's side, he clasped a hand on Felix's shoulder. "Oh my dear boy, you do not look well. Is everything all right? Is there something I can do for you?"

Felix fidgeted with the lighter. It was a good thing he didn't sweat; the thing would have been disgusting by now.

Richard smiled and patted him again. "Come now. You can ask me anything you want."

Felix swallowed. He might as well forge ahead. "I want you to help me find someone."

Richard looked surprised. "Who?"

Felix hesitated. Should he tell him that John was a witch? "Just a man I met," he said at last. "He smelled very delicious, but I wasn't able to get to him, and now he seems to have vanished."

"Hmm. I might be able to manage something. Do you know his name?"

"It's John. I don't know his surname."

"I'm afraid that's not a lot to go on," Richard said. "I don't suppose you happen to have an item of his?"

Felix curled open his hand. "I do, actually." He gave the lighter to Richard.

"Excellent. Come with me."

Felix followed Richard to his old desk in the back of the room. Felix had a brief flash of a memory of moving that desk when Richard bought it, many years ago—picking it up all on his own and hoisting it up the stairs while Cat and Richard laughed and the delivery man gawked. It had been new then. It was old now.

Richard sat down and shut his eyes, taking a moment to settle as he breathed in deeply. He laid his arm on the table, the lighter clutched firmly in his fist. His grip became tighter as he breathed deeper and quicker. A strange, creaking groan escaped his lips. The amber ring on his finger glowed brightly for a moment.

All at once, the tension appeared to leave him. The glow from the ring faded. He opened his eyes but didn't look to Felix. "How interesting," he muttered, rubbing his thin mustache thoughtfully. "How very extraordinary."

"What?"

Richard looked up at him. "Your John is a witch."

"Oh."

Richard's gaze sharpened. "You don't seem surprised."

"Well, I suspected," Felix confessed. "He wasn't afraid of me, you see. He told me I couldn't hurt him if he wasn't frightened of me. That seems like something only a witch would know."

"Is that so?" Richard leaned back in his chair and looked thoughtful. "That would mean he's had training—he's not a naive talent." Richard cocked his head in concentration. "There's more. He's under a curse."

"What sort of curse?"

"I can't tell exactly, but it feels...familiar, somehow." He was silent for a moment as he stared off into the distance, lost in thought. "Whatever it is, it's very strong," he said at last. "It's no wonder you were attracted to him, what with that sort of darkness hanging over his head." Richard looked at Felix again. "How is it you found him?"

"I just ran into him on the street while he was on his way home. I visited him again at his home, but he hasn't been there in weeks, as far as I can tell."

Richard reached for a pen and paper. "He has, actually," he said as he began writing. "But I imagine he's been avoiding you. Fortunately, I have another address for you to try." He handed Felix the paper.

"'Five Star Diner?'" Felix read aloud.

"His place of employment, no doubt." Richard handed the lighter back to Felix. "And what do you plan to do once you find him? You've said yourself that he is not frightened of you."

"Maybe I just didn't try hard enough!"

Richard smiled mildly. "Best of luck to you, then. Do let me know how it goes."

Felix left the library feeling triumphant. He couldn't wait to see the look on John's face when he showed up.

THE RESTAURANT WAS easy to find—it wasn't far from where John lived. The sign declared it the Five Star Diner, but that description did not seem wholly accurate. Felix stepped inside; the restaurant was one small, ill-lit room. The only person in the place was a young Latina woman lounging at one of the tables, looking bored. Her long black hair had a streak of blue dyed into it, and her bangs were nearly long enough to obscure her eyes. She looked up as he entered the restaurant.

With a sigh, she made her way over to the host stand. "WelcometotheFiveStarDinermynameisLo," she said in one breath. She turned and started to walk away. Felix figured she meant for him to follow her, so he did.

She sat him down in a booth in the back. She patted her apron. "Shit, I forgot the menu. I'll be right back." She returned to the stand and came back, menu in hand. Felix accepted it, although he wasn't planning on eating. While he could ingest food, he gained no nourishment or enjoyment from it.

As Felix examined the menu, Lo pulled a pad of paper out of her black apron. "Want anything to drink?"

"Maybe," he said. "But I'm actually looking for someone. Is there a John here?"

"Yeah," she said, but offered nothing further.

"Can you send him out?"

"This isn't his section."

Felix looked around the empty restaurant. "Well, he's not exactly busy, is he?"

"It's not his section," she repeated.

"Then can I move to his section?"

Lo let out a long sigh. "Look. There have only been five customers the whole night, and I need the tips. It's my turn, and my section, so I'm not moving you."

Felix took out his wallet and dumped a bunch of cash on the table. "Here. Now bring John out."

Lo picked up the money and pocketed it. "He's on break."

Felix gritted his teeth. "I can wait."

"Well, then you'll have to order something. You can't just sit here and take up a seat."

"Then pick something for me," he snapped.

"You got it."

Felix fidgeted in his seat for an agonizing twenty minutes; he'd never been good at waiting. But at last, he was rewarded when John emerged from the kitchen, carrying a tray. Felix picked up the menu Lo had neglected to take back and opened it, obscuring his face. When John arrived, he lowered it slowly.

"Hello, John," he said. He gave him a smile with just a hint of fang.

He had hoped John would at least be a little startled, but John just leveled a cool gaze at him. "What do you want?"

Felix tried not to be discouraged. "It appears you cannot hide from me."

"Guess not," John said.

Felix set the menu down. "Aren't you at least a little disturbed by that?"

"Not really."

"Don't you want to know by what terrifying means I was able to track you down?"

"It wouldn't take a Sherlockian genius to figure it out. I was wearing a shirt with the name of this restaurant on it when we met."

Actually, he hadn't noticed, but he wasn't about to tell John that. "Well, if you aren't afraid, why have you been hiding from me? And don't deny it—you haven't been home in weeks!"

"Yes, I have."

"No, you haven't—I've been watching your place, and I haven't seen you enter or leave."

John rubbed his temple. "Were you watching my place during daylight hours?"

"Of course not!"

"Exactly."

It took Felix a moment to get it; if John had only left or entered during the day, he wouldn't have seen his comings and goings. "Oh." Then he brightened. "But that means you were deliberately avoiding me. Surely that means you are at least a little bit afraid of me."

"I'm *annoyed* by you." John set the tray on the table. "I figured you would lose interest eventually."

Felix grinned. "Then you figured wrong. I have not lost interest."

"I'm going to ask you one more time—what do you want from me?"

The grin left Felix's face. He hadn't thought that far ahead. What *did* he want? "Would you like to get a drink sometime?" is what he finally came up with.

John stared at him. "You're asking me out?"

Felix smiled, no fangs this time. "I suppose so. My name is Felix, by the way."

"So let me get this straight. You try to attack me, stalk me, threaten my family and friends, track me down at my place of work, and now you want to know if I will go on a date with you?"

Felix gave him a helpless shrug. The whole thing was a surprise to him, too.

John pointed to the door. "Get the actual fuck out of here, and don't come back."

"You can't kick me out—I'm a paying customer!"

"Last time I checked, vampires weren't a protected class under US law, so we absolutely do have the right to kick your undead ass out on the street."

Felix crossed his arms. "And last time I checked, you're just a waiter and you don't have the authority to do that!"

"*Fine.*" John whipped around and stomped off.

Felix slumped back in his seat. That had not gone well. He probably should leave, but he didn't want John thinking he'd won. He picked up the hamburger John had brought. It was limp and greasy, but he tried a bite anyway. He immediately spat it out. It was terrible. He wondered if anyone had summoned the police on them, like on Cat's show. Good thing he was immune to poison.

A few minutes later, a man as greasy as Felix's hamburger appeared from the kitchen and made his way to Felix's table. He was thin with the exception of a perfectly round pot belly that his pants couldn't quite contain. A strip of dead-fish-white skin covered in wiry black hair peeked out from under his shirt.

"Hello, sir," the man said with an apologetic smile on his face. "I'm Mike, the owner of this establishment. John tells me that you got into a little argument." The man looked over his shoulder before turning back to Felix and continuing in a lower voice. "So what, you had a date gone bad or something?"

"Something like that."

"And now he won't give you a second chance. I get it." Mike smiled at him. "He's cute, yeah? One of those—what do you people call them? Twinks?"

Felix had no idea what he was talking about, but since the man seemed surprisingly sympathetic to his situation, he smiled and nodded.

"Look, here's the deal. Why don't you get out of here for now, and I'll work on him a little. Then you can come back tomorrow, and who knows?"

"You'd do that for me?"

"Sure! And maybe you could bring some of your friends—you know, nothing like a quality burger before you hit the club, right? We specialize in the late-night crowd."

Felix didn't have any friends, but decided not to mention it. He stood up. "That is really too kind of you."

Mike patted him on the back with one hand and shook his hand with the other. "Oh, it's no problem. Just cool it for a little while, and I'm sure you two will work it out."

Felix pondered the situation as he walked out of the front door. None of that went as he expected it to. He wondered what Mike planned on saying to John and then realized he could stop wondering and just find out for himself. He zipped around to the back of the restaurant and eavesdropped.

"—not asking you to fuck him," Mike was saying. "Just string him along."

"No," was John's emphatic answer.

"Oh, come on! The guy dropped $200 on a burger. Business sucks right now. Take one for the team."

"How about this idea—instead of pimping out your waitstaff, try serving food that doesn't taste like cat vomit."

"Hey!" Another voice—male and gruff. "My food don't taste like cat vomit!"

"You're right," a female voice said. It sounded like the waitress. "It's more like dog shit."

"Yeah, well, maybe I should make my food taste like dicks—then I bet you'd cram it into your face all the time."

"Fuck you, Vince."

"Just a little bit of flirting," Mike continued as if he hadn't been interrupted. "That's all I ask."

"*No*," John repeated. "And I don't want him here at all. I want him banned."

"Why? Is he dangerous?"

There was a long pause. "No," John said. "No, he's not. You shouldn't be afraid of him at all. He's kind of nuts, though—he thinks he's a vampire. So he might try to scare you, but don't let him."

"Sounds like a fruity fruitcake," Vince said. "Get it? Because he's—"

"Oh yes, very clever," John interrupted. "You're a regular Oscar Wilde."

"Who?"

"All right," Mike said. "If you feel that strongly about it."

"I do. And we all have to be together on this—no letting him in."

"Okay, okay, I got it. Keep the rich guy out," Mike said. "But when I go out of business, none of you sorry losers will have jobs. Just keep that in mind."

Lo spoke again. "Hey, where's Gabriel?"

"I sent him home," Mike said. "In case you haven't noticed, there's not a lot of dishes to be cleaned, and I'm not paying for him to stand around."

"There's still another three hours before we close," Lo pointed out.

"Then I guess John's on dish duty," Mike snapped. "And now I'm going home. Try not to evict any more customers, all right?"

Felix fell back into the shadows as Mike exited the restaurant out the back. Once he was gone, Felix returned to his post. He sneaked a little closer to the back door and pushed it open just a little so he could peek inside. Only John and the man with the gruff voice remained in the kitchen—that was presumably Vince. Vince was a hulking young man with slicked-back black hair and a faint mustache. He was just the sort that Felix loved to dine on—huge and full of dark, delicious blood. He tried not to get distracted.

Vince and John didn't speak for a while. John busied himself by cleaning some errant dishes while Vince leaned back and did nothing. Well, not nothing, exactly—he was watching John. Watching him rather intently.

"You know," Vince said after a while. "If that guy ever comes back, I could always go out and have a little chat with him, if you know what I mean. I bet he'd piss his pants as soon as he sees me."

John didn't turn to look at him. "Thanks, Vince, but it would be better if you didn't say anything. We just have to ignore him. He'll get bored eventually."

"I don't know. What if he's, like, obsessed with you or something? You might need me to look out for you."

"I can handle myself, thanks."

They lapsed into silence again as John spritzed some cleaner on a counter. Vince cleared his throat. "So where did you meet this guy? A club, or on that one app that's like gay Tinder?"

"If I were you, I'd stick with apps," John said. "Because real-life conversations are not your forte."

Vince's mouth opened and shut a few times, like a fish sputtering its last after it had been hooked. "What are you trying to say?" His voice rose with each word.

"Nothing." John set aside his last dish. "I'm going for a smoke."

As John walked past Vince, Vince blocked his way. "You're not going anywhere until you tell me what you meant by that."

"Christ, Vince, it was just a joke." John tried to step past him again, but Vince shoved him backward.

"Well, it wasn't funny. I'm not gay." Vince moved forward, crowding him. "I bet you wish I was. I bet—"

He didn't get to finish that thought, because Felix swooshed in and grabbed Vince by the throat before slamming him against the wall. John was sent flying backward to tumble to the floor. Vince tried to cry out, but Felix tightened his grip so the only sound he managed to make was a distressed gurgle. His face was turning a very amusing shade of purple. Felix smiled widely, baring his fangs. Vince's eyes nearly bugged out of his head. He thrashed against Felix's grip, but it was, of course, useless.

"It wasn't at a club," Felix said as he raised him higher. "We just ran into each other. As you can see, I've never had problems picking up men." Felix felt extremely pleased with himself for that line. He hoped John had heard it.

Felix inhaled deeply, the essence of Vince's fear teasing him, tempting him. He was reminded suddenly of how long it had been since he had fed. The exact circumstance of what had brought him to this moment grew very hazy. He was a vampire; his prey was squirming in his clutches. Before Felix knew it, he found his fangs in Vince's neck.

His meal was interrupted by a thwack on his head. Reluctantly, he removed his fangs from Vince to see what had caused the interruption. John stood there, armed with a broom.

"Put him down!" he said sternly.

Felix felt a little embarrassed. He truly hadn't meant to feed from the man, but surely John couldn't blame him. He opened his mouth to apologize, but John thwacked him in the face. It would normally take a much harder hit to bother Felix, but the broom bristles got in his eyes, scratching him. He dropped Vince, who crumpled to the floor, unconscious. Felix and John's gazes locked. John kept the broom poised, but he wasn't afraid. Unfortunately.

Just then, Lo appeared in the doorway.

"What's going on back here?" She looked at Felix. "You again. I thought we told you to get lost." Her gaze skittered toward the floor. "Vince?" She moved rapidly across the room and dropped to his side. "Jesus fuck, he's bleeding!" She looked up at Felix. Fear radiated off her. "Your teeth—"

"There's nothing wrong with his teeth," John interrupted. His gaze never left Felix. "I told you, he thinks he's a vampire. They're fake. There is no reason to be afraid of him. He's going away, and he's never coming back."

"I am not," Felix huffed. "And I'll come back whenever I please. And don't think that broom-to-the-face trick is going to work twice. I'm faster than you."

John dropped the broom and headed to the other side of the kitchen, where a shoulder bag hung on the wall. He riffled through it for a moment.

Felix came up behind him. "What are you doing?"

"Getting something."

"What?"

"This." He turned around and sprayed Felix in the face.

Felix screamed. His face felt like it was on fire, and he couldn't see. He tried to zip away but banged into a wall. "What did you do to me?" he wailed. "Is this some sort of spell?"

"It's pepper spray." John thwacked Felix again and again until he was eventually corralled out the door. "Don't come back or I will call the police. And remember what we talked about before. Morgue. Sun. Poof."

The door slammed shut. Felix stumbled behind a dumpster. He rubbed at his eyes, but that only made things worse. Nothing to do except wait it out; as a vampire, his healing was accelerated, so it shouldn't take too much longer.

Eventually, the agony subsided. He took the lighter out of his pocket and flicked it a few times. *This is so unfair*, he thought sourly. He'd only been trying to help! Maybe he *should* just leave John alone. The man was clearly deranged.

Felix stumbled as his whole body cramped. The taste of Vince's blood had stirred the hunger he'd been ignoring for far too long. As he set off into the streets, thoughts of John faded. In fact, thoughts of any kind evaporated, leaving only hunger and the hunt.

Four: Toil and Trouble

JOHN WAITED UNTIL the vampire was well out of sight before he went back inside to start damage control. What a pain in the ass. The worst part was he was sure he hadn't seen the last of...what had his name been? Felix? He wondered if this was curse related or if his luck was really that shitty.

When he re-entered the kitchen, he found Lo at Vince's side, holding a cloth firmly to his throat.

"He's gone?" she asked.

John nodded.

"Then what the fuck are you doing just standing there? Call 911! I didn't want to let up the pressure on this wound—he's bleeding pretty bad."

John got down beside them. "Let me see." He lifted the cloth slightly. It looked bad with the fang marks and the bruising from where Felix had tried to squeeze the life out of him, but not so bad that John couldn't manage; his magic was a little rusty, but he should be able to manage a rudimentary healing spell. He positioned himself so Lo's view was blocked. He muttered the spell as quickly and quietly as he could.

"Let my words be my might/use my power to heal this bite."

The holes in his neck began to close and the bruises started to fade. John pulled the cloth away. "Looks like it wasn't as bad as we thought," he said. "I don't think we need to call 911."

Lo pushed John aside to look for herself. "No way," she said, shaking her head. "No, I saw the marks on his neck and the bruises, and there was blood all over your psycho ex's face."

"He's *not* my ex. And maybe you saw wrong. Look for yourself—it's not that bad."

Lo waved the bloody towel in John's face. "If it's not that bad, where the fuck did all of this blood come from?"

John took a deep breath. He felt depleted from the healing spell, but his work wasn't done yet. He had to get Lo and Vince to remember this encounter differently; he did not feel like putting Lo and Vince in the know about the supernatural. Fortunately, memory alteration wasn't that difficult in these sorts of circumstances. People had a natural desire to discount anything highly unusual and/or frightening. John just had to tap into it.

He put his hand on her arm—having physical contact tended to help. "Everything's fine. Vince and that guy who came in earlier got into a fight, but everything turned out all right."

"That crazy asshole tried to rip Vince's throat out with his teeth!" Lo exclaimed. "How is that all right?"

"That didn't happen. It was just a normal fight."

Lo stared at him for a moment. Then she reeled back and punched John in the shoulder so hard he fell back a little.

"Ow!" he said. "What did you do that for?"

"Stop telling me that shit I saw happen did not actually happen! What is wrong with you? And what did you just mumble at him? Why are you acting so shady?"

John blinked at her. Yeah, he was out of practice, but that should have worked. He met her gaze with all the willpower he could muster.

"Everything is fine," he said with as much force as he could manage.

"I swear to Christ, I am going to punch you in the fucking face if you say that one more time."

Their gazes locked. Her will was unbending. That meant only one thing.

Shit. The last thing he needed was a vampire stalker, but the second to last thing he needed was an unrecognized, untrained witch in his life.

Just then, Vince groaned. John had to think fast. "Okay, I'm going to level with you," John said to Lo. "But what I'm going to tell you Vince does not need to hear. Play along, and then I'll fill you in, okay?"

She looked hesitant, but at last she nodded.

Vince's eyes blinked open. "What happened?"

John helped him sit up. "That guy came back," he said as he rubbed Vince's shoulder. "You were right. He's obsessed with me. But you fought him off."

Vince rubbed his head. "I did?"

"Oh yeah. You sent him running. Isn't that right, Lo?" John looked at her pleadingly.

"Uh, yeah. Sure."

Vince sat up a little straighter. "Yeah," he said slowly. "Yeah, I remember. I really fucked him up, didn't I?"

"You sure did." John helped Vince to his feet. "I was so impressed. You beat him so bad you shouldn't ever be afraid of him again."

Lo pretended to gag. John ignored her.

Vince was practically glowing now. "Fuck yeah. I knew that he wouldn't stand a chance against a real man like me."

"But he did get a couple of hits in," John continued. "You feel a little dizzy. You think you should probably go home and lie down."

Vince frowned. "Mike's not going to like that."

"He'll never know. We'll just close up early tonight."

"Sounds good to me," Lo chimed in.

The three of them got the restaurant ready for closing. Vince grew more and more pleased with himself every minute. John had leaned pretty hard on the desires that were already spinning around in Vince's head in order to make sure John's version of events stuck. Hopefully his suggestion that Vince shouldn't be afraid of Felix would stick, too. Vince was a homophobic prick and a bully, but that didn't mean John wanted him to end up as vampire food.

The three of them gathered their things and went out the front. As Lo locked the doors, Vince leaned up against the wall, gazing at John in a way that made him less than comfortable.

"So do you need me to walk you home?" he asked. "I mean, he might come after you again."

"I think you scared him off."

Vince pushed himself off the wall and moved toward John. "It's no problem," he insisted.

John put a hand on Vince's arm, who got a little dreamy-eyed at the contact. As usual, John felt a little sorry for him.

"Go home, Vince," he said. "And don't mention any of this ever again, to me or anyone else." That last command was a stretch, as suggestions like that tended to fade with time, but it couldn't hurt to try.

Vince blinked rapidly. He turned and left without a word.

That took care of one problem. John turned around to face the other, who had her arms crossed and was tapping her foot.

Neither of them said anything for a moment. Lo spoke first. "So is this going to be an urban fantasy kind of deal, or are we talking sci-fi?

Because with the vampire and the spells, I'm thinking urban fantasy, but I guess it could be blood-sucking aliens and mind-control rays, too." Her tone was flippant, but John could see she was shaking.

John smiled thinly. "More fantasy, although probably not as exciting as you'd expect. Tonight was abnormally eventful."

"No shit." Lo took a deep breath and let it out again. She appeared calmer. "So. Urban fantasy means you put some sort of spell on Vince to erase his mind?"

"I didn't erase his mind! I just...helped him remember differently."

Lo did not seem as though she appreciated the difference. "Whatever. And your ex is a vampire, right?"

"I told you, he isn't my ex. I didn't even know his name until tonight. He followed me home one night and has been harassing me ever since."

"Aren't you afraid of him?"

"Vampires can't hurt you if you aren't scared of them. If he ever tries anything on you, just tell him to fuck off."

She snorted. "Not a problem. What do I do if I ever meet a werewolf?"

"Highly unlikely in a city. You'd actually have to go hunt down a werewolf; they mostly keep to themselves."

"What about a mermaid?"

John raised an eyebrow. "Are you worried about being attacked by a mermaid in the middle of LA?"

"What if I go to the beach?"

John sighed. "A merperson would never make it as far as the beach. If you're ever on a boat and you see one, ignore them. If they see that you've seen them, they'll try to drown you, and they'll probably succeed. They are a people who value their privacy."

"What about fairies?"

"I don't know, they're mostly in the UK, but I imagine a flyswatter would probably do the trick on the smaller ones."

Lo started laughing, just a giggle at first, but soon she was laughing so hard she had to steady herself against the wall.

"*Shit*," she said, wiping tears from her eyes. "Is this really happening?"

"'Fraid so." John looked up and down the street. The vampire Felix didn't seem to be around presently, but it was probably only a matter of time before he showed up again. "Is there somewhere we can go to talk a little more privately?"

She crossed her arms. "How about you tell me how to defend myself against a wizard first?"

She had good instincts. A witch's worst enemies were generally other witches.

"I'm a witch, actually. Not a wizard. And so, it seems, are you."

Lo's eyes grew big. "Excuse me?"

"I couldn't control you," John explained. "I'm out of practice, but it still should have worked on you. The fact that it didn't means you have magical talent."

"You're shitting me."

"I think you've made it pretty clear that I am terrible at lying to you. Do I really seem like I'm lying now?"

Lo took a moment to process that. "You know, when I was a kid, I always hoped that an owl would bring me a Hogwarts letter. This is kinda disappointing." She smiled a little.

John shrugged. "I could hoot and flap my arms if you want."

"Nah. That would just make this night weirder, and it's been about as weird as I can take." She nibbled on her nails for a moment, seemingly in the midst of an internal debate. At last, she started to walk off to the right. "My car's this way. We can go to my place if you want."

It was a short trip to her apartment—a studio, like John's, but she'd made an effort to actually personalize the place. She'd painted one wall a deep maroon. Posters of bands he'd never heard of hung on the walls, along with a few old photos of a woman and a little girl—Lo and her mom, maybe.

There was only one chair: it was black wicker and looked like an enormous bowl with a cushion in the middle. John sat down on it, placing his bag on the floor beside him, as Lo went to the fridge.

"All I got is beer. You want one?"

"Sure."

Lo grabbed two cans and handed one to John. John noticed for the first time how ragged her fingers were; the nails were bitten into near nonexistence. She hadn't stopped with the nail, either—all her cuticles were shredded, like she'd stuck her hands in a cage full of bloodthirsty hamsters.

Lo sat on the bed on her black-and-white striped comforter. She opened her own can and chugged the entire thing, finishing with a belch. "Okay, Dumbledore. Tell me how it works."

John took a long drink. He'd never had to explain this to anyone before. For him, magic had been a part of his life as long as he could remember. If his mother had ever sat him down to explain it, he didn't remember. It would be like hearing how gravity worked—interesting, but you didn't really need to understand it when it happened all around you.

"You have to be born with it," he began.

"And by 'it,' you mean magic."

John nodded. "Usually it runs in families, but it can pop up in the general population, too. Some people are just born with the ability to...I don't know, bend reality? Does that make sense?"

"No," she said. "But please continue."

"It's like you're enforcing your will on the world," John tried again. "Like you want things to be *this* way, and the world says it's *that* way, but if you concentrate hard enough, you can make the world change its mind."

"Can you show me?"

John held up his beer can. "*Are you ready for a surprise?/Change this can to the color of my eyes.*" The metal shifted shades into blue.

Lo laughed. "Pretty cool!"

John made a noncommittal noise in response. It had been the first spell he'd learned, at the age of five. He'd run around the apartment, a gleeful little dictator demanding that every object should reflect the color of his eyes—the couch, the refrigerator, his formerly red truck, and at last his mother's hair. She'd looked like a mermaid when she swept him up in her arms, laughing and kissing him on the cheek, her hair brushing his skin like seafoam.

"So do you always have to make a little rhyme?" Lo asked.

The seafoam memory dissolved. John shook his head. "No. The rhyming is just to help hone your concentration. Some people use talismans, other people will meditate a little. There are certain plants that have magical properties you can use to channel your power, if you want to make potions. It doesn't matter as long as you get a clear idea of what you want to happen."

"You didn't rhyme when you were messing with Vince's head."

"That's will magic. It's different. For that, you have to tap into the person's own willpower and manipulate it. It's not so much that you're using yours as you're manipulating theirs."

"So you can just make anyone do whatever you want?"

"Not exactly. Depending on how strong a person's will is, it might not work. It goes easier if you try to make them believe something they really want to believe."

"Which is why you laid it on so thick with the hero stuff for Vince."

"Yeah."

Lo looked thoughtful. "That sounds like it has a lot of possibilities."

John pressed his lips together in a thin line. He had to impress on her what a bad idea that was. "No, it doesn't. You have to understand—when you twist people's will like that, you twist, too. Use it too much and you can...change."

"What do you mean?"

"You become callous. Cruel."

Lo raised an eyebrow. "So I'll become a wicked witch?" she said with sarcasm.

"I'm serious. Magic is dangerous. I try to use it as little as possible."

She held up her hands. "Okay, okay—I won't try to make the world do my evil bidding. But why bother telling me I have power if you don't want me to use it?"

"Because it can be dangerous. You need to learn discipline so you can control it. Spells are created through concentration, but that's not the only way your power can be used. In moments of intense emotion, your will could cause some serious damage without meaning to."

Lo grew very still. "Like what?"

"Well, have you ever gotten so angry that you made a wish you later regretted and then it came true?"

Lo looked away. She started nibbling her thumb again and didn't stop until she really started to bleed.

"Shit," she said when she noticed. She disappeared into the bathroom. When she came out, all her fingers were wrapped in Band-Aids. "Sorry, I know it's gross. I've tried everything to stop biting my cuticles, but nothing seems to work."

"That's not uncommon," John said. "Witches tend to have a lot of nervous energy." John's own fingers were twitching. "Do you have a balcony or something? I could use a cigarette."

After John retrieved his pack of cigarettes from his bag, Lo led him outside to the tiniest balcony John had ever seen. He lit a cigarette.

Lo held out her hand. "Give me one."

He handed it over. She leaned close as he flicked the lighter for her. She inhaled and immediately started coughing. "God, these things are gross." But she didn't put it out.

They smoked for a while, looking out over the city.

"So do you know any other witches?" Lo asked after a while. "I mean, is there like a magic society, or something?"

"There's a council," John said. "But I avoid them."

"Why?"

"Witches aren't a particularly friendly lot. There are exceptions, of course, but you're as likely to meet a bad witch as a good one. And you can forget it if you have any kind of problem that would require help." John flicked his cigarette. "The council only exists to deal with extreme problems, like a witch who's gone seriously off the deep end, but even then, they don't do much." He frowned. "Although one of the few proactive things they do is scan for unrecognized witches, such as you. I wonder why no one has found you yet."

"Why do they do that?"

"Like I said, untrained witches have the capacity to cause major damage. It's in everyone's best interest that people with magical abilities receive at least some magical training. If you're lucky, you get an actual mentor who knows what they're doing."

"And am I lucky?" she asked, peering at him.

"I don't know. I've never actually taught anyone."

"Who'd you learn from?"

"My mom." John put out his cigarette in his beer can. "And she can't help us because she's dead."

Lo chewed on the corner of a Band-Aid. "What a coincidence. So is mine."

They sat there for an uncomfortable moment, neither of them meeting the other's gaze. John stood up. "I should probably get going."

"I can give you a ride."

John hesitated. "Okay, but just as far as the restaurant. I can walk from there."

"Why?"

"That vampire's going to be back. I don't want him taking an interest in you."

"I thought you said he couldn't hurt me."

"He can't, but he can be extremely annoying."

Lo drove him to the restaurant and put the car into park. "Well, thanks for letting me in on the magic thing, I guess," she said. "Or alternately, fuck you for dropping this atom bomb on my already decimated life." She was smiling—a joke. Sort of.

"You're welcome, and I'm sorry." He gave her a weak smile. "A lot of it will be fun, I promise."

"Unless it pushes me to the brink of insanity. That doesn't sound like so much fun."

"That won't happen. I mean, *I'm* normal, right?"

Lo shrugged. "Yeah, sure."

John laughed a little. "What's that supposed to mean?"

She hesitated. "I get these feelings about people. I don't really know how to describe it. Maybe it's magic or whatever. Don't take this the wrong way, but there's this darkness hanging over you. It's a little scary."

John was taken aback. Since he had no idea what to say to that, he got out of the car without responding. "I'll see you tomorrow."

She gave him a concerned look. "Are you sure you don't want me to drop you off closer to home?"

"I'm sure." He shut the car door. Lo took off, leaving him alone on the sidewalk.

John started the walk to his place. As predicted, the vampire soon appeared by his side.

"Are you a glutton for punishment?" he said through clenched teeth.

"Don't try to spray me again," Felix said. "It won't work now that I'm expecting it. I'm very fast."

"I suppose it would be useless to tell you to leave me alone."

"Probably," Felix agreed. "Why did you attack me? I saved you."

"You didn't save me. Vince is just a self-loathing closet case. He's harmless."

"Not true. He pushed you."

"So what?"

"He wanted to hurt you more. I can tell that sort of thing, because I hurt a lot of people."

"Yeah, I know. You nearly killed him. Am I supposed to be intimidated or impressed?" John snapped. "Because I'm neither."

"I *am* sorry about that. I wasn't going to eat him, but I haven't fed in quite some time." Felix, to his credit, did look contrite.

John stopped to fumble around in his bag for another cigarette. Quick as lightning, Felix pulled a lighter from his own pocket and flicked it open, holding it in front of the cigarette that now perched between John's lips.

John stared at the lighter. "Is that my lighter?"

"Yes." He moved the flame forward, encouraging him.

But John removed the cigarette from his lips. "Do you just carry it around with you?"

"I do. Would you like it back?"

John hesitated. "No." He began to walk again, putting the cigarette back between his lips and lighting it himself with his own lighter.

Felix kept pace with him. "But it means something to you," he insisted. "It says, 'Love, Rob.'"

John wouldn't look at him. "I know what it says."

"Who's Rob?"

"None of your damn business."

"Did he know about your curse?"

John felt like he'd been hit in the chest with a sledgehammer. He stared at Felix, who was looking mighty pleased with himself.

"How the *fuck* do you know about that?"

"Oh," Felix said airily. "I have my ways."

Who had told him, and why? Only another witch could have sensed the curse—but what kind of vampire was in cahoots with a witch? John almost asked him, but he shook himself out of it. Whatever was going on, he was better off not encouraging Felix further.

"Never mind," he mumbled as he began to march away again. "I don't care."

Felix zipped in front of him. "It was a witch," he said, all the smugness gone and replaced with an air of a puppy in desperate need of validation. "I asked him to find you, and he told me he felt a curse on you."

John blew a cloud of smoke into Felix's face. While he coughed, John marched onward.

Felix zipped in front of him again. "So what's your curse?"

"Ask your witch."

"I did. He said he wasn't sure."

John didn't reply, continuing his grim march onward.

"Is it something really bad?"

"No. It's a nice curse."

That seemed to puzzle Felix for a moment. "Ah. You're being sarcastic."

"No shit."

"So what is it, then?"

John gritted his teeth. "I am forever plagued with annoying vampires."

"You're being sarcastic again."

John finished his cigarette, threw the butt on the ground, and then started another one. He refused to look at Felix. He didn't want to encourage him.

They walked in silence some more. "What are you thinking about?" Felix asked.

"I'm thinking about how I'm going to have to both quit my job and move." He wondered if he could teach Lo magic over Skype.

"Why?"

"Why do you think?"

Felix thought about it for a moment. "To get away from me?"

"Bingo."

"It won't work. My witch will find you again."

"I could move back to Cincinnati."

Felix pouted, but that pout quickly twisted into a grin of triumph. "But you don't want to go to Cincinnati, because you don't want to see Rob, which is why you're here in the first place!"

John flicked his cigarette butt out into the street. "Then I'll move to Paris. Or Bangkok. Or the moon."

"You can't live on the moon. How would you get there?"

They had arrived at John's apartment. Felix got to the door first and leaned one hand on the door casually.

John sighed. "You aren't going to leave me alone until I say yes, are you?"

Felix just smiled—no fangs.

John rubbed his temple. He had to think of some way to get him out of his hair. It was too bad vampires were immune to will magic. Their attention spans were short, though—maybe he could play on that.

"All right. I'll go out with you. But you have to prove yourself first."

If Felix had a tail, he'd be wagging it. "What do you want me to do?"

"I want you to find a rose bush."

"You want me to bring you flowers? That seems a bit old-fashioned."

John shook his head. "I wasn't finished. When you find a bush, go to it every night at midnight and put three drops of your blood on one of the blooms. Do this for one hundred nights. On the hundred and first night, the rose will turn blue. Bring it to me."

"A hundred and one nights?" Felix said. "But that's—" He held out his fingers as if trying to calculate the weeks, but gave up. "It's a long time!"

John shrugged. "That's my offer."

"What do you want a blue rose for?"

"It's a witch thing."

"Why don't you bleed on a bush yourself if you want it so bad?"

"It requires vampiric blood," John said. "I'm not a vampire, in case it escaped your notice."

Felix examined John's face. "You don't think I can do it."

"I don't, actually."

Felix bristled. "Well, you're wrong. I can do it. I *will* do it. And when I bring you that rose, I want a kiss, too."

"Fine. One rose. One kiss. Now will you let me into my apartment?"

Felix reluctantly lifted his hand off the door. John put his key in the lock and opened it.

"See you in a hundred and one nights," Felix said as John entered his apartment.

"Sure I will." John slipped inside and slammed the door shut in Felix's face. He put down his things, but he could still feel Felix's presence on the other side of the door. With a sigh, he went to the window and opened it.

Felix appeared immediately. "Yes?"

"You need to leave. If I see you before then, the deal is off. Got it?"

Felix scowled, but the threat worked. John watched him zip away; it really was a bizarre sight, seeing someone move that fast. He shut his window and collapsed face-first on his bed. Astray jumped up beside him and let out a curious *mrow*?

"Don't ask," he said. "It's been a long night."

Five: Perchance to Dream

"I HAVE EXCITING news!" Felix exclaimed as he burst into Cat's room.

She was sitting on the sofa as usual, the television blaring. She had one foot up on the coffee table as she painted her nails a cherry red.

"Hmmm?" Cat didn't even look up.

Felix stalked over to the TV and shut it off.

It took Cat a moment to even realize what he had done.

"Hey," she said, lifting her head at last. "I was watching that." Her eyes were glassy. There was a significant dent in her pill dish.

"This is much more interesting than your programs."

Cat let out a dramatic sigh. "I will be the judge of that. Have a seat."

Cat lay back on one of the voluminous pillows to make room for Felix on the sofa. She put her foot in his lap. Felix picked up the nail polish and took up where she had left off.

"Richard was able to find my John. I tracked him to the restaurant where he is employed."

"Did that unnerve him?"

"Well, no, not exactly. There was a bit of a scuffle, actually. But it does not matter! He agreed to go on a date with me!"

"A date? I thought you wanted to scare him."

"Oh, I've given up on that," Felix said. He finished her pinkie toe. "Other foot."

Cat obliged. "He wants something from you, doesn't he?"

Felix's face fell. "How did you know?"

"Witches always have agendas." Cat narrowed her eyes. "I don't like this one bit."

"He isn't like Richard," Felix said assuringly. "If he were, he would be the one trying to lure me to him, yes? But since I am the pursuer, I am not in danger. You needn't worry. I have it all under control."

She pressed her lips together but didn't respond directly. "Will you hand me my pill dish?"

Felix did so, grabbing a few for himself. They were chalky and blue today; he crunched them until they were a bitter powder. For undead creatures such as themselves, a great deal more drugs were needed to obtain the desired effect. When he finished Cat's toenails, he grabbed the bottle of wine for a long swig.

Cat lay back on the sofa and draped an arm over her face for a moment, as if collecting herself.

"So what does he want?" she asked eventually.

"He wants me to bleed on a rose bush for one hundred days."

"Did he say what it was for?"

"He said that it would make a blue rose, which I am to give to him to prove my worthiness."

Cat popped another pill. "Hmm. Well, it is true that roses are important to mortals nowadays." She gestured at her current television program, where a man in a tuxedo was handing roses to women. "Although it really should be the other way 'round, with him bestowing the rose on you once you prove yourself worthy. They never say anything about bleeding on them, though."

"He said it was a 'witch thing.'"

"Witchery," Cat said darkly. "Who can make sense of it?"

"I thought I'd ask Richard. He is a witch, after all. Perhaps he can help."

Cat made no response. They watched the rest of her romance program. When it was over, Cat switched over to a very diverting program about a man who was good at training dogs.

"Why do you want him?" Cat asked after a while. "What makes him worth the risk?"

"Well, he's very handsome—sandy blond hair, eyes like the ocean..."

"There are many lovely young men in the city who pose no danger to you."

"I can never truly be myself with mere mortals," Felix pointed out. "With a witch, I can."

"And why would you want that?"

Felix didn't say anything for a moment. "I'm lonely, Cat," he finally said. "I'm tired of this old house—the emptiness and the darkness."

Cat looked away. "You could always leave. There's nothing keeping you here. I would not blame you."

"I would *never* leave you," he said ferociously. "I could never—it's impossible to even think it for a moment!"

She smiled sadly. "Then to empty houses and darkness you must reconcile yourself."

"No, I must *not*. And neither must you! You aren't confined here, Cat. Yes, you are bound to Richard, but that doesn't mean you can never leave this house." He took her hand. "Come with me. Let me show you the city. There are so many marvelous things you've missed—they don't have to be mere pictures on your television. You can experience them yourself! It could be like old times—"

Cat yanked her hand back suddenly. "We can never go back to how we were," she said sharply. "*Never.*"

She looked so angry that Felix wasn't sure what to do. "Cat..."

"Go talk to Richard, if you must," she said, her voice cold. "And don't come back. I won't be awake."

Instead of standing, Felix pulled her into his arms, resting his head on her chest. "I'm sorry."

She rested her head on his as he lay there and listened to the heart that thumped in her chest—a heart that wasn't her own.

"Does it still hurt?" he asked.

"With every beat. Remember that when you're chasing your witch."

He sat up and met her gaze. "I will. He's not wicked, Cat. You'll see."

She sighed and waved her hand. "Go, then."

Felix rose from the sofa and made his way to the door. He hesitated briefly; was Cat right? Should he just end this before it became too complicated?

He shook the feeling off. This was the first time he'd truly wanted something since as long as he could remember. He had to see it through.

FELIX FOUND RICHARD in the theater, watching a movie.

It was not as large as a commercial movie theater—the screen wasn't quite as wide, and there were only fifty seats. However, it did have an enormous pipe organ, which couldn't be said for the local AMC.

Richard was sitting in his usual spot, three rows back and in the center. He was munching on some popcorn.

"Good evening, Felix," Richard said without turning his head. "Why don't you join me?"

Felix slid into the velvet-covered seat beside him. He watched the movie for a moment—a talkie, but still black and white. The actors were in the middle of an extravagant song and dance number.

Richard gestured at the screen. "Why did I never produce any musicals? I always scoffed at Mayer over at MGM for his devotion to the form—so sentimental! Yet here I am, an old man, wishing for a bit of sentiment. Movies are all so cynical nowadays. Where's the joy?" He sighed and waved a hand. The projector stopped, plunging them into darkness. It didn't matter. They were both used to darkness.

Richard turned to Felix at last. "Well? Did you find your witch boy?"

"Yes."

"How did it go?"

Felix rubbed his neck. "It...could have gone better. But he did agree to see me again!"

"What did he want in return?"

Felix looked at him with surprise. "How did you know he wanted something?"

"Witches always do."

"That's what Cat said," Felix muttered unhappily. He shook it off. "He wants me to put my blood on a rose for one hundred and one nights and then bring him the blue rose it produces."

Richard's eyes widened in surprise. "Ginerva's Rose?" He sat back in his seat. "That lore is all but forgotten. Your witch boy grows more interesting by the moment. I would be happy to help." Richard stood and glanced down at his pocket watch. "If we hurry, we can start tonight. Let's go to the gardens."

They took the golf cart. Richard was not as mobile as he once was, and the estate was vast. The mansion and the theater were only two structures that made up Happy Endings. There was also a swimming pool, a tennis court, and a nine-hole golf course. Floodlights were installed everywhere so Felix and Cat could enjoy putting on the green or swimming in the pool when the sun was down. Cat used to "sunbathe" sometimes, her alabaster skin nearly glowing in the artificial rays. That was a long time ago, though.

They reached the entrance to the gardens. Richard stopped the cart and stroked his chin.

"Hmm, I suppose it doesn't really matter which type of rose. However, since we have options, we might as well put some thought into it. Now the albas should be around here somewhere—fine flowers, but they don't really feel like proper roses to me—too delicate. Then there are the floribundas over by the stallion fountain, but those feel too frilly and frivolous for our purposes." He tapped his finger to his lips, lost in thought. "Of course!" he said after a moment. "The grandifloras. I think this calls for something grand, don't you?"

Felix shrugged. He knew nothing about roses.

Richard steered the cart to the left. "If I recall correctly, they're in the greenhouse."

Felix tensed. "Actually, the floribundas sound nice."

The corners of Richard's lips curled upward. "No, I think the grandifloras would suit us best. Besides, it's at the other end of the garden, and it's been ages since I've set foot here. A midnight tour of the flowers should be pleasant, don't you think?"

Felix wrapped his arms around himself and said nothing. Richard started the cart again, down the cobblestone path. He stared dully at the swarms of flowers as they passed. Motion lights flickered on as they went forward, but the light they provided was meager. Felix knew that the blooms were very colorful in proper lighting, but they were robbed of their vibrancy in the dark. He didn't see much point in looking at them.

After some time, they reached the end of the gardens. Off to the left was a small cottage, where Richard's Extras were housed. And to the right was the greenhouse. Felix shivered. It had been fifty years since he'd been in the greenhouse. He had hoped never to step in it again.

Richard exited the cart, but Felix hesitated.

"Oh, come now," Richard said, his mouth curled upward again. "You aren't still frightened, are you? It's been fifty years, at least."

"Fifty-three," Felix said.

Richard looked annoyed. "I did apologize. Has there been a single cross word between us in all that time?"

Felix shook his head.

"Then you have no need to worry."

Still, Felix did not move. "Is it still there?"

"What, the glass coffin?"

Felix nodded.

Richard sighed. "Yes, it's there. It was a difficult enchantment—I wasn't about to destroy it."

In case you needed it again, Felix added mentally. Richard was right that it had been many years since he confined Felix to it. Felix, being a vampire, healed quickly once he'd been released, but he hadn't forgotten what it felt like to burn. He'd tried to smash it once, a few months after the "unfortunate incident," as Richard called it. It was shatterproof, of course. He hadn't gone near it again.

Richard consulted his pocket watch. "It's nearly midnight. Do you want your witch boy, or don't you?"

Felix took a deep breath, which was a silly thing to do since he didn't need to breathe. He zipped to Richard's side in a blur and gained some satisfaction at Richard's momentary surprise.

Richard gestured to the door. "Shall we?"

Richard turned on the lights, setting the greenhouse awash in an artificial glow. When they reached the roses, Felix could see why Richard had chosen them. They were radiantly beautiful—movie roses, just like a leading man might give his true love. He hoped John would be pleased.

Richard looked up at the sky through the glass. "The moon seems about right. Can you cut your finger, or shall I?"

As an answer, Felix protruded his fangs and pricked a finger against one. He squeezed it over one prominent bloom; the blood splattering against the petals— red on red.

"That should be sufficient," Richard said after a few moments.

Felix took his hand away. "Are you sure? It doesn't look any different."

"It will take time." Richard smiled. "And we certainly have an abundance of time, don't we?"

He couldn't argue with that.

They made their way back to the golf cart. Just as they were about to depart, a dark figure stumbled from the cottage across the way. It staggered toward them, slow and rambling.

Richard sighed. "It seems our newest Extra is sleepwalking."

The man suddenly lurched forward with a surprising surge of strength. He pointed at Richard. "You," he sputtered. "You lied to me."

"You're having a bad dream, Michael," Richard responded. He got out of the golf cart. "You should go back to sleep."

The man stared at him, dazed, but then he shook his head. "No—not a dream. This is real."

"And it's very unpleasant, isn't it?" Richard moved toward him slowly. "It's always been unpleasant for you out in this terrible world, hasn't it? You were having a wonderful dream. Return to it." His voice was gentle, but there was real command behind it. So much so that Michael wavered. He seemed about to obey, but then he caught sight of Felix.

"You!" he screamed. "You look like that monster bitch who bit me!" He turned and staggered in the opposite direction, clumsily at first, but soon gaining more speed than Felix thought him capable of. He disappeared down the cobblestone path.

Richard turned to Felix. "Well? What are you waiting for? Go after him. And do be gentle—I need him to last a while longer."

Felix did as he was told. A second later, he was on top of the man, who fell to the ground at the sight of him.

"Oh Jesus, oh God," he begged. "Save me, save me..."

Felix pounced on him, sinking his fangs into his neck. He fed until the man went limp. After he checked to make sure he was still breathing, he scooped the unconscious man into his arms and returned to Richard.

Richard gestured toward the cottage. "Let's tuck our Extra into bed."

Felix followed Richard into the cottage. Twelve beds lined the single room. Only one was empty. The others contained the still figures of the other Extras, all of them in various stages of decay. Their shallow breathing was the only sound in the room.

Felix dumped the man on the empty bed. Richard took a bit more care situating him, tucking him in as he murmured words Felix didn't care to listen to. The ring on Richard's finger glowed as he spoke. The man was fitful at first, still fighting him. All at once he went slack, giving in at last.

Richard sat at his bedside for a few more moments, stroking the man's hand. "I give them such lovely dreams," he said. "Their lives were all in shambles, and now they know only peace. You'd think they would be grateful."

He stood and walked to the door, pausing briefly at one of the other beds. It held a girl who was just barely out of childhood. She was skeletal, her breathing shallow.

"This one's almost used up," Richard commented. "I suppose I should get another. Cat doesn't really like them young, but their energy is most potent that way. It's barely enough to keep my old bones going as it is. It's getting harder every year."

They left the cottage and returned to the cart. Richard drove them back up to the manor. Felix was about to leave when Richard stopped him with a hand on his shoulder.

"I have a favor to ask of you."

Felix tensed. He should have seen this coming. "What is it?"

"If things go well after you give John his gift, will you invite him here for dinner?"

Felix's eyes widened in alarm. "Why? Are you going to hurt him?"

"Of course not!" Richard shook his head as if it were the most absurd question in the world, in spite of the fact that a whole Council of witches found him so toxic that they quarantined him. "No, I would merely like to talk to him. It's been so long since I've had another witch to speak to."

"Why do you want to speak with him?"

"For the same reason you do, I imagine," Richard said. "I'm lonely. How many decades has it been since we've had guests?"

"I will extend the invitation," Felix said stiffly, although he did not intend to do any such thing.

Richard smiled. "Excellent. I look forward to meeting him."

Felix tried to look agreeable. He casually strolled into the house, but as soon as he lost sight of Richard, he zipped into his room and shut the door. He paced the floor, trying to think of what to do. Unfortunately, the only thing he could think of was to lie and say that John declined the invitation. Would Richard leave the issue alone after that? He couldn't be sure. But he wasn't going to allow Richard's meddling to ruin his chance with John. He had already taken so much from him.

Besides, John was a witch. He could defend himself. Couldn't he?

Six: The Drowning of Natalie Wood, and Other Tragedies

IT WAS NEARLY time for Lo's first lesson. John examined the contents of his kitchen table. He had his stack of spell binders, a box of crystals, a map, and a notebook, all neatly arranged. He'd straightened up the apartment and spelled away the smell of tobacco. He'd even made a little snack—Ritz crackers and apple slices. He probably wasn't going to win Hostess of the Year, but at least the place looked presentable. This shouldn't be a big deal, but he still felt nervous. He'd never taught anyone before.

There was a knock on his door a little after ten. He opened the door to find Lo standing there, a messenger bag slung over her shoulder. It seemed strange to see her out of her uniform—she was wearing a T-shirt with a unicorn on it, ripped jeans, and combat boots.

"Yo," she said.

John smiled. "Please, come it."

Lo set her bag by the door. "So where do we start?"

"Why don't we have a seat?"

They sat down at his kitchenette set. Lo picked up one of the binders. "What are these?"

"Spells."

"I gotta say, when I picture books of magic, I don't tend to think of three-ring binders."

"Like I said, spells aren't really dependent on knowing the right words. You can make up your own—actually, it tends to work better that way. I just thought, to start with, it might be easier to show you mine. These are some of the easier spells—pick one and we'll try it."

Lo leafed through the binder. She stopped at one page in a laminated sleeve. "Some of these are in different handwriting, though."

John didn't say anything for a moment. "A lot of them are my mom's."

"Oh." Lo's fingers traced over the friendly loops of his mother's writing. "I'd like to try this one, if that's okay with you."

John glanced at the faded yellow page—it was *Pocket Full of Sunshine*. A happy sun decorated the corner of the page.

"This was one of my favorites as a kid," he said with a sad smile.

Lo peered at him. "We don't have to do this one."

"No, no—it's fine. It'll be fun."

"So what do I do?"

"Read it through a few times until you have it memorized. Then we'll work on channeling your energy."

Lo took a few minutes to read, her lips moving as she committed it to memory. "Okay, got it."

They put the binder aside. "Now close your eyes and focus on your breathing."

Lo groaned. "Oh no. I am shit at meditating."

"Then don't think of it as meditating. You're focusing your will. Don't worry. I'll talk you through it."

Lo looked skeptical, but she obediently shut her eyes. In spite of her protests, within a few minutes of John's instruction, her breathing was even and her notoriously twitchy fingers lay still, folded on her lap.

"Good," John said. "Now think of the spell. Visualize it as detailed as you can. Let me know when you can see it."

Lo took a few more breaths. "Okay, I got it."

"When it feels right, start the spell."

Lo inhaled. On the exhale, she murmured the words. *"There's joy in my heart, time to unlock it/put a little sunshine in my pocket."* Nothing happened. She opened one eye. "It didn't work."

"Keep trying. Breathe."

She tried again and again. John could see her shoulders tensing in frustration. But then Astray jumped in her lap as the last words of the spell left her lips, and suddenly there was a flash of brilliant light. Lo opened her eyes and laughed in delight at the glow in her pocket. She reached in and pulled out an orb of light. Astray purred her approval.

"Wow!" she said, beaming.

"See? It just takes a little practice." John scratched Astray behind the ear. "And a little help sometimes. Pets can give you a little boost."

"So witch's familiars are a thing?"

"You could call it that."

Lo let the light dance in one hand as she petted Astray with the other. With every stroke, the orb got a little bigger.

"This is *amazing*," she said. "I mean, does it always feel this good?"

"Sometimes. You have to watch your energy, though—you only have so much willpower in every given day. If you overexert yourself, trust me—you will pay for it."

Lo sighed. "It figures." She shut her hand; the ball of light vanished.

"Do you want to try another?" John asked.

"In a minute." She picked at her thumb. "There's something I want to ask you about."

"Go ahead."

"It's just—well, I keep thinking about that...you know. Vampire." She laughed a little. "I just pulled sunshine out of my ass and that still seems crazy."

"What about him? Has he bothered you?"

"No. It's just—I mean, is he out there killing people?"

He shrugged. "Probably not."

Lo raised an eyebrow. "Probably?"

"Vampires usually just take what they need from someone. They don't need to drain them totally."

"Oh, so he's only serially *assaulting* people, not serially killing them. That totally makes it not a big deal."

"I never said it was okay."

"But you shrugged!" she said, loudly enough that it disturbed the cat. "You just literally shrugged it off."

"What do you want me to say? I can't stop him."

"But you're immune to him," she pointed out. "Scratch that—*we're* immune to him. Shouldn't we try to stop him?"

"Just because he can't hurt us doesn't mean we can hurt him. You've seen how fast he moves, and vampires are insanely strong."

"But we have magic."

"It takes a lot of power to coerce a vampire. I don't have it in me."

"Yeah, but it could work on other stuff—like, we could make a trap for him. Stick his feet in concrete or something."

"And then what? Slay him?"

"Well—yeah."

John shook his head. "It's a bad idea."

"Why? Don't you think we have a responsibility to do something since we know about it?"

"There are hundreds of nonsupernatural robbers, rapists, and killers out there. Do you feel like you need to don tights and a cape and go out there and stop them?"

"No, but the police can go after those guys. They can't go after a vampire."

John sighed and rubbed his face. "Look, I get where you're coming from. You find out you have these powers and you want to use them. The fact that you want to use them to help is admirable. But whatever your intentions are, magic can and does backfire in ways you can't predict. And once you start trying to wield magic as a weapon...that's a really slippery slope."

"So we do nothing, then? Just let him munch his way through LA?"

"If it makes you feel any better, vampires are mostly attracted to people with an air of darkness around them."

"Like you."

He looked away, saying nothing. Astray leapt off Lo's lap and curled up in John's. He ran his hand over her fur; some warmth tingled up his fingers. Love sparks. Not that he deserved it.

Lo dipped her head until her gaze caught his. "Are we going to talk about it?"

"I'd rather not."

"Well, too fucking bad." She crossed her arms over her chest. "We're talking about it. I'm not leaving until you tell me what's up."

John leaned forward and put his head in his hands for a moment. He could tell she wasn't going to let it go. Might as well tell her the truth and get it over with. "I'm cursed."

"Cursed?"

"Yeah. It's a family thing, and the less you know about it, the better."

"Why?"

"Because if I tell you, you're going to want to try to stop it, and there's nothing you can do."

"Why are you so sure? I'm new to this whole magic thing, but I'm good at figuring shit out."

"It is literally written into the curse that any attempt to fight it makes it worse," he said, more harshly than he intended. "Just do me a favor and drop it, okay?"

He felt a twinge of guilt at Lo's wounded look. Astray jumped off his lap and headed for the bathroom, giving him what he could have sworn was a reproachful look over her shoulder.

John sighed. "I'm sorry. It's just that I've been down that road, and that road is full of land mines, and there's nothing at the end that justifies me dragging anyone along it with me."

"Okay," Lo said. She nibbled the Band-Aid on her right thumb. "Is that what killed your mom?"

John's gaze lingered on the little yellow sun in the corner of the spell for a moment. He blinked rapidly and looked away. "Yeah."

"And it's going to kill you, too."

"Think of me like a cancer patient who has been through all the chemo, all the radiation, every surgery and alternative medicine and experimental drug, and the only thing any of it has done is cause me more pain. I just want to let things take their course. Can you respect that?"

Lo looked as if she were about to protest, but she swallowed it back. "I guess so." She smoothed her hand over the page. "What was your mom's name?"

"Adelaide."

"That's pretty. My mom's name was Lourdes." She smiled. "We didn't really sit around and make sunshine together, but she taught me a lot. She was really political—she was big into Latino rights in particular, and any time there was an injustice of any kind, she was there to grab a sign and get loud. She took me to protest as soon as I could walk. She didn't teach me magic, but she taught me how to be strong." She looked away and laughed a little. "Maybe a little too strong. She used to call me Brillo Pad, because I was so abrasive." Lo met John's gaze again. "How old were you when you lost her?"

"Twelve."

"That's when I lost mine, too. They said it was an aneurysm."

Neither of them said anything for a moment. It was Lo who broke the silence. "Can I ask you something?"

"Sure."

"Your mom and your grandma...do you ever, you know, hear from them?"

"They're dead."

"I know, but we're witches and there are vampires and werewolves and mermaids and fairies. I thought maybe there might be ghosts."

"Yeah, there are. But they're very hard to communicate with. We witches don't know much about the afterlife—same as anyone. Ghosts are somewhere between there and here, and being stuck probably isn't a good place to end up. If you love someone, it's best to hope that they moved on."

"But even if they've moved on, is it still possible to talk to them?"

"Sure, if you want to rip them from whatever peace they've found."

Lo bit her lip. "Point taken." She started flipping through the binder again. "How about we try another one?"

Over the next three hours, they worked their way through four or five more spells. Lo was a quick study. She even managed to craft her own spell by the end—she levitated the cat. He hoped she wasn't too adept for her own good. His grandma had always said that was his mother's problem. Considering where she ended up, John couldn't disagree with her assessment.

By lunchtime, they were both spent. They decided to call it a day. Well, at least as far as the magic went—they'd both be starting shifts at the diner in a few hours.

"We should get lunch," she said.

John shook his head. "No thanks."

"Are you sure? My treat."

"No, no—I'm good." John tried to smile. The truth was that between all the magic and the unavoidable trip down memory lane, he was feeling totally drained. What he wanted more than anything was to curl up into the fetal position under a heap of blankets.

Lo chewed on the tip of her pinky. "I know that my sparkling personality and total normalcy probably makes you think I've got a ton of friends, but actually, I'm a little lonely."

"Another side effect of magical ability," John said. "We tend to put people off."

She snorted. "Well, at least I have something to blame it on now. I just meant that—well, it was nice. Hanging out." Suddenly, her arms shot out. Before John could react, he found himself enveloped in a tight hug. After a few awkward moments, John returned her embrace.

"Thanks," she said, her voice muffled against his shoulder.

John extracted himself from her embrace. "No problem."

She grinned. "See you at work?"

"Yeah, see you."

He shut the door behind her. That had gone well. He felt lighter, somehow. Like the vise of grief that squeezed his heart had let up a little. As he gathered the binders to put them away, one slipped from his grasp.

He put the others away before coming back to it. It had fallen open to the page with the sunshine spell. When he reached to pick it up, it felt...warm.

He shut it firmly. They'd spent a lot of time on that page; it was only natural that the binder would fall open to it. As for the warmth—well, it was probably residue from the spell. Or maybe he imagined it. But maybe...

He shook his head, dislodging the thought. John marched the binder over to the closet and shoved it behind all the others, in the darkest corner he could find.

"This world is a pile of shit," he said out loud. "Only an idiot would hang around if she had another option."

A strange stillness settled over the already quiet room. Something brushed his leg; he jumped. But it was only Astray, who meowed and started to purr. When he picked her up, her purr went from a vague rumble to full-blown jet plane.

"I didn't mean you," he said, kissing her head.

She leapt out of his arms. She meowed again as she padded over to her food dish. John followed her. One of the things he liked about cats was that they were not complicated. He couldn't say the same thing about people, living or otherwise.

JOHN FIGURED HE'D seen the last of Felix.

It was true that he had been unusually persistent for a vampire, but focusing on a task for a hundred and one nights was basically impossible for a vampire. He might as well have told him to bring him back a moon rock. He was surprised that a small part of him felt...well, not sad, exactly, but a little wistful. He didn't need an amorous vampire in his life, but it had been sort of exciting. Nothing excited him much anymore.

Over the next couple months, his life settled back into its old routine, except now he had Lo. She was a good student, picking up glamours and other small magics with alacrity. He kept putting off teaching her soul magic; he told her she wasn't ready, which was true. While her talent for getting the knack of a spell quickly was impressive, her ability to hold onto the spell needed work. Her concentration wandered too much. And frankly, her do-gooder attitude worried him. One unintentional lesson he'd learned from his mother was that do-gooders got done good themselves. He didn't want her to rush out and try to save the day, only to have things go wrong.

John had done such a good job of convincing himself Felix was gone for good that he was genuinely surprised when, one hundred and one nights since the last time he'd seen him, Felix showed up on his doorstep.

John had just gotten changed out of his work clothes into a T-shirt and a pair of sweats when there was a knock on his door. It was 3:30 a.m.—he'd thought it had to be Lo so he didn't bother looking through the peephole. As soon as he opened the door, he was confronted with Felix's grinning face. He had one arm behind his back.

John just stared at him dumbly for a moment. "What are you doing here?" he asked finally. He couldn't have done it. It wasn't possible.

Felix brought his hand around, and there it was: the rose. It looked almost black in the dim light of the doorstep, but when John stepped closer—of course he stepped closer; he couldn't help himself—he could see that it was, indeed, blue.

"I told you I could do it," Felix said.

John ripped his gaze away from the rose. Felix was still smiling at him. He was preternaturally still—it was one of the most reliable ways to spot a vampire. Human beings could never be that still, even if they tried. Humans' hearts beat, their lungs breathed, their eyes blinked. Vampires didn't have to do any of those things.

Felix held the flower closer to him. "Go on."

John hesitated. He hadn't allowed himself to think it was possible, but here it was, right in front of him—the panacea for all curses. Perhaps even his.

No. He shouldn't even think it. He knew what could happen. In fact, it might be too late already. He should chuck it into the bushes, slam the door, and bolt it. Maybe that would be enough to fool the curse.

But he didn't do any of those things. He took the rose. It was the same blue as the ocean; it even shimmered.

"May I come in?"

John nodded vaguely, only realizing too late what he'd allowed. Felix breezed past him into the apartment. He opened his mouth to protest, but what would be the point? He shut the door.

Felix was stalking around his apartment, his gaze flicking over his meager belongings.

"It's small," Felix said at last.

"No kidding. I hadn't noticed."

"You're joking again!" Felix laughed. "You are very funny."

"Thanks," John said, because what else could he say? The whole situation was surreal. He searched around the apartment for something to put the rose in. Eventually he settled on a two-liter bottle of Coke; he emptied the soda into the sink and filled it with water. Although did the rose even need water? From what he had read, it would never wilt. He set it on his windowsill. He couldn't quite tear his gaze away from it. It seemed even lovelier now that it was under direct light. It was as if he could *hear* it sparkle...

"Does it please you?"

John jumped and turned to find Felix mere inches from him; he hadn't realized Felix had gotten so close.

John swallowed. "Yes. Thank you."

"What are you going to do with it?"

"Nothing," John said, a little more loudly than was probably necessary. "I'm not going to do anything with it."

Felix frowned. "Then why did you make me go to all that trouble?"

A very good question. "I just wanted to see if it could be done," was what he finally came up with.

Felix shook his head with exasperation. "I will never understand witchery."

John didn't want Felix to get too comfortable in the apartment, so he slipped on some flip-flops and gestured toward the door. "Why don't we talk outside?"

Felix frowned. "Why?"

John picked up a pack of cigarettes from the counter. "I want to smoke."

Once they were outside, John shut the door and then lit a cigarette. He had no idea how he was going to get rid of Felix, who still seemed very pleased with himself. Felix clapped his hands together, bringing his clasped hands to his chin. "So! Where shall we go?"

"Go?"

"On our date."

"Oh. Right." John's head still felt cloudy, as if he wasn't sure this was a dream. "I don't know. There's not a lot open this time of night. Or morning, technically."

Felix steepled his index fingers and tapped his lips in thought. "Ah, I know! Do you like the beach?"

"Yes," John said. "But it would be hard to get there; I mean, I don't have a—"

Before he could complete that sentence, he felt himself lifted off his feet and was soon whooshing through the air. He was too surprised to do anything but yelp and reach out to hold on to something. His arms wrapped around what he suspected were Felix's shoulders. He couldn't tell because his eyes were firmly shut, and he didn't plan on opening them.

Some short time later, they stopped. John opened his eyes. He found that he was wrapped around Felix like a baby koala.

"—car," John finished weakly.

"Neither do I," Felix said. "Useless machines. Noisy. Smelly."

John let go of Felix; it took a moment for him to get his balance. His flip-flops had flown clean off his feet, leaving him without shoes. His cigarettes were also nowhere to be found. He looked around. They had arrived, somehow, on a beach. Which beach it was, John couldn't say. Just how fast and how far could Felix move?

He looked over to find Felix giving him a smug look. "I've impressed you, haven't I?"

"You've made an impression," John admitted. The beach was long and thin; steep cliffs surrounded them. The moon was full, but it was still very dark. He could see no houses or any other signs of human life. A shiver ripped through him; it was cold.

"A walk on the beach by moonlight. Very romantic, don't you think?"

John watched the black water churn, lapping up onto the gray sand and nearly hitting his bare toes. "I don't have a jacket and I'm barefoot," John said. "I'm fucking freezing."

Felix frowned at that. "Oh." He thought for a moment. He took off his jacket and draped it over John's shoulders. "There! Is that better?"

"Are you going to give me your shoes, too?"

Felix scowled. "Instead of complaining, why don't you whip up a spell to make it warmer?"

John hesitated. He'd been doing a lot of magic with Lo lately. Low levels, sure, but given that he'd sworn off it, using it in a nonteaching and nonemergency setting seemed like a slippery slope. On the other hand, he was voluntarily standing on a beach with a vampire—he was clearly taking a night off from good sense, anyway.

"Well?" Felix prodded him when he didn't respond. "Are you a witch or aren't you?"

"Okay, okay, let me think." John took a deep breath. *"I've got a date sent straight from hell/I do not want to freeze as well."*

The chill left John's bones. When he opened his eyes, Felix was making a face at him.

"That wasn't a very nice spell."

"Magic works best if it has some real feeling behind it," John said. Although it remained as dark as before, he felt as if he were sunning himself on a warm day. Even the sand under his feet felt warm. He wiggled his toes. It felt...good.

Felix offered John his arm. "Shall we?"

John took it. What else could he do?

They walked along in silence for a little while. John racked his mind, trying to think of where Felix had brought them. He'd only been to the beach once since his arrival in California, but it was a crowded, tourist-filled beach in the middle of the day, right next to a lively boardwalk. There was no boardwalk here, or any other sign of civilization. Felix could move fast, that much was clear, but he doubted they were too far from home.

Felix was staring at him again. "Will you tell me about your curse now?"

John hesitated. There were many reasons that kept him from telling people about the curse. The first was that no one would believe him. That clearly didn't apply in this situation. The second was because he feared collateral damage, which is why he hadn't wanted to tell Lo. Felix was a vampire, though; he couldn't be hurt in any meaningful way.

Felix continued to look at him expectantly. John gave in. "It started with my great-great-great-great-great-great grandmother, Abagail. She was a witch in New England, around 1775. She somehow got entangled with another witch—a real nasty asshole. Things didn't work out. He didn't take it well. So he cursed her, and all of her descendants." He took a breath; he could recite the whole thing from memory.

"Abagail Palmer, a woman fair
Has used her beauty to ensnare
My heart, and cruelly threw aside
The chance to be my blushing bride
And so on her I put this curse:

She used me ill, but she'll have it worse
When her cruel heart learns at last to love
A premonition she'll have—what of?
Of violent death. Her love's embrace
Will bring a vision of a face:
The man who will cause her bloody death
To love will mark her final breath
But even this is not enough
To punish her for her rebuff
To each descendant, this curse extends:
To love a man is to meet your end.
But a small mercy I will give:
Embrace your fate, and you may live
A relatively peaceful life
Accept your fate, or else bring strife
Upon yourself and all you love
No mercy will come, from below or above
Only Death's sweet embrace
Will bring you to a state of grace."

"Ah," Felix said thoughtfully. Then, a few moments later, "And what does that mean?"

"It means whenever a member of my family falls in love, she has a vision of the man who will kill her. All the women in our family die by violence."

"But you're safe, then!" Felix said. "You're a man."

"That's what I thought, too," he said. "But the curse is activated when a member of my family falls in love with a *man*. That usually means the object of the curse is a woman." John smiled humorlessly. "But not always."

"Because you fell in love with a man."

"Yes."

"Good gracious! Does that mean that when you fall in love with me, I will be compelled to murder you?"

John really should have been annoyed by Felix's presumption that he was going to fall in love with him, but a part of him found it sort of cute. "No. Falling in love is the trigger, but the actual murderer will be someone else." He looked off into the distance for a moment. "Well, in most cases, anyway." He shook himself out of it. "Anyway, I've already had my vision, and it isn't you."

"That's a relief—the part about it not being me, I mean. Your vision is still rather distressing." Felix rubbed his chin for a moment, and then his whole face brightened. "Aha! We should break the curse! That would solve everything!"

John pinched the bridge of his nose. "Believe it or not, you are not the first person to have that idea. However, it's a really fucking bad idea. Think about the wording. It's worse if you try to fight it. Much, much worse."

"How can it be worse than death?"

"Not all deaths are created equal. My grandmother, for instance, made no effort to avoid the curse. She died at age seventy, hit by a drunk driver. She was killed on impact. No suffering, and no one else died." He paused. "My mother fought it, though. She started fighting as soon as her mother told her, when she was fourteen. She researched everything she could about counter-curses. She cast spells. She sought experts. She swore she would never fall in love. But then she met my father. They got to know one another, and before she knew it, she had fallen for him. Then she had her vision. It was him. He was the one who was going to kill her.

"Of course, that made her fight harder. There was part of her that didn't believe it could be true. They even started a family. But as soon as my mom became pregnant, he started to change. He got violent. She broke it off with him when I was a baby, but he wouldn't stop coming for her—for both of us. When I was two, he nearly killed her. He went to jail for it, but when he got out ten years later, he came after her again. He murdered her, and then he killed himself." John stared off into the ocean. "I was there when it happened," he added quietly. "I watched him kill her."

He looked up at Felix. It was difficult to see his expression in the low light. This was something he never told people, although for a while he couldn't avoid people knowing. The whole thing had been in the news for ages; it had been unusually gruesome. He hated the way that knowledge made people treat him—their voices always high-pitched with exaggerated sympathy and an undercurrent of fear, like somehow tragedy was contagious.

"Well, that's unfortunate," Felix said eventually.

John let out a breath he hadn't been aware he was holding. Maybe he should have been offended at his callousness, but instead he felt relieved. He looked at Felix with a different perspective. He was a vampire, which made him heartless. A man without a heart was a man who couldn't grieve. John liked that idea a lot.

"But you have decided not to fight, I take it?" Felix continued. "That means you may live for a very long time!"

John shrugged. "Maybe."

They had reached the end of the beach; it wasn't very long. There appeared to be hiking trails that led inland, but the details were lost in the darkness. He gave up trying to solve the mystery himself.

"Where are we?"

"Oh, an island."

"An island?" John said with surprise. Felix moved fast, but he was sure they couldn't be too far from home. There was only one place it could be. "Is this Catalina?"

"Yes."

John looked around the rocky beach with new appreciation. Catalina was a small island off the coast of Los Angeles. It was a popular tourist spot, with a small resort town—Avalon—on the southeast side of the island, but the majority of it was a nature preserve. There was an additional tidbit of trivia that made it particularly interesting to John. "This is where Natalie Wood died."

"Who?"

"The actress. She and her husband were out yachting in the bay there, and then she mysteriously drowned. Her body washed up in a little cove. No one has ever solved the mystery of what happened."

"Why does that interest you?"

"I'm a fan of Old Hollywood, and I have a tendency to be morbid." He looked behind him at the cliffs, squinting to see if he could make out any signs of civilization. "How far are we from Avalon?"

"Far enough. No one comes here. That's why I like it." Felix smiled at him. "We're all alone."

A shiver ran down John's spine, though not from the cold. Which was ridiculous—he *knew* Felix couldn't kill him, even without the curse. As long as he didn't fear him, he was safe.

But at the same time, he was on an isolated beach in the middle of the night with a vampire. True, Felix would not be the one to kill him, but there were fates other than death that were always a possibility.

And John had accepted that rose. In fact, he ordered its creation. His heart began to beat a little more quickly. Had he triggered something?

Was this all part of the curse—that he'd be used as a vampire's plaything until the man of his dreams came to deliver the killing blow?

No. He tried to shake himself out of it. He was being ridiculous. As long as he remained calm, it would be fine. And he really didn't think Felix would hurt him.

At least not intentionally.

Felix cocked his head, examining John. "Are you all right?"

John swallowed. "I'm fine," he managed with a weak smile.

Felix's head remained cocked as his continued to look at him. "No, I don't think so," he said. "You're afraid. I can feel it."

John's heart rate spiked. He took a deep breath, but it only made things worse, like blowing on a fire.

"I'm fine," he said again, but his voice was shaking.

Felix frowned. "Are you frightened of that man who will kill you? You needn't be. He won't get to you tonight." Felix gestured. "As you can see, we are truly alone."

"Yeah, I get that."

"And yet you still tremble." Felix put his arms around John, his face hovering inches from John's own. John felt frozen in place by Felix's green gaze. "You have nothing to fear." Felix's voice was now a low rumble, like the growl of a lion. "If he comes, I will tear him limb from limb." He smiled, showing just the faintest hint of his fangs. "I can do that, you know. I'm very strong."

John laughed a little, more from tension than anything else. "Yeah, I know. Thanks."

Felix smiled a little wider. John felt Felix's arm travel down until it settled around his waist. He pulled John forward until their bodies were flush with each other. He tilted his head. "I think I'd like my kiss now," he breathed. Or no, he *didn't* breathe, because he was *dead*, a monster, and he literally had John in his clutches—

—and then his mouth was on John's, and it was like he'd been hit by a bolt of lightning. Adrenaline surged through him, and to his great shock, he found himself kissing back. Felix made a pleased sound and rolled his hips forward, his desire more than evident. And damn it if John wasn't just as hard. Sweet Jesus, he was literally embracing death and getting a boner from it. How hopelessly fucked up was that? But for the first time since resigning himself to his curse, he felt *alive*, shocked out of the dullness of what was left of his life.

Felix slipped the jacket from John's shoulders; it fell to the ground. He slid his hands down to John's waist again and tugged at the hem of his shirt.

"Off," he growled, barely breaking the kiss.

John pulled back. "What? You want to—here?"

"Why not? There's—"

"—no one here," John finished for him. "Right." Did he really want to do this? Adrenaline surged again; he felt like he'd been dropped out of an airplane.

Felix kissed his neck as he moved his hand downward to cup John through his sweatpants. "You desire me," he said with just a hint of smugness. "You can't deny it."

He had a point. Even so, John opened his mouth to protest, but Felix dropped to his knees, his face level with John's groin. He yanked down his sweatpants with alarming swiftness and took his cock into his mouth. John gasped. His hands found themselves on Felix's head. He wasn't sure if his intention was to push him away, but that didn't end up happening. John slipped his fingers through his silky hair as Felix bobbed his head up and down. He started to move more quickly—preternaturally quickly, in fact. The sensation was like nothing John had felt before—it was utterly relentless and overwhelming.

"Stop!" he managed to choke out. Felix immediately complied—but moments later, John found himself flat on his back on the sand with Felix over him. John's chest heaved as he struggled to catch his breath.

"I want to fuck you," Felix said.

"But—we don't have any—"

Felix reached over to his jacket and produced a bottle of lube and...a condom? That cocky bastard had come prepared!

John gestured to it. "You know you can't get or spread STDs, right?" *And why would he even care if he could?* John added mentally.

Felix shrugged. "Men insist on them nowadays. It isn't as if it's a burden."

"That's very considerate of you," he said. He hesitated. "Do you...you know, feed on your partners?"

Felix made a face. "Of course not. Would you fuck your dinner?"

John laughed. "I guess not."

Felix leaned down and kissed him. John gave up his internal debate—this was clearly happening. He wrapped his arms around Felix and returned the embrace.

They parted to strip, coming together again when they were both naked. John's senses were so confused—the night air should have been cool, but it wasn't thanks to the spell, and Felix's skin pressed against him should have been warm, but it was unnaturally cold. That thought sent another rush through him. *I'm about to fuck a monster.*

That monster was now brushing his cool fingers against John's straining erection, causing John's hips to jerk upward. Felix looked as though he were about to say something smug, so John put one hand on the back of his head and pulled him into a firm kiss. He put his other hand over Felix's grip on his spit-slicked cock and encouraged him to move.

Once Felix took up the rhythm, John let his hand fall away. John moaned, moving his tongue forward into Felix's mouth—

John jolted back with a yelp. He'd just pricked his tongue on one of Felix's exposed fangs.

"Sorry," Felix said as he continued to stroke him, not missing a single beat. "They tend to come out when I get excited. I don't do much kissing."

John brought a finger to his mouth; when he drew it away, there was a trickle of blood. He looked back up at Felix. Haltingly, John reached a hand up to Felix's mouth. He touched one of the fangs, starting at the root and ending with the sharp end. He pressed his finger against it until it pierced the skin.

Now *that* caused Felix to fumble. "What are you doing?"

"I don't know." His heart was racing. John pushed his finger into Felix's mouth. Felix's lips closed around it and sucked for a moment. Suddenly John found himself flipped over, face-first in the sand with his wrists pinned down.

"I told you I don't mix feeding and fucking," Felix hissed in his ear.

John lifted his ass until he came into contact with Felix's cock. Felix moaned as John ground against him, thrusting back to meet his movements.

"Get the lube," John panted.

Felix released his wrists to do as he was told. As soon as Felix had the condom and the lube in hand, John tackled him, straddling him as Felix landed with an *oomph* on his back. John plucked the condom from Felix's hand and threw it over his shoulder—they were both dead men walking, so what did it matter? He slicked his fingers and briefly prepared himself. When he was done, he put more lube on Felix's cock, lined it up, and pressed down in one long, slow slide. He had never needed much preparation. He liked it when it hurt.

When he was fully seated, he took a moment to breathe. John planted a hand on Felix's chest for balance and began to move, slowly at first, then picking up speed. Felix's hands settled on John's hips as he thrust up to meet John's movements. They set a rhythm with surprising ease, hovering right on the sharp line of pleasure that separated longing from satiety.

When they were close to crossing that line, John pulled off and rolled on his back, pulling his legs up. As Felix entered him again, John put a hand around the back of Felix's neck and pulled his face close to his own, kissing his neck and keeping him close as Felix found his rhythm again. Those fangs were out, still so close and sharp. John couldn't keep his eyes off them.

John threw his head back, exposing the long line of his throat. "Bite me," John panted.

Felix faltered. "I told you I don't—"

John grabbed Felix by the hair and yanked him until his fangs were directly over his jugular. In fact, they actually scraped the skin—not hard enough to make him bleed, but hard enough to leave a mark. "Do it. I want to see if you can."

Felix snarled. The tips of his fangs broke the skin, but he went no farther. Still, John began to bleed, if only a little.

John laughed. He felt like he was high. The moon hung over Felix's head like a web, and the stars spun like spiders, but Death hadn't caught him. Not yet. Every beat of his heart said *not yet*.

Felix had started thrusting again, lapping at the trickle of blood as he moved inside John, faster and faster, and then suddenly they were both *there*, flying over the edge, falling like stars, messily exploding on impact.

Afterward, Felix rolled off him. They both lay there for a very long moment. Water lapped at his feet; the tide appeared to be coming in. John couldn't bring himself to move. Neither, apparently, could Felix.

"That was very confusing," Felix eventually said.

John started laughing, and Felix joined in. Their laughter fed into itself, growing more and more until they were practically howling. John punched the air with both hands, letting out a rapturous yowl. He felt *amazing*.

Felix grabbed his jacket, feeling around in the pockets. Before John could ask what he was doing, Felix pulled out his phone and snapped a picture of the two of them, lying together on the sand.

"Why did you just take our picture?" John asked.

"Oh, it's for my sister. I want to show her what you look like. She is afraid of witches, but I'm sure once she sees you, it will put her fears at ease. It is very clear that you are not wicked. You can see it in your face."

There were so many surprising things about that statement that John wasn't sure where to begin. "You have a sister?" he said at last. "Is she a vampire, too?"

"Of course. Her name is Cat. She's really terrific."

John wasn't sure what to make of that. One vampire taking care of himself was plausible enough, but two of them? "Do the two of you live together on your own?"

Felix's goofy expression faltered. "No. She's married."

"*Married?* To a normal person?"

"Not exactly. He's a witch."

"The one who helped you find me? The one who told you I was under a curse?"

"Yes."

As John processed that information, Felix flipped through his phone until the picture of the two of them came up. The flash made them both look eerily luminescent.

"We are a good-looking couple," Felix said, grinning.

John couldn't share his grin. "Did your brother-in-law help you with the rose?" John asked carefully.

"He did. He said it was Ginerva's Rose..." He trailed off. "Wait—is the rose a counter-curse?"

John slapped a hand over Felix's mouth. "Don't say that out loud," he hissed. "Promise you won't."

Felix's eyes widened in surprise, but he nodded his head. John released him.

"He didn't tell you what it was for?"

Felix shook his head. Something was *definitely* not right with this scenario. This witch had sent Felix off like he was some sort of errand boy who didn't need to know what he was delivering. If this man was responsible for getting the rose to John, he must have ulterior motives. But what could they be?

"I'm going to ask you something," John said. "And I need you to be honest. When we first met, did your brother-in-law send you?"

"What? No! He didn't even know about you until I asked him to find you."

There was no trace of dishonesty in Felix's voice, and somehow John thought Felix was probably not the best of liars.

John stood up. "We should get dressed," he said as he grabbed his clothes.

Felix followed suit, shooting John a confused look. "Is something wrong?"

"Maybe." His warming spell was wearing off, and his feet were wet and cold. He pulled on his sweatpants. "What does your brother-in-law look like?"

"He's old now. Silver hair, blue eyes. He's quite a bit shorter than he used to be."

John felt a modicum of relief. Not the man of his dreams, then. That was kind of a long shot, anyway—after all, why would the man destined to kill him offer him a cure? But that was just the kind of irony the curse liked.

"What do you mean, 'now'? How long ago did he marry your sister?"

Felix zipped up his jeans. "Oh, some time ago," he said airily.

"How long ago?"

Felix didn't say anything as he put on his shirt.

When he still hadn't responded after a few minutes, John prodded him again. "How long ago?"

Felix turned on him suddenly. "I don't particularly wish to discuss my brother-in-law!"

John took a step back at Felix's sudden burst of temper. "Why not?"

Felix sighed. "You witches and your curiosity—some things are best left alone. Ask me no more about Richard. You wouldn't like the answers."

John started to ask why, but managed to stop himself. There would be time to wheedle the information out of him. After all, Felix wasn't the brightest star in the sky. He'd already let the man's name slip. And regardless of what Felix thought, this definitely was something John needed to know.

Felix put a hand on John's shoulder. "You're shivering again," he murmured, all trace of anger gone. He put his jacket over John's shoulders. John put a hand on his, encouraging him to keep his arm around him.

They sat like that for a little while, looking out at the sea. "She was wearing a jacket when she died," John said eventually.

"When who died?"

"Natalie Wood. A red down jacket over her nightgown. Some people think her husband killed her in the heat of an argument, but that seems like a strange outfit for a late-night fight. But then, it's a weird outfit for a suicide, too—why put on the jacket if she was heading off to drown herself?" John absently patted his pocket for a cigarette, but of course he hadn't brought them. "Then again, Virginia Woolf wore a jacket, and she definitely drowned herself. She put rocks in her pockets to weigh herself down."

"And Virginia Woolf was also an actress?"

"No. She was a writer." John huddled in closer. "I don't think it would be a bad way to go, in cold water especially. There would be that sudden shock of cold, a couple of panicked minutes, and then just numbness. It would save anyone from having to clean up afterward—not like hanging, or a bullet to the head." God, he wanted a cigarette. This was a cigarette sort of conversation. "Do you know what she wrote once? *'Someone has to die in order that the rest of us should value life more.'* I always thought that was an extremely shitty sentiment."

"This is very gloomy talk," Felix observed.

"Sorry. I'm a gloomy person." He got to his feet. "We should go."

Felix agreed; he scooped him up, and soon they were soaring through the sky. John kept his eyes open this time. The world looked so small beneath them.

Felix landed in the shadows of his apartment building. They walked the remaining steps to his front door.

"Well, good night," John said awkwardly. "Or good morning, I guess."

"Can I see you again?"

To John's own surprise, his immediate reaction was to say *yes*. This whole thing was such a terrible idea, but he had enjoyed himself tonight. He had honestly thought that wasn't possible.

Fuck it. Why spend the rest of his probably short life being miserable? "Thursday is the next full day I have off."

Felix's responding smile was almost boyish. "Another date, then?"

"Yeah, sure."

Felix lifted him up and spun him around. "This is marvelous," he said. "Absolutely wonderful! You won't regret it."

"Put me down," John said, but he couldn't help but smile a little. What was wrong with him? And for that matter, what was wrong with Felix? This was not how vampires were supposed to behave. He'd always assumed they were nearly brain-dead and totally heartless, but Felix looked so honestly happy.

Felix set him down. "Until Thursday, then," he said, giving John's hand a kiss. With that, he was gone.

John stepped into an apartment, still half-dazed. In his life of weird happenings, this was up there.

The rose was still sitting on the windowsill, shimmering in the light. John stared at it for a long while. Should he try it? All he would have to do was take a few of the petals and brew some tea...

He took the rose and put it under the kitchen sink—out of sight, out of mind. Hopefully. When that was taken care of, he stripped off his clothes and climbed into the shower.

As the sand washed off him and down the drain, he ruminated on what Felix had told him. What was the deal with Richard? Whatever he was up to was something so dark that even a vampire didn't care to talk about it. Could John even be sure it was Ginerva's Rose? There was a strong sense of magic coming from it, but it could be a different spell. A witch's worst enemies were always other witches. Why Richard would want to enchant John was beyond him, but nothing about this situation was trustworthy. He needed to find out more about the man before he determined if it was safe. For all he knew, this was the curse at work, using Richard as its vessel. But why? To weaken him for the final blow? To punish him for allowing the tiniest bit of hope into his life?

By the time he was clean, his normal gloom had settled over him again. He got dressed and curled up on his bed. Dawn was on its way. He always slept better when the sun was out. As he shut his eyes, he imagined the waves again, and Felix's skin against his, and that orgasm that blew all his misery into smithereens for one brief, glorious moment.

It had been a nice mental vacation from himself. In spite of his better judgment, he found himself looking forward to Thursday.

Seven: Flight of the Mastodon

THURSDAY ARRIVED. FELIX met John at his apartment, eager for more romance. He thought maybe they would go to dinner. Felix didn't really eat, but he knew that dinner at a fancy restaurant could be very romantic. However, John had different plans. He wanted to go to a museum. Felix thought it was a very odd place to have a date, but he had learned long ago that it was best not to question the strange impulses of witches. Besides, it didn't really matter where they went, because John wrapped his arms around Felix and kissed him, and that's what *Felix* wanted the most.

Felix zipped them across town. They arrived at the La Brea Tar Pits around 11:00 p.m. It was billed as "the world's most famous Ice Age excavation site," centered around giant pits of tar where many prehistoric beasts had met their ends. The museum was closed, obviously, but John used his witchery to convince the security guard that his life would be much easier if he didn't notice that John and Felix were there. They had full run of the place—the museum, the gardens, and the pits themselves.

They wandered through the exhibits—blackened skeletons pulled from the pits and reassembled. There were helpful pictures of what the animals would look like in life, had they not had the misfortune of falling into tar pits. They walked past a saber-toothed tiger.

"Oh, I like this one," Felix said, admiring its fangs. "Very majestic."

John squinted at the inscription. "Their fangs could be almost a foot long. That *is* pretty impressive." He moved on to the next exhibit. Felix hung back for a moment, protracting his fangs and giving them a quick feel. Once you accounted for the size of the beast, his were a perfectly respectable length, surely?

He caught up with John as he perused the dinosaur statues. "You know, there actually aren't any dinosaurs here," John said. "They existed millions of years before all these mammals. But they bill themselves as a fossil pit, so people demanded dinosaurs. Why let the truth get in the way?"

"That's very interesting," Felix lied. They continued their stroll. John seemed so lost in thought that Felix wasn't sure what to say. "I must confess that I find this a rather strange place for a date," Felix said eventually.

John stopped to examine some fossilized ferns, looking at them with a great deal more interest than Felix thought they deserved.

Just when he thought John was not going to answer his question, he spoke. "My mother and I used to go to museums. We'd always come in after hours so we could look at all the exhibits without anyone bothering us. It was her way of educating me. I didn't ever go to school until after she died; we were always on the run. I guess she thought if we kept moving, the curse might not catch us."

Unlike John's previous observation about the dinosaurs, that was very interesting. However, it was also very gloomy and did not answer his question as to why John would think that a place that reminded him of his murdered mother was a good spot for a romantic date. Felix decided to let the subject rest. The last thing this date needed was more ruminations about his dead mother.

They reached a wall of dire wolf skulls. There were dozens of them, all lined up neatly against a display case that glowed a deep orange.

"*The way of all flesh*,'" John intoned solemnly, and then he laughed.

"What's funny?"

John gestured to the wall. "A mastodon gets stuck and starts bellowing, and that would attract these wolves and the tigers, who would then get stuck, who would then in turn be attacked by vultures, who would also get stuck... There's something almost slapstick about it, don't you think?"

"I suppose," Felix said, although it didn't seem that funny. John's sense of humor was better than his, though, and he didn't want to seem stupid.

"And then they all would slowly starve." He didn't laugh about that, but grew thoughtful instead. "That's a fate worse than death. I've always liked the idea of fates worse than death. It makes death seem a lot easier to swallow."

"Yes, but then they *did* die. So it isn't really a fate worse than death— just a nasty fate, followed by death."

John shrugged. "If you want to split hairs, sure. My point is that while they were stuck, it was definitely worse than being dead. Everything dies eventually."

"Not me," Felix said a little smugly.

"Oh, sure you will. Humanity is doomed. Climate change, nuclear war, maybe even an asteroid. And even if you managed to survive all that, you'd have no one to eat, and you would starve. Slowly."

Felix's face fell. He'd never thought of that before.

John kissed him on the cheek. "But not yet," he said. He pulled Felix by the arm. "Come on—let's go see the pits."

The grounds surrounding the pits were as pretty as any park, but there was an ominous odor emanating from the large pools of tar. Bubbles appeared on the surface here and there, burbling briefly before they popped. The shiny black surface had an odd sort of beauty to it. He could understand why an animal might be attracted to take a closer look.

They made their way to the east end of the largest tar pit, where there were three realistic statues of mastodons. A plaque beside them read: *The mother has become trapped; her mate and offspring watch helplessly.* The father and the baby mastodon stood at the edge, looking very grim indeed. The baby held out its trunk pitifully, reaching for his doomed mama.

They both stared at the statues for a while. The breeze blew. Bubbles blurped.

"Why does it always have to be the mother?" John said suddenly, with unusual passion. "They always kill off the mom in all of these forced pathos scenarios. And why? Whose idea was this? They have a whole fucking museum of black skeletons, but they felt like that wasn't grotesque enough—no, they've got to have a statue of a baby watching his mom caught up in a fate worse than death. People bring their kids here. What were they thinking?" He put a hand on the baby's head. "I hope he left," he said, his voice softer now. "The only thing that could be worse is if the mom knew her baby was going to toddle in after her."

John took his hand off the baby's head. He pulled out a pack of cigarettes and a lighter.

"Do you really think that's wise?" Felix asked. He gestured to tar. "Isn't this all...flammable?"

"Fuck it," John said as he flicked the lighter once. "I know I don't die by tar fire."

"But as you very recently pointed out, I am not as immortal as I once believed, and vampires are very prone to catching on fire." He smiled in what he hoped was a persuasive fashion.

It worked. John put the cigarettes and lighter back in his jacket.

Felix looked at John with concern. His mood had taken such a sudden dive and now appeared to be as black as the tar that surrounded them. Seeing him so miserable did strange things to Felix's insides; he felt stirred in a way he couldn't remember feeling. Besides, if things continued in this vein, John wouldn't have sex with him tonight. He had really been looking forward to that. Drastic measures were clearly called for. He knew what he had to do.

He had to save that mastodon.

Felix pushed off the ground and launched himself at the statue. When he was on top of the thing, he looked back at John and was pleased to see that the gloomy expression on John's face had vanished. It had been replaced by one of complete bafflement, which wasn't quite where he wanted John to be, but it was better than misery.

"What are you doing?" John called after him.

Felix patted the mastodon. "I am going to rescue this poor creature and reunite her with her offspring."

"You do know that it's not a real mastodon, don't you?"

Felix rolled his eyes. "Of course I know that. I'm not *that* stupid."

"Then why?"

"Because this statue is making you sad, and I don't like to see you sad."

John was speechless for a moment. "If a two-ton mastodon couldn't get herself out of the tar, what makes you think you can?"

"I told you. I'm extremely strong." He turned around and grabbed the statue by its trunk. "I can also fly."

He took off into the air, the trunk firmly in his grasp. Or at least, he tried to. The thing remained stuck. He strained, harder than he ever had before. It began to move—barely. After a few moments of not making much progress, he tried a different approach, floating upside down above the statue and pulling directly upward. It moved a little more, but as soon as he let up, it started to sink again.

He looked over to John with dejection, only to find that he was laughing. "I don't think you'll be able to do it."

"Well, are you a witch or aren't you? Help me!" He started to pull again.

John hesitated for a moment, but then he spoke. "*All we need is a little luck/And a little spell to make the thing unstuck.*"

Felix went flying backward as the statue was suddenly released, taking the thing with him.

"Come down here!" John shouted, laughing. "Someone is going to see!"

When he got control of himself, Felix flew back to the ground. He set the mastodon down with a thud. They arranged the baby and the mother in a joyful reunion.

John put his arm around Felix when they were done, his good mood restored. "There. That's much better." He laughed again. "This is going to mess with people's heads so much."

John pulled him in for a deep kiss. Felix had to pull away before his fangs started to protrude.

"Let's go dancing," Felix said.

John looked surprised. "You dance? Like, at clubs?"

"Of course! How do you think I meet sexual partners?"

"And you're able to pass yourself off as a completely normal human being?"

Felix made a face at him. "Of course I can. Can you?"

John laughed. "Touché."

They left the pits and headed downtown. John insisted on taking human transportation and walking at a natural pace, which Felix protested at first. To his surprise, he actually enjoyed going slowly, taking in the sights of the city for once instead of focusing solely on fulfilling his appetite for either blood or sex. Also, John continued to hold his hand; he hadn't fed in a long time, but that gentle pressure of John's hand in his made him feel as warm as if he was fresh off a kill.

The club was not particularly crowded, being a Thursday night, but there were still plenty of people on the dance floor. They went to the bar first for drinks. "I'll have two vodka martinis, a Bloody Mary, and three Snake Bites," he told the bartender. "Oh, and a Sex on the Beach," he added, winking at John. "And what will you have?"

John looked surprised. "Uh, I'll have a margarita." When the bartender left, John asked Felix, "So all those drinks you ordered are for you?"

"Yes."

"I didn't think you could eat or drink."

"Oh, I can. It just doesn't nourish me. But one does not drink alcohol for nourishment, do they?"

John laughed. "No, definitely not. So can you get drunk?"

"Yes, but it takes a lot of effort. Hence all the drinks."

Once their drinks arrived, Felix downed the shots immediately before turning to his Bloody Mary, which he began to drain with alacrity. John took a sip of his drink. "You might want to slow down," he murmured. "People are looking at you."

"Why should I care?"

"We're trying to pass ourselves off as normal, sane human beings, remember?"

Felix reluctantly set his drink down. John rewarded him with a stroke of his foot against Felix's shin, which Felix found surprisingly arousing. It probably had a lot to do with the way John was looking at him as he did it, his eyes peeking out at him from lowered lids, the edge of his teeth biting ever so slightly on his lower lip...

"John!"

Felix and John both started at the sudden intrusion. A man with red hair and freckles stood in front of them. "Hey," he said. "I was hoping to run into you, but you haven't been around lately."

John smiled weakly. "Yeah, guess I haven't." He turned to Felix. "Felix, this is...um..."

The other man's smile faltered. "Mitch."

"Mitch! Right."

Mitch soldiered on. "You slipped out of my apartment so quickly I never got a chance to get your number. Or to say goodbye, even."

Felix narrowed his eyes. So this was one of John's conquests. It shouldn't surprise him that someone as beautiful as John would have many lovers. That didn't mean Felix had to like it.

John rubbed his neck. "Yeah, sorry, I had...stuff."

Mitch looked wounded. "Look, I know we met in a bar and moved fast, but then we really talked, you know? I thought we had a connection."

"I'm sorry," John said again. "I've been busy."

Mitch looked back and forth between John and Felix. "Yeah, I can see that." He turned to Felix. "Make sure you use a condom. John gets around."

Felix shot to his feet and towered over Mitch. He was good at towering. "I could throw you across this room so hard you would splatter on the wall like a mosquito on a windshield," he growled. "But I won't, because I most certainly don't have preternatural strength." His smiled, with just a hint of fang. "For I am a completely normal and sane human being!" he pronounced to both Mitch and the bar at large.

Mitch stumbled backward and fell on his ass. He scrambled to his feet and ran away.

When Felix turned back to John, he found John laughing. "Oh my God, you are a weirdo," John said, but from his tone, Felix could tell it was a compliment.

They finished their drinks—John stole a few of his —and got on the dance floor. Felix loved the way John moved, his body melting into the flow of the music as he danced. Felix took John's lead, dancing to complement John's moves. Soon they were up against each other, dancing in perfect harmony.

"You're a really good dancer!" John shouted over the music.

Felix gave an extra grind with his hips. "Why do you sound surprised?"

John just laughed. He whipped around and backed his ass up into Felix. With a growl, Felix held John flush against his body. John moaned and bared his neck. Felix brushed it ever so lightly with the tips of his fangs.

John turned around, draping his hands over Felix's shoulders. "Let's get out of here."

Felix most heartily agreed. "But where?"

"My place." He bit Felix's earlobe and breathed in his ear, "Get us there quick."

They stumbled out of the club. As soon as no one was looking, Felix whisked John up in his arms and zipped to his apartment. Felix groped John from behind as he fumbled with his keys. He got the deadbolt opened and moved to the doorknob, but he wasn't moving fast enough for Felix's taste. He began to nibble at the nape of his neck.

John dropped his keys with a breathy laugh. "We're never going to get inside if you keep that up."

Felix took the doorknob, turned it until it snapped, and pushed the door open.

John gaped. "You just broke my door—"

He pushed John inside and maneuvered them so they hit his bed with John flat on his back. He covered John's body with his own, kissing and grinding against him until he was a panting mess. When he seemed sufficiently dazed with desire, Felix tore his shoes and pants off quick as lightning. There was a nightstand beside them; Felix made an educated guess that he'd find what he needed there, and he was right. He got the lube and slicked his fingers.

John drew his legs up, giving Felix full access. Felix pressed two fingers into him, lingering just long enough to warm him up. Felix didn't bother taking off his own pants. He unzipped his fly and pulled his pants down far enough to free himself. It only took a moment to slick his cock, and then he thrust inside. John gasped and wrapped his legs around Felix, encouraging him.

Their coupling was furious and savage, like they were no more than beasts. John came first, shooting his seed all over his belly, staining the shirt he still wore. Felix followed soon after, thrusting deep as he could as he spent every last drop he had.

He stayed where he was as John's legs grew slack, relishing being inside him still. He was so *warm* and wet and alive. Felix could swear he felt him pulse around him. John smiled lazily up at him.

"C'mere," he said, half sitting.

Sadly, Felix slipped out of him, but he didn't have much time for regret as John's mouth covered his own.

Felix's fangs had yet to retract, so John got unintentionally poked on the lip. Or maybe not so unintentionally, because John pulled back and smiled a little, a trickle of blood dripping down his chin. Felix didn't need an invitation; he licked it up, pressing his tongue against the little prick of blood.

John pulled back suddenly, looking over his shoulder. "Oh my God," he said. "The door..." Felix turned to see what he was talking about. The door was wide open.

John started laughing. "Well, we might have given someone a pretty good show." His expression suddenly shifted from amusement to alarm. "Close the door!" he said as he got to his feet.

Felix tried to do what John asked, but the door wouldn't close completely. "It won't stay shut."

"Just hold it, then!" John held a tissue against his lip as he scurried around the small apartment. "Astray!" he called in a high voice. "Astray!" He went into the bathroom.

Felix was about to ask what on earth he was talking about when John emerged holding a gray cat in his arms. "I was worried my cat had gotten out. Felix, meet Astray."

The cat hissed at him, then scrambled out of John's arms and fled under the bed. "Sorry," John said. "She's not used to visitors."

Did that mean that John didn't bring his lovers here? He hoped that was so; the idea made him feel special. "Can you fix this?" Felix asked, indicating the door.

John came over to examine it. "It looks pretty busted, and I'm not really good with repairs."

"Don't be silly. You're a witch, aren't you?"

Again John hesitated, dabbing at his lip with the tissue. Why was he always so reluctant when it came to spells? He relented after a moment. "*With my touch, the metal bends/And as it does, the doorknob mends.*" The doorknob became good as new. John locked it, as well as the deadbolt. When he was finished, he looked down at Felix's crotch.

"You can put that away now," he said with a smirk.

Felix looked down at his still-erect cock jutting out of his jeans. "But I'm sticky," he complained.

"We can fix that. Get naked and follow me." John headed back toward the bathroom, his bare bottom peeking out from under the hem of his shirt. Felix followed him, stripping as he went, although his boots tripped him up and he ended up falling on the bathroom floor.

John laughed at him as he turned on the shower. "Take your time. We aren't in a hurry, are we?"

Felix grinned up at him. "I suppose not."

He got his boots and jeans off just as the water got warm. The shower was small, but that wasn't a bad thing. John's lip began to bleed again under the hot spray, and Felix licked at it. Hunger surged through him, but he couldn't attack John even if he had wanted to, which he most certainly did not. He really would have to hunt soon, but the idea of it had lost appeal as of late.

"Why do you like this?" Felix said between laps.

"Showering with the guy I just fucked?"

"No. Bleeding for me."

John got quiet. "I don't know," he said, his gaze cast downward. "I just... I guess I have trouble feeling things sometimes." He pulled away from Felix and shut off the water. He got out of the shower without giving Felix so much as a glance. Felix cursed inwardly. He shouldn't have said anything.

When Felix stepped out, John was drying himself off. "There's another towel in the closet," he said, still not looking at Felix. His expression was blank, all traces of the good humor of earlier gone.

Felix scowled to himself as he went back into the main room. Why did witches have to be such moody creatures? He found a towel easily enough and dried himself, wrapping it around his waist when he was finished. Since the closet was open and John had, after all, given him permission to look inside, he nosed around. To his surprise, he found some canvases and sketching pads leaning up against the wall. He picked up one of the sketch pads and started to flip through it.

"What are you doing?"

Felix whipped around to see John standing behind him, his hands on his towel-wrapped hips. He had a bunch of toilet paper sticking to his lip, like he'd nicked himself shaving.

"I didn't know you were an artist."

John tried to snatch the book away, but Felix zipped over to the bed. If his witch was going to be moody anyway, he might as well satisfy his curiosity. "Who is this boy?"

John heaved a great sigh and sat down beside Felix. "If you really want to know, it's Rob."

"The Rob from the lighter?"

"Yup."

Felix examined the sketches. He stopped on one that was more of a proper drawing, with color and scenery. The young man sat under a tree, basking in sunlight. He had red hair and too many freckles, and his limbs were gangly. Quite homely overall, in Felix's opinion.

"I suppose you'll go back to Cincinnati now that you're cured."

"Cured?"

Felix turned the page. "Oh, don't bother trying to deny it. Heaven knows why you witches are so secretive. I asked Richard about the rose, and he confirmed it would cure your curse."

John sighed and tilted his head upward. "Right," he said, his gaze fixed on the ceiling. He didn't say anything for a long time. "I wouldn't go back to Cincinnati."

Felix's face broke out into a huge grin, but he muffled it quickly. From John's tone, this was to be a serious conversation. "And why is that?" he asked somberly.

Again, John was silent. "Rob and I met in community college," he finally began. "Biology 101. I'm really terrible at science—being able to twist reality interferes with the ability to actually understand how it works, apparently. Rob was a great student, so I asked him for help." Another pause. "My grandmother had died the previous year. My mom was murdered by my dad six years before that. That left only me. I emancipated myself so I wouldn't have to go into foster care. I was utterly alone and planned to keep it that way. I never told my grandmother I was gay, because I knew what it could potentially mean: that the curse could get me, too. I couldn't risk falling in love."

John rolled over to look at Felix. "But I thought that surely I could have a couple of friends? I met a few girls, but we didn't really hit it off. And Rob was, well, not exactly handsome, in the classic sense."

"That is exactly the impression I got," Felix said.

John gave him a severe look. "Yeah, well, looks are a really shitty way to judge someone."

Felix made himself somber again. "Oh, yes, naturally. Do please continue."

John rolled over again, his gaze back at the ceiling. "It started with meeting for lunch. It turns out he was really sweet—just insane levels of sweet, like you don't think it's even possible for someone to be that nice." John ran rubbed his eyes. "I actually did a spell on him, just to see how sincere he was. What kind of shitty person does that?"

"So was he? Sincere, I mean."

"Extremely. And he was funny, but not mean. Just this tall, goofy guy with the world's nerdiest laugh." John had to stop again. When he continued, his voice was shaky. "The study sessions moved to my apartment, which was just as terrible as this one. So then he invited me home, and I met his family. They were this huge Irish clan—he had like five siblings and a mom and a dad, and they were amazing, like this totally perfect family. I guess there was some drama when he came out in high school, but they were all over it by this point. And when they learned I didn't have anyone, they sort of adopted me." He laughed a little. "His mom was so mad I was a smoker. She'd slip Nicorette gum into my bag when I wasn't looking.

"A semester passed like that. They invited me for Christmas. On Christmas Eve, Rob kissed me." John shut his eyes tight. "And on Christmas morning, I knew I was going to die." John rubbed his face vigorously. "Shit. I need a smoke." John got a cigarette and crawled back into bed, sitting cross-legged in the center. "My present from him was that lighter. It was kind of a joke to annoy his mom, but it said love. He loved me. I loved him. And now that I knew I would be murdered, I couldn't stay. I'm sure me breaking up with him and disappearing was hard on him, but it's way better than finding out I was horribly murdered."

Felix sat up and put a tentative hand on John's shoulder. It turned out to be the right thing to do because John snuggled closer, letting Felix put an arm around him. They sat like that until John was finished with his cigarette. John lay down, encouraging Felix down with him. He put his head on Felix's chest. John's skin felt so toasty warm against his own, like he was sunbathing. Or at least, he imagined that's what sunbathing would feel like. Sunbathing wasn't a common activity back when he was alive.

"It's weird that your heart doesn't beat," John said into his chest. "I keep waiting for a thump, but there's nothing."

"Does it bother you?"

"No." John kissed his chest, right over his inert heart. "It's actually a really great metaphor for my new life philosophy."

"And what is that?"

"Stop anticipating. I've spent so much time mourning the fact that I don't have a future, but what was I really missing? The future is a fiction people think they can write, but it doesn't work that way. No one really *has* a future. The present moment is the only guarantee, so why not focus on that instead?"

Felix wasn't sure he liked this kind of talk. "That is true enough. But surely you feel at least a little bit brighter about the future now that your curse has been lifted."

John pulled away from Felix. "I'm going to get dressed."

Felix fished his own clothes off the floor as John went to his closet and pulled out some sweatpants and a T-shirt.

"You have taken the cure, haven't you?" Felix asked.

"What can you tell me about Richard?" he said in lieu of an answer.

Felix scowled. "I told you, I don't want to talk about Richard."

"Why not?"

"I don't want him meddling with you."

"What do you mean by that? How would he meddle?"

Felix didn't know how much he should say. "He has a way of getting into people's heads. But he's much diminished these past few years. He never leaves the house. As long as you stay away from him, you should be safe."

"So you're saying if I don't stay away, I'd be in danger from him? Why?"

Felix hesitated. He couldn't tell John about the Extras—John seemed very moral for a witch, and he might take it upon himself to do something about it. Or worse, break up with him.

"I don't know. Witches seem to take delight in meddling with one another. Back when Richard was in his prime, there were always ridiculous feuds amongst his witch colleagues. Best that you stay out of it. He can be truly awful."

"If he's so terrible, then why do you stay with him?"

Felix shrugged. "He's very wealthy. He provides us with everything we need. And of course, there's my sister. I would never leave her."

"And why does *she* stay with him? Is it because she's afraid to leave him?"

"I don't know," Felix lied. He didn't want John to get involved. No good came of defying Richard; he knew that from personal experience.

Felix hoped that John wouldn't press the matter further, and he didn't. Instead, he crossed his arms and looked away. "You should probably get going. It's going to be dawn soon."

Felix got out of bed and crossed the room. John still had his arms crossed over his chest, so Felix put a hand on his cheek, caressing him. Felix tipped his chin upward and kissed him. John at last uncoiled and kissed him back, putting his arms around him. John's small wound had scabbed over and Felix's fangs were retracted, so it was a real kiss this time, soft and human.

"Can I see you again?" Felix asked.

"Sure."

"Marvelous." He gave John another quick kiss on the lips. "Until next time, then."

He looked back once after he left. John hadn't closed the door yet; his figure was framed with the soft light of his apartment. His cat had emerged from under the bed and sat by his side, glaring at Felix with intense amber eyes. The image only lasted a moment; John shut the door, leaving Felix alone in the night.

Eight: A Last Time for Everything

THE FIVE STAR Diner was having a surprisingly decent night. Mike's new strategy to market to clubgoers seemed to be working. It made a lot of sense, actually—most of them were too drunk to notice how terrible the food was.

Also surprising was John's mood. He felt...well, not happy, exactly, but not steeped in misery either. He was having *fun*. Real, actual fun. A part of him knew a romance with a vampire was a bad idea, but it was in keeping with his new philosophy. *Tomorrows* were imaginary. Best live with *todays* instead.

He had yet to make his mind up about the rose—that was definitely a *tomorrow* problem. He had done several diagnostic spells on the rose, trying to determine if it really was Ginerva's Rose, but his results were inconclusive. But even if he was totally sure it would cure him, who's to say he wouldn't be hit by a bus tomorrow? Or get cancer or choke on a grape or succumb to a thousand other random fates that claimed people's lives every day? Mostly, he was sick of thinking about it. He was enjoying himself for once. He flicked his tongue over the scab on his lip and smiled a little to himself.

"That looks like a nasty cold sore," Vince said, interrupting John's thoughts.

John shrugged. "I've had worse."

"Did you know that cold sores are herpes? I thought that was an interesting fact. So you know, you might want to quit sucking dicks until that heals up."

The delicate balance of John's not-quite-good mood faltered. Usually, he could brush Vince off, but not today. He marched up to him and got in his face.

"What the fuck is your problem?" he snarled. "Can I finish one goddamn shift without you harassing me?"

Vince actually took a step backward, his eyes wide with surprise at John's uncharacteristic aggressiveness. Even Gabriel, the dishwasher, took an unusual interest in the situation; normally he just listened to his headphones and tuned the rest of them out.

Vince's gaze skittered away from John's face. "Take it easy, man. I'm just busting your balls."

"No, you're not. 'Busting balls' is something you do with your friends. And I am definitely not your friend, Vince. So unless it's work related, I don't want to hear another word from you. I am *done* with you. Now where is my goddamn order?"

Vince finished plating the burgers and fries. John snatched it up and stormed out into the dining room, passing Lo on his way.

"Whoa," she said. "You okay?"

"I'm fine," he snapped. He was equally short with his customers, although they didn't seem to notice.

He'd cooled down a little by the time he went back to the kitchen, passing Lo again on her way out with another order.

"Good for you," she said before she entered the dining room.

John put his tickets up. He was satisfied to see that Vince seemed too mortified to even look at him.

After a couple of hours, the business died down. Lo went on her break and Gabriel went back to his phone, leaving John essentially alone with Vince. At first, John thought Vince wouldn't have the courage to bother him again, but then he spoke up.

"'m sorry," he mumbled, his shoulders slouched and his gaze cast down at his feet.

John rolled his eyes. "Whatever."

He hoped that would be the end of it, but Vince continued. "You're right. I was being an asshole. I don't know why I say shit like that."

"It probably has something to do with you being an asshole, as you correctly self-diagnosed."

Vince's face turned red. He slumped even further. "Yeah, that's probably it," he said. "It's like Dad always said, I'm pretty worthless."

John sighed and rubbed his temple. He steeled himself against pity, but Vince was the very definition of pitiful in that moment. "You aren't worthless, Vince."

"Yeah, pretty sure I am. You don't have to feel sorry for me. It's my own fault."

"I don't—" John started to say, but that was a lie—he really did feel sorry for him. "Look, can you just explain to me why you talk to me like that?" John was pretty sure he knew the reason, but he wondered how aware of it Vince was.

Vince shrugged. "Dunno. I want to talk to you, but I can never think of anything to say."

"How about, 'How are you today?' That'd be a good start."

Vince blinked dumbly at him for a moment before catching on that he was being given a second chance. "Uh, how are you today?"

"I'm fine. It was nice that the place was busy for once."

"Yeah," Vince said, warming to the conversation. "And no one sent back an order."

"I know, right? A successful night at the Five Star Diner. Who would have thought it?"

"Yeah." Vince smiled a little. "So are we cool?"

"Not exactly. But ask me again in a couple of weeks."

Vince's smile grew wider. "Yeah, okay. Sounds good."

"And, Vince?"

"Yeah?"

John bit his lip, unsure if he should continue. It wasn't his job to coax Vince out of the closet, but he somehow doubted Vince would ever get any support from his usual crew. "If there's something you ever want to tell me that you feel like you can't tell anyone else, I'll listen. Okay?"

Vince's smile faltered. "Don't know what you mean by that, but sure, whatever."

When Lo came back, Vince was whistling to himself while he busied himself cleaning. She raised an eyebrow at John. John just shrugged.

At the end of the night, Lo gave John a ride home.

"I can't believe you forgave him," she said. "He's had it coming for a long time. The guy is a piece of shit."

"Don't be so hard on him. I know he has a hard time."

"Why? Because he won't come out of the closet? Boo-fucking-hoo. He needs to get over himself. I've been out since I was twelve."

John looked at her in surprise. "You are?" He immediately felt embarrassed. "Wow. I am the most self-centered person in the world to not have picked up on that."

"Oh, stop it," she said, waving her hand. "You are not. It just hasn't really come up. I'm not exactly swimming in pussy, am I?"

John snorted. "That doesn't excuse me. You are my only friend; I should be able to keep track of the most basic things about you."

Lo grinned at him. "So if I'm your only friend, that automatically makes me your best friend, right?"

"It also makes you my worst friend."

She punched him in the arm. "Smart-ass," she said affectionately.

He rubbed his shoulder. She could really pack a punch.

"Seriously, though—I grew up with guys like Vince. Just because he's a sad sack doesn't mean he can't hurt you."

John sighed. "Let's stop talking about this. I don't want a bunch of negativity harshing my groove."

"*Harshing your groove?*" Lo laughed. "Have you been possessed by the spirit of a dead hippie?"

John grinned. "Not that I know of."

She grinned back. "You seem good lately. I like it."

"Me too."

They reached John's place. He started to get out, but Lo stopped him.

"I know it's late," she said. "but there's this spell I've been working on, and I could use your input. I'm trying to make a potion, and it's tough finding weird plants in the city."

"I'd love to help, but can it wait until tomorrow? I have a date."

Lo raised an eyebrow. "At two o'clock in the morning?"

"Yeah."

"Sounds more like a booty call. Is that why you've been in such a good mood lately?"

"It probably has something to do with it," John admitted.

She gave his shoulder another punch. "Good for you. The spell can wait. Have fun!"

Lo peeled off down the street. John started to unlock his apartment when suddenly he felt arms close around him and a cool kiss on the nape of his neck.

John squirmed out of Felix's grip. "Jesus, you scared me," he said with a laugh. "You weren't supposed to be here for another half an hour."

"It isn't as if I have much else to do." Felix put his arms around him again and drew him in for a kiss, on the mouth this time.

"You're so cold," John said when they parted. He took one of Felix's hands and held it up. "Your fingers are practically blue."

Felix shrugged. "I have not fed in some time. It needn't concern you."

John opened the door. "Well, come on in. I need to get changed."

John took a quick shower and got dressed in a T-shirt and jeans. He emerged to find Felix admiring the painting he'd been working on. "This is very good."

"It's just a painting of the ocean; nothing exactly earth-shattering about it."

"It's not just any ocean. It's a view from Catalina, is it not? The beach where we had our first date?"

John blushed, which was not something he did often. "Yeah, I looked it up. I'm pretty sure we were at Ripper's Cove. Pretty apropos name, I thought."

"But you painted it in sunlight." Felix hooked a finger in the belt and pulled him in for another kiss. "I like seeing it in sunlight," he said when they parted.

And now John was pretty sure his face was even redder. He turned away. "We should go."

"And where are we going this fine evening?"

"The Natural History Museum."

Felix's expression faltered. "Another museum?"

"I like museums," John said a little defensively.

Once they arrived, John performed his usual tricks to get past the security guards and cameras. They had the full run of all three stories of the place. They went to see the dinosaurs first. The skeletons were enormous. John went past the ropes and put a hand on the leg bone of a T. Rex. He couldn't really explain the strange comfort he took in fossils. He guessed he liked the idea that after millions of years, these bones endured. A life after death. Sort of.

"Alas, poor T. Rex," John said solemnly. "I knew him well."

Felix put hand beside his on the long bone. "It's really quite extraordinary."

"Yeah. It's weird to think about. There's a whole chain of events that had to happen for it to end up here. It had to die at just the right moment, and fall in just the right place, for it to end up preserved enough for people to find its bones, dust them off, and bring them here. It's a meeting millions of years in the making." He gave the bone a pat. "And I'll never see it again."

He walked away down the hall with Felix close on his heels. "Why won't you see it again?"

"I don't have any reason to. That's the thing about sightseeing. You go, you see, and you generally don't see again."

"If you want to come back, it really isn't any trouble."

"That isn't the point. Even if I came here every day, at some point it would be the last time I saw that dinosaur. There's a last time for everything. At least in cases like this, I can mark the moment for what it is instead of having it just blow past me unrecognized."

Felix frowned. "What do you mean?"

John sighed. "It's like—well, for example, there was this customer we had for a while. I have no idea how our restaurant managed to attract a regular, but somehow we did. He was this average-looking guy, probably in his fifties. He wasn't talkative, but he was polite and always tipped well. But then one day, he just stopped coming. I don't know what happened—if he moved or died or just decided he didn't like the restaurant anymore."

Felix's frown deepened. "So you wished to see him again?"

"No. Like I said, he didn't talk much. We weren't friendly. But there was a day when I saw him for the last time, and it bothers me that I don't remember." John shrugged. "Every day, we have dozens of little 'lasts.' The small stuff isn't important, but hidden in all those insignificant endings are huge losses you don't even recognize."

"Like what?"

John had to think about it. "Like one day my mom picked me up, put me down, and then she never picked me back up again. That happened to you, too. To everyone at some point." John hugged his arms to his chest. "No one remembers the last time their mothers held them. That seems wrong."

They stopped in front of another looming skeleton that leered down at them, almost as if smiling. They considered it for a few moments.

"Perhaps this is the last time I will ever see a dinosaur," Felix said. "But it occurs to me that it is also the first time I have seen one. Are there not as many firsts as there are lasts?"

The corners of John's mouth quirked. "Why, Felix, that is downright profound."

Felix drew John into a kiss. "And that is the first time I have kissed you in the presence of a dinosaur." His hand wandered down to John's ass. "And the first time I have groped you in the presence of a dinosaur..."

John started laughing. Felix gestured grandly to the fossil. "Gaze upon us, ye mighty primordial beasts! You have survived the ages to witness our love!"

They were both laughing now. Felix kissed him again. They parted at last and looked up at the bones. "Have you really never seen a dinosaur fossil before?" John asked.

"No. Gazing at ancient bones seems more of a witchly interest." Felix brought John's hand to his lips and kissed it. "My goodness, this is gloomy. Is there something less morbid to look at?"

"There's a bunch of gemstones downstairs." John pulled him forward. "Come on."

"Now *this* is interesting!" Felix beamed at the dazzling array of gems and jewels on display. Like a kid in a candy store, he put his hands and face against a display case exhibiting several rows of gorgeous rocks—some chunky and substantial, others as delicate looking as spun sugar, twisted into strange and beautiful formations. "Look how shiny they are!"

"Very shiny," John agreed.

"You don't suppose they would miss a few, should we happen to take a particular liking to any of them?"

"They would," John said firmly.

"But look at this one—it looks just like a flower. Isn't it lovely?"

"They're staying here."

Felix pouted.

They came upon an enormous crystal ball, displayed alone in a case. John squinted at the inscribed plaque. "Says here that this is the world's largest flawless quartz sphere."

"How delightful! Is it true that witches can read fortunes in crystal balls?"

"Sort of. They're usually of the vague and ironic kind, where you don't appreciate the meaning of the vision until after it's happened. That sort of thing is worse than useless, in my opinion."

Felix cocked his head, still fixated on the ball. "And only witches can have these visions?"

"Well, yeah. It *does* take magic to do it." John turned away and wandered over to the next exhibit.

"What does it mean if I can see a lady inside the ball?"

John whipped his head back around. "What?"

"There's a lady in there," Felix said again. "She seems very friendly. Look, she's waving!" Felix waved back. "Hello!"

John froze. There was no need for him to look, because he knew what he would see. Blonde curls and a wide smile, exuding warmth and curiosity—and much too interested in the world of the living. If she had made herself visible to Felix, she must be exuding a lot of force.

He didn't want to encourage her, so he grabbed Felix's hand and pulled him away. "Wow, would you look at this room over here!" he said, hoping to distract him. "Looks like it has the shiniest rocks of them all!"

It worked. "Oh yes—and there's jewelry!" Felix pranced into the room.

John glanced back over his shoulder at the crystal, but only briefly. It was possible that Felix was imagining things. He didn't want to take a closer look to find out otherwise.

Their last stop was back on the first floor, in the Mammals of North America Hall, which housed various taxidermy specimens, all meticulously arranged in artificial habitats. Or, well, not really habitats, seeing as dead animals couldn't actually *inhabit* anything. Un-habitats, maybe. He snorted.

"What's funny?" Felix asked.

"Nothing."

They walked past the displays—moose and elk, foxes and wolves, seals and walruses. They stopped in front of the grizzly bear display. One of the bears was standing upright; John hadn't fully realized how large they were up close.

"You know, I've always thought museum exhibits were better than zoos. Since dead animals can't hide, you can get a really good look at them."

"You have quite a penchant for dead things, don't you?"

John grinned at him. "Lucky for you." He took Felix's hand. "Come on. Let's go do it under the T. Rex."

To his surprise, Felix hesitated. "How about we go out to the gardens?"

"Why?"

"I would like to see them." He gestured around the museum. "And doesn't this all feel a bit suffocating? I feel like I can barely breathe."

"You don't breathe, though."

"That's hardly the point. It's a beautiful night. Why shouldn't we be outside in the garden, instead of in here with all these dead things?"

John smiled a little. "Can't argue with that."

It was a nice night outside, although downtown LA always smelled like gasoline, and the night sky was gray and starless. Still, the air was pleasantly cool, and the gardens were pretty enough. They avoided the perimeters, staying out of view of the street, and found a place to sit under a tree. A plaque informed them they could observe many wild birds here; it was hard to see in the dark, but John could hear chirping.

"I wonder what bird is out this late," John said.

"It's a mockingbird," Felix immediately responded.

John laughed. "And how do you know that?"

Felix sniffed in mock-offense. "I may not be as clever as a witch, but I *do* know things. Especially things about the night."

"If you know so much, can you tell me why it's singing this late?"

"For the same reason all birds sing." Felix kissed his shoulder. "To attract a mate." He gave him a smoldering look.

John's dick suddenly took interest in the situation. Felix moved forward, sliding a hand between John's legs before undoing his fly. John's eyes fluttered shut. He moaned and tilted his head back, exposing his neck. A toe-curling shiver rolled through him as he felt the tips of Felix's fangs on his skin—

—which suddenly vanished as someone tackled Felix, knocking him backward into the brush. It took a moment for John to recognize the tiny figure sprawled on top of Felix.

"Lo?"

Lo didn't look at him. "*I call on you, tree roots below grass/Rise up now and trap this guy's ass!*" she screamed. The tree's roots lurched upward from the ground, clasping Felix's hands and feet before disappearing back into the dirt, effectively trapping him. Felix roared and surged forward, but was unable to break the tree's grip. His fangs were fully extended as he hissed and snarled. Lo picked up a nearby rock and stuffed it in his mouth. As soon as he was secure, she scrambled backward.

"Are you okay?" she asked John, her chest heaving. "Did he hurt you?"

John's mouth opened and shut several times before he was able to form a response. "What are you doing here?"

"That spell component I was telling you about—I figured out I could find it here at the museum's botanical gardens." She furrowed her brow. "What are *you* doing here?"

There was a retching sound; they both turned to look at Felix, who had managed to spit the rock out.

"John, tell this witch to free me at once!" he cried.

Lo's head whipped back to John, her brow furrowing deeper. "But...there's no way he could be attacking you. Vampires can't hurt you. You aren't afraid of them." She looked him over carefully this time. "Your fly is down." The truth slowly dawned on her. "Oh no. Oh *hell* no."

John hastily zipped up his pants. "Lo—"

"If the next words out of your mouth are some variation of 'it's not what it looks like' or 'I can explain,' I swear to Christ I will put you in the dirt right next to him."

With a great grunt, Felix freed one of his hands, sending splinters of wood and clumps of dirt flying into the air.

"You would do best to watch your tongue! John is a very powerful witch, and I am his lover—he will not look very kindly on another attack against me!"

John pressed the heel of his hand against his eyes. "Felix, please stop talking."

"His *lover*," Lo repeated. She laughed a little. "Wow. Just—wow. I am out of here." She turned around and ran off down the path, toward the street.

"Lo, wait!" John started jogging after her.

"What about me?" Felix shouted after him. "I could still use some assistance!"

John ignored him. It was best if Felix was held up for a minute anyway.

It didn't take John long to catch up with her. She had slowed to a swift stride.

"Lo, please talk to me."

"What is there to talk about? You've been fucking a vampire. You've been *lying* to me about fucking a vampire."

"I never lied to you."

"You said you two were never involved!"

"And we hadn't been at that point!" He put a hand on her arm. "Please, can we just stop and talk for a minute?"

Lo came to an abrupt halt. She crossed her arms and turned her full glare on him. "Fine. Talk. What do you have to say for yourself?"

·

Her glare was so vicious that John found himself struggling for words. "I wasn't deliberately trying to hide this from you."

"Don't waste my fucking time. Of course you were, because you knew if I found out, I wouldn't approve. And I don't." She gestured wildly in Felix's direction. "He's a vampire! He attacks people and sucks their blood!"

"He can't help that. It isn't his fault that he's a vampire."

"Oh, so I suppose it's his *victims'* fault, then?"

"No! That isn't what I said." John rubbed his face. "I know how this sounds. I do. But it's been a long time since there's been anyone in my life—"

Lo looked hurt. "I guess I don't count."

John shook his head wildly. "No, no—that's not what I mean! Of course you count! But you're a friend, not a—"

"—a *lover*?" Lo finished for him with a sneer. "You know there are easier, less morally complicated ways to get your rocks off, right?"

"It's more than that. Because of my curse, I can't let anyone get close. But I don't have to worry about him. He's not in any danger. I can just be with him without thinking about what will happen when I'm—" He broke off.

"When you're dead." Lo crossed her arms a little tighter and looked away. "But you don't worry about what will happen to me, I guess."

"Of course I do."

She uncrossed her arms and took a step toward him. "Then tell me your curse," she said. "Please—*please* let me help."

"I don't want to hurt you, either. I didn't intend to be your friend, but I can't help that you needed a magic teacher."

"So you're only my friend out of obligation?"

John just shook his head, unable to speak.

She leveled a cold look at him. "Well, I think I've learned everything I need from you, so you don't owe me anything else."

She turned to leave, but John stopped her with a hand on her arm. "I'm sorry," he said. He could feel tears pricking the back of his eyes. "I'm so sorry. It was never my intention to hurt you."

"Yeah, well, the road to hell is paved with good intentions, isn't it? No, scratch that—your intentions are so shitty that any road they paved would be full of potholes."

"That's not fair."

She jerked herself out of his grip. "Oh really? Being with him is the same thing as saying you don't care about who he hurts. That makes you worse than him, because like you pointed out, he doesn't really have a say in it. But you do."

"What are you saying?"

"You need to stop him."

"How?"

"I don't know. You figure it out."

"Or else you will?"

"Maybe."

"I can't let you do that."

She laughed a little. "Because he can't help being a vampire, so he deserves your protection? I've read the curse—only people who have committed an act of great evil as mortals become vampires after they're bitten. Have you asked him about that? Do you have any idea exactly who or what you've crawled into bed with? Do you even care?"

John had nothing to say to that.

Lo shook her head. "You know that darkness I feel around you? I don't think it's just the curse."

She turned to leave again. This time, John didn't stop her.

He walked back down the path to Felix, who had just finished extracting himself from Lo's trap.

"How terribly rude!" Felix brushed the dirt from his clothes. "Wasn't that the waitress from your restaurant?"

John stumbled over to the bench and sank down to sit. "Yeah."

"Witches and their feuds," Felix scoffed, plonking himself beside him. "Should I even bother asking what it was about?"

"It's about you, actually."

"Me? What have I ever done to her?"

John didn't answer right away. He stared at Felix for a long moment. "We need to talk."

Felix cocked his head. "About what?"

John didn't even know where to start.

"Not here," he said at last. "Let's go back to my place."

"Shall we walk?"

"No. Let's get there quickly."

He wrapped his arms around Felix's neck as he scooped him up and whisked him away. They got to his place too soon; John didn't want to let go.

But he did let go. He unlocked the door, and they stepped inside.

Felix appeared to at last recognize something wasn't quite right. He cupped John's face in his hand. "You've grown so solemn."

John stepped back and lowered his gaze. "I need to sit down."

They sat down on the bed. Felix tried to take John's hands in his own, but John pulled away. "How did you become a vampire?"

Felix seemed surprised at the question. "I was bitten, naturally."

"Not everyone who's bitten becomes a vampire. You should know that."

Felix rubbed his chin. "You know, I'd never really thought about it, but I suppose you're right. There would be a great deal more vampires running about if that were the case! How does one become a vampire?"

"You have to die from the bite."

"That explains it, then. I most certainly did die—let me tell you, it is not a pleasant experience!"

John paused. "You also had to have recently committed an act of great evil." John leveled his gaze at him, determined not to look away. "Did you?"

Felix froze, which only accentuated how unnatural he was. He was so still that he might as well have been made of stone. "Well, there might have been some—unpleasantness," he said eventually.

"Explain."

Felix looked up at the ceiling, avoiding John's unwavering gaze. "Are you sure you want to know? I can't imagine why dragging up some nasty business from so long ago is necessary."

"It is." John made his voice firm, even though the rest of him was shaking.

Felix rubbed his face and was quiet for a long moment. At last he began to speak. "It was after the catastrophe with the acting company."

"Acting company?"

"Yes. Cat was an actress. I was—well, I was good for nothing, really, but I helped out here and there. Our parents died when we were sixteen and left us very little. We could have ended up in worse circumstances, but Cat's beauty and talent saved us from the worst of it."

"What year was it?"

Felix had to think for a moment. "1860 when we left the group."

John took a moment to absorb that. "And how old were you then?"

"Twenty-four or thereabouts. It's difficult to remember exactly."

"What happened with the acting company?"

"Cat was having an affair with the manager. His wife found out." Felix rubbed his neck. "And I was having an affair with his son. Really, it was best for all parties concerned that we moved on. We decided to go west—this was the time of the gold rush. We had some money saved up; we thought we'd stake a claim and hit it rich. However, it turns out that mining for gold is very taxing, especially since I was the one doing all the mining. We came up with a better idea."

"Which was...?"

"Scamming people. Buy up a worthless claim, plant just enough gold to make it look like it would be worthwhile, and then sell it at an inflated price. It worked very well, although you really have to keep on the move.

"We had a lot of success. Somewhere along the way, we made a very strange friend. His name was Lucien. We only ever saw him at night, and wherever we went, he was always there to meet us at the next town. But the sight of him was never unwelcome. We became...intimate. Cat didn't like him. He always wanted money. In fact, he was always pushing us to get more. I don't understand why he didn't just steal it, since he was a vampire."

"When did you find out that he was a vampire?"

"After he killed us."

"Why?"

"I don't know. Everything was going fine, until one day one of our dupes tracked us down, demanding his money back. He threatened us, and well—" Felix broke off. "You have to understand that it was a very chaotic scene. I didn't mean to kill him, but he went after Cat."

John frowned. Would killing someone in self-defense qualify as a 'great act of evil'? "What happened then?"

"Lucien arrived. Something strange came over him—perhaps it was all the blood. He attacked us. We woke up the next night in coffins. No one had gotten around to burying us yet, so we made our escape." Felix looked at him imploringly. "I never meant to hurt anyone. And it was all such a long time ago."

John looked away. "But you still hurt people. All the time."

Felix was quiet for a moment. "I suppose I do," he said at last. "I can't really help it."

"Yeah," John said softly. "Yeah, I know." A wave of exhaustion came over him. He lay down on the bed. Felix curled up behind him, and John didn't push him away. He felt like his bones had turned to ice; any movement and he'd shatter into a million pieces. John had given up on his *tomorrows*. Now *today* was gone as well. There was no place left for him.

Felix kissed the back of his neck. "I'm sorry to cause you pain."

John didn't respond at first. He turned Felix's words over in his mind slowly. He was sorry. He was *sorry*. An idea dawned on him.

He turned over to face Felix.

"You really are, aren't you?" He tried to keep the excitement out of his voice.

Felix looked puzzled. "Yes."

"But you shouldn't be."

His puzzled expression deepened. "I shouldn't?"

John shook his head. "No, no—that's not what I meant. I meant that it shouldn't be possible for you to feel sorry. You aren't supposed to be able to regret, but you do!"

"I don't understand why that's a cause for celebration. It's not a particularly nice feeling."

John's mind was whizzing now. "Maybe I've been misinterpreting the vampiric curse. I mean, you're the first vampire I've ever met. Most witches haven't even seen a vampire—maybe we've all been wrong." John's gaze darted over Felix's face. "Or maybe something's changed in you." John kissed Felix. "You feel something from that, right?"

"Of course," Felix said, still sounding puzzled, but more cheerfully so.

"How do I make you feel?"

Felix smiled and looped an arm around John's waist, pulling him closer. "Feel for yourself."

John swatted him. "I'm not talking about how I make your dick feel. I already know *that*. Do you care about me? About what happens to me and about how I feel?"

Their gazes met. John was shaking. Everything depended on Felix's answer.

"Yes," he said.

John grinned. He kissed Felix and then scrambled out of bed to the closet. He searched through the bookcase until he found the binder he was looking for. When he found it, he went back to the bed.

"Let's see," he said, leafing through the pages. "Okay, here it is."

Felix looked over his shoulder. "Here what is?"

"Your curse. There's got to be a way around it."

"What do you mean?"

"If we can get it so you don't have to hurt anyone anymore, then everything will be okay. We can stay together."

"What do you mean by that?"

John ignored him as he scanned the text. "Maybe we could feed you animals...no, no it says 'human' here. We could try a blood bank, I guess."

"They keep blood in banks now? Why would they do that?"

"For when people lose a lot of blood, like in an accident. We could just steal some for you." John frowned at the page. "Although it seems to be really specific about coming from 'the living...' Well, I mean, the people who donated it are still alive, so that's got to count, right?"

"What did you mean by not staying together?" Felix asked again. "Are we coming apart?"

John looked up from his binder. "I can't stay with you if you keep hurting people."

"But I told you I can't help it! I have to feed. You know that. You've always known that. What's changed?" When John didn't answer, Felix supplied the answer. "It's that witch girl. She said something to you, didn't she?"

John closed the binder. "She didn't say anything I didn't already know in my heart. This isn't sustainable. I can't keep ignoring it."

"I don't kill them," Felix said. "I don't think they even remember. And if that's so, then where's the harm?"

John's optimism flagged. "Felix, it's wrong to assault people. It doesn't matter if you don't kill them."

Felix got to his feet. "This isn't fair! I've already cut down. I haven't fed in weeks, for your sake!"

"So then you *do* know that it's wrong."

Felix opened and shut his mouth, but no sound came out. He started pacing like a caged beast.

"It's not *ideal*, obviously," he said. "But you can't hold it against me—haven't I been good to you? Haven't we had a wonderful time together?"

"Yes, of course, which is why I'm trying to fix this—"

"There's no changing what I am!" Felix roared. John jumped at his sudden outburst. His heart began to race in spite of himself; Felix's voice had sounded downright demonic.

Felix's angry expression melted away. "And now I've frightened you."

"No," John said, but his voice was shaky. "You just startled me."

Felix shook his head. "I feel it. You fear me."

John tried to smile. "If you didn't frighten me when you were actively trying to suck my blood, how could I possibly be frightened of you now?"

"I don't know, but you are." He dropped to his knees in front of John and buried his head in his lap. "Don't be frightened. *Please* don't be frightened."

"I'm not," John said. But that wasn't true; he was still shaking. Why?

Felix was shaking too. It took John a moment to realize he was crying.

"I felt nothing before I met you," Felix said, his face still muffled in John's lap. "I don't want to go back to it—to that endless night. I was in a cage, but I didn't notice the bars until you showed me."

John ran a hand over Felix's hair. "Hey, don't cry," he said. He moved his hand to Felix's face, tipping it upward. "We'll figure this—" He cut off abruptly and gasped in horror. Felix's face was covered in blood. He looked down at his own hand, which was wet and red as well. *Tears of blood.* Instinctively, he pushed Felix backward.

"Shit," he said. He got down on the floor beside Felix. "I'm sorry, it just surprised me."

Felix looked at him sadly. "And now you're repulsed."

John wanted to deny it, but found that he couldn't. He took Felix's hand and stood, encouraging him to stand with him.

"Come on—let's go to the bathroom and get cleaned up."

Felix allowed himself to be led to the bathroom. John washed his own hands first before grabbing a washcloth. He wet it in the sink.

"There," he said as he gently wiped the blood from Felix's face. "And don't get sentimental on me again—I'm out of clean washcloths."

Felix put a hand on John's, stopping him. Their eyes met. "I love you."

John's heart sped up. He pulled away, turning his gaze back to the sink.

"Why are you still frightened?"

"I'm not *frightened*. You just keep startling me." John began washing the cloth in the sink. The blood swirled around the white porcelain, obscenely red.

"Do you feel the same for me?" Felix asked. When John didn't answer, he put a hand on his shoulder. "John—"

John jerked away. "I'm sorry," he said immediately. "It's just—this is a lot to process. I need a little time to think." John forced himself to smile. "Don't worry. We'll figure something out."

"Do you wish me to leave?"

Felix looked so sad and so lost. John pulled him into his arms. "We'll figure it out," he repeated. There was still blood in his hair. It wasn't the same as blood from a fresh wound—it smelled like a mixture of metal and rot, sharp and cloying. He pulled away and tried not to be sick.

"When can I see you again?"

"I don't know—next week? I'll text you." At Felix's incredulous look, John replied a little more forcefully. "I *will*. I don't have a night off for a while, and I just need a little time—"

"—to 'process,'" Felix finished flatly.

"Yeah."

"Very well, then." Felix left with a *woosh*, so quickly it was like he had vanished into thin air.

John sank to the floor and put his head in his hands, sucking in deep breaths. When he had calmed down, he stood and undressed. His clothes were covered with blood; he got out some hydrogen peroxide and worked on the stains, but he wasn't sure he could save them. After a long, hot shower, he went to the bedroom and picked up the binder from where it had fallen on the floor. He grabbed his cigarettes, too, and brought them all over to the kitchen table. He smoked steadily as he read every line of the curse carefully. But the words all seemed to blur together, as fuzzy as his head. At last he gave up, pushing the binder away.

The thing was, Felix was right. He *was* scared of him. He was scared of the damage he was doing—Lo spoke the truth; he was complicit now. And he was scared for himself. When Felix had tried to attack him when they first met, the only thing he could threaten was his life, which John had already given up on. Now Felix actually *could* hurt him.

He could break his heart.

Nine: Blood Work

FELIX DIDN'T SLEEP that day.

Between the fight with John and the fact that he hadn't fed in weeks, he was exhausted. If anything, his body should be shutting down. Instead, no matter what he did, his body stayed uncomfortably animated, his mind buzzing with unpleasantness, although he was so tired and the thoughts were so quick he could barely make sense of them. He crept into Cat's room; she was asleep in her bed, but Felix had no desire to wake her. He curled up on her sofa and turned on the television, letting its relentless glow hypnotize him as he munched on Cat's pills.

He was well and truly stoned when Cat arose at last. He didn't rise to greet her. She sat down beside him. "Felix? Whatever is the matter?"

He shifted so that his head was in her lap. "I don't think my witch wants me anymore."

"Poor brother," she said. She stroked his hair. "What happened?"

"Another witch has inserted herself into the situation. She finds my existence monstrous, and has convinced John to think likewise."

"Witches against monstrosity? My goodness, we live in strange times."

Felix turned over so that he faced upward. "Don't make fun of me. I'm extremely miserable."

Cat sighed. "Have you considered this might be for the best? There is no way this situation has a happy outcome." She touched his cheek. "Your skin is like parchment. When was the last time you fed?"

"I don't remember. Anyway, I can't. I promised I wouldn't."

"So your witch would have you shrivel for his amusement."

"No. He wants to feed me blood from a bank."

"Oh yes, blood banks," Cat said. "I've looked into those."

Felix gaped at her. "When?"

"Some time ago."

"Why didn't you tell me?"

"I *did* tell you, a long time ago," she said. "But you were not in a mood to listen."

"He asked about how we became vampires."

"And you told him?"

"Some of it. He told me to become a vampire, one must have committed an act of great evil as a mortal."

Cat snorted. "Well, we certainly qualify."

"I was defending you."

"Oh yes, from poor Jedidiah. That might be forgiven. But what of our neighbor, the sweet old widow Mrs. Williams, who came to investigate the commotion? And our landlord who followed her? And his son?"

"We were panicked!"

"We were stupid and cared for nothing other than ourselves. We lied and we stole and we ruined people without a single care. Maybe the murders weren't even the worst of it. Maybe our lives were evil enough without a bloodbath."

Their gazes met. "We really are very wicked, aren't we?" Felix said.

"I'm afraid so."

"It's strange how it never seemed to bother me before."

"Not so strange," she said. "Witches are agents of transformation and destruction. If he wants to be rid of you, you should take the opportunity to escape."

"He doesn't wish to harm me. He wants to save me."

"Oh, my brother." Cat kissed him on the forehead. "That's quite impossible."

They both looked up as the door creaked open. Richard stood in the doorway. He was not alone; a girl of about seventeen stood beside him, her face slack.

"Felix!" Richard said, all smiles. "I didn't expect to see you here. Your nights have been quite busy as of late."

Cat turned to Felix. "You should leave."

"Nonsense," Richard said as he entered the room. The girl wandered in after him, quiet as a ghost. She sat down on the armchair while Richard approached them. "Why shouldn't he stay? Like old times."

Cat stood up. "You know it is my explicit wish that Felix be kept out of this business."

"And I have indulged you, as I indulge all your charming eccentricities. But since he is here, why not have him join you? I can find another for him; it won't take me more than an hour."

"No," she said. She looked over at the girl. "And I won't touch this one. She's too young."

"Don't be ridiculous. She's no younger than the last one."

"Yes, she is. And I told you I won't take anyone under twenty-five anymore."

Richard clenched his jaw. "Shall I ask to see their identification before I take them?"

"If you must." Cat turned her back to him and went to her vanity, where she sat. She picked up a brush and tended to her hair.

Richard stalked over to her and took her by the shoulder, forcing her to face him. "You will not ignore me!"

"I haven't," she responded, just as viciously. "I've given you my answer. You said I had a choice in our victims, and I reject her. She is too young."

"She wishes for death," Richard countered. "That is your requirement, yes?"

Cat shook herself free from his grip. "She. Is. Too. *Young*," she repeated, every word a bullet.

"Shall I bring her back on her twenty-fifth birthday, then?" Richard sneered. "Because in all honesty, I'm not sure she will make it that long. She is addicted to drugs. Her new boyfriend beats her and pimps her. Even if she miraculously survives, her life will be filled with nothing but pain and misery." Richard's tone shifted, becoming a bit softer. "We can bring this poor girl mercy, you and me. One more brief moment of pain, and I will give her the most beautiful dream..."

Cat laughed bitterly. "Oh yes, a beautiful dream." She gestured around her. "Like the one you gave me."

He looked at her coldly. "You liked it well enough."

"I did," she said. "Until you gave me your heart." She began to brush her hair again very vigorously. "Although I'm sure it was a great surprise to you that giving me that shriveled, black organ would awaken human sentiment in me. God only knows it never did for you. Now get that girl out of my sight."

Richard snarled and retreated across the room. He stopped at the display Cat kept from the production of *Hatshepsut, Egyptian Queen*. He took the dagger and approached the girl.

"Stand up," he commanded her. She did without hesitation, although tears were streaming down her cheeks. Richard held the blade to her throat. "If you won't do it, why don't I just end her useless life right now?"

Cat was up and across the room in the blink of an eye. She snatched the dagger from him and held it to her own chest. "Or I could cut out this useless heart and end our miserable existences instead!"

Richard swore. He waved his hand; the dagger glowed hot. Cat dropped it with a cry.

"You ungrateful bitch!" Richard pointed at Felix. "Since you care nothing for yourself or your husband, perhaps you'll think of your dear stupid brother. Do you remember what your suicidal impulses cost *him*?"

Two small streams of blood trickled from the corners of her eyes. She wiped them aside.

"Then get me someone else," she said coldly. "I'll do your nasty work, but not on her."

Richard stalked out of the room. The girl followed. She let out one small sob—the first sound she'd made. Richard waved his hand and she was silent once more.

As soon as he was gone, Cat turned to Felix. "Are you sure you want a witch?" she asked flatly.

Felix had no response to that.

Cat sat down on the sofa and turned on the TV. She grabbed her pills and curled her legs up, almost in the fetal position.

"Would you go with him?" she asked Felix, without turning from the screen. "Make sure he keeps his word and doesn't leave her dead in a ditch somewhere."

The absolute last thing in the world Felix wanted to do was spend a moment alone with Richard, but how could he refuse? He kissed her cheek before he left.

He found Richard out front, putting the girl into his limousine.

Richard looked at Felix with annoyance. "I suppose she's sent you to make sure I'm sufficiently obedient to her ridiculous whims?"

Felix nodded.

Richard sighed. "Well, get in, then."

Felix climbed inside with Richard following. Once they'd shut the door, Richard pressed the button for the speaker. "Back to the slums,

Philip." The limo pulled out from the driveway, down the hill, and out the gates.

Richard opened a cabinet and pulled out a bottle of cognac. "Would you like a glass?"

Felix declined.

Richard shrugged and poured one for himself. "That was certainly some nasty business with your sister. I can't understand why she's being so difficult. You see my point, don't you? I mean, look at her." Richard gestured to the girl. She was shivering—unsurprising, since she wasn't wearing much. Cat was right—she did seem young. Her face still had the roundness of childhood. Her dirty face was tear-streaked, but her eyes had the glassy look of the Extras.

"She does seem very young."

Richard scowled. "Oh, not you, too. I swear, you vampires—your brains are so rotten it's amazing you're able to function." He took a sip of his drink. "What I can't understand is why she is so intent on 'sparing' you. You're the one without a heart, after all."

Felix said nothing. It puzzled him too sometimes, but it felt disloyal to say so.

Richard rubbed his brow. "What a mess. Your sister may not like it, but we are going to need them younger. I'm old—older than I ought to be. It's taking more power to keep these old bones of mine moving." He laughed a little. "I had thought sixty-five years would be enough time to figure out how to add youth to my now eternal life, but it still eludes me. Although maybe not for long."

Felix wondered what he meant by that.

Richard swirled his drink, looking moodily into the amber liquid. "Did you know she was happy when I first proposed the plan to give my heart to her so we could live together forever? She loved me then. It seems strange that she was capable of it when she was heartless. It seems backward, doesn't it?" Richard looked up from his drink and leveled his gaze at Felix. "Do you love your witch boy?"

"Yes," Felix said quietly.

"Do you know why he hasn't taken the cure yet?"

Felix was stunned. "I thought he had."

Richard shook his head. "I searched for him yesterday and felt the curse still hanging over his head. He lied to you, then?"

"I-I don't know," Felix said, fumbling for words. "I never asked. I just assumed—" He broke off, his thoughts too scattered to continue.

"He's probably suspicious of me." Richard actually smiled a little. "Which means he isn't stupid. That's good." Richard took another long drink. "I think the time has come at last for you to bring him here. I have a proposal for him—one I think you'd like as well. How would you like to live with your witch boy for all of eternity?"

"How do you mean?"

"If I joined the two of you the way Cat and I are joined, I believe I'll have enough energy to make both John and I immortal *and* eternally youthful." Richard smirked. "Surely that's a better outcome than succumbing to a curse. Do you think he'll be responsive to that?"

"I don't know. He's very moral and very stubborn."

Richard hummed ambiguously. "He might change his mind once he learns how dark that curse of his is getting. By the way, has he told you what it is?"

Felix hesitated. John probably wouldn't want him to say, but if there was any hope that Richard could help him, Felix was willing to risk it. He told Richard the whole story.

When he was finished, Richard didn't look surprised. Instead, he looked almost pleased with himself. "As I expected. Yes, that is a nasty curse indeed. He must be very suspicious of me indeed to resist a cure."

"He was hoping that by not fighting it, his death would be peaceful, like his grandmother's."

"There's very little hope of that. You should tell him. It might persuade him to be more open to my proposal."

The limo came to a stop.

"Here you are," Richard said to the girl as he opened the door. "Back to your hellhole."

The girl stumbled out. As soon as her feet hit the pavement, she ran. Felix searched himself for some emotional response. He knew he *ought* to feel bad for her. Was that the same thing?

Richard sighed. "And now my hunt begins anew." He pressed the button for the speaker. "Philip, the same as before. Start bringing them in for an interview." He turned to Felix. "I wish your sister was not so picky. It's very tiresome having to determine the extent of their despair. Ah well." Richard licked his lips as he looked out the window. "New blood. Yes, that's what we need. You should go to your witch now—it's still early."

Felix exited the vehicle. As much as he didn't want to take orders from Richard, he was right; Felix needed to talk to John immediately. He zipped off into the night.

Felix crouched in an alley outside of John's restaurant. He decided interrupting his shift would be counterproductive, especially with that horrid girl witch there. It seemed like ages before John and the rest emerged. He made to go after John, but he decided it was best not to approach him when the other witch might be watching. He zipped over to John's apartment and waited in the bushes across the street.

Eventually, he saw John walking down the street. Instead of heading to his doorstep, he walked immediately to the bushes where Felix was hiding. "Why are you hiding in the bushes?"

Felix stepped out into the street somewhat sheepishly. "How did you know I was here?"

"I enchanted a crystal to alert me when you're around."

"You have an alarm for me?" Felix didn't like the sound of that.

"Not an *alarm*. Just—an alert. No big deal." He motioned with his head to his apartment. "If you want to talk, we should probably do it inside."

They crossed the street and entered the apartment. John's cat gave him a reproachful look when she saw Felix. She jumped off the bed and crawled underneath it.

John crossed his arms. He didn't seem particularly upset to see Felix, but neither was he pleased. His expression betrayed nothing at all—not how he felt, nor how he lied. His cool blue eyes were as impassive as the sea on a windless day.

"I thought we weren't going to see each other for another week," John said.

"Am I unwelcome?"

John sighed. "That isn't what I said."

"Then why haven't you kissed me?"

John gave him a peck on the cheek. He retreated to the kitchen; Felix followed him.

"Actually, I've already started working on our problem," John said as he opened the fridge. He pulled out a couple of plastic bags, dark and red. "I managed to get some donated blood. Had to use a little will magic to get it, but it wasn't hard. We can work out a system if this works."

He handed the cold bag to Felix. It was blood, most certainly, but it was so cold, and so foreign outside of a human body. "How am I supposed to drink this?"

John opened a cupboard and pulled out a mug. "Here."

They undid a valve on the bag and poured it into the mug. John looked at him eagerly. Felix took a sip—and immediately retched.

"What's wrong?" John asked.

"Too cold."

"Oh." John took the mug back. "Maybe we can put it in the microwave?"

They tried it. When they took the mug out again, the blood had congealed into a sticky mess. The smell of blood was normally enticing, but this made Felix feel sick.

John seemed undaunted. "Yeah, probably should have realized that was a bad idea. Let's try putting it in warm water."

John filled up the kitchen sink with hot water.

"What if this doesn't work?" Felix asked.

"Don't be so negative." John placed the other bag in the steaming water. "We'll figure it out."

"And what will I do once the curse takes you?"

John's head whipped up. "What do you mean?"

"Don't try to deny it. Richard told me that you're still cursed, which means you didn't use the cure I brought you."

John didn't say anything. His gaze lowered to the sink. "It's like you said before—it might take many years for the curse to get me."

"Richard says your curse is getting darker." Felix put his hands on John's shoulders, forcing him to look up. "Why won't you take it? And why did you lie?"

John shrugged out of Felix's grasp. He went over to his nightstand and removed a pack of cigarettes. He didn't speak again until he'd taken a few drags. "I haven't taken it because I don't trust Richard. I wanted to make sure the rose is what it appears to be."

"I made it exactly as you specified."

"Did Richard help you?" When Felix didn't respond, John said, "That's what I thought."

"I didn't notice him casting any additional spells."

"You should know by now that witches can be tricky. Everything you've said about him sets off red flags."

"Do you really think anything he could do to you would be worse than a violent death?"

"Yes! Haven't you been listening to me? There are fates worse than death. Everyone dies. Not everyone is enchanted by some deranged witch."

Felix thought about the Extras. Richard said they were better off, while Cat seemed to think the opposite. Who was right?

"Richard won't die," Felix said.

"What do you mean?"

"He's come up with a way to live forever. He's already 118." Felix hesitated. "He wants to teach you, too."

Those cool blue eyes were no longer still. Now they raged like a storm. "Did he send you here?"

"Not exactly."

"Then how, exactly?"

"He told me you hadn't taken the cure, and that I should find out why."

"So you could convince me to go along with whatever he has planned?" John sucked on his cigarette, inhaling it so quickly that it almost instantly turned to ash. He stubbed it out in the ashtray with great force and then advanced on Felix, his hands suddenly all over him.

"What are you doing?"

"Searching you. Did he give you any objects to hide in my apartment? Anything to slip into my food?"

"No, of course not!"

After coming up with nothing, John pulled his hands away. He was breathing heavily. "So you think that your brother-in-law just wants to share immortality with me, out of the goodness of his heart?"

"I—"

John jumped in before he could respond. "And just so you know, any spell that would disturb the natural order so much as to give a human immortality is by definition dark magic—the darkest there is." John narrowed his eyes. "Do you know how he does it?"

"He gave Cat his heart."

John blinked. "What? How?"

"Years ago, when they got married, he made a spell that put his heart in her, and it gave him eternal life. But something's gone wrong—he's aging, but not dying. He needs new energy to bring back his youth—"

"He wants to suck up my youth and you're wondering about fates worse than death? There's one right there!"

"No! No, he said that you would both benefit."

John laughed. "And you believe him."

"If he means to join you the way he joined himself with my sister, then yes, I do. It had no ill effect on him—why should it for you?" Felix looked at him imploringly. "Is it a fate worse than death to be joined to me?"

Instead of responding, John stalked back over to the kitchen sink. He pulled out the bag of blood and poured another mugful.

"Here," John said, thrusting the mug in Felix's direction. "Drink this and we'll see."

Felix took the mug. He looked back and forth between the mug and John's face. Slowly, he brought it to his lips. He took a sip. It tasted foul—like something rotten. Regardless, he pressed on. He managed to get the whole mugful down and even held it down for a minute. Then he ran to the bathroom and vomited it all into the toilet.

John was standing over him when he was finished. He handed him a towel. The anger in his face had been replaced by despair. "An eternity of watching you prey on people. Yeah, that counts." He left the room.

Felix wiped his mouth with the towel and set it on the counter. When he returned to the main room, he found John sitting on the bed, smoking another cigarette.

Felix sat down beside him. "I don't think Richard would poison you if he intended to use you. The cure is probably safe."

"Maybe." John took a long drag of his cigarette, his gaze firmly fixed on the carpet. He didn't speak again until his cigarette was finished. "Do you really think you love me?"

Felix hesitated. It felt like a trick question. "Yes," he said carefully. "Yes, that is what I think."

"How do you feel about your victims?"

Felix blinked at the sudden change in subject. "I feel nothing at all for them. Why should I?"

"Yeah," he said. "That's what I thought."

From the look on John's face, it seemed as if that was the wrong answer.

"I have to survive," he pointed out, quite reasonably. "What's one moment of pain for them if it lets me live, when I cannot live without it?"

"It's more than one moment of pain. That's something that will haunt them forever, even if they aren't sure what happened. It's a violation." John lit another cigarette. "And I keep letting you do it."

"So I'm supposed to starve, then," Felix said, angry now. "Would that make you happy? Would you love me if I was nothing more than a shriveled corpse? Because as I'm sure you are aware, cutting off my supply of blood won't end me. It throws me into an agony of never-ceasing starvation! It's torture."

John cocked his head. "That's happened to you?"

Felix cursed at himself internally. If he told John about it, it would surely make him less inclined to trust Richard. "Yes, it's happened. I do not wish to speak of it. Does my pain mean less than that of my—" He stopped and tried to think of a better word than *victims*. "—my blood providers?"

John burst out in bleak laughter. "Blood providers— that's some pretty good PR spin." Something shifted in his expression. "Blood providers..." he repeated. "So your attacks don't kill people, right?"

A little flicker of hope sparked in Felix. "Yes, precisely! There's no lasting damage, as far as I'm aware."

"Could you feed from me?"

That flicker of hope abruptly flamed out. "I can't attack you," Felix said. "That's how this all began, remember?"

"But you can bite me when I give you permission. We've done it before."

"Yes, but I haven't seriously fed on you."

"We could try."

"I don't think that's a good idea."

"Why not? You just said there's no lasting damage."

Felix hesitated. "I must confess I don't know that for certain. I don't linger after I've fed." He averted his gaze. "It will also hurt. Probably quite a lot."

"I don't see a lot of other options." John got up and went to the closet. He pulled out a shoe box and a clean washcloth and then sat back down beside Felix. Out of the shoe box, he took a necklace with a crystal pendant. He held it to his lips and whispered something. The crystal glowed white.

"For the pain," he said as he put it on. "Won't take away all of it, but it should help." He returned to the shoe box and retrieved a bandage. He put the washcloth and the bandage on the nightstand beside them. "For the wound. I assume if I stay still, you won't tear my throat out the way you nearly did Vince's."

Felix winced. "I will be exceedingly careful."

"Good." John put a hand on Felix's shoulder and encouraged him to lie down with him.

They gazed into each other's eyes for a very long moment. Felix desperately tried to think of a way around this. But he was a vampire—heartless and witless. What match was he for the cunning of witches?

"If this works, do you promise to take the cure?"

"One thing at a time." He bared his throat.

Still, Felix hesitated. "I don't think I can."

"You were attracted to my blood the first time we met," John said. "Has that changed?"

"No," Felix admitted. "You still smell enticing."

John laughed a little. "So it's by smell?" He moved a little closer to Felix, wrapping his arm loosely around his waist. "What do I smell like?"

"Sweet. Ripe. Dark."

John nuzzled him. "So what are you waiting for?"

"You aren't frightened. It's difficult if you aren't frightened." Felix brushed the hair from John's face. "And why aren't you? You were frightened of me yesterday."

"I still am," John said quietly. "You terrify me."

Once he said that, Felix could feel the truth of it. It wasn't the same fight-or-flight terror of a victim trying to escape, but a deep, almost quiet fear—one that came not from animal instinct, but from the heart. Once Felix felt it, his fangs bared. And it had been so long since he'd fed, his body ached with the emptiness and the cold, and John was so *warm* against him. John's heart beat quicker and quicker, a relentless drum that battered against the last of his resistance. With a growl, he drew John to him and sunk his fangs into his flesh.

John cried out—or he tried to. It was always the same with Felix's victims—their screams died in their throats before they could voice them. But the blood gushing over his tongue and down his throat dissolved any concern Felix might have had. His thoughts had stopped as he satiated himself at last. The only thing inside him was *need*. John struggled in his grasp. Felix just held him tighter.

He was broken from his feeding trance by a fierce yowl and claws scraping over his face. He pulled back from John as his entire head was engulfed by John's cat, who was biting at his neck. By the time Felix had extracted the cat from his head, he'd come out of his feeding-induced trance. He looked to John.

The cat sat down in the middle of his chest and hissed at Felix again. It seemed like John was still breathing. He tried to approach him, but the cat looked as if she would scratch his face off.

"I want to help, you stupid creature!" Felix shouted, although he had to admit that given what had just happened minutes before, it seemed like a ridiculous statement. At that moment, John heaved in a deep breath.

"John!"

John sat up, coughing violently. The cat curled up at his side and purred. He put his hand on her. Felix once again tried to approach; the cat growled.

"It's okay," John said to the cat. He stroked the little beast until she settled down.

At last, Felix was able to go to him, although the cat stayed firmly curled at his side, glaring at him as her tail twitched. "How do you feel?"

John picked up the washcloth and held it to his throat. "Hurts. Guess my spellwork needs more practice."

"I'm sorry."

"My idea." John smiled at him weakly. "Could use some water."

Felix dashed to the kitchen and returned with a glass of water. John struggled to sit up; Felix propped a few pillows up behind him. When John's grip on the glass faltered, Felix held it up to his lips. After he'd drunk his fill, Felix set it on the nightstand.

"How are you feeling now?" he asked.

"Still hurts. But I'm okay." He tried smiling. "I should get a cookie and some OJ. Plus a little sticker—'I donated.'"

"What's OJ?"

"Orange juice. They give you orange juice when you donate blood."

"I can get you anything you require. I'll gather all the oranges in Los Angeles if you need them!"

John's attempt at a smile succeeded a little more this time. "Just a joke." He pulled back the washcloth and examined the red stain. "Looks like it's not bleeding too badly." His hand searched the bed until it found the bandage. He handed it to Felix. "Help?"

Felix affixed the bandage with great care over the wound he'd created. When that was done, he lay back down beside John so they were facing each other once again.

John frowned. "Your face—it's covered in scratches..."

"It's nothing," he said dismissively. "How are you feeling now?"

"The same as when you asked that question a minute ago." John peered at him. "Did it work? Did you get enough?"

Felix nodded vaguely.

"How much time do we have until you need more?"

"A few weeks."

John let out an enormous sigh. "That's good. Gives us time." He shut his eyes. "I need to rest."

"And the cure?" Felix asked. "You will take the cure now, won't you?"

But it appeared that John had drifted off to sleep.

Felix stayed for a long time, watching him sleep. He left only when he felt dawn approaching. The blood was flowing through him, relieving him of the ache and the cold that had plagued him these last few weeks. Although his physical suffering had ceased, the torment in his mind had increased a hundredfold. This could not happen again. If John's cat had not stopped him, Felix might have seriously injured John. But if he didn't feed from John and returned to his predation, then John would cast him out of his life. And then there was John's curse—would he take the cure? And what of Richard and his plans for John? And what of Cat and her deep, unending sorrow? Felix was utterly helpless in the face of it all.

He went to Cat's room. The place was trashed—the coffee table was smashed in two; the frames of her movie posters were shattered, the souvenir prop pieces broken and scattered about the room. When Felix stepped forward, his boot crunched a piece of a wine bottle.

Cat herself was passed out on the couch, her pill dish nearly empty. Felix curled up beside her and finished the last of the pills, chasing it with the last of the wine bottles. The world grew fuzzy and began to fade, like the lights going out in a movie theater before the show began.

Ten: Outrageous Fortune

JOHN WOKE UP with a hell of a headache.

Astray was curled up beside him, a little ball of purring warmth. Her purr grew louder when she felt him stir. He petted her until he felt strong enough to sit up—which only made his headache worse.

"Ow," he said.

Astray meowed at him severely.

"I don't need any lectures from you. I'm suffering enough already."

She jumped off the bed and sauntered over to her food dish, meowing again. With a great deal of effort, John got up. He went to the kitchen to fetch the cat food. With that done, he retreated to the bathroom to look at his wound. It hadn't bled through the bandage, which was good. Less good was that the pain crystal had worn off; it had only dulled the pain before, but now that it had faded the pain was in full force. He could try to enchant another crystal, but healing spells generally required the caster to be in good health, which John certainly wasn't this morning. He took a bunch of Advil instead.

John went to get some breakfast of his own, only to find that his cupboards were mostly bare. Distressingly, he was also out of coffee. He ate some dry cereal, which tided him over for the moment. It was unavoidable: he needed to go to the store. But not yet. First, there was something he had to do.

Until now, he had been focusing his attention on the rose itself, but maybe that was the wrong strategy. If he could locate Richard, he might be able to get a feel for his magical signature and then determine if he felt it on the rose. Scrying for him would be difficult, since he knew nothing about him other than his first name, but now that he knew he was engaging in some serious dark magic, he could just search for that. He got out his shoe box of magical implements, selecting a crystal pendant and a map of LA. He smoothed the map over the table and gathered the leather strap of the pendant in one hand. After closing his eyes and taking a few deep breaths, he muttered a spell.

After a few moments, the pendant began to sway, slowly at first. It circled around and around, drawing closer and closer to the map. Suddenly it plunged downward, as if it weighed fifty pounds. It landed in Beverly Hills; he didn't get the chance to see where exactly, because the entire map burst into black flames. He let go of the leather strap and jumped to his feet, stumbling backward as the flames grew larger. He was just starting to think of how he was going to put out the fire when it vanished as suddenly as it had appeared. The map was gone. In its place, a sentence was etched into the wood of the table, in looping, elegant writing: *Curiosity killed the cat.*

Well, shit. This appeared even worse than he thought.

He sat back down to give himself a chance to get a hold of himself. Once his heart felt like it was no longer going to beat out of his chest, he got up again. He needed to think. He also needed coffee. A walk to the store might do him some good. He put on his hoodie and put his cigarettes in his pocket before heading out.

The sunlight was brazen in its relentless brightness, making his already aching head feel worse. With every step he took, the pain in his neck spread, pulsing down and radiating outward, making him sway like a strand of seaweed thrashing back and forth with the tide. He took a moment to steady himself. Hopefully the Advil would kick in soon.

He arrived at the store. As he wandered the aisles, his shopping basket grew heavier and heavier. With annoyance, he realized he wasn't going to be able to carry very much home. He settled on coffee, a half-gallon of milk, some bread, a few apples, and lunch meat. That should hold him over for a little bit. He probably wouldn't be able to work tonight. Briefly, he thought about calling Lo. Would she even answer his call?

He was making his way back down the street when a white limo cruised up beside him. He didn't think much of it until it slowed down, keeping pace with him. The rear window opened, exposing the face of an elderly man. It was hard to determine his exact age. His hair was a luminous white, as were his teeth. He had a thin, white mustache. A few wrinkles adorned his face, crinkling especially around his bright blue eyes.

A well-preserved rich white man was not a particularly unusual sight in Los Angeles. What was unusual, however, was the stench that rolled out of the window. It wasn't the normal ammonia-tinged odor of the elderly. This was rot—like a dumpster in summer or bloated roadkill on the side of the highway.

The old man smiled. "Good morning, John. I trust I need no introduction."

"Apparently I don't either, since you already know who I am." He tried to sound nonchalant, but his heart had started to race. Running was out of the question—he was still weak. Besides, it was common knowledge that running from predators was a bad idea. "So now that we've got that nonintroduction out of the way, I would ask you to kindly fuck off and leave me alone."

"My, how rude we are," Richard said mildly.

John ignored him. He started moving at a brisk stride. The limo kept pace with him. "It's rather juvenile to telephone someone if you don't wish to speak with them," Richard continued. "Metaphorically speaking, of course."

"I didn't hang up," John said. "My phone exploded. Metaphorically speaking."

"Ah. I do apologize. My metaphorical number is unlisted—you caught me quite by surprise. Perhaps I responded with a bit more force than was necessary. But now that that misunderstanding is behind us, why don't we have a conversation? I'd like you to be my guest for the afternoon."

"Not interested."

Richard pursed his lips in annoyance. "Felix said that you were stubborn."

"Then you know you're wasting your time. You can't compel me."

Richard sighed and put his head back in the window, which closed. The limo sped up slightly and pulled up to the curb. The door opened, and Richard emerged. He was shorter than John had expected. He extended a hand. An enormous amber ring graced his middle finger. The way the sun hit it made it seem to glow. Or maybe it wasn't the sun, because when Richard flicked his fingers, John suddenly stumbled and face-planted on the concrete.

"There's compulsion, and then there's *compulsion*," Richard said. "One involves a gentle manipulation of the mind. That is how I prefer to persuade, but you are no doubt correct that a battle of wills would leave you psychically wrecked and give me a dreadful headache. Your body, however, is much more easily manipulated. Please don't make me drag you in here. It would be undignified."

John got onto his hands and knees, breathing shakily. Richard hadn't even said a word and he'd tossed him down like a rag doll with a flick of his finger. If he could get in his apartment, he could try to set up some wards—it was a long-shot, but better chances than he had now.

"I have groceries," John said. "Let me put them away."

"Nonsense." Richard snapped his fingers. The driver got out of the car—he was a huge man in a ridiculously old-fashioned uniform: a double-breasted coat and a pillbox hat, like something out of the movies. "Philip, retrieve this young man's groceries." The driver obeyed, placing them in the trunk. Richard looked down at John and raised an eyebrow. "Does he need to retrieve you as well?"

Gingerly, John got to his feet. He didn't take a second look at Richard as he made his way to the limo; he couldn't bear to look at his smug expression.

The inside of the limo was appropriately decadent, with wood paneling and leather seats. Richard got in as well, bringing that horrible smell with him. A moment later, the limo started again, and they set off down the road. John kept his gaze fixed out of the window, trying to figure out where they were going.

"Would you like some water?" Richard asked eventually. "Or a bit of a nosh, perhaps?"

"No thank you. I'd probably vomit. It smells like a dumpster in here."

"Ah," Richard said. "My apologies. Give me a moment." Suddenly, the odor vanished. "It's been some time since I've kept company with the magically sensitive."

John still refused to look at him, keeping his gaze fixed on the window. "I still feel sick."

He heard Richard sigh. "If you are trying to deduce where we are going, I can tell you. I'm taking you to my estate in Beverly Hills, not dragging you off to some dungeon. You are to be my guest today. You should feel fortunate; there are people who would pay very good money for the tour I'm going to give you."

"How generous of you."

"It is. I am a very generous person."

They spent the rest of the ride in silence. Richard wasn't lying; John recognized their route to Beverly Hills. They turned onto a twisted driveway that was almost like a road itself. An abundance of trees lined the drive, so after only a few moments, the main road was obscured, as if they'd left the city entirely. They reached a cast-iron gate with a name boldly arching over the entrance: HAPPY ENDINGS. John gaped. It couldn't be—

"Welcome to Happy Endings," Richard said. "It was a perfectly charming name when I built it, but I understand that the term now refers to a sexual act performed at the end of a massage. What a vulgar age we live in now."

John's gaze flickered back and forth from the sign to the man sitting beside him. John was a witch, under a curse, and sleeping with a vampire. He should be incapable of being shocked. But he was.

"Is there something the matter?" Richard asked.

"You're Richard Livingstone," John said at last. "Founder of Livingstone Productions."

Richard's expression brightened. "You know my work? How delightful! It sometimes feels as if most everyone has forgotten me."

"My grandma got me interested in old Hollywood," John said faintly. His mind was buzzing—it wasn't every day you learned a major player in early Hollywood history was secretly a master of the dark arts. "But you died ten years ago." John looked at Richard again. He wasn't a vampire. So what was he? "Are you dead?"

"Only legally. There comes a point when people start to question your longevity. Best to make it seem as if I passed away."

Something else dawned on John. "And your wife, Catherine Neville, the eccentric actress who would not let a single ray of sunshine mar her fair complexion..."

Richard smiled. "It was difficult to shoot all of her movies in sound stages or at night, but we managed."

The gate opened, permitting the limo to drive through. John couldn't help but gawk at the estate—it was like going into another world. You would never guess the place was in the middle of Los Angeles, California—it seemed more like the English countryside. What made the whole experience even more surreal was the fact that he knew this place already, from the well-worn copy his grandma had given him of *Homes of the Stars*. Happy Endings had always been his favorite.

The limo stopped at the front doors of the mansion. Philip exited the vehicle and went 'round to open the door for them.

"Thank you, Philip," Richard said. "That will be all."

Philip bowed slightly. When he rose again, John got a look at his face. It was impossible to tell his age; he seemed neither young nor old. His brown eyes seemed wrong somehow—unfocused and vague. His skin had a strange gray hue to it. He wondered how aware he was and how he felt about what was happening. John couldn't be sure, but he had a feeling he might be looking at a fate worse than death.

Richard spoke again. "Shall we begin with the mansion or the grounds?"

"What?"

"For the tour. Which would you like to see first?"

John opened his mouth to protest but shut it again. Very little scared him anymore, but right now, he was frightened. He didn't think he could fight his way out of this situation. Maybe it would be better to simply play along.

"The grounds," he said weakly.

Richard smiled. "Excellent choice. There's a golf cart just around the corner."

The cart was there waiting for them, just as Richard had said. John got into the passenger side as Richard took the wheel. They started out, heading west from the mansion down a dirt path.

"Happy Endings is just a little over fifteen acres," Richard began. "Construction began in 1928. As you are no doubt aware, I had already built my empire by then. Money was no object. I managed to snag Julia Morgan to design it for me. It's not quite as grand as her work on Hearst's estate up in San Simeon, but I never intended it as such. After all, who really wants to live in a castle?"

John offered a vague nod. He frowned as he looked around. It seemed familiar; of course he knew it from his grandmother's book, but he felt it more intimately than that. Like he'd been there before. But that was impossible, wasn't it?

"We did visit San Simeon on several occasions," Richard continued. "Hearst himself was such a bore, but Marian was a delight. She and Cat got along splendidly." Richard gestured to his left. "There's the golf course—I haven't played in ages, but I keep it well maintained all the same. Do you golf?"

"No."

"It's not too difficult to pick up. Felix is actually an excellent player; I'm sure he'd be a good teacher."

"That might be hard since I can't see in the dark."

"Oh, but it's never truly dark here. Not if I don't want it to be. There are floodlights everywhere. All it takes is the flick of a switch and it can be nearly as bright as day. When I met Cat, I promised to bring daylight back into her life." His hands flexed around the wheel. "I always keep my promises."

Past the golf course, they came across an enormous swimming pool. "It's the largest in Southern California," Richard said. "One hundred and fifty feet long. It's surrounded by a tunnel with underwater windows so you can see the swimmers. Cat doesn't breathe, of course, so she could stay under there for hours. I loved to watch her swim—she is so preternaturally graceful, and all the more lovely underwater, her movements so slow and dreamy. I did a very famous photo shoot of her in promotion of *Mermaids of the Blue Lagoon*. Perhaps I could show you later."

"I've already seen it." He remembered it vividly from one of his grandmother's books. The pictures had always struck John as eerie. Now he knew why.

From there, they drove past the tennis court and a bowling green. They came at last to a small amphitheater.

"Cat was an actress even before her death. It was her wish to return to the stage, so I had one built for her. We used to put on plays, just for fun, with some of the top movie stars of the time. We liked Shakespeare especially. Can you imagine Clark Gable as Hamlet? Or Buster Keaton as Nick Bottom? And Cat, of course, as Rosalind and Ophelia and Juliet..."

"And you as Romeo?"

"Once or twice," Richard admitted. "Although I'm not much of an actor. Besides, I prefer Hamlet." He cleared his throat and began to recite grandly:

"To be, or not to be—that is the question:
Whether 'tis nobler in the mind to suffer
The slings and arrows of outrageous fortune
Or to take arms against a sea of troubles,
And by opposing end them."

He turned back to John. "What do you think of that?"

"I think you're right—you aren't much of an actor."

Richard put a hand over his chest in mock despair. "I'm wounded. But I meant what do you think of the sentiment? To be or not to be? Which do you choose?"

John crossed his arms over his chest. "I think either way, you get fucked."

Richard let out a bark of laughter. "An astute observation. But what if I were to tell you there is a way to avoid the slings and arrows without drowning yourself in a sea of troubles?"

"What do you mean?"

"All in good time." Richard did a U-turn and made his way up the other side of the estate. To their left was an archway, beyond which John could see flowers and greens.

"The gardens," Richard said with a gesture. "You're not ready for the gardens."

"Why not?" he asked, but Richard acted as if he hadn't heard him.

When they were nearly upon the mansion again, Richard headed to the left, where there was a small building with marquee lights. Richard stopped the cart.

"And here is my movie theater. I thought we could take in a show. I think you will find it very interesting."

He exited the cart and walked toward the front door. John followed. The theater only had about fifty seats, but the screen was large. A pipe organ stood against the back of the room, next to the projection booth. An old-fashioned popcorn machine was set off to the left.

"Why don't you make yourself comfortable?"

John sat down. Richard disappeared into the projection booth, emerging a few minutes later. He sat down beside John and waved his hand. The lights went down, and the movie reel started.

"Cat's first feature," Richard said. "Sadly, it's something of a lost film. It didn't do very well. It was a silent film when the talkies had just started to take off." He waved his hand again. John jumped as the pipe organ suddenly came to life.

It wasn't much of a trick, turning things on and off with a wave of his hand. John was sure he could have done it himself, but not silently—not as effortlessly as Richard seemed to. His ring flickered faintly—clearly, the power came from there, but what was fueling it?

A title card appeared on the screen: *The Deathly Lover*.

"I wrote the screenplay myself," Richard said over the sound of the pipe organ. "It's based off a story by Gautier." He paused. "It's strange—when I came into my magical power, I was sure that would be what made my fortune. But aside from a little nudge here or there to make sure the right deals were made, *this* was the magic that shaped me—the magic of movies, with the ability to touch millions."

The Livingstone Productions logo came on the screen: a great boar with enormous tusks.

"Why did you pick a boar for your mascot?" John asked.

Richard took a moment to answer, and then said, "I was born on a pig farm. Up in North Dakota, where the winters are so cold. Have you ever been to a pig farm?"

"No."

"It's disgusting. All that smelly, dirty flesh. The terrible thing is that pigs are intelligent, and yet we have tamed them so completely that they just wait to be slaughtered. Now a boar, on the other hand—*that* is a formidable creature. There's no taming a boar."

After the credits finished, the movie began in earnest. The scene opened on a church. A card gave the place and time of the story: *France, 1843*. A young man was being ordained as a priest. A memory stirred in John.

"Does this seem familiar to you?" Richard asked, as if he'd read his thoughts.

"Yes," John said slowly. "It does." He half remembered clutching his mother's arm in terror in a darkened theater. "You cast a vampire in a movie about vampires."

Richard smiled slyly. "I couldn't resist. She was born to play the role. Or rather, she had died to play it."

John ignored Richard's smug self-satisfaction, his full attention directed at the screen. The priest character was taking his final vows. As he prayed, the great Catherine Neville entered the church.

"Luminous, isn't she?" Richard said.

John said nothing, but Richard was right. She was gorgeous, her dark, wavy hair framing her pale face. Her eyes were wide and clear, her lips the same Cupid's bow as Felix's. But even with as beautiful as she was, there was something off about her. She looked wrong. As a child, he'd tried to tell his mother after the movie was over. She reassured him several times that she was just an actress, it was just a movie, silly John, sweet John—she had kissed him and tickled him until he forgot all about it, but now it came rushing back, the horror he'd felt when he'd laid eyes on the lady who wasn't a lady. He had seen death for the first time that day, even if he'd been too young to recognize it.

The priest character did some elaborate miming that showed that he had been struck by her beauty. He walked toward her, then turned his back, his face twisted with anguish. The camera cut back to Cat, who pouted. A title card appeared: *"I am beauty and youth; come to me, and together we shall be Love!"*

"Now who could resist that?" Richard said softly. "Certainly not me."

"Somehow I find it hard to picture you as an innocent seduced into darkness."

Richard laughed. "You would be correct. If anything, it was the other way around. There's something perversely innocent about vampires—they're terribly destructive, but it isn't as if they can help it."

The film went on. The priest character went back to his room, where he beat his chest and rent his garments melodramatically.

"Where did you meet her?" John asked.

"At a party. She and Felix came in with some idiot—I can't even remember his name. He had money and pretensions of being a movie producer. I knew she wasn't entirely human the moment I saw her, but I couldn't quite place it. I asked her what she was. Do you know what she said?" Richard laughed a little. "She said she was a star. And she is! Look at her!"

Cat was back on the screen, beckoning to the young priest from outside his room. He resisted heroically as she writhed seductively. And then, suddenly, Felix was there, behind Cat.

Richard scoffed at Felix's appearance. "This is the only film I ever put him in. He's handsome enough, I suppose, but he had no idea what to do with himself."

Felix did look awkward. He even took a peek at the camera. John's memory flashed again—that was why Felix had looked familiar when they first met.

John stood up. *"Stop the show, and give me silence/before I have to turn to violence!"* The room was plunged into darkness and silence. "Can we stop these games? Just tell me what you want."

Richard waved his hand, turning the lights back on. "I want to help you with your curse."

"How much did Felix tell you?"

"Enough. Although he didn't have to tell me. I knew it already."

John furrowed his brow in confusion. "What?"

"I wasn't sure at first. When Felix came to me and asked me to find you, I felt the darkness of the curse on you. I couldn't pinpoint exactly what it was, although the feel of it was familiar. It evaded me for a while, but then I remembered."

"Remembered what?"

"Your mother came to me many years ago," Richard said. "You came as well, although of course you were just a child—five or six years old at the most. We watched this movie together, in this very theater."

John felt dizzy suddenly. He sat down again. "My mother came to you for help?"

"Yes. The council warned her against me, but she persisted. It was very brave of her."

John took out a cigarette and lit it, his hands shaking. "What did you tell her?"

"After I met her and heard her story, I offered her my assistance, of course. I had two vampires and dozens of rose bushes. All I needed from her was one hundred and one days."

"Did I—" He broke off and took another drag of his cigarette, trying to calm himself. "When I was here as a child, did I meet Felix?"

"No. Your mother wasn't too keen on the idea, particularly after your reaction to the film. You seemed like a sensitive child."

John breathed a small sigh of relief. That would have been *too* weird. "And she turned your offer down."

"Yes. She said she would find a better way." He spread his hands. "But since we are here together, it seems she did not."

"Why did she refuse?"

Richard didn't answer right away. "Your curse has darkened since I first searched for you," he said eventually, avoiding the question. "You don't have much time."

"Maybe that isn't as much of a threat as you think it is," he muttered.

Richard peered at him a moment. "Oh dear." He had the nerve to chuckle. "I think I have misjudged you. I thought you a canny witch suspicious of an unknown magical artifact. But no—your love affair with a vampire, your refusal of a gift that could cure you, your cigarettes. It appears you have a run-of-the-mill death wish. What would your mother say to that? She loved you very much, you know."

John felt his face flush. He stubbed the cigarette out on the armrest. It left a mark on the wood. "I want to go home," he said as he stood up.

Richard stood as well. "Of course. You aren't my prisoner. But first, tell me—if you really wish to die, then why did you ask Felix to make you the cure?"

"I didn't think he could."

"But you thought he might. Were you merely trying to hasten the curse by breaking the clause that forbade any attempt at escape? Or were you, perhaps, holding out some hope?"

John felt pinned in place by Richard's blue gaze. "I don't know."

"You should know your death won't be easy. That curse around you is dark and bitter. Felix told me you witnessed your mother's death. Tell me—how did she die? Is that something you want for yourself?"

John blinked rapidly. Before he could help it, a tear escaped his eye and ran down his cheek. It was quickly followed by another. He broke away from Richard's stare and stumbled over the seats into the aisle. He brushed the tears from his face, willing them to stop, but they kept coming, one after the other. He steadied himself with one hand against the wall, trying to breathe, but it was useless. He started to sob.

He felt a hand on his back. "Poor child," Richard murmured. "Alone with this darkness all these years. It would be enough to drive anyone to despair." He produced a handkerchief from his pocket and offered it to John. After a moment's hesitation, he took it.

After he'd pulled himself together, he looked up at Richard again. "She didn't accept your help—why?"

"She didn't like my offer. But perhaps you will feel differently. Will you at least hear me out before you consign yourself to your fate?"

John didn't say yes. But he didn't say no, either.

They left the theater and got back into the cart. "I think you're ready for the gardens now," Richard said.

They headed back out, away from the mansion. Richard drove the cart through the arched gate that marked the entrance. It was laced with beautiful blooms, vibrant in the sunlight. Why, then, did the words *Abandon all hope, ye who enter here* suddenly flash in his mind?

"I'm quite proud of my gardens," Richard said. "I have sunken gardens, rose gardens, terraced gardens. I also have a lovely greenhouse—I can grow any plant you could dream of. I used to delight in doing some of the gardening myself, but alas, I have grown too old for that to be possible."

John looked around at the well-manicured gardens. "So you hire gardeners."

"Of course."

"How does that work, seeing as you're 'legally' dead?"

"The estate was inherited by my nephew."

"You have a nephew?"

"Of course not. I invented him. I am very good with illusions; the staff all see me as a middle-aged man, and I was able to forge my nephew into existence. I came up with the plan ages ago—I had expected to find the secret to making myself young again by this point."

"Which is why you need me."

"Yes. Felix and Cat are twins. They were born together, and they were risen back from death together. The link between them is very powerful—and magically potent as well."

John took a moment to absorb that information. "Is that why he can love?" he asked, to himself more than Richard. "Because his sister has a human heart?"

"Perhaps. One isn't able to love without a heart, or so I've heard." Richard rapped his fingers on the steering wheel as he thought. "You know, if I really think about it, I'm not sure she ever loved me. At least, before we were married. Certainly she was *fond* of me, but that's not quite the same, is it?"

John crossed his arms over his chest. "So you want me to give my heart to Felix, which would make me immortal like you."

"Yes. And with the four of us linked, I think there will be enough energy to give us the youth that we need."

"That *you* need."

"You'll need it too, eventually."

"How do I know you won't just suck the youth out of me?"

"We'll be linked. That would only hurt me."

"And that's what you offered my mother. You wanted to put her heart in Felix."

"As a matter of fact, no. I hadn't thought of that particular solution at the time."

"What did you want from her, then?"

"Her companionship. I asked her to live here with me. Oh, don't look at me like that," Richard said with annoyance at John's horrified look. "I didn't sexually proposition your mother. I already have a wife, the love of my life who quite literally holds my heart. I merely craved human interaction."

"Why?"

"Vampires aren't exactly intellectually stimulating company." He smiled. "And you were a very sweet child. Happy Endings is so lacking in youthful vitality. I'd never had any particularly parental urges, but it would have pleased me to educate you. It would please me still."

John hugged himself tighter and was silent.

They rode past many beautiful flowers and plants, but they were interspersed with strange fountains depicting unsettling scenes. John's feeling of foreboding grew worse as they went farther and farther inward.

At last, Richard stopped. To their right was a greenhouse. To their left was a cottage.

"What is this?" John asked.

Richard exited the cart. "This is where the Extras reside." He began to walk toward the cottage. John followed.

He wasn't prepared for what he saw when he entered. Twelve people lay in twelve beds. They were all fast asleep. But there was something wrong about them. There was a stench, just like the smell of Richard. Rot. Decay. John gagged.

"Who are these people?"

"The Extras, as I said. Cat and I share immorality, but her own feeding is not enough to sustain us. I must take my own nourishment. She feeds on the blood of the guests I select for us, while I take their life power."

John was too appalled to form a response.

"I know that it looks bad, but this is actually compassion at its most pure," Richard said. "Each and every one of the people in this room explicitly wished for death. They chased it in the streets, called it upon themselves in their homes and their lives. They were abused, addicted, abandoned, ashamed."

"And so what, you put them out of their misery?" John spat.

Richard seemed to miss the sarcasm in John's voice. "Yes, precisely."

John looked again at their prone forms. "They still look pretty miserable to me."

"Looks can be deceiving." Richard walked to the bedside of one woman. "This is Jennifer. Her father abused her terribly, driving her to the street at age fifteen. She had no family, no friends. She was forced into prostitution. All she wanted in life was a family to love. She has one now. I have crafted her the most beautiful dream, where she has a husband and children, a house in the suburbs, all of the safety and love denied to her in life."

He moved on to a man. "And this is Anton. He's a veteran. He came back from war scarred, both in his body and his mind. He frightened people. No one would help. Now, he is whole. His dream is of his life as a young man—the youth he missed. His pain is forgotten." Richard gestured to the room at large. "Every lost soul here will never feel a moment of pain again."

"While you suck the life out of them."

"They don't feel it. Inside their minds, they live the lives they've always wanted, and they meet their ends happy. I probably don't need to remind you how rare that is. And I assure you, I only take on the direst cases."

John looked down at Jennifer. He couldn't tell what she was feeling, although it was true that she didn't look like she was in pain. "What makes you think you're qualified to determine who is so broken they deserve to die?"

Richard sighed. "No one deserves to die," he said. "And yet, we all do eventually."

"Except for you."

Richard smiled. "Except for me. And Cat, Felix, and potentially you. Tell me, John—if it weren't for your curse, would you still have that death wish? Do you truly wish to end your life?"

John's voice had suddenly left him; any words he had died in his throat. But he found himself shaking his head, although he wasn't sure if he was rejecting the question or giving Richard his answer.

Richard put a hand on his arm. "I realize this is a lot to take in. I want to be clear: I am proposing a partnership. The rose you have in your possession is pure; I have not placed any additional spells on it. Enchanting you would be counterproductive, as the kind of magic I would use to grant you immortality must be entered into voluntarily. I know that Felix is willing; he's quite in love with you. Do you share his sentiment?"

"I don't know." John's voice was so soft he could barely hear it himself.

Richard patted his arm. "Why don't we go find him? He's probably sleeping, but I'm sure he wouldn't mind being woken up. And you can meet Cat as well. The four of us can talk this over."

They rode back up to the mansion. John's thoughts were a jumble. This was *wrong*; he could feel it in every fiber of his being. The magic Richard was wielding was the definition of darkness; it literally stank. He tried to block out all the arguments Richard had made. But there was a small, dark part of himself who was listening.

The inside of the house was as grand as it looked on the outside. John steeled himself to be unimpressed, but once again, he failed. It was even more impressive than the pictures in his grandmother's book. The domed ceiling with a chandelier, double staircase, and marble floor made it seem more like the entrance to a fairy-tale castle than a home in Beverly Hills. Paintings decorated the walls—John couldn't help but move in for a closer look. Richard Livingstone was famous for his collection of pricey works of art. He stopped in front of a Cubist picture of a woman pouring water from a mug.

"Before you ask, yes, it's an original Picasso," Richard commented. John jumped; Richard was much closer than he had thought. "Cost me a pretty penny, too. You're something of an artist yourself, aren't you?"

"Felix told you?"

"No. You have a bit of paint on your trousers."

John looked down. It was true, although it was such a small amount he was surprised Richard had noticed. "Yeah, I paint a little."

"You could have a studio here, if you like. There are forty-four rooms, all of which will be at your disposal. Not to mention my vast fortune— you will have access to that as well. You will have every comfort and everything your heart desires here."

"And all it will cost me is my heart and soul."

"You wouldn't really be losing your heart. It would be in the breast of the man you love. That's very romantic, don't you think? And as for your soul...well, I've never been a big believer in souls. Are you sure you have one to lose?"

They went up the stairs and to the right and then down a long hallway. They stopped in front of a door. Richard went in without knocking. John began to follow, but Richard came out again a moment later.

"He's not here. That probably means he's in Cat's room. Follow me."

They went farther down the hall until they reached another door. Richard opened it, then froze.

"Not again," he muttered under his breath.

"Not what again?"

Richard shut the door. "Nothing. It appears they are indisposed. We can wait until tonight—if you like, I can show you my extended art collection—"

Before Richard could stop him, John pushed the door open. What he saw was a complete disaster. The room was in complete ruins—everything was smashed to pieces, like a small tornado had whipped through the room. Two figures were slumped on the sofa.

John looked at Richard in confusion. Why wasn't he alarmed? "What happened?"

"It seems that Cat has thrown a tantrum," Richard said evenly. "No need to worry. She's done it before. It's best if we let them sleep it off." Richard pulled a rope on the side of the door; a bell rang somewhere in the distance. "The mess is cleaned up easily enough. Come, let's go to the library—I would love to show you some ancient books I've discovered..."

John ignored him. He made his way to the sofa, kneeling beside it. Felix and his sister were curled up together. There was something brown and crusty on their faces. When John touched it, it flaked away. It was dried blood. They'd been crying.

John shook Felix's shoulder. He was completely still and pale—he wasn't breathing, but vampires didn't breathe... "Felix, wake up. *Wake up!*"

"I doubt you'll be able to rouse them." John looked up; Richard was standing over him.

"Why not?"

Richard reached down and picked up what looked like a candy dish. John saw a few white and blue candies—except when he took a second look, he saw that they weren't candies at all. They were pills. John looked around and noticed all the empty wine bottles surrounding the couch, several of them broken.

"They get a little carried away sometimes," Richard said.

John felt light-headed, the *wrongness* of it churning his stomach. He shook Felix again. "Please wake up."

John heard footsteps coming down the hall. Several women in maid uniforms entered the room. None of them seemed surprised at the mess. In fact, none of them seemed to be reacting in any way at all. They began cleaning without a word.

"They can't see us," Richard said. "And before you ask, no, they aren't cursed or controlled. I pay them well. I've just placed a light enchantment on them, to spare them the worry of strange scenes."

"This happens a lot?"

"Not frequently, no. But Felix and Cat are both somewhat off-putting. It's best if the staff doesn't notice them."

"And so you're just going to leave them here like this."

"Of course not. We'll put them to bed." Richard waved his finger. Cat floated upward until she was facing Richard, almost as if she were standing on her own. "I wish this hadn't been your first introduction to her. She's still as lovely as she was the moment I met her." He put his arms around her. She flopped about in his grasp, like a puppet with its strings cut.

John looked on in horror. "And why does she throw 'tantrums'?"

"She's confused. It's her brother, I fear—he's still half wild, and the connection between them is strong. If Felix were to be properly settled, perhaps she would see reason more clearly." Another wave of his hand and her feet floated upward until she was horizontal. Richard put his hands under her, carrying her as a groom carries his wife over the threshold. He brought her to the bed and laid her down. "And when I am young again, things will be different," he said softly. "Like they were before."

John was too horrified to speak. Richard came to John's side again. "Shall we put him to bed, too?"

He didn't wait for John to answer. With another wave of his hand, Felix was hoisted into the air, without as much care as he'd given to Cat. He headed for the door, Felix floating behind him. None of the maids noticed; they kept to their work, sweeping and collecting the debris.

John followed Richard to Felix's bedroom next door. Richard dumped Felix on the bed unceremoniously.

"Now, then," Richard said, turning to John. "Why don't we have some lunch? And then I can give you that tour—I'm sure you'll find my art collection fascinating."

"I want to go home," John said. He realized how pitiful he sounded, so he forced a smile and continued with a stronger voice. "Just for now. I need some time to think. Please."

Richard considered him for a long moment. "Very well," he said at last. "I'll have Philip take you home. Felix will come for you tonight. We can all talk then."

John nodded vaguely, although he had no intention of setting foot in this horrible place again.

Richard took him to the limo and sent him off with a wave. The drive was quiet. John felt too emotionally concussed to think properly. When they reached his apartment, Philip got his groceries out of the trunk and carried them in. He bowed to John and turned to leave.

"Wait," John said.

The man stopped and turned to John again.

John examined him some more. Philip was different than the maids, clearly; none of them had the same glazed look, or the same gray skin. What had Richard done to him?

"How long have you been with Richard?" John asked.

For a moment, John didn't think he would respond, but then he spoke. "I don't recall." His voice was raspy and flat.

"Do you work for him of your own will?"

"I don't recall," he said again. He continued to stand there, completely still, as if waiting for an order.

It was clear that John wouldn't get any information out of him. It was also clear that he was beyond help. "You can go now."

Philip bowed and left.

John sat on the bed, staring dully at the floor. Astray jumped up and nuzzled his hand, but John barely felt her.

John sat there for a long time, trying to decide what to do. He could take the cure. He had a strong feeling that Richard wasn't lying about tampering with the rose; it was probably clean. But what then? Run? He would have to be quick, and he would have to go far—Richard might be able to trace him, but John had the suspicion that Richard's sphere of influence was not large. His power would diminish if he was separated from the source of it.

But that would leave Felix behind. Poor Felix, both a monster and a captive, who was far beyond John's ability to save. Abandoning him would haunt John for the rest of his life—not that he had one. He'd been living as if he had no future—he had a job that was leading nowhere, and he'd never finished school. His family was dead. He'd left Rob. He'd alienated Lo. He had no one.

He tried to think about what he would do if he started his life over again, but he couldn't work up any enthusiasm. Mostly, he just felt tired.

He went to the kitchen and opened the cupboard where he'd put the rose. It was still as full and beautiful as when Felix had given it to him. He stared at it for a long time.

After a little bit, he placed it on the table. He got out his messenger bag and tucked the rose inside. Astray was weaving in and out of his legs, meowing and purring. He picked her up and kissed her. She was a good cat. He'd have to find a home for her. He got out his phone and called for an Uber to take him to Forest Lawn.

He didn't go to his grave. After all, he had the rest of eternity to spend there. Instead, he went to the lake with the Little Mermaid statue. He sat on the perfectly manicured grass and just gazed into the water for a while as the statue's reflection rippled in the light breeze. Eventually, he reached into his bag and brought out the rose. Slowly, he plucked each of the petals, tossing them into the water. He watched them float away. When he was finished, he stood up and stretched his arms to the sky. He felt so empty he thought he could float away on the breeze, out into the water where he would dissolve, like foam on the sea.

Eleven: The Cage and the Key

THE SUNSHINE WOKE Felix up.

It took him several moments to recognize the light for what it was. First, he assumed it was the television set, except the glow of this light was constant, not flickering. Was he perhaps under a streetlamp? No, this light was warmer than that. But then again, it couldn't be sunlight, because he was currently not on fire.

He blinked sleepily as he puzzled out the situation. He sat up and took in his surroundings. He was on the beach, laid out on the golden sand under an impossibly blue sky. He held his hand up in the light and examining it. No, it was certainly not on fire.

"A dream," he finally concluded. "I'm having a dream!" This itself was also odd, seeing as he had not had a dream since he'd died. However, a dream seemed more plausible than any of the alternatives that he could think of.

He stood up and stretched. Somewhere in the back of his mind, he was aware that in the waking world he was desperately unhappy about something, but for now, the day was beautiful and the sun was warm. He smiled; it felt good.

He decided to take a walk. He strolled along for some time, letting the soft crash of the waves along the shore soothe him. He wondered how long it would be before he woke up. He hoped it would be a long time.

Gradually, he became aware of a noise—an uneven, metallic clanking, coming from somewhere ahead of him in the distance. He sped up his walking; before long, he came upon a woman sitting cross-legged under the shade of a palm tree. She wore faded jean shorts and a bright yellow tank top. Her long blond curls were pulled back in a messy ponytail. In one hand, she held a crowbar. She was using it to pry at something she held in her lap.

She looked up. As soon as she saw Felix, she smiled widely and got to her feet, leaving the object she had been tinkering with on the ground as she bounded over to him. She was extremely pretty, but there was something strange about her: she had scars on her wrists, her elbows, her knees, her ankles, and her neck. It was like she had been stitched together, like a rag doll.

She gave him a quick squeeze, as if they were old friends. Her smile was dazzling; Felix wasn't usually susceptible to feminine charms, but this young woman was delightful. She took him by the hand and led him over to the tree. She gestured at the object. Now that he was closer, Felix could see what it was. It was an empty birdcage.

"Are you trying to open that?" he asked.

She nodded and held out the crowbar.

"You want my help?"

She nodded again.

He bowed. "I would be delighted to assist you, but I have no need of a crowbar." He picked up the cage and tore the door open quite easily.

The woman clapped in delight. Felix smiled widely. "As you can see, I'm extremely strong."

The woman's shoulders shook with laughter. She curled her arm, miming making a muscle and pointed to Felix, as if agreeing that he was indeed very strong. That's when Felix noticed that her laughter was silent.

"Can't you speak?" he asked her.

Her smile faltered for a moment. She shook her head briefly, but then her smile was back. She reached for the birdcage. Felix went to hand it to her, but she shook her head. She mimed breaking a bar.

Felix frowned. "You want me to break it apart?"

She nodded. She curled her arm and pointed to her muscle and then at Felix again, shrugging.

"Of course I'm strong enough!"

She grinned and gave him a thumbs-up.

It took a little while, but eventually he removed every bar of the cage. The woman took each bar as it was removed. Once the whole cage was in pieces, she laid all the bars on the sand in front of them.

"Now what?" Felix asked.

She rubbed her chin as she looked at them. Felix also stared at them thoughtfully, even though he had no idea what he ought to be thoughtful about. After a few minutes, she sighed and sat down under the tree, resting her head on her knees.

Felix sat down beside her. She seemed gloomy, which in turn made Felix feel gloomy. "Is there anything I can do?"

She shook her head, her curls bouncing. She tapped her finger on her head.

"It's a puzzle, then," Felix said. "Alas, I am not as smart as I am strong."

Her smile was like the sun peeking out from dark clouds. Suddenly, a thought came to Felix.

"I've seen you before," he said. "You were in the crystal ball at the museum! I remember, I saw you waving!"

She nodded.

"I waved back," he said. "Did you see me?"

She laughed and nodded again. She squeezed his shoulder.

"Are you a witch?"

She tilted her hand back and forth, which Felix interpreted as "somewhat." But how could someone be "somewhat" a witch? Now Felix had his own puzzle to work on.

After a little while, an expression of "Eureka!" came over her face. She got to her feet excitedly, motioning for Felix to join her. She pointed to the bars and mimed picking them up. As Felix gathered them, she began to trace a shape into the sand. Felix brought the bars over and peeked over her shoulder. It took him a moment to puzzle out the shape she was drawing: it was an enormous key.

When she was finished, she took the bars from Felix and arranged them in the outline. After she was done, she stopped and rubbed her chin.

"You want to make a key?" Felix asked.

She nodded.

"Wouldn't you need to melt the metal first?"

She smiled widely, nearly jumping with excitement. She gathered the bars and thrust them into Felix's hands. With a snap of her fingers, suddenly the scene shifted. Felix looked around; they appeared to be in a blacksmith's forge. The forge itself was cold and dark. She gestured at it.

"You want me to heat it up? Can't you just snap your fingers again?"

She shook her head.

Felix sighed; dream logic was confusing. "Fire is not one of my strong suits, dream or no."

She pointed at his pants pocket. Felix put his hand in it and pulled out a lighter. Not just any lighter—the one he'd taken from John. He opened it and lit it.

As soon as the lighter lit, the forge itself lit up. The woman laid the bars in a tray. Soon they were melted. With Felix's help, she poured the metal into a mold of an enormous key. When they were finished, she blew on it. The heat left it at once, leaving a fully formed metal key. When she picked it up, it shrank in size. She held it out to Felix.

Felix hesitated. There was something about this moment that felt hugely important. Gently, Felix folded his hands around hers, so that they were holding the key together. Their gazes met. Her smile was as sunny as ever, but Felix could see tears shimmering in the corners of her eyes.

"I will keep it safe," Felix said solemnly, although he wasn't quite sure what "it" was. He started to pull back, but she moved with him, pushing gently until their hands were on Felix's chest. Felix opened his hands so that the key could press against him. The key grew warm; with another gentle push, it somehow passed into him. Felix gasped; it didn't hurt, but it did feel strange. It settled inside him, pulsing with a gentle heat, spreading warmth through his whole body.

The tears that had been in the corners of the woman's eyes were rolling down her cheeks now, but she was still smiling. She brushed them away. She touched her own chest, then Felix's. Then she put her arms around him, hugging him close. Felix returned her embrace.

When she let him go, Felix felt himself being pulled away, floating upward and backward. He looked over his shoulder and saw a distressing darkness. He looked back to the woman, who was growing smaller and smaller.

"Wait!" Felix called out. There was so much he wanted to ask her; true, she couldn't speak, but they'd been able to communicate. "Who are you? Will I see you again?" But by then, she was too far away for him to see any response.

FELIX'S EYES OPENED. He sat straight up. He looked around; he appeared to be in his bedroom. It was very dark and very real. All at once, the events of the previous night came back to him. He lay back down and screwed his eyes shut, hoping maybe he could fall asleep again and return to the dream world. Unfortunately, it soon became apparent he was stuck.

He got out of bed and changed his clothes. When he felt more presentable, he left his room and went to Cat's. The room was back in order, with no trace of the mess of the previous night. This was not especially surprising. Richard usually had things cleaned up after nasty scenes.

Cat was awake and sitting on the sofa, watching TV. Her hair was a mess, sticking up in all directions. Felix sat down beside her and then put an arm around her. She leaned her head against his shoulder.

"Do you want to do your hair?" Felix asked.

"Not tonight." She put a hand on her arm. "You're warm," she said, puzzled.

"I fed last night." He felt a stab of shame as to who that blood had come from, and at what price.

"Yes, but you feel—different."

Felix didn't feel like talking about how disastrously it had gone; the memory of it made him feel sick. He changed the subject. "You're warm as well. Did you feed?"

"Richard brought me someone else after you left."

"Yes, I gathered. The room was in quite a state."

"You came back?"

"You were passed out. I joined you, but I woke up in my room. I suppose Richard moved me."

"Yes, well, he does consider you part of the mess." She sighed. "At least he'll leave us to ourselves for a little while."

Unfortunately, she was wrong, because just then, Richard came through the door. He did not look happy.

"Well," he said. "It seems the two of you have recovered. You made quite a mess."

Cat ignored him, keeping her attention on the television. Richard stomped over, blocking the view. "I don't like being ignored."

"Why are you here?" Cat snapped. "You got what you wanted. Let me be."

"As a matter of fact, no, I did not get what I wanted," Richard snapped back. "And your ridiculous melodramatics are to blame."

"What are you talking about?"

"I brought John over for a tour today."

Felix felt his stomach drop. "He agreed to come with you?"

"He required some persuasion," Richard admitted. "As I have told you, I have no desire to harm him; I was merely giving him a tour."

"So you made your proposal?" Felix asked.

Cat looked back and forth between the two of them. "What proposal?"

Richard casually examined his nails. "I offered to join Felix and John the way you and I are joined."

Cat shot to her feet. "*No*! You cannot!"

"Of course I can," Richard said mildly.

"You promised you would leave my brother out of this!" Cat said, her voice growing louder.

"The situation has changed."

Cat shrieked. She picked up a vase and threw it at Richard's head, but he batted it away with a flick of his finger.

"Now, now, my darling. Let's not have any scenes. You aren't thinking reasonably about this." He turned to Felix. "You love your John, do you not?"

Felix nodded.

"And you want to be with him forever?"

"No!" Cat said. "Not like this!" She turned to Felix. "You can't imagine the pain—"

"Which will last for a few weeks only," Richard said.

"You're wrong," Cat spat. "It remains. It grows worse every day!"

Richard rolled his eyes and continued speaking to Felix as if she hadn't interrupted. "If you truly love him, you should be glad to endure it. After all, what is a few weeks in the face of eternity?"

"An eternity of hell." Cat was crying now, trickles of red falling down her cheeks. She threw herself on the sofa and wept.

Richard just sighed. "It's up to you, Felix. Ignore your sister. Go to John and invite him back. Assure him again that the rose is untouched and he can use it safely. And then we will work to change his mind." He made to leave but then turned back. "Oh, and I feel I must mention that if John refuses my offer, I will be most displeased. It will earn you a trip to the greenhouse. You will have pain either way. Just something to keep in mind."

Cat looked up, blood streaking her face. "Oh, you are cruel!"

"And you are ungrateful," Richard shot back. "Your unhappiness is your own making. Perhaps once your brother is bound, you'll come to your senses." With that, he left.

Cat rushed to Felix as soon as he was gone. "You mustn't do this! You have to leave—forever. I cannot bear to see you succumb to my fate!"

"I'm not abandoning you."

"Is it abandonment if I bid you to go? I will never speak to you again should you go through with this!"

Felix took her in his arms and shushed her until she was more composed. He couldn't imagine why she was so opposed to his and John's joining, but he knew he would not get many answers from her in the state she was in.

"There must be another way around this," he said. "I'll talk to John."

She laughed bitterly through her tears. "And he will convince you what a marvelous idea it is, I'm sure."

"Didn't you hear Richard? He said we must change his mind. If that's true, then it means John refused him!"

Cat sobs abated. "He refused immortality?"

"As I have told you, he is not wicked. He would not harm me any more than you would."

Cat rested her head against Felix's chest again. "Can it be true?" she said, half to herself.

"It is." Felix pulled away so they could look each other in the face. "I must go to him now and convince him to use the blessing. And once he is free of his curse—well, we can take it from there. We will find a way to make this right."

"Do you really think he can help?"

Felix hesitated. He was about to tell her how poorly John's last idea had turned out, but there was something in her face that he hadn't seen in a very long time. It was hope.

"Yes," he said decisively.

"Then go to him," she said.

So he did.

FELIX CALLED JOHN'S phone first. It went straight to voice mail. That wasn't entirely unusual as John had an unnatural indifference to his phone. He had perhaps forgotten to plug it in. No matter; Felix would simply track him down. He went to John's apartment first. John had not been well when he last saw him, and an encounter with Richard probably didn't help matters. He couldn't imagine him going to work under those circumstances. And yet, he wasn't home. Felix was certain of it, because when John didn't answer the door after ten minutes of knocking, Felix let himself in. He must have gone to work after all. That could be good news. Perhaps he had found a way to heal himself.

Felix zipped over to the restaurant and hid in the alley in back. He thought it best not to march in the front door, considering how his last visit had gone. It was only a matter of time before John took a cigarette break.

Except he didn't. The hours wore on, and John didn't make a single appearance. Felix took a few discreet looks into the kitchen. He saw the cook, the dishwasher, and the terrifying witch, but then there was this other woman working as a server who Felix had never seen before.

Had John been fired and replaced? Had he quit? Where *was* he? Felix was starting to get a very bad feeling. He tried to sort out why he felt that way. Then it hit him.

When he had been at John's place, the cat was missing.

Now Felix started to panic. If he took the cat, that meant he could have left the city. Why and where, he hadn't the faintest idea. Felix was at a complete loss as to what to do. He tried to think, but after twenty minutes, he gave up. He considered consulting Cat, but while she was smarter than Felix, she was hopeless at life outside the gates of Happy Endings. That left only one course of action.

He needed a witch. And there was only one he knew who wasn't Richard or John.

He was going to have to approach this with the utmost care. He considered trying to get Lo alone, but that would lead swiftly to his entrapment and/or slaying. But if other people were around, she would be reluctant to use magic.

He thrust out his chest and walked through the front door with the most courage he could muster. The restaurant was nearly empty, with a lone customer eating spaghetti in one of the booths. Lo was on hostess duty. She stared at Felix for a good thirty seconds, as if she couldn't quite believe he was there. She opened her mouth to say something, or possibly cast a spell, but before she could, Felix dropped to his knees.

"O great and powerful witch," he began. It never hurt to flatter a witch. "I am throwing myself at your mercy. I fear for John's safety, as he has disappeared quite suddenly, and he may be in great danger."

She continued to stare at him. "You have got to be shitting me," is what she finally said.

She seemed angry, so Felix lay down on the ground for the full grovel. "Entrap me, torture me, slay me if you must, but John must be made aware of the terrible danger he is in, and I have only you to turn to. I do not pretend to understand witches' feuds, but surely since you are both good witches, you would be displeased to see his curse fulfilled."

"You know about his curse?" She sounded more interested now.

He nodded. Or he tried to, which was hard when he was face down on the ground. "Yes, my lady."

She hesitated for a moment, then heaved an enormous sigh. "For Christ's sake, get up off the floor. You are making a scene." Felix did as he was told, brushing himself off. He took a peek at the spaghetti eater, who was still slowly eating his meal, oblivious to the world. Lo gestured to one of the booths in the back.

They sat down. "You have ten minutes to explain yourself. If you bullshit me, I will destroy you."

That seemed fair. He opened his mouth and then shut it again. "I'm not quite sure where to start."

Lo rubbed her temple. "How about with the curse, which is the only reason I'm agreeing to talk to you?"

"Right."

So he told her, starting with the curse, then moving on to the rose, which of course meant he had to tell her about Richard, and then his sister, and then since he was on a roll, he told her about how they became vampires and the Extras and Richard's sinister plan for John and the little he knew about John's meeting with Richard the previous day.

"...and Richard said his curse has become very dark now and will probably strike at any moment, which is why I must find him and encourage him to use the blessing before it's too late."

Lo didn't say anything for a few moments. She leaned back in the booth and ran a hand through her hair.

"Wow," she finally said.

"So do you know where he is?"

"Yeah. He quit. Said he found a better job, but was going to take some time off before it started. He dropped his cat off with me this morning."

"Where was he going?"

"Catalina."

Felix's stomach dropped. "He can't go to Catalina! That's where Natalie Wood died!"

"What the fuck is that—" She broke off. "Never mind. I don't have any more time to listen to you ramble." She stood up.

Felix followed suit. "Where are we going?"

She started walking toward the kitchen. "*We're* not going anywhere. *I* am going to call John and we'll figure this out."

Felix followed her. "That's not fair!"

The old man eating the spaghetti called after them. "Excuse me, miss—could I get my check?"

"In a minute," she snapped. She went into the kitchen.

Felix zipped in front of her. "Please," he said. "I want to help. I meant it about throwing myself at your mercy. You can do whatever you like to me, but I need to know that John is safe. You see, I am terribly, terribly in love with him." Felix did his best to look pitiful. "Please?"

She was about to respond when a masculine voice interrupted. "What the *fuck* are you doing here?"

Felix turned around to see the cook headed straight toward him. He shoved Felix back a few steps. "I thought I told you never to show your sorry face here again. Or do I need to teach you another lesson?"

"Lesson?" Felix echoed with confusion.

"Yeah. I'm a professor at the University of Kicking Creepy Stalker's Ass, and I'm ready to take you to school again."

Felix's brow furrowed. "I'm fairly certain I nearly ripped your throat out the last time we met." He shot a glance at Lo; he probably shouldn't have brought that up. "For which I do sincerely apologize," he added quickly.

The cook shoved Felix again. "What the fuck are you talking about?"

Lo stepped between them. "I can handle this, Vince."

"No offense, Lo, but you are like five foot nothing. This is a man's job."

Lo's entire body tightened. Felix prepared for a witch's wrath, but Lo took a deep breath and turned her attention to the woman who had replaced John, who was watching the whole scenario unfold with a look of alarm on her face. "Jennifer, that customer wants his check. Why don't you go give it to him?"

She hastily fled. Lo turned next to the dishwasher, who did not seem as nervous as he did bemused. "Gabriel, call Mike and tell him I'm having a family emergency and I had to go."

"Uh, sure," he said. He also left the room.

At last, she turned back to Vince. "And you get back to work."

Felix recognized the power underlying her words. It reminded him of when Richard spoke to his victims. Vince blinked. He turned around and went back to his station.

Lo turned to Felix. "Come on. Let's go."

Felix brightened. "I can come?"

"Only because you'll cause trouble otherwise."

"I might be of use as well," Felix said, eager to prove himself. "Between the two of us, we're certain to find him."

Vince looked up from his work. "Do you mean John? You're taking him to *John*? You can't take this stalker right to him!"

Felix scowled. "I am not a stalker. He is my lover, which is more than you will ever be, you miserable closet case."

The color first drained from Vince's face, and then suddenly came rushing back. "You motherfucker—"

Lo pointed at him. "Stop talking." He shut his mouth. She turned to Felix and pointed at the door. "And you stop making trouble, or you will know my wrath. Got it?"

Felix obeyed. As he left, he took one last look at Vince. He was staring so intensely at Felix that his eyes were nearly bugging out of his head. He looked like an angry toad. Felix couldn't help but laugh; what an absurd person.

Lo led him down the street to her car, a beat-up old thing that at one point in its life was red in color. Felix really disliked cars, but he got in without complaining. She took out her phone and tried to call John, but she was also unsuccessful. "I guess we'll go to my place and try to think of a plan."

They sat in silence for the first ten minutes of the ride.

"May I ask you something?" Felix finally asked.

Lo sighed. "What?"

"What's a closet case?"

Lo started laughing; it became so raucous that Felix was afraid she would crash the car. She stopped at last, wiping the tears from her life.

"Oh my God," she said. "Fuck my life." But she didn't sound angry. Felix was relieved, even though he didn't get an answer to his question.

They arrived at Lo's apartment. Felix sat down at the table while Lo searched her closet. John's cat came out from under the bed. Felix expected her to hiss at him, but instead she started purring and rubbing his legs. He gave her a little scratch on the head, which she seemed to enjoy.

Lo came to the table with a small chest. Inside were her witch's implements.

"What are we going to do?" Felix asked her.

"I don't know," she said. "Scry for him?"

"But we already know where he is."

"Yeah, but not his exact location." She rubbed her face. "Christ, what a mess."

A thought occurred to Felix. "There was something I forgot to tell you earlier. Perhaps it will help."

She gestured at him to continue.

"I had a very unusual dream. There was this woman with a birdcage—"

"Blond ponytail, yellow shirt, smiles a lot?" Lo interrupted.

"Yes! However did you know?"

"Because I had the same dream." She looked a little shaken. "Shit." She rubbed her temples. "I didn't have any luck with the birdcage. How about you?"

"Oh, I opened it. I'm very strong."

"And then what happened?"

Felix explained about the forge and the key. "What do you think it means?"

"I think it means I need different tools." She went back to the closet and came back with a long cardboard box.

Felix frowned at it. "What is a oo-gia board?"

"Ouija," she corrected him. "It's for contacting spirits."

Felix thought back to the woman's ambiguous answer as to whether she was a witch.

"Oh I see! She's a dead witch! But what on earth does she want from us?"

"I think I might know." She put a plastic planchette in the middle of the board, which was covered in letters and numbers, with the words "YES" and "NO" in opposite corners. "Put your fingers on the edge of it, very lightly. It's going to move around, but you don't want to jerk at it. And stay quiet."

Lo shut her eyes and took a deep breath. "Are there any spirits with us?"

The planchette flew across the board to the YES before returning the center.

"I'm guessing I'm talking to Adelaide," Lo said.

The planchette flew to YES again.

"Who's Adelaide?" Felix asked.

Lo met his gaze. "It's John's mother."

Before Felix could absorb that information, the planchette began moving around again, this time to a succession of letters. It was too quick for Felix to register it; fortunately Lo had no trouble.

"Ripper's Cove?" she said. "What's that?"

"It's where I took John on our first date," Felix said.

Before Lo could respond, the planchette moved again. This time, Felix caught what it spelled.

HURRY.

"Shit," Lo said. "How are we going to—"

Felix grabbed her around the waist and zipped out of the room, launching into the sky the moment they were out of the building. She was screaming and cursing at him, but Felix barely registered it. He knew what John was doing.

He was beating the curse to the punch.

As soon as they reached the beach, Felix dropped the still cursing Lo off on the sand. A light flashed in the air above them, briefly outlining the form of the woman, wispy and golden. She gestured; Felix felt as if there were a hook in the middle of his chest, pulling him forward. He shed his boots and his jacket and made a great leap into the ocean, following the pull of the hook. The salt stung his eyes, but they were much hardier than mortal eyes, and he had no trouble seeing under the dark water. It didn't take him long to find John, his limp form waving with the tide. He put his arms around John and swam to the surface, bursting from the waves like a dolphin jumping from the surf.

He laid John out on the beach. He did not look good; his face was blue and he wasn't breathing. Lo was shouting, running toward them, but she was knocked down by another burst of light and heat, which to Felix's great surprise was emanating from *him*. He didn't question it; he simply followed the pull again. He kissed him, and as their lips met, the light passed from him and into John.

The light faded. For a brief moment, Felix feared they had been too late, but suddenly John gasped. He started coughing; Felix turned him on his side as he retched up seawater.

Lo reached them at last. "Is he okay?" Her voice was hoarse from screaming.

John's eyes fluttered open. He looked up at both of them.

"Hey," Lo said, half laughing, half crying. "Are you with us?"

The color was returning to his cheeks, fading from blue to pink. Still, he said nothing. Instead, he began to sob.

Felix gathered him in his arms. "It's all right," he said, burying his face in John's wet hair. "You're alive. We saved you."

This only made John cry harder. "No. No, you didn't."

Twelve: Mixed Blessings

JOHN SAT ON Lo's bed in her apartment, covered with a blanket. Felix sat at his side, his arm around John's shoulder. Lo was busy in the kitchen, slamming cupboards and banging pots as she scrounged up some tea. He should be wondering about when and how Lo and Felix's strange alliance came to be, but he was too tired to think. The feeling returned to John's skin as the numbness of the cold sea faded away, like he was being pricked with a thousand needles as the feeling returned, coming back to life as the numbness of the cold sea faded away.

He wished he was still there.

"Are you still cold?" Felix asked as he rubbed John's back. "I can get you another blanket. I can get you ten blankets. Or a robe—do you have a robe? I should have brought you one." Felix had gone to John's apartment earlier to get him some dry clothes. He himself was wearing a pair of John's sweatpants and a T-shirt, both of which were comically small on him. He looked down at John's bare feet. "Your feet!" He smacked himself in the face. "How stupid of me—I should have looked around to see if you had slippers." He got down on the floor and wrapped John's feet in his warm hands.

"Lo," Felix called. "Do you have any slippers? Or socks? John's feet are cold."

"In a minute!" she snapped. "I'm trying to get this fucking tea made."

Felix took it upon himself to root around in Lo's chest of drawers. He triumphantly pulled out a pair of pink fuzzy socks. He had to stretch them to get them over John's feet.

"There. Is that better?" When John didn't respond, Felix climbed back up on the bed, putting both his arms around John from behind. "Say something," he said very quietly. "Please?"

But John couldn't think of anything to say. A stab to his heart joined the pain of the prickles of his skin. He had gotten involved with Felix because he'd been convinced he couldn't hurt him. Leave it to John to fuck up even that. No matter where he went or what he did, he brought only pain to people around him.

Lo stormed over to the bed. "Here." She thrust a mug in John's direction. "Drink this." When John didn't make a move to take it, she snapped her fingers in his face. He flinched. "You aren't catatonic, so take this fucking mug of tea I made you and *drink it*."

Not doing what she said seemed more effort than doing it, so he slowly raised his hands and accepted the mug. She stomped back across the room.

"Let me help you with that," Felix said. He blew on it until the steam faded and then helped John bring the mug to his lips. It smelled of cinnamon and other spices; it tingled on his lips as he drank.

When his tea was finished, Lo snatched the cup back from him. She threw a piece of paper at him.

"I found your suicide note," she said. "Tucked into those binders you gave me, so that I could have a chance to study while you were on 'vacation.'"

John's hand curled around the paper. "I'm sorry," he said—his first words since they'd brought him there.

"Oh you're sorry, all right."

"You should have let me go."

Lo exploded. "Oh for fuck's sake. If you want to stew in self-pity some more, go ahead. But this isn't just about saving you—that's only the beginning of the metric ton of problems that your chickenshit ass wanted to dump in my lap." She started counting out the reasons on her fingers. "Firstly, there's the matter of your boyfriend, who is still a predator, and I told you I wasn't going to let that go. Much to my surprise, the bloodthirsty vampire is more interested in stopping himself than you are. And then it appears that there's a serial-killing witch who has been preying on the city for decades—you knew about this, but instead of trying to stop him, you chose self-annihilation, leaving it to me to do something about it."

"I didn't leave that to you," John said. "I had no idea you'd find out about it."

Lo laughed. "Even better! You weren't willing to do anything at all! You were so caught up in your own self-pity you didn't give a single thought to the evil and the suffering you would leave behind." She stopped her tirade. When she spoke again, her voice quivered. "And you lied to me. You told me straight to my face you'd be back in a few days. How could you?"

"I'm sorry" was all John could offer.

She snatched the suicide note from John's hands. "Well, if you try it again, you can forget about all these final requests. I would've made sure that your remains never made it to this Forest Lawn place. And I'm not going to take care of your fucking cat. She's going straight to the pound, and you know the city has a stray problem. Odds aren't good for her."

That finally shocked John out of his stupor. "You would let my cat *die*?"

"Does that make you angry?" she said, getting in his face. "Does that piss you off?"

John felt his face flush. "Of course it makes me angry!"

"Good." She leaned back. "Get angry and stay angry. *Fight* this."

John looked down at the floor, unable to meet her gaze. "Do you want to know what happened when my mom chose to fight?" he asked quietly. Lo and Felix were silent, but John continued anyway. "As soon as my father was put in jail for trying to kill her, she ran. My grandmother begged her not to—said it would be so much easier if she just stopped fighting and let things take their course. But she had me to take care of. She didn't want to wait the ten years for him to get out. I was two years old; my mom packed up me and what little she owned into an old car, and we hit the road. We never stopped. She visited the most powerful witches she could find, as well as doing her own research. She was determined to beat it." He paused. "Do you know what's funny? I never for a moment knew we were in danger. She always kept our lives full of fun and happiness. My mother was the smartest, most determined, and most positive person I have ever known. She thought—no, she *knew*—she would beat this curse that had laid waste to our family." John looked down at the floor. "She was wrong."

Lo and Felix both were still silent, but looking at him with sorrow in their eyes. He wished he could change the end of the story, spare them the way he himself had not been spared, but of course that was impossible. "I was twelve. My mother had seemed off for about a week or so. I think she must have sensed it, or maybe she knew my father had been released. We stopped staying in hotels—we camped out instead. I don't know what her thinking was. Maybe she thought if we stayed off the grid, he wouldn't be able to track us down. Or maybe the curse was just maneuvering her into where she needed to be.

"We'd just set the tent up when we heard a car coming toward us. We were isolated, no one around for miles. I knew something was wrong at that point. The car stopped, and a man got out. I didn't recognize him at the time, but it was my dad. As soon as she saw him, she started hurling spells—no one cast spells as well as she did. But nothing happened. I tried to cast a spell too, but I wasn't any more successful. We made a break for the car, but it was useless. He tackled her and started hitting her, like he was crazed. She told me to run, but I didn't. I tried to fight him off, but he tossed me away like I was nothing. I'll never forget the look in his eyes—it was like he was dead. Once he beat my mother so badly she couldn't get up, he came for me. He tied me up."

John stopped, took a deep breath, and rushed through the rest. "He cut her to pieces, starting with her tongue. He made me watch. And when he was done, he took a gun out of the car and shot himself. It was hours before I got myself untied. Several hours more before I was able to get back to the main road and signal for help. I tried the cars, but neither one of them would start."

He had to stop for a moment. He couldn't look at Lo or Felix yet; otherwise he would lose it. When he collected himself, he continued. "After that, I went to live with my grandma. She told me the whole truth about the curse." He looked down at his hands, still blue around the nail beds. "Fighting is what got my mother killed. And losing her is what destroyed me. I'm not afraid of death. I've already been annihilated." He turned around in Felix's arms until he was facing him. "I miss my grandma," he said, his voice cracking. "I miss my mom. I don't want to fight, I don't want to be anything. I just want it to be *over*." He was sobbing now.

Felix wrapped his arms around John again. John allowed himself to be held, pressing his face into Felix's shoulder as he wept. He tried to get himself under control, but it was like he was possessed. Lo surged forward, wrapping her arms around him from the behind; John was sandwiched between them now, the warmth of their bodies carrying away the last of the stinging pain of coming back from the cold.

"I'm sorry," he gasped when he could speak again. "I'm so sorry. I didn't want to hurt either of you."

Lo pulled back; her own face was wet with tears. "I wasn't really going to let your cat die. I just don't want you to give up."

"I'm sor—"

Lo hit John's shoulder lightly. "Stop saying you're sorry. Let's just move forward, okay?"

John shut his eyes. How could he make her understand that there was no forward? This was all so exhausting. He leaned more fully into Felix, taking comfort in his warmth—

—which was deeply weird. John looked up at Felix again. "You're warm," he said in disbelief. "How are you warm?"

Felix and Lo exchanged looks. "We don't know, exactly," Lo said. "But it probably has something to do with the same way we found you."

John frowned. "You didn't just scry for me?"

"No." Lo chewed her finger. "Your mom hasn't stopped fighting."

John felt as if his heart had stopped. "What do you mean?"

"Her spirit came to both of us in our dreams," Lo continued. "There was some weird symbolic shit with birdcages and keys that I don't really get, but it seems like she put some kind of power inside Felix. She led us to you, too." She paused. "What I don't understand is why she came to us when she could have gone to you."

John covered his face with his hands. As if things couldn't get worse.

Felix gently tugged John's hands from his face. Felix looked so puzzled and concerned. "She came to us at the museum. You knew it, didn't you? But you distracted me away. Why?"

John just shook his head, unable to respond. Was she watching them right now?

"Was that the first time she's tried to contact you?" Lo asked.

When John spoke, his voice was weak and thin. "No. She's tried several times."

"And what, you've just ignored her?"

"I didn't want her to watch me die, the way I had to watch her die." John looked down at his hands. "And I was angry at her," he admitted. "Angry that she never told me before it happened."

They were all silent for a long time. Felix spoke up at last. "Are you quite certain that Richard tampered with the rose? Surely it's worth the risk, if your curse is as dark as he said it is?"

"I don't think he tampered with it. But it's not relevant anymore anyway, since I destroyed it."

Lo looked at him as if he'd lost his mind. "You *what*?"

"I just tried to kill myself," John snapped. "I think it's pretty clear why I didn't think I needed it."

Lo took a deep breath. "Sorry. No more blaming. We're moving forward. But did it occur to you that you're not the only person in this room who's cursed?"

"What are you talking about?"

"Vampirism is a curse, right? So why wouldn't Ginerva's Rose work on Felix?"

John opened his mouth to explain why not, but then he realized he couldn't think of any reason. "I...hadn't thought of that."

She gestured to Felix. "So all we need is him, a rose bush, and a hundred nights, and then we can cure you, him, and his sister, right?"

Felix jumped in. "And once Cat is cured, then wouldn't that bring an end to the eternal life Richard is sharing with her?"

A very strange feeling came over John. If he had to guess, he'd say it was something like hope. "I don't know."

"But it's worth a try, isn't it?" Lo was getting excited now.

"And perhaps you are no longer cursed," Felix said. "You were dead when I pulled you out of the water. Whatever your mother did to me allowed me to bring you back."

John frowned. "That seems too easy."

Lo headed for her closet. "We should be able to do a quick spell to figure it out."

Lo got out a crystal. She shut her eyes for a moment. *"Has the curse been reversed?"* The crystal levitated off the table. For one hopeful second, it remained clear, but then it began to darken, becoming blacker and blacker before cracking and dropping to the table.

"I guess that answers that," Lo said.

Felix scratched his head. "If I didn't break the curse, then what on earth did your mother do to me?"

"Can you explain the dream?" John asked.

Felix and Lo both shared their experiences about the locked birdcage, and Felix explained the forging of the key.

"I had no idea it was a magical dream when I had it," Lo said. "But now that I do, it seems pretty obvious that the cage is the curse, which would make the key—"

"—a blessing," John finished for her.

"Can she do that?" Lo asked. "I mean, she's dead."

From across the room, the cat meowed. They all turned to look at her. She was batting at the planchette of the Ouija board that was still laid out on the table. It was moving.

Haltingly, John stood up, the blanket dropping from his shoulders. Felix and Lo followed him. John's heart was racing as he sat down. Astray jumped off the table and curled up under his chair. John did nothing except watch the planchette inch along the board, as if being pushed with great difficulty. She was here. His whole heart ached with an unnameable feeling: a mix of longing and apprehension, of love and grief, of relief and guilt. And buried somewhere under all that mess of emotion, desperately trying to break out of the cellar he'd locked it in since the day his mother died, was *joy*. His mom was here. She was with him again.

He put his hand on the planchette. As soon as he did, a pulse of energy went through him. And then in the chair across from him, he saw his mother, wispy and ethereal, but clear enough that he could see every detail of her face. She smiled at him.

John blinked rapidly; the tears that had been gathering in his eyes spilled over. "Hi, Mom," he said. He laughed a little because it seemed so inadequate.

The planchette moved: *Hi.*

John laughed again, even as more tears coursed down his cheeks. She laughed, too—silently, but the echo of her laughter played in John's memory. Her laughter was the soundtrack to his childhood; he had buried all his memories of her as deeply as he could because he found thinking of her too painful, but now he wondered why. It felt good to remember. It felt good to see her.

The planchette moved again: *Get pen and paper.*

"I'll get it," Lo said, who was standing over his shoulder. When she came back with the requested items, she sat down at the third seat at the table. "I'll transcribe. Whenever you're ready."

The planchette began to move more fluidly now. John had trouble keeping track of the letters; all he could do was gaze at the image of his mother. She was just as he remembered her, except for the scars. What did that mean? What was the afterlife like that she had to put herself back together after she was dead? He had another chilling thought. What would it have been like if his suicide had been successful? If he couldn't pull himself together while he was alive, what chance did he have once he was dead?

It was a long time before the planchette stopped. John looked at Lo. "What does it say?"

"It's a blessing, I think," she said.

The planchette moved again, although the tug of the planchette was weaker than before. This time, John was able to follow the words: *Have to go now.*

"Wait!" John cried. He'd just gotten her back; it wasn't long enough. "Don't leave."

She smiled again. *I never leave. Always with you. Love you.* Her wispy form faded. The planchette went still.

John didn't remove his fingers right away, willing it to move again. Felix put his hand over John's, startling him. "Are you all right?" Felix asked.

John tried to smile. "Not yet."

"But 'yet' means you will be in the future?" Felix looked so hopeful that John could barely stand it. He managed a little nod. Felix drew John's hand up and kissed his palm. John marveled at how warm that kiss was; it sent a pulse of heat through him. Felix looked like he wanted to do more, but Lo loudly cleared her throat, pulling them both out of the moment.

"You guys are going to want to hear this."

Felix sat down in the chair that John's mother had vacated. Lo began to read:

Knight of the night, I call on you
Through you I can defer the curse
But the shedding of blood I can't undo
My powers alone were far too few
Life blood runs red, but the dead runs blue
Knight of the night, I call on you
It's the only way, Richard knew
Though I thought he meant only to coerce
But the shedding of my blood I can't undo
My life is gone, but my power is renewed
With help, I can make this curse reverse
Knight of the night, I call on you
Become my vessel. We will cut through
This blight that has made my son's life a hearse
But the shedding of blood I can't undo
But there's only so much I can do
Curses like this are too perverse
Knight of the night, I call on you
But the shedding of blood I can't undo

They all took a moment to absorb it. Lo finally broke the silence. "Well, I don't have a fucking clue what that means."

"That's witchery for you," Felix agreed. "Who can make sense of it?"

"I can," John said. "She's using Felix as a vessel. It actually makes sense."

"Using blood-sucking fiends as a vessel for a blessing?" Lo sounded incredulous. "That doesn't seem right."

"You're thinking of it wrong," John said. "If you leave the morality issue out of it, undead creatures are powerful vessels for all sorts of magic, particularly magic that has to do with life and death. As undead creatures, they exist outside the natural order. The magic animating them is extremely potent. It's why Ginerva chose vampire's blood when she made her blessing. After my mother died, I found a bunch of her notes, which explained it. I think part of the reason we moved around so much was that she was on the hunt for the undead so she could make her own cure, but the undead are pretty notorious for being disagreeable."

"Not me," Felix said. "I'm extremely agreeable."

John couldn't help but smile a little. "Yeah. Which is what makes it better. Power freely given is always stronger than power taken."

Lo looked skeptical. "If the undead are really that powerful, why can't she just use Felix to break the curse right now? If that Ginerva lady could manage it, why can't we?"

"Really powerful spells have to be sealed with blood."

"I've got blood," Lo said. "So do you."

"When I say 'sealed with blood,' I mean a whole human body's worth of blood. Ginerva died to create her blessing. The man who cursed my family had to have sacrificed at least one human life to cast it."

"Which is why it's so hard to break."

"Exactly. And that's probably why the curse didn't break when I—" John's voice gave out.

"When you took your swim," Lo finished for him.

"Right. No blood."

Lo looked down at the paper again. "*The shedding of blood I can't undo.* What does that mean?"

John bit his lip. "I don't know. It sounds kind of ominous."

"But she said she could 'defer' it. That sounds promising." Lo put her hand on his. "If she bought us at least a hundred days, then we have a real chance of beating this. But you have to believe it. Do you?"

John looked back and forth between Lo and Felix. "Yeah," he said at last. "I do."

Felix got up from his chair. With great solemnity, he got on one knee in front of John. "I pledge myself to you completely and utterly. I will never leave your side until we are free of these foul curses."

John looked down at him, not sure what to say. Felix was so earnest; he felt a fresh stab of guilt at being willing to abandon him.

John was still enormously bad at feelings, so all he could manage was a faint "Okay."

From Felix's reaction, you'd think that John had just pledged his undying love. Felix kissed his hand with fervor.

They were interrupted again by another throat-clearing from Lo. "I hate to say it, but I'm not sure that's a good idea. If Felix doesn't show up at Richard's, he'll know something's up. He needs to go back and stall."

Felix's face fell. "But whatever shall I say?" he asked Lo. "I'm afraid that I'm not very clever."

"Then keep it simple," Lo said. "Tell him John's open to it, but you just need a little more time to work on him."

"That won't keep him at bay very long. He's growing impatient."

"Just buy us a couple days until we can think of something else. Trust me, I'm good at figuring shit out."

Felix turned back to John. "Do you agree?"

John bit his lip. The thought of Felix going back to that nightmare palace made him feel sick, but Lo was right. "Yeah. I don't see any way around it."

Felix dropped his gaze and very quietly asked, "You won't leave again, will you? I don't think I could bear it."

"Don't worry, he's not going anywhere," Lo said. "I'm not going to let him out of my sight." She sighed. "We have to go into work tomorrow. Supernatural shenanigans aside, I still need a job. You probably do, too. Shouldn't be too hard to 'persuade' Mike to take you back."

Felix got to his feet. "Money is no issue!" He got his still-soggy wallet from the table and handed Lo some wet bills.

"Uh, thanks," Lo said, pinching the bills between her thumb and forefinger. "But sorry to say this isn't going to pay my rent. Yours either," she said to John. "And I refuse to depend on handouts from a serial-killing witch."

"But surely that will leave you both in danger!" Felix cried.

"As soon as the sun sets and you get Richard off your case, come to the restaurant. You can escort us home. But for Christ's sake, stay out of sight this time; we don't need another scene with Vince."

"There was a scene with Vince?" John asked.

"I handled it," Lo said.

Felix still looked uncertain. John got to his feet. He put a hand on Felix's arm. "Don't worry," he said, trying to sound confident. "We have a plan."

Felix put his arms around him, holding him tightly. "If you say I must go, then I will go."

"Only for a little while." John pulled back a little so that he could look Felix in the eyes. "Thank you."

In response, Felix kissed him with such passion that John couldn't help but be swept up into it. At last, he drew back. "Until tonight," Felix said. With that, he left.

When he was gone, Lo crossed her arms and gave John a look. "You told me vampires were heartless."

John sighed. "They are."

"He doesn't seem heartless."

John rubbed his face. "I know. Is that why you changed your mind?"

Lo nibbled at a finger. "He's not what I expected. And Jesus, the whole situation with his sister is like a horror movie. You're right—*they* can't help what they are, but *we* can. I believe it."

John looked away. "You were right about me being a coward. It's just like—" He paused for a minute, trying to put together all of the feelings inside him, so many of them buried. He felt like an archaeologist, uncovering his own soul piece by piece. "It's like falling down a well in slow motion. There's enough light to make out your surroundings for a little while, but as you fall farther and farther, that light gets smaller. It was just a pinpoint at the end. I couldn't even see my own hand in front of my face." He shook his head and laughed a little. "I mean, my metaphorical hand. I'm sorry. I'm not making any sense."

Lo rubbed his shoulder. "We both could use some rest. I'll take the couch; you can keep the bed." She looked down at the pink socks on John's feet. "And the socks."

They both laughed a little. John took a long look at Lo. "Are you okay?"

"I will be when this is over."

"I'm sorry," he said. "For everything."

"No more apologies," she said firmly. "If you really are sorry, you'll focus on beating this."

John hesitated for a moment before speaking again. "Can I ask you something?" When she nodded, he continued. "Where did the Ouija board come from? That's not something you and I ever did together."

Lo was quiet for a moment. "I got it because I was hoping to talk to my mom. Remember when I told you she had an aneurysm?"

John nodded.

"Yeah, well, she had that aneurysm right after we had a huge fight. And when you first told me about magic, and how it could have dangerous consequences..." She wiped a tear from her eye. "I thought maybe I'd killed her."

John took her hands in his own. "Oh, no. Lo, you should have asked me! You loved her, didn't you?"

"Of course I did."

"Then you couldn't have killed her, no matter how angry you were."

Tears flooded Lo's eyes. "Are you sure?"

"Yes."

She started to cry. John held her until she was finished. "Shit," she said as she grabbed a tissue. "I fucking hate crying. Snot drips in your nose; it's so gross."

They both laughed.

"Were you able to find her?" John asked.

"No. And I tried, believe me."

John squeezed her hand. "That's a good thing. It means she moved on."

"Moved on to where?"

"I don't know," John said quietly. "No one does. The only thing I'm sure of is that being a ghost is not a great fate. It's a half existence, neither in this world nor another one. I hope when this is all done, my mom will be able to rest in peace."

"I hope so, too." Lo gave him a mischievous look. "So this one time my high school was hit by a meteorite. That was probably me, right?"

John laughed. "Yeah, that's a possibility."

They hugged again. "I'm going to go get ready for bed," Lo said. She started toward the bathroom, but then she turned and grabbed John in a fierce embrace. "I'm sorry, too," she said. "I fucking dumped water on you when all you needed was a light." When she pulled back, her eyes were wet again. She wiped them with the back of her hand. "Okay, *now* we're officially done with apologies." She gave him another squeeze. "We'll be okay."

She sounded so sure that John almost believed her.

Thirteen: The Man of His Dreams

FELIX CREPT INTO the mansion.

No matter how much confidence Lo seemed to have in him—and it was a very strange thing to have the confidence of such a formidable witch—Felix had absolutely no idea how he would mislead Richard. He had to talk to Cat; she would know what to do.

But just as he was about to reach her bedroom, Richard came up behind him. "Well? How did it go?" He looked him up and down. "And what on earth are you wearing?"

"Sweatpants," Felix said.

"Why?"

"I got my other pants wet. And then I forgot them." Felix paused. "We went swimming."

"And you forgot to take off your clothes?"

Felix shrugged. "As you have told me many times, I am not very clever." An idea suddenly came to him. "Actually, he pushed me off a boat! He thought it would be amusing." That made much more sense. Richard would surely understand a witch enjoying toying with him, since cruel games were a particular pleasure of his.

Richard snorted. "Are you sure he didn't push you in because you were being an imbecile?"

"Oh no, it was all in jest. He was in a very good mood; he is certainly very interested in your proposal!"

"Excellent. I assume he will be joining us for dinner, then."

Felix rubbed his neck. "Ah, no."

Richard's gaze hardened. "Why not?"

Felix paused. "He has work."

"Is he as addled as you? Why on earth should he go wait tables when he will soon have all the wealth he could ever want?" Richard moved forward, his eyes narrowing. "Are you lying to me?"

Felix backed up, but Richard kept edging closer. "No! He really is going to work tonight!" Felix's back hit the wall.

"But he didn't agree to dinner, did he? Did you ask him at all?"

"I—I..." But Felix had no answer.

Richard cocked his head. "There's something different about you." He put his hand on Felix's face. Felix smelled the rot of his breath, sour and damp against his skin. "You are warm. But it isn't just blood."

Felix was on the edge of bolting, but suddenly the door to Cat's room opened. They both gaped at the sight of her. She was dressed as neither of them had seen her in decades. True, Felix and Cat would play dress-up when she was bored, but it was always a pale imitation of the height of her glamour. She was back at that peak now in a stunning silver gown, her hair impeccable, her lips a deep, seductive crimson and her eyeliner a perfect cat's eye. Felix wondered how she had managed it on her own. Perhaps she finally learned how to use the web camera.

She smiled at Richard, bright as the flash of a camera. "Richard, darling, why on earth do you have my brother pinned against the wall?"

Richard took a step back from Felix. "We were just talking."

She pouted. "Will you be long? I wish to speak to you."

Felix was deeply puzzled. From the look on Richard's face, he shared in Felix's befuddlement. She had not spared him a kind word in over a decade, as far as he could remember.

Richard cleared his throat. "You...want to talk to me?"

Cat smiled again. She beckoned with one long, elegant finger. "Come here."

When he was close, Cat draped her arms over his shoulders. "I have thought about what you said, and you are right. My misery is my own making. It's just that I miss the glamour of our old life. I want things back the way they were."

Richard gazed at her in wonder. "You do?"

In response, she pulled him into a long, deep kiss. When they parted, Richard's mouth was smeared red. "It was so hopeless before, with you withering before my very eyes. But then I thought about what you said, about Felix's witch. Can he truly help us?"

"Yes," Richard said, his voice growing more excited. "Yes, he can. I can be young again for you, Cat. That will solve everything, won't it?"

Cat giggled. "I think so." She kissed him again. "We had such fun, didn't we? And poor Felix, always the third wheel. It really is time for him to have someone of his own. Imagine the four of us—"

"*Yes*," Richard moaned. "I will bring back the old days to you—all the glamour, all the glory." He tried to kiss her neck, but she gripped his chin in her hand, her red nails pressing into him.

"Do you swear it?"

His legs nearly buckled. "I do."

"And yet," Cat said as she tightened her grip. "It seems as though you are intent on frightening him away. If this John is put off by your heavy hand and flees, then we will lose our last chance. Is that not so?"

Richard gasped. "I-I suppose."

Cat leaned in until her mouth was against his ear. Felix could see her fangs just barely protruding. "Then leave the seduction to Felix and me and you make sure that spell of yours works." She nipped him on the ear. A drop of blood spilled onto the white shoulder of his shirt. With that, she pushed him backward.

He stood there stupidly for a moment, swaying.

"What are you waiting for?" Cat snapped. "Off with you. Felix and I have plans to make."

"Yes," Richard mumbled. "Yes, of course." He moved forward and took her hand, kissing the inside of her wrist. "My Cat, how I have missed you..."

She pulled her hand back. "Not until you're young again."

"Yes, of course." He shuffled off down the hallway, seeming half-dazed. He took one last longing look at her before disappearing around the corner.

Felix felt dazed himself. Cat took his hand and led him into the bedroom, shutting the door behind them.

"What on earth was that all about?" Felix said with not a little bit of alarm. "Are you wicked again?"

Cat rolled her eyes. "Of course not. He repulses me. I thought you might need a distraction. Was I wrong?"

"No! It was perfectly timed."

"Then your John has a plan?" Her eyes had a brightness to them that Felix hadn't seen since they were both children, when she was planning her grand career as they lay in bed together, too weak from hunger to move. Their desperation was different now, but that fire in Cat was back.

Felix wasn't sure where to begin. "Somewhat. Let's sit down."

He told Cat of John's suicide attempt, his ghostly mother, and the blessing she had bestowed upon him.

"I thought you felt different." She put her hand over where his heart used to be. "A blessing," she said, her voice filled with wonder. "To think that creatures of darkness such as ourselves would be capable of harboring grace."

He put his hand over hers. "We will not be creatures of darkness much longer."

She gave him a searching look. "Do you think it's truly possible?"

"I do," Felix assured her. "Can you keep him distracted for one hundred days?"

Cat bit her lip. "I can try. But he will get impatient."

"Perhaps John will agree to a meeting without committing. We can all do our part in stringing him along."

She threw her arms around him. When she pulled back again, she was smiling so bright and open that Felix couldn't help but smile, too. "What will we do when we're mortal?" he asked.

"Let's go to the beach," she said. "I will wear a bathing suit and lie out in the sun until I'm red as a lobster."

"We can bring a picnic basket," Felix added. "I can't remember what it's like to enjoy food. What shall we eat?"

"Sandwiches and potato chips. And iced cream! I've never had iced cream."

"Won't it melt in the sun?"

"We'll eat it quickly, and then wash our sticky fingers off in the waves."

They both laughed. "I can't wait for you to meet him," Felix said. "John, I mean. And Lo as well."

Cat's smile faded a little. "You're quite certain they're good?" Her gaze dropped. "Witches have a way of turning."

"I am. They have no desire for power or fame. They would never use us the way Richard has used us."

Cat's smile returned. She squeezed his hands. "You should rest. You must be on guard to keep John safe."

"You're right." He kissed her cheek. "You should rest as well."

He retired to his room, shedding John's ill-fitting clothing and changing into clothing of his own. Before he climbed into bed, he plugged his phone in. Strangely, the blasted contraption didn't seem to be picking up a charge. In fact, the battery power started draining instead of rising. He was too tired to deal with it. He shrugged; he would see John and Lo the moment the sun set anyway. Surely they wouldn't need to contact him before then.

JOHN AND LO arrived at the restaurant at two thirty in the afternoon, right before their usual shift started. They'd both gotten a solid six hours of sleep and felt refreshed. John felt more rested than he could remember feeling in ages. It was hard to believe that he'd been ready to kill himself less than twenty-four hours ago. The sudden shift felt so odd, but right. For the first time since his mother died, he felt *whole*, like he'd been pieced back together.

He flashed Lo a grin before they entered. "So you handle Mike, and I'll handle Vince. Are you sure you can manage it?"

Lo scoffed. "Shit, I could handle Mike even if I didn't have powers. I have to warn you—Vince resisted pretty hard when I commanded him last time. Are you sure you have enough of your strength back?"

"I'll be fine," John assured her. "Vince's will isn't exactly made of iron. I'm sure I can twist it around enough that he won't give us any problems."

"So you're ready, then?"

John nodded. "Ready."

They headed for the kitchen. Mike came out of his office. "Well, looks like the no-good, lazy bums have come crawling back."

"I had a family emergency," Lo said. "I only missed half a shift."

"Only half a shift? That was poor Jennifer's first day and you left her all alone!" He turned to John. "And you! Just up and quitting on me with no notice? After all I've done for you?"

"I'm really sorry," John said.

"Yeah, we both are." Lo touched Mike's shoulder. "Why don't we go into your office and talk about it?" The command under her voice was subtle but strong. John grinned to himself. She'd have no problems. He went ahead and got ready for his shift.

A few minutes later, Vince entered the kitchen. He stopped in his tracks as soon as he saw John, seeming frozen in place. "You're back," he said, his voice wavering.

John waved at him. "Hey."

Vince shook himself out of it. "So I guess Mike's just gonna let you back on like you didn't abandon us."

"I think 'abandon' is a little strong of a word."

"Whatever." Vince stomped over to his workstation. The day cook, perhaps sensing drama, got out of there as quickly as he could.

Lo emerged from Mike's office, who was now all smiles and announced that everyone was getting a raise. John raised his eyebrows at Lo, who met his gaze with a smirk and a shrug. Mike declared himself done for the day and left.

Everything went fine for a couple of hours. It was unusually busy. Through it all, Vince kept to his work, although he did have a very stormy expression on his face. But John didn't need him to be happy; he just needed him not to give them any trouble. Maybe he wouldn't have to manipulate his memory at all. Even though he told Lo he was confident, the truth was he still felt a little weak from everything that had happened. Besides, he never liked to interfere with people's minds unless he absolutely had to.

Business started to slow down. Lo took hostess duty, leaving John in the kitchen with Vince and Gabriel, who had his earphones on and was oblivious, as usual.

"So how's your boyfriend?" Vince spat.

John sighed. "Lo told me what happened with him showing up. But seriously, everything's fine, Vince. You don't need to worry about me."

"You think I'm worried about you?" Vince let out a bark of laughter. "Nah. Why would I? Looks like you have exactly what you want."

"Then let's drop it, okay?"

"Fine." Vince busied himself scrubbing a stove. He wasn't quiet for longer than five minutes. "Here's what I don't get, though. This asshole comes barging in, harassing you, and you beg me to protect you—"

Begged? John tried not to roll his eyes. He could only imagine how Vince's memory of his first encounter with Felix had played out. John was sure it involved him swooning like a romance heroine at Vince's heroics.

"—but then a few months later, turns out you're still seeing him. So I gotta wonder—what was that whole thing about? Was it like some kind of game? To see what you could get me to do for you? Or to make that asshole jealous?"

Looks like there was no avoiding it. John crossed over to Vince and put a hand on his shoulder. "I know you were just looking out for me," he said with a little sweetness and a lot of magical heft. "But everything is fine. In fact, he didn't even come in yesterday. You just thought you saw him." He pushed his will forward—

—and Vince pushed back with a force of will John didn't think him capable of. Vince jerked away from John's touch. "What the fuck? Yes, I did."

John blinked at him in surprise. Clearly he was off his game. Maybe the memory alteration he was going for was too far from what had actually happened. He put his hand back on Vince's shoulder and tried again. "Sure, he was in here, but you scared him off again."

Again, John felt himself shoved out of Vince's mind. His paper-thin will suddenly felt like it was made of Teflon. "That is not what happened. Lo was taking him to see you. And he laughed at me. He fucking *laughed* at me." Vince caught John's wrist in his hand. "Why do you keep touching me? Is there something you want?"

John tried to twist away, but Vince's grip was like iron. "Let me go."

Vince's grip only tightened. "What kind of lies did you tell him about me? 'Cause he seemed to think I wanted to fuck you." Vince jerked him forward. "That's what you wanted him to think, huh? That you have some big, hot guy just following you around like a lost puppy? Bet you thought that would make him really jealous. Maybe you were looking for him to give you some extra cash. I mean, he's rich, right? Is that it? He can *afford* you?"

"*Let go.*" John threw the full force of his magic behind the command. It didn't work.

John's mind scrambled to think of a spell that would stop him. Fortunately, he didn't have to as Lo came in the door.

"What the fuck are you doing?" she shouted.

Immediately, Vince released him. "Nothing."

Lo swooped over to them. "It didn't look like nothing." She turned to John. "Are you okay?"

"I'm fine," John said, but his voice was shaking.

She glared at Vince. "Don't talk to him for the rest of the night," she said, the magic crackling under her words.

"You can't tell me what to do, bitch," Vince snarled.

Gabriel seemed to have broken himself out of his phone-induced trance long enough to enter the fray. "Hey, man, that's not cool," he said to Vince.

"Mind your own goddamn business!"

Gabriel held up his hands. "I'm not trying to get in your business, but you don't want to start with me."

Vince fumed. "Whatever." He balled up his apron and threw it aside. "I'm going on break."

As soon as he left, Gabriel said something in Spanish to Lo, who laughed a little and responded with a shake of her head. He put his earphones back on.

"What did he say?" John asked.

"He asked me if I wanted his friends to fuck Vince up. I said no." She gnawed at her thumb. "Maybe I should have said yes, though. My magic didn't work. I'm guessing yours didn't, either."

John shook his head.

"What the fuck is going on?"

"Vince feels really, really strongly about this. It's hard to bend someone's will when they're that worked up. What exactly happened?"

Lo sighed. "Felix called him a closet case."

John rubbed his temple. "Shit. Yeah, something like that would probably do it."

"But my magic still worked on him after it happened, and trust me, he was plenty worked up then, too. This seems...off."

She was right, but what else could they do? "Let's just get through tonight."

"Okay, but you take the front of the house. I don't think you and Vince should be in the same room."

John took over host duty. A couple of customers came in. Vince recovered from his tantrum enough to cook, but every time John entered the kitchen to retrieve an order, he felt Vince's gaze burning on his skin. It was five thirty. Sunset was still a few hours away. He hated feeling like a damsel in distress, but he'd feel a lot safer once he knew Felix was out there.

Around seven, the restaurant cleared out abruptly. At seven thirty, a young man in a dark hoodie walked in the door. His hair was a light blond; combined with his bone white, pockmarked skin, he looked almost like a skull. His blue eyes fixed on John, his pupils almost pinpricks. John knew this man very intimately.

He'd been haunting his nightmares for years.

Everything in the room seemed to fall away. The beating of John's heart pounded in his ears, obliterating all other sound. The tenuous hope he'd just had the courage to reach for this morning felt as insubstantial as a sunbeam, leaving him grasping and clutching at nothing.

"Hey," the nightmare man said with a smirk. "Aren't you supposed to, like, welcome me to the restaurant or something—" He glanced down at his name tag. "—*John*?" The way he said his name, mocking and cruel, sent a shiver down John's spine.

"W-welcome," John said, trying to stuff his panic down. "Party of one?"

"Nah," the man said. "I'm actually here to see Vince. He's your cook, right? Is he back there?"

The man didn't wait for John's answer; he just brushed past him and went straight to the kitchen. John didn't know what to do. Run? But Lo was back there. Besides, he knew there was no running from this. He had to stay cool, stay smart. He tried to calm himself, but his hands were shaking.

He followed in the man's wake, entering the kitchen. Vince and the man were pounding each other on the back, grinning. John didn't see Lo. Gabriel was watching the two men with a concerned look on his face. Gabriel took off his apron and went out the back door.

"I thought you weren't supposed to get out for another year!" Vince was saying.

"I got out on good behavior."

Vince snorted. "No fucking way I believe that."

The man grinned slyly. "You got me. It was a technicality, man. The big man's lawyers took care of it. Loyalty pays."

"So what brings you around?" Vince asked. "If you're looking for a job, I could probably hook you up here. I think our day cook is about to quit."

The man started laughing. "A job? *Here*? I just got out of prison. Why would I want to crawl back into a shithole?"

Vince's smile faltered. "Yeah, well, it's work. Kind of tough to come by when you've got a record. It's not so bad."

"Sure, if you're content to be a bottom-feeder for the rest of your life."

Vince turned away, busying himself with some cleaning. "It's just for now. I'm thinking about going to school."

The man laughed even harder. "You, in school. Right." He put a hand on his shoulder. "Listen, I've got an offer of some real money, and I thought maybe you'd want in on it."

"Oh yeah? Doing what?"

"What do you think?"

As they spoke, John slunk across the room, trying to be as inconspicuous as possible. He retrieved his phone from his bag, which hung on the wall. The time was 7:37—about twenty minutes until sunset. He began to write a text to Felix; he knew Felix couldn't get there before sunset, but at least he could let him know what was happening so he would be prepared. As he was typing, his phone suddenly shut down, even though it had been fully charged. He was reminded of the cars when his mother had been killed, that had both inexplicably broken down. With shaking hands, he put the phone back in the bag. It would clearly be no use to him.

Lo entered the kitchen; she must have been in the bathroom. At the sight of her, the nightmare man whistled. "Hey, Vince—you gonna introduce me to your fine-ass coworker?"

"That's Lo," Vince said.

Lo rolled her eyes. "Is this asshole a friend of yours?"

"Don't be such a bitch," Vince said.

The nightmare man laughed. "No, no, it's cool. I like them spicy." He bowed. "My name is Zach, and I am at your service."

Lo flashed him a fake smile. "You're at my service? Awesome. Go jump off a bridge."

"Oooh, *muy caliente!* Are you sure there's not another way I can *service* you?"

Lo scowled and turned to Vince. "What is he doing here?"

"You don't gotta ask him; I'm standing right here," Zach said before Vince could say anything. "Me and Vince go way back. We used to move in the same crowd, but no one's seen him in a while. So I tracked him down."

John felt like a ghost in the corner of the room, unable to move, to stop this. Lo finally caught sight of him; her expression shifted from annoyed to concerned. She crossed the room.

"What's wrong?" she asked quietly.

John didn't get a chance to respond. Zach's gaze had followed Lo across the room and was now on them both, as intense as high beams on a car. "That's a good question. What *is* wrong with you? You look like you're about to piss yourself." Zach rubbed his chin. "Know who he reminds me of?" he said to Vince. "That kid Harrison." Zach slapped Vince's arm. "Remember that one time when he actually did piss his pants?"

Vince looked away, his expression complicated. "Yeah, I remember."

While they were somewhat distracted, John managed to speak. "It's him," he said as quietly as he could.

Lo's eyes grew round. "Shit," she whispered back. "What do we do?"

"What are you girls whispering about?" Zach called over to them. He was grinning again; in fact, he hadn't really stopped grinning since he had arrived. He snaked toward them until he was beside Lo. He put one hand on the wall beside her, blocking her exit. "I was just heading to a party, and I'm looking for a date. Been a long time since I've seen someone as pretty as you. You look uptight. I could show you a real good time."

"I'm at work," Lo said tightly.

"So what? I don't see your boss here." He turned his attention to Vince. "How much cash is in the register, do you think?"

"Uh-uh," Vince said, shaking his head. "No way. Not interested."

"Oh, come on! Is this really going to be the rest of your life? Working in some shitty restaurant while you try to scrape through community college? How often you see that work out for people like us?"

Vince's expression wavered. "I don't know, man."

"Listen. You do what you want, but you know the kind of money you got a shot at if you come with me. And the kind of life you could have? Shit, we go down to Mexico and live like kings. And you'd get *respect*. You think you'll ever get that here? Stop asking the world for what you want, and start taking it."

Vince's gaze darted over to John. He wet his lips. "Okay, I'm in."

Zach whooped his approval. "And how about you, babe?" he asked Lo. "Are you sick of waiting tables?"

"No."

Zach pouted. "Come on, don't be like that." He twisted a lock of Lo's hair around his finger and tugged.

She reared back. "Fuck you."

Zach sighed. "I didn't want to have to do this." He pulled out a gun from the back of his pants and pointed it at her. "Get the keys to the register."

Just then, Mike walked in the back door. Gabriel must have gone to get him earlier. He took in the scene with wide-eyed horror. "What the fuck is going on here?"

Zach turned to Vince. "This your boss?" he asked casually.

"Yeah."

Zach turned the gun on Mike and shot him twice in the chest. He went sailing backward, hitting the floor with a sickening thud.

"Jesus fucking Christ!" Vince shouted. "What the fuck did you do that for?!"

Zach's smile hadn't wavered. If anything, it had grown wider. "You said you were in—and we're going *all* in this time. Gotta show the big man we're ruthless motherfuckers."

While the two of them were distracted, John grabbed Lo's hand and pulled her through the door to the dining room; they both ran as fast as they could, but Zach caught up with them before they could reach the front door. He grabbed Lo's arm, yanking her backward.

"You're not going anywhere," he snarled.

Lo punched him in the face. Zach cursed as he raised his hands to his bleeding nose. Lo struck again, knocking the gun from his hand. John and Lo made another mad scramble for the door, succeeding this time.

Lo took off down the street, with John close behind her. "Where are we going?"

"To my car," she said. She patted her pockets. "Shit, I don't have the keys..."

John grabbed her hand and pulled her into an alley. "We can't go far," he said. "Felix thinks we're at the restaurant. He won't be able to find us."

"But we can't stay here, either!"

"I know, I know." John looked around. The sky was fading into night, but not quickly enough. "*Shadows, please open wide/Find for us a place to hide,*" he tried. It didn't work.

"We have to get somewhere populated," Lo said. "Maybe a bunch of witnesses will slow him down."

John shook his head. "This is the curse. There isn't any slowing him down. We get in a crowd and a lot more people are going to die."

"As opposed to just us?" Lo's voice was bordering on hysterical.

"Or just me. I'll distract them—"

Lo shook her head. "No way. I'm not leaving you."

The discussion was made moot when the dark figures of Vince and Zach appeared at the entrance to the alley.

"There you are." Zach's face was covered in blood, but he was still grinning. He pointed the gun right at Lo's head. "Look what you did to my face. I should shoot your head off right now, you little bitch."

John threw himself between Lo and the gun. "I'll show you where the key is. Just let her go—you only need one of us."

"You think I'm so dumb that I can't find a key on my own?" Zach laughed. "Nah, I don't need you for that. What I need is to make sure you aren't running off to the cops. I can shoot you now, or you can get your asses over here and do as you're told. If you play it right, maybe you'll get to live."

John turned back and mouthed "stall" to Lo, hoping she understood. She gave him a shaky nod.

They moved forward slowly. When they got close, Zach grabbed Lo and pushed her in front of him. He wrapped his jacket around the gun and pressed it into her back. "We're going to walk out of here like there's nothing wrong, and you're not going to make a sound, got it?" He glanced over his shoulder. "And that goes for you, too."

Vince grabbed John, gripping his arm so tightly that John knew he'd leave bruises. They fell in line behind Zach and Lo as they made their way back to the restaurant. The light of the sun still stained the sky. He hoped Felix would be on time—that is, if the curse didn't divert him somehow. John tried not to give in to despair, but he had just learned how to hope again; he wasn't very good at it yet.

They entered the restaurant. Zach turned the sign from OPEN to CLOSED and shut the blinds as well. John looked at the clock on the wall. It was ten minutes 'til eight—fifteen more minutes of sunlight. He just had to stall.

"I'll go get the key," he said.

Zach smirked. "I like your improved attitude, but I think Vince better go with you and make sure you don't try to run out again." He brought the gun out from under his hoodie, making it visible. "Be good for him, or else we're leaving two bodies behind."

John made eye contact with Lo and then looked at the clock. Her gaze followed his; from her expression, it seemed like she understood. He didn't need her trying to fight this and end up getting herself killed.

Vince and John entered the kitchen. Mike's body was lying just where they'd left it, but the pool of blood had grown larger. When he looked over at Vince, he saw that he was staring at it, too. He was pale and shaken. Maybe John could reason with him.

"This isn't right," John said lowly. "I know you know that."

"Just shut up and get the key." Vince was staring at the floor, away from both Mike's body and John.

"And what happens after that?" John dipped his head until he met Vince's gaze. "I know you're mad at me, but do you really want to see me dead?"

"I won't let him kill you."

"He isn't going to leave any witnesses. That might include you, too. Do you really think you can stop him?"

That was apparently the wrong thing to say, because Vince suddenly surged forward, crowding John back into Mike's office.

"Yeah, I can fucking stop him. I'm not his flunky. We're equals. He respects me."

"It didn't sound like it from what I heard."

"He was just telling the truth. Truth that I needed to hear."

John kept his voice as nonconfrontational as possible. "I don't know that what he said was true."

Vince laughed. "Are you going to give me some pep talk about how great my life will be if I'm a good boy? 'Cause it really isn't turning out that way."

"Are you sure he's right about the money? Do you think any crime boss is going to rain money and praise down on some psycho who killed someone in an armed robbery for a couple hundred bucks?"

That seemed to give him pause, but then he shook his head. "Doesn't matter. I'm not going to rat him out, and I said I was in. There's no going back."

"We could overpower him," John said. "If we take him by surprise—"

"Did you just hear what I fucking said?" Vince snarled. "I'm not betraying him. We've been through some shit you can never understand."

"You're right, I can't," John said, keeping his tone even. "But this isn't *right*. I know you aren't a bad person—"

That was mistake number two, because Vince shoved him against the wall. "And how do you know that? Because you're suddenly my friend now?" He laughed bitterly. "I can see why your boyfriend treats you the way he does. You get very sweet when you're scared."

And John *was* scared, his breath coming in shallow gasps. No matter how hard he tried to tamp down on the panic, it kept bubbling back up again. "Vince, *please*—"

He cut off abruptly when Vince cupped John's face in his hand. "I like it when you say my name like that," he said, his voice softer now. Vince ran his thumb along John's lip, staring at it for a moment. He leaned in and kissed him.

John kept perfectly still. When Vince pulled back at last, his chest was heaving. "We'll get the cash and get out of here," he said, pressing his forehead against John's. "You just do like I tell you and I'll keep you safe, okay?" He kissed him again.

They were interrupted by Zach, who was now standing at the door with Lo. "What the fuck are you doing?" he said, laughing. "You know this isn't prison and we can get you a girl, right?"

Vince pulled away, his face flushing a deep red. "This isn't your fucking business, Zach."

"No need to get all defensive," Zach said. "Do whatever the fuck you want to him, but not now. We really need to get out of here—there's time for fun later."

Vince turned to John. "Get the key."

John fumbled through Mike's desk, taking as long as he could. He looked at the clock on the wall; it was 8:00. Four minutes to sundown. But was it enough? Was Felix there? Or would they be gone by the time he arrived?

"Hurry the fuck up!" Vince yelled in his ear. John tried to think of another way to stall, but his rational mind seemed to white out under the blur of his fears—he knew Zach would kill him, but he didn't know when. What was going to happen to him between now and when Zach pulled the trigger? How long would it take? Days? Weeks?

His fingers found the key; Vince was looking right at it, so there was no hiding it. Vince snatched it from him and threw it to Zach.

"Finally," Zach said. "Let's go." He shoved Lo back out of the door. Vince grabbed John by the arm, his touch not gentle anymore. John looked at his face. His eyes had a strange, dull look in them now. It reminded him of the look in his father's eyes that day he'd killed his mother. Was this the curse making him do it, or were the decisions truly his own?

He supposed it didn't matter. The curse was an acid, dissolving John's life, and now Lo's and Vince's, too. Even if Felix arrived, who was to say it wouldn't burn through him as well?

Fourteen: Wanted—Dead or Undead

FELIX WAS COVERED in vines. Black ones, with stinging nettles that twisted unnaturally, as if animated by some dark power.

Or as if they were in a dream of some sort, which he imagined to be the case. He didn't have much time to contemplate the symbolism, because a beam of light began to sear through them, one by one. He was unsurprised to see John's mother standing above him, brandishing a fiery sword like some avenging angel. In fact, she was wearing armor. This sudden turn toward military symbolism was deeply troubling.

He sprang to his feet. As he craned his head to look above them, he saw more vines woven together in a dark dome that was rapidly growing more and more dense, although it couldn't quite block out the sunlight that streamed through the cracks.

"What do we do?" Felix asked.

In response, she grabbed his hand. They leaped upward toward the vines. Felix noticed that he, too, held a sword of fire. The two of them hacked away until they were able to burst from the vines. They flew up, toward the glaring sun, which grew larger and larger...

Felix sat up straight in bed, fully awake. There was a tugging at his chest. He followed the pull to the window. The sun was still out, but only barely.

"I still can't leave," Felix tried to explain, but the pull was incessant. Clearly something was deeply wrong and required his immediate attention. He glanced around the room, looking for something that might shield him. After some frantic searching, he decided at last on a sheet from his bed. He wasn't sure exactly how much protection it would afford him; hopefully, it would be enough.

Holding the sheet over his head, he took a leap out of the window and was soon soaring through the sky, following the pull on his heart. It led him straight to the restaurant. He touched down in the alley and went through the back door. The pulling in his chest was so intense that it hurt now, like a fishhook inside him.

As he burst through the back door, he nearly tripped over a body—it took him a moment to realize it was John's boss. The smell of blood was thick and heavy, like rusted iron. He heard noise coming from the dining room. He rushed through the door.

John and Lo were there with two men. One of them was Vince, who was standing behind John, his arm hooked around his waist. Felix didn't recognize the other man. He stood behind Lo, pointing a gun at her. Curiously, both John and the man with the gun were glowing red.

The man with the gun seemed like the most immediate threat, but the tug inside him led him to Vince first. He rushed toward him, prying him and John apart. As he touched both of them, he felt a spark rush through him, like an electrical current. The red glow passed from John, through Felix, and then at last into Vince.

Chaos erupted. "Who the fuck is that?" the other man shouted, pointing his gun at Felix. As soon as he was distracted, Lo dashed out of the way, grabbed John, and pulled him to the ground. Vince tried to throw Felix off, but Felix had him now, wrapping his arms around him from behind as he bared his fangs.

The other man screamed. He fired his gun twice, hitting Vince in the chest. The bullets passed through him into Felix, who stumbled backward. Vince staggered and fell to the floor.

The other man stared at Felix for a split second, trembling. He shot four more times, right into Felix's chest. The force of it threw Felix back a few steps, but it by no means took him down. The blood draining from him spiked Felix's hunger; he bared his fangs and leapt at the man, easily disarming him as he sank his fangs into his neck. The man tried to scream, but all that came out was pitiful gurgle, the last sound of a dying animal, because Felix had bitten into him with such viciousness that his throat was torn open. The blood gushed into his mouth as he drank his fill more deeply than he had in months. He needed it; the loss of blood from the bullet wounds made the hunger in him scream. And the blood— it was intoxicating—so dark and rich, more satisfying than anything he'd had in ages...

Dimly, he heard sirens and shouting, but it wasn't enough to stop his feast. What did stop it was a stinging sensation in his back. He turned around with a snarl to find a very shocked-looking policeman staring at him with wide eyes. Felix lunged toward him, his bloodlust not yet sated.

"Felix, no!"

John's voice was like a bell, ringing clear amidst the chaos. It was enough to stop him for a moment. Their gazes met, but then John's gaze darted over his shoulder. He shouted "No!" again, but it wasn't directed at him. He turned just in time to be sprayed with bullets, this time coming from the gun of the second policeman.

Three hit him in the chest. As he reeled from the blast, another two hit him from behind.

A vampire body could withstand a lot of trauma, but even it had its limits. He fell to the ground. His head lolled to the side. The police approached him, their guns still drawn, but there was little he could do about it. He tried to move, but his limbs would not obey him.

"*STOP!*" John shouted.

The police froze in place. John rushed over to Felix, nearly slipping in the wide pool of blood that was emanating from Felix's body.

"Felix!" John put his hands under Felix's arms, trying to pull him up. Felix tried to assist, but the blood was still pouring out of him. The policemen remained still—unnaturally still. Felix saw a fly out of the corner of his eye; it was completely still as well, as if it were trapped in crystal. The whole room seemed to be holding its breath.

Except for Lo. She got back to her feet and looked with astonishment at the frozen room. "What did you do?"

"I don't know," John said, his voice shaky.

"How long do you think it will last?"

"I don't know," John said again. "We have to go—help me."

She came to Felix's other side and slipped an arm under his shoulder. John did the same; between the two of them, they managed to get Felix to his feet. They hauled him into the kitchen.

"Let me get my keys," Lo said. "We can take him to my car." They leaned Felix against the wall while she dashed across the room to grab her purse. Felix tried to stay standing, but he began to slide downward. John struggled to keep him upright but ended up sliding down to the floor as well.

"Felix!" John put a hand on his face. "Are you still with me?"

Felix tried to focus on John, but it was difficult. "...save you?" he slurred.

"What?"

"Did I save you?"

Tears began to course down John's cheeks. "Yes," he said, laughing a little through his tears. "You saved me."

Lo came back; they got Felix to his feet and headed out to the alley. Lo and John were clearly struggling with the weight of him. He tried to move his feet, but it was hopeless.

"Where are you parked?" John asked.

"Not far." Lo cursed. "We need a spell—something to make him lighter or to make us faster." She cursed again. "I can't concentrate!"

"Let's just get him to the car."

After a few minutes, they reached the car. Unfortunately, they were not the only ones there. The police had broken out of their spell—or perhaps it was different policemen altogether. Felix couldn't be sure. There were lots of sirens and lots of shouting.

"Stop, stop!" John screamed again, but it didn't work this time. Lo was screaming something, too, but the police kept advancing. The flashing lights seemed to blend together as Felix's vision grew blurry. All the shouting and the sirens started to fade into a distant rumble, like a passing thunderstorm. He slipped from John's grasp, falling, falling...

He blacked out before he hit the concrete.

WHEN FELIX OPENED his eyes, everything was cold and black.

Felix was not used to true darkness. He was a creature of the night, of course, but that meant his vision was perfectly fine in the dark. To be unable to see anything at all sent him into a panic. Why couldn't he see? What had happened to him?

He tried to sit up, but immediately hit his head. He couldn't move much at all; he was confined on all sides. A coffin? No, it was metal. He put his hands above his head and pushed as hard as he could, but it wouldn't give. He was so weak, and so *cold*...

He struggled some more, to no avail. Eventually, he was forced to stop, having expended all his energy. Which in and of itself was alarming—he was a *vampire*. He was strong, not *weak*, but the cold permeated through him, into him, making him slow and sluggish. Every part of him ached; he felt hollow, drained... He shut his eyes and tried to think, although that was difficult as well. His thoughts felt as frozen as the rest of him.

The events at the restaurant came back to him gradually—his vanquishing of John's attackers, the police shooting, the mad scramble to get away, and then nothing. He thought some more. It was likely that he had been declared dead. Which meant he was in a morgue.

As he was working up the strength to make another attempt to break free, the door at his feet opened. He was pulled into fluorescent light, plunged from pure darkness into blinding light.

A woman in a lab coat loomed over him. Behind her were two men, dressed in suits.

"I don't understand why you had to drag me out of bed for this," the woman was saying. She sounded irritated. "It isn't as if he's going anywhere." The woman's expression suddenly changed from grouchy to unnerved. "Did he just blink?"

She didn't get an answer, for Felix leaped off the table and lunged for her throat. He sank his fangs into her neck and got a few gulps of blood before he was pried off by the men, each of them holding one of his arms. The blood he'd gotten from the woman was enough to return a little of his strength; he shook the men off and then pounced on one of them, tackling him to the ground as he bit his neck.

He was able to get another few mouthfuls of blood before the other man assaulted him again. Felix pivoted from his current victim's neck to his attacker. Out of the corner of his eye, Felix saw the woman stagger out of the room. It occurred to him that the commotion was probably going to attract a lot of attention. He needed to leave. Fortunately, he was nourished enough that his strength had returned. He zipped out of the room, brushing past the woman, down the hall, and up a flight of stairs.

It took him a moment to orient himself. He was in a hospital. A few people caught sight of him and began to scream—an understandable reaction, given that he was covered in blood. He located the nearest exit and burst out into the night. A moment later and he was airborne, soaring through the sky.

He touched down in front of his home. As soon as he was inside, he headed straight for Cat's room. She stood up from her customary position on the sofa. "Felix! What's happened to you?"

Felix opened his mouth to respond but then started to sway. Cat caught him and laid him out on the sofa. "You're bleeding!" Her hands fluttered over his body. "Have you been shot?"

"Yes." He looked down. While some of the bullet holes were healing, others were instead bleeding again.

"Whatever shall I do?" she cried.

"I don't know—I've never been shot before!"

Cat ripped his shirt off to take a better look at the wounds. "There are bullets in you," she said. "Perhaps I should take them out?"

"Yes, I should think so!"

Cat rushed over to her vanity; she returned with a pair of tweezers and dug into Felix's flesh, fishing out the bullets. It hurt tremendously. He shut his eyes so he wouldn't have to watch.

At last, she finished. Felix opened his eyes in time to see her clunk the last bullet on the coffee table. He looked down at his chest. The holes that had been bleeding were closing over. He laid his head back on the sofa, the panic in him settling.

Cat peered at him anxiously. "How are you feeling?"

"Better."

"What on earth happened?"

"I saved John. The man who was destined to kill him was at the restaurant, and I killed him first."

"Does that mean the curse is broken?"

Felix allowed himself to smile. "I think it does." His smile quickly faded. "But I don't know what's happened to John or Lo. The police came shortly after I killed the man. That's when I was shot. John and Lo tried to help me escape. I don't think the police took too kindly to that."

"Did the police take them away?"

"I don't know." Felix got out his phone and called John, but it went straight to voice mail. He didn't know Lo's number. "I should go look for them."

"Are you strong enough?"

Felix sat up. Now that the bullets were gone, he felt much better. "I'll be fine."

Cat hugged him. "Do hurry back."

Felix changed his clothes and set back out into the night. All being told, only about five hours had passed since his arrival at the diner. He had the rest of the night to search.

Unfortunately, his efforts proved fruitless. The restaurant was criss-crossed with yellow tape, although no one was there. He went to both John's apartment and Lo's, but both places were empty. He didn't know where else to look. The police must have taken them, but he couldn't be sure which police station held them, nor did he have any idea how he would break them out even if he did find the right one.

He headed back to the mansion a little before sunrise. Cat was anxiously awaiting him.

"Well?" she asked.

Felix shook his head. "I couldn't find them."

They sat down together on the sofa.

"We must think this through logically," Cat said. "Perhaps we can search on the computer and discover which police station they were taken to."

"But then what? I have no desire to repeat the experience of being riddled with bullets!"

Cat bit her lip. "I don't know." She glanced at the clock. "We'll have some time to think on it; it's nearly dawn."

"Do you think we should tell Richard?"

"That depends on which you think is worse: having them held prisoner by the police or delivering them into Richard's clutches?"

They gave each other gloomy looks. Neither option seemed ideal.

Felix kicked off his shoes and stretched out on the sofa, his head in Cat's lap. Neither of them had much else to say, so they turned on the television. Felix was just about to fall asleep when he heard the door open. He sat up as Richard entered the room.

"Good morning," Richard said, his voice unusually mild. "How was your evening?"

Felix wasn't sure what to say. "It was fine," he said after a moment.

"Really? Are you sure there isn't anything you want to tell me?"

Felix shot a look at Cat, but she appeared just as helpless as he felt. "Why do you ask?"

Richard pulled out a newspaper that had been tucked under his arm and handed it to Felix. "I thought that perhaps you might know something about this."

Felix opened the paper. One story dominated the front page: "THREE DEAD IN DINER MASSACRE." Below that, it continued: "Corpse of the murderer stolen from morgue; two accomplices held for questioning." Accompanying the article were mug shots of John and Lo.

"Oh yes, well—there was that," Felix said. "But I'm fine now, which is what I meant."

Richard picked up one of the bullets from the coffee table. "You mean after you escaped from the morgue and fished the bullets out of your body?"

"Actually, Cat got the bullets out."

Richard rubbed his temple. "What were you thinking, ripping someone's throat out with the police present? And why is John being held as a suspect in a robbery? What the devil happened?"

Since there was no escaping it, Felix told Richard the extent of what he knew, although he omitted the part with John's mother.

Richard looked very thoughtful. "So I assume you were successful in getting John to use the rose. How strange that it would use you as its vessel. I had thought Ginerva's Rose destroyed curses without the need for bloodshed." He smiled. "This is good news, although I can't believe how clumsily you handled it. And what was John thinking, resisting the police?"

"He was trying to save me."

"Which would have gone much easier if he'd just let them take you. We could have collected you later very easily." Richard sighed. "And I'm assuming since he's still locked up, that means his powers are taxed. Unsurprising, since he apparently decided an all-out assault was the best course of action."

"What do you mean?"

"Did you read the article? He flipped one of the police cars with his magic and then led them on a wild car chase." He chuckled. "I can only imagine their confusion at all of this." Richard took the paper back from Felix and looked at it. "Who is this 'Dolores Riaz'?"

"She's a friend of John's."

"How much does she know?"

Felix hesitated. On the one hand, perhaps Lo did not wish for Richard to know of her existence. On the other hand, he didn't want her languishing in jail. "She knows everything. She's a witch."

"Another witch?" Richard looked at her picture. "My, my. You know, I have been the only witch in Los Angeles for decades, and now I've found another? Why, with three of us, we'd practically be a coven."

Felix highly doubted that either John or Lo would be pleased with that idea. "How are we to free them?"

"I'll just pop around the police station and pick them up. Shouldn't be too much trouble."

Felix fidgeted. "And what if they don't want to go with you?"

Richard's blue gaze turned icy. "And why would they prefer prison over coming with me?"

Felix couldn't think of a good answer, so he looked to Cat.

"What Felix means is that he has not yet had the chance to make your case in the most persuasive way possible," she said.

"You mean *our* case," Richard said.

Cat met Richard's gaze calmly. "Yes, of course. We wouldn't want him to feel cornered."

Richard's gaze lost some of its coldness. "I suppose. But the fact of the matter is that he *is* cornered. We must get him out of that police station. I imagine they are still questioning both John and his friend, but before long, they will ship them off to a proper prison. That would be more difficult for me, even with all the powers at my disposal."

He was right, of course. Felix dreaded the idea of John being locked away, but he honestly did not know how John would react to such a "rescue."

"May I come with you?" he asked.

Richard raised an eyebrow. "Might I remind you that you are still a wanted man? Or your corpse is, at least. Besides, the sun is out in full force."

"Can't you do some sort of spell?"

"If I had that kind of power, don't you think I would have used it back when Cat was making pictures? No, I'm afraid blocking the power of the sun is something too great for me."

Felix almost mentioned the glass coffin Richard had created for his punishment; he'd certainly been exposed to the sun through *that*. But strictly speaking, it only protected him enough not to be burned to a complete cinder—only a partial one. And that certainly wouldn't help their current predicament.

"He could cover up," Cat suggested. "I used to do that on occasion. Do you remember that one dress I wore to the premiere of *Mermaids of the Blue Lagoon*—with the high collar, the gloves, the head scarf, and the sunglasses?"

Richard rubbed his chin. "Yes, I suppose that could work. I'll send Philip to pick up an outfit for you. Does that suit you?"

"Yes," Felix said.

Richard clapped his hands. "Good! Then it's all settled. I should go get ready myself. It's been some time since I've been amongst the public." With that, he left the room.

"I don't know about this," Felix said as soon as he was gone. "I don't think we should bring them here. They'll be trapped."

Cat patted his hand. "It won't be forever. Let Richard break them out of prison and bring them here. We'll all play nice until tonight, and then you and the witches can escape."

"I won't leave you here!"

"It won't be forever—just one hundred days. And lest you forget, I used to be an actress of some renown. Richard will have no idea I was involved. Enough time for you to make the blessing." She smiled. "And then we'll all be free!"

Felix couldn't quite match Cat's enthusiasm. Happy Endings was Richard's realm. Everyone who entered—from the celebrities in their golden days to the servants that staffed them now, to him and Cat themselves—became Richard's creatures the moment they stepped through that wrought-iron gate. Would they truly be able to outwit him?

PHILIP DROPPED FELIX and Richard off in front of the police station. Felix clutched his scarf tightly around his face. In spite of all his coverings, he still felt intensely uncomfortable. His sunglasses were very dark, but even so, the light hurt his eyes. Was the world really this terribly bright? How did anyone stand it?

They entered the building. Felix hung back as Richard approached the front desk. He tried his best to look casual, although his head-to-toe black apparel probably spoiled his efforts.

"I would like to speak to the investigator in charge of the cafe massacres," he said to the woman sitting at the desk.

"Do you have information pertaining to the case?"

"Yes, that will do," Richard said with a vague wave of his hand.

"Can I get your name?"

"No."

The woman gave him an odd look but didn't press him further. She picked up her phone. "Go ahead and have a seat; we'll be with you shortly."

Twenty minutes later, a portly man approached them. He gave Felix a long once-over before turning his attention to Richard. "I'm Detective Frank Johnson," he said, offering his hand to Richard.

Richard rose and took his hand—a bad move on the detective's part, seeing as Richard's influence only grew stronger when he made physical contact with someone. "A pleasure to meet you," he said warmly.

"I understand you have some information that might help us out?"

"Yes. Is there somewhere we can speak privately?"

"Of course. Right this way."

They started toward the back, but the detective stopped when he saw Felix following them. "Who is he?"

"Don't concern yourself with him."

The man opened his mouth, seeming prepared to argue, but the protest appeared to dissolve before he could voice it. He turned back around and continued down the hall.

They arrived at their destination—a nearly bare room, furnished only with a table and a few chairs. They all had a seat.

The detective smiled at them. "I didn't catch your name earlier."

"That's because I didn't give it. You don't want to know my name."

The man blinked rapidly. "Okay," he said after a moment, as if the answer Richard had given him had been in any way normal. "So what information can you give us?"

"You are holding John Richmond and Dolores Riaz at this station, correct?"

The detective gave him a condescending smile. "I thought that you had info for us, not the other way around."

"It's not exactly a secret, is it? I read it in the paper. I just wanted to verify."

"Yes, we're holding them. Now why don't you give me the information you claim to have?"

"No. I want you to get Mr. Richmond and Miss Riaz and bring them here."

The man just stared at him for a minute. He laughed uncomfortably. "I can't do that."

"Of course you can," Richard said. "You know where they are. You have the ability to release them. Go fetch them and bring them here. Now."

The detective's expression became very complicated. He clearly was at war with himself and Richard's words, but Richard's words won out, as they always did. "Wait here," he said and left the room.

"There," Richard said once he was gone. "Didn't I tell you it would be simple?"

Felix was glad for the dark glasses and the scarf he was wearing; he was sure his expression would give away his true feelings. Dealing with the police was not the hard part of this scenario, although he suspected saying so would only make the situation worse.

After about fifteen minutes, the detective returned with John and Lo, who both wore handcuffs. Richard and Felix both got to their feet when they entered. "John," he said with a wide smile. "Fancy running into you here."

John's face had gone completely white. Lo started shaking her head. "No," she said. She turned to the detective. "Take us back to our cells, now."

"You will do no such thing, Detective Johnson," Richard said. "You will shut the door, and then you will stand quietly in the corner until I say otherwise."

There wasn't even a moment's hesitation this time. The detective shut the door and went off to the corner.

"Turn around," Richard further specified. "And don't listen." When he was satisfied with the detective's obedience, he turned to Felix. "You can reveal yourself now."

Felix took off his various head accessories. John let out a cry and rushed to him. "Oh my God, Felix! I thought you were dead!"

"I still am."

John started laughing. He made as if to embrace him, but was impeded by the cuffs. Felix seized the chain and broke it in two. They wrapped their arms around each other. For a moment, the whole world seemed to fade away and it was just the two of them.

Richard cleared his throat. "This is all very romantic, don't you think?"

John pulled away from Felix. Something had shifted in him; the sunny look of relief had faded. Felix's own smile faltered. Had he done wrong to bring Richard here? But what other choice did he have? Surely John understood that.

John turned to Richard. "So you're here to break us out." He didn't sound enthused.

Lo spoke up. "We aren't going anywhere with you," she spat at Richard.

Richard approached her. "Miss Riaz, we seem to have gotten off on the wrong foot, somehow. Perhaps we should make a proper introduction—" He reached for her cuffed hands.

She jerked back. "Don't you fucking touch me. I don't need an introduction. I know who you are, and I want you to stay far, far away from me."

Something in Richard's eyes hardened. Since this morning, Richard had been in a very good mood, smug and self-satisfied. But now his mood had shifted. Felix didn't like it at all.

"My, my," Richard murmured. "What have they been telling you about me that has made you so hostile?"

"You're a serial killer."

Richard scoffed. "A serial killer? What a ridiculous notion. I'm not in the habit of raping corpses and sending taunting letters to the police."

"You kill. Serially. Therefore, you are a serial killer." She spoke louder, directing her attention toward the police officer. "He's a serial killer!" The man didn't respond.

Felix winced, waiting for Richard to lash out. But he didn't, his expression kept deceptively mild. Richard directed his attention back to John.

"From the young lady's reaction, I'm starting to think that you have not considered my offer in the spirit with which I made it."

John's face was a mask, his tone equally inscrutable. "We can talk about it, but not here."

Richard nodded. "Agreed."

Lo exploded. "No, not agreed!" She turned to John. "We can't go with him!"

Richard spoke before John could respond. "Would you prefer to take your chances here?" he asked, addressing Lo. "The fact that you're still incarcerated suggests that your powers have been exhausted."

"For now."

"My dear, I hope you don't take this the wrong way, but you don't have the capacity to work your way out of this particular situation. Influencing one or two people to secure your release might be possible once you've had a chance to collect yourself, but what then? You will have made yourself a fugitive. Your faces have made the front page of the papers and are probably all over the World Wide Web, or whatever you call it. Do you have the power to influence an entire city, Miss Riaz?"

Lo's eyes flashed with anger. "Which is why I asked the detective to bring us back to our cells. We don't need to escape. We didn't really do anything *that* wrong."

"You threw a police car at them."

"How are they going to prove that? Claim it was magic? Somehow I don't think that's going to fly. Witch trials aren't a thing anymore. Once this whole mess has calmed down, they'll charge us with maybe resisting arrest or obstruction of justice or whatever. It was a confusing scene. I'm sure we can talk our way out of it. Probably won't even have to use magic."

"*Or* they could decide to throw the book at you. Aiding the escape of a criminal, possible accessory to robbery—perhaps even murder."

"That seems like a stretch."

"A stretch easily made." Richard smiled. It was not a pleasant sight. "Just the slightest pressure of a thumb on the scale of justice, and your outlook seems not so rosy. And my thumbs can be quite heavy, my dear."

"Are you *threatening* us?"

"No. I am saving you. That thumb could easily tip the balance in your favor as well."

"Fuck you, you piece of shit. We aren't going anywhere with you."

Richard hummed ambiguously. He turned to the detective in the corner. "Detective Johnson, would you come here for a moment?"

The man obeyed, stopping at Richard's side. His eyes were glassy and unseeing—Felix recognized the look.

"Now Miss Riaz, Detective Johnson here is a fine specimen of law enforcement. His will is not easily swayed, and yet as you can see, I have him completely in my power. I just convinced this upstanding detective to bring two criminal suspects to meet with a civilian witness whose name he doesn't even know. Then I sent him off to stand in the corner like a naughty child, and not even your accusation against me has roused him." Richard's mild smile turned ever so slightly into something more menacing. "What else do you think I can get him to do? Use your imagination. Think big."

Lo lapsed into silence. "You're disgusting," she finally said, although with none of the bravado of her earlier words.

Richard smirked. "Back to your corner, Detective Johnson." The man obeyed. Richard turned his attention back to John. "Now, I think we are both agreed that any further conversation should be held elsewhere. Shall we head to Happy Endings?"

"I'd like to speak to Lo for a minute."

Richard waved his hand in assent. Lo and John went to an empty corner of the room and began speaking in low tones. All the while, Richard's gaze remained riveted on Lo. "You should have told me about her," Richard said to Felix. "She's remarkable. So fresh, so untouched—"

Felix twisted his scarf in his hands. "Are you going to hurt her?"

"That depends entirely on your witch boy."

Lo and John ended their conference and returned to the other side of the room. "Can you make it so it's like we were never arrested?"

"You flatter me. I am unfortunately not as powerful as that. What I can offer you is invisibility. They won't be able to find you."

Lo spoke up. "And how are we supposed to make a living?"

Richard smiled. "You won't have to. That time of your life is over. I can provide everything your heart desires."

"My heart desires to get away from you," Lo snarled, but John put a hand on her arm and shook his head. Her temper went from a boil to a simmer.

Richard clapped his hands. "So we're in agreement. Let's get out of this vulgar place."

Richard summoned the detective again. "We're leaving now. You will wait ten minutes before leaving this room. You will forget having ever met me or any of your actions since I've been here. Do you understand?"

The man nodded.

Richard removed both Lo and John's cuffs with a touch of his hand. They left the police station without so much as a second glance from anyone. Felix covered himself up again before they went back out into the sunlight. Philip was waiting for them outside in front of the limo. He opened the door.

Richard and Felix got in straight away. John followed them, but Lo hesitated. She was shaking. For a moment, Felix thought she might bolt.

John took her hand. "It will be all right," he said quietly. She took a deep breath and allowed herself to be guided inside.

The door shut. With that, they were off to Happy Endings.

Fifteen: Happy Endings

JOHN HELD LO'S hand as they rode in the limo.

Felix sat across from him. He had taken off his sunglasses and loosened his scarf; the windows were tinted, but John could still see that it pained him a bit to expose even that much. He was looking at John with a hopeful expression John couldn't bring himself to return.

Richard sat beside Felix, but his gaze was fixed on Lo. "Dolores, Dolores, Dolores," he said in a lilting voice. "Such a lovely name. Do you know its meaning?"

She said nothing, keeping her expression stony. Richard continued as if she had responded. "It means 'our lady of sorrows.'"

That did get a reaction out of her. "And what does your name mean? 'Creepy-ass psycho motherfucker?'"

Richard tutted. "We are going to have to do something about your language."

"I'd like to see you try!"

Richard leaned forward with the anticipation of a spider about to enjoy a meal.

And something in John finally snapped. Ever since the bloodbath at the restaurant, John had been floating like someone underwater, moving in slow motion, his vision blurred and hearing muted. But the threat in Richard's eyes dragged him to the surface, forcing him into the cold, bracing air, and all at once everything was clear.

He looked at Lo's pale, angry face, and the defensive hunch of Felix's shoulders. In spite of all his efforts, John had managed to find two people who loved him, and they were put in terrible danger because of him. Once upon a time, that would have filled him with paralyzing self-loathing. Not anymore.

"I need to get my cat," he said abruptly.

Richard's attention shifted from Lo to John. "Your cat?"

"Yes. I left her at Lo's place. If we're going to be staying with you, I need to get her. And some other things."

Richard sat back and considered John silently. After a moment, he pressed the button for the intercom.

"Philip, we will be making a stop before we return home." He released the button. "What's the address?"

Ten minutes later, they pulled to a stop. Richard pressed the intercom again. "Philip, park the car and then come around. You will be going with John to help him retrieve his things."

"I need things, too," Lo said quickly. "And John can't get in. He doesn't have the key."

Richard raised an eyebrow. "And neither do you, my dear. I expect it's still back at the police station. Fortunately, locked doors rarely present a problem to witches. You are staying here with Felix and me. I'm sure that John can fetch whatever you need." Before Lo could respond, Richard waved his finger. Lo jerked backward, her back completely flush to the seat. She tensed as if she was trying to get up, but was unsuccessful.

"I apologize for the restraint, but I'm afraid I don't trust that you won't try to walk away from my hospitality."

She struggled again, but it was useless. "You son of a bitch!"

"*Language*, Dolores," Richard chided. "I can silence you as well, you know. It would not be very pleasant."

Lo bit back whatever insult she'd been about to spew out, and Richard smiled. "Good. Now tell John what you need."

"Some clothes," she said haltingly.

"And other stuff," John said, looking into her eyes, trying his best to communicate for her to sit tight. "Stuff we can use."

She nodded slowly. "Yeah," she said. "Those, too."

"Let me come with you," Felix said, looking to John with pleading eyes. "I can help."

John shook his head. "The sun is out. Covered or no, it isn't good for you to be out and about too much."

"But—" Felix began to protest.

John put a hand on Felix's face. His skin was back to being cold. "It's okay," John said softly. "I'll be right back."

The door of the limo opened. John got out and walked into Lo's building, with Philip trailing behind him. When he reached Lo's door, he spelled it open, and they went inside.

Despite John's reassurances to Lo and Felix, he actually didn't have a plan yet. He looked at Philip. It was probably hopeless, but it couldn't hurt to try again.

"With your help, we could get away. We could take you with us."

"I am to help you get your cat, and then bring you back to Mr. Livingstone," he said a flat tone.

It seemed clear that John wasn't going to get anywhere with him. He handed Philip the carrier and then started to look for Astray. He found her at last curled under Lo's bed.

"Hey, kitty," John said softly as he reached for her. She pulled back and made an annoyed noise. He sighed. "Trust me, I don't want to go either."

After a few minutes, he coaxed her out. Philip had picked up the cat carrier and held it open. She yowled as he lowered her in.

"Sorry, kitty," he said as he closed the door. "We need her food and her litter. They're in the bathroom."

While Philip was in the bathroom, John grabbed a backpack and a duffle bag from Lo's closet. He gathered his spell binders and the Ouija board and shoved them inside. He still had no idea how exactly he planned on outwitting Richard, but hopefully between his magical research and maybe some help from his mother, they'd be able to figure something out.

Next, he filled the duffle bag with as many clothes as he could fit. When Philip emerged with the food and the litter, he'd already put the backpack on and slung the duffle bag over his shoulder. Philip picked up the carrier, and then they were off.

They returned to the limo. Astray made her displeasure known very loudly for the rest of the ride to Happy Endings. It saved them from more conversation, at least.

After driving through the gates, Philip stopped the limo in front of the mansion. He came around and opened the door. Felix zipped out of the limo and inside the mansion immediately while Philip picked up the cat carrier and the duffle bag and carried them inside. Richard followed behind him. Lo, however, hung back.

"No," she said, shaking her head.

"It's okay," John said quietly. He couldn't have her freaking out and doing something stupid. John and Felix were essential to Richard's plans; he wouldn't hurt them. Lo, on the other hand, was expendable. "We'll figure it out."

"Are you two coming?" Richard called as he held open the door.

John slung the backpack over his shoulder and offered a hand to Lo. Reluctantly, she allowed herself to be led into the mansion. Once they were inside, Richard shut the doors. The sound echoed through the foyer.

Felix was standing at the staircase. He had shed his coverings. Even though they were indoors now, he still looked pained. He gave John an awkward half smile. John couldn't bring himself to return it.

"Welcome to my home," Richard said, gesturing around them. "A paradise on Earth, although it has been a lonely one as of late. Until now." He smiled at Lo. "Now, I know you have your reservations—" She scoffed loudly, but Richard ignored her and just spoke louder. "—but once you have seen what I have to offer, I think you will change your mind."

"Not fucking likely." Lo words were filled with as much bravado as before, but a desperate quality had crept into her voice. John couldn't blame her; he was feeling a bit desperate himself. However, he thought antagonizing Richard was not the right way to get out of this, so he put his hand on Lo's arm.

"Let's wait and see, okay?"

He'd hoped Lo would understand that he was stalling, but she gave him this wild, wounded look. But he couldn't say any more—not with Richard standing right there.

"Very reasonable of you, John," Richard said with a smirk. "Philip will see to your cat while we see to mine." He gestured to the stairs. "Come—I want to introduce you to my wife. She's dying to meet you."

They went up the stairs and down a long hallway until they reached a grand door. Richard knocked but did not wait for a response before sweeping in. "Cat, darling, our guests are here."

Cat stood from the sofa where she'd been lounging. She was wearing a dress right out of the golden age of Hollywood, with her hair and makeup done to match. John stopped in his tracks when he saw her. Of course, he'd seen her before on the screen, but seeing her in person was beyond eerie. She was like Felix in female form, with her raven hair and bright green eyes. It was uncanny. And with the way she was dressed, it seemed like she had jumped straight off the movie screen.

She glided toward them, her face lit with a bright smile. She went to John first. "You must be John. How wonderful to meet you at last." She held out her hand. John dropped the backpack on the ground and took her proffered hand, and then she turned to Lo. "And you must be Miss Riaz. I can't tell you how excited we are to have you."

Lo had also been staring at Cat in bewildered fascination, but she snapped out of it. She looked back and forth between her and Felix, her expression dark.

"Yeah, I bet you are. To have us, I mean. You've all got this planned out nicely."

Richard interrupted. "Well, it was more fortuitous circumstances, but what a happy accident of fate." He clapped his hands. "Let's get to it, shall we?"

"Get to what?" Cat asked.

"Why, putting John's heart into Felix, so they can be joined as you and I."

John felt a jolt of alarm and was about to protest, but Cat beat him to it. "You mean right this moment?" she said with a pout. "Aren't we going to have a wedding?"

Richard raised his eyebrow. "A wedding?"

"Men marry one another nowadays, you know. I've seen it on television. And I can't imagine having my brother joined to his truest love without a proper wedding."

Richard rubbed his chin thoughtfully. "You're right, of course," he said after a moment. "It shouldn't take too long to plan. My chef isn't given nearly enough to do. It will only take a few hours for the staff to get out all our old dinnerware. And if I call now, I'm sure I'd be able to secure a musical act of some sort."

Cat smiled again. "Sounds perfectly lovely!"

Richard took her hand and kissed it. "And we can renew our vows as well."

For the briefest of moments, Cat's expression hardened. "Of course, my darling," she said with excessive sweetness.

"I'd best get started on the arrangements." He turned and started to leave the room. John breathed a small sigh of relief. With Richard gone, they could at least have a chance to regroup and try to think of a way out of this.

But Lo had other plans. She picked up an empty wine bottle from the coffee table. *"Change this bottle to iron from glass/Make a blade so I can kill his ass!"* The bottle turned into a blade in her hand as she ran across the room to Richard, who barely had the chance to turn around before she was on him. She stabbed him several times in quick succession, right in the middle of his chest.

He collapsed to the floor. Lo grabbed John's hand and ran out the door, pulling him after her. "We have to get out of here!"

He stumbled after her. "But Felix—"

"He's with them now!" she said, not slowing for a minute. "Don't you see? That's why he got Richard to break us out of jail—to bring us to him. Don't fall for it!"

They made it down the stairs and almost out the door when they were stopped by the imposing figure of Philip. "*Let us pass—*" she began, but then there was a great roar coming from the top of the stairs.

"*SILENCE!*" It was Richard, who did not seem to be injured in the least, although his shirt had been ripped to shreds. The expression on his face was so dark and twisted he barely seemed human. Felix and Cat stood at his side.

Lo's lips continued to move, but nothing came out. Undeterred, she brandished her blade again and surged toward Philip, but he easily disarmed her and held her arms behind her back. She reared back, kicking, her mouth opened in a silent scream. John tried to speak, but unsurprisingly, his voice was gone as well.

"Bring her to me," Richard said to Philip, who obeyed at once, dragging Lo up the stairs. Richard's piercing gaze turned to John. "And what of you? Do I have to have you dragged up here as well?"

John shook his head. He mounted the stairs and trailed after Philip.

They all ended up back in Cat's room. Philip kept a firm grip on Lo, who continued to fight, but it was clear she was losing energy. Cat and Felix stood behind the couch, their expressions so blank John couldn't read them.

"Sit down!" Richard barked at John. He felt a jerk as a magical force tugged him to the sofa and kept him there.

Richard began to pace the room. It was a long time before he spoke again, calmer this time. "I should kill you," he said to Lo. "But that would really be a waste. You are wild and undisciplined, but it's been so long since there's been another feminine presence in the house. Both Cat and I would enjoy that."

At that, Lo renewed her kicking, not that it did any good. Richard made a gesture at Lo; she stopped moving. "Put her in the chair and then kneel in front of her," he said to Philip, who obeyed.

"No doubt John has acquainted you with curses," Richard continued. "Now, there are little spells of mischief and mayhem that don't require much other than a keen mind, but curses are something altogether different. We'll need blood for this."

At that, John tried to get up and call out instinctively, but he found himself both stuck and silenced. Felix zipped across the room and placed himself between Richard and Lo.

"No!" he said.

"Shut up," Richard snarled. "Or you will find yourself in the coffin, Lo's life will be forfeit, and I can think of some rather unpleasant things to do to John as well while I wait for obedience to be burned into you."

Felix cowered at that, slinking back.

Cat stepped forward, but not with aggression. She put a hand on Richard's shoulder. "Really, darling, is this strictly necessary? I'm sure if you just give me some time to explain things to her, she will come around."

Richard took her hand and kissed it. "While I have always found you quite persuasive, I'm afraid Lo will find you less so. And she is not a mere mortal whom you can overpower. She's a witch, and she is dangerous. I won't have her harming you."

Cat drew back. "Anything you say, dear."

Richard turned back to Lo and Philip. "As I was saying. I think that nothing less than a curse will be able to tame you." He shot a brief look at John. "And while you are being a bit more agreeable than your friend, you still seem to show a certain reluctance." He clapped his hands. "So! Let's kill two birds with one stone, shall we?"

He held up one finger. The nail began to grow until it was six inches long, gaining a metallic sheen as it grew. He held the nail to Philip's throat, who offered no resistance. Then he began to speak:

"The wages of sin are said to be death
But who pays the sinner; who writes the check?
If you think it's you, dear, you are bereft
Of sense, but if you want to risk your neck
Then why not aid your friend's true love? Because
Felix will soon possess a human heart
He still needs blood, but he will find what was
Once an easy feat will make him fall apart
So now I call upon your bravery

To find the victims he will still need
I know you'll find the task unsavory
But even vampires with hearts must feed
If you refuse, my lady of sorrows
You will not live to see tomorrow."

As he said the last word, he raked his nail across Philip's throat. Blood spurted all over Lo, drenching her in it. She was shaking, her mouth opening and shutting in screams that could not be heard.

No one moved for a long moment. Richard's chest heaved; it was the most effort John had ever seen from him. At last, he waved a hand. Lo slumped forward, down onto her knees, apparently released from Richard's hold. She wasn't fighting anymore.

Richard towered over her. "That's better. Perhaps I will give you back your voice if you behave yourself tonight."

Lo did not react, but Richard didn't seem to expect her to. "Now then," he said, his voice cheerful. "I have a wedding to plan. Cat, get her cleaned up and dressed in something suitable. And something in white for you, I think."

"Of course, darling."

Richard turned to John, rubbing his chin in consideration. "You'll be a bit more difficult to dress. The ideal would be to have a suit tailored for you, but naturally that would be difficult given the time constraints. Off the rack will have to do. I'll send Philip—" He caught himself. "Or I suppose I won't, will I? I'm going to have to train another manservant. How annoying."

John looked at Philip's body. Whatever half-life he had was probably nothing to be grieved, but John still felt ill.

Richard followed John's gaze. "Yes, that's a bit unsightly." He knelt beside the body. "*Ashes to ashes,*" he murmured. The body dissolved into a fine powder. "*Dust to dust.*" He blew on the ashes, which dissipated into the air. He stood up and turned his attention back to John. "Which would you prefer for your wedding—a classical string quartet, or something a little jazzier?"

John patted his throat.

"Oh, right." Richard waved his hand. John sucked in a croaking gasp. Richard looked at him expectantly. "Well?"

"Whatever you want," he wheezed.

Richard rubbed his chin. "Jazz, I think," he said, mostly to himself. He began walking to the door. "And roses, of course. Lots and lots of roses..."

As soon as he was gone, John moved forward and took Lo into his arms. Philip's body might have been gone, but the blood remained, all over Lo—staining her clothes, slicking her skin, matting in her hair. It got on John too, now. He shut his eyes, but there was no escaping the smell.

He felt arms wrap around him from behind as Felix embraced him. In response, Lo stiffened in John's arms. She pushed both of them off and stumbled to her feet. She opened her mouth and screamed—or tried to, but of course her voice was still lost. She grabbed an empty wine bottle from the coffee table and smashed it on the floor.

"Lo—" John said, trying to calm her, but she continued her rampage, flipping the entire coffee table over and sending its contents crashing to the floor as well.

Cat watched it all dispassionately. "You can rage all you want. It won't help. Believe me, I've done it often enough to know."

Lo stormed over to the backpack John had brought. After riffling around in it for a moment, she produced a pen and a few papers she'd torn from one of the binders. She began to scribble furiously and then handed the paper to John.

Bitch-ass motherfucker forgot I was literate, I guess. He can't shut me up.

She smiled grimly. John actually laughed a little.

She took the paper back and scribbled some more.

What now?

Cat looked over John's shoulder at the paper. "I will stall Richard until this evening, and then John and Felix can make their escape." She looked at Lo. "I was going to help you too, but now there's nothing for it. Felix and John will have to go on their own. I can give you pills, if you like. No sense in going out sober."

"She's not going to die," John said firmly. "I'm going through with the ceremony."

"You are *not!*" Cat said with sudden ferociousness as she rounded on him. "I will not allow it!"

John took a few surprised steps backward. Felix inserted himself between the two of them. "I still don't understand why you're so against it. I know there will be pain, but I can bear it."

"And it will only be for one hundred days," John added. "That's enough time to make cures for all of us."

Cat laughed bitterly. "You still don't understand, do you? Once you are heartless, you will have little interest in a cure. In fact, you will betray us at the first opportunity."

This surprised John. "Why would you say that?"

Cat didn't respond right away. She scooped some of the blue pills that had scattered over the floor and swallowed them dry. "I know you'll find it hard to believe, but Richard wasn't always as he is now. He was never a good man—he was a user and a cheat, thinking only of how to bring riches and glory to himself. But that is not so unusual. It barely qualifies as bad in this wicked world.

"But after he lost his heart, he changed. He became cruel in a way he'd never been before. What little conscience he had was silenced completely. He had no care for anyone's pain—not even mine." She wrapped her arms around herself. "Especially not mine."

She wiped one eye, her finger coming away bloodied. "And I changed as well. I'd never thought of my victims for more than a moment when I was heartless, but after Richard put his heart in me, their fates began to haunt me. For the first time, I became a true killer—my feedings were no longer brief attacks in the night. They were *murders*, which perhaps would not have bothered me if I were heartless. But of course, I wasn't any longer."

She covered her face with her hand as her shoulders shook. "And now I am consumed with guilt and grief—so much that sometimes I feel I may drown in it. What he's doing to those people—he thinks it's a kindness, but it isn't. Those dreams he gives them—I find myself inside them too, sometimes, connected to these people I have sentenced to a living death. They may have their fondest wishes, but they can *feel* it's wrong, and they can feel themselves wasting away. It's beauty masking unspeakable terror." She pulled her hand away; her face was streaked in blood. "And for me, it is unending. I won't have you putting Felix through that! That has been my one consolation in all of this—that he was spared this evil."

"And you think that letting Lo die won't weigh on his conscience?" John shot back. "I know it would weigh on mine."

"You could make him forget," she said. Her eyes were wide now, pleading. "You witches are so clever with mortal minds. You could make us both forget all of this darkness and pain, and we'll start over new, innocent again—"

"No," John said, aghast. "I'm not going to wipe your minds. I don't know that I can. And even if I could, I wouldn't."

"So that's it, then? You're just going to unload all your pain onto Felix and me, and live an eternal life of heartlessness, content to spend centuries feeding off mortal lives? Because that is exactly what will happen if you allow the ceremony to take place." She pointed at Lo. "How many hundreds of lives are you willing to sacrifice to save hers? And if she's truly a good witch, then how will she feel being bound to Felix in his murderous deeds?"

They all sat with that for a moment. At last, Lo wrote something and handed it to John.

She's right. You have to go.

"No!" John said. He looked around at the three of them. "I have spent years of my life giving in to defeat. Not anymore. Every single person in this room is going to make it out of here alive. There's no such thing as an unbreakable curse. We just have to think."

They all jumped as the backpack tipped itself over, spilling its contents on the floor. The Ouija board skittered across the floor, landing at John's feet.

"Looks like Mom might have an idea," John said.

Felix righted the coffee table so they could lay the board out. The planchette began moving around immediately. Lo wrote down each letter. When the planchette stilled, she handed the paper for John to read.

"*Memories are held in the heart,*" he read.

"What on earth does that mean?" Cat asked.

John thought about it. "I could tie my memories of this whole conversation to my heart," he said slowly. "So when I give it to Felix, I won't remember the plan."

Cat shook her head. "No. The risk is too great. And even if it worked, what's to happen when we're cured? If we could slip away as I planned, we might have the chance, but it's too complicated if we have to undo the heart transference. We'll still have Richard to contend with, and he is awfully powerful."

Lo wrote something and passed it to John.

Not w/o her. No vampire=no immortality.

John passed the paper to Cat. "He'll still have the power of the Extras," she said. "He can still feed from their power. And his wrath will be terrible once he's found what we've done."

Lo wrote again.

Then we get rid of them.

"You'd kill them?" Cat asked.

She shook her head and wrote.

We wake them up.

"How?" John asked.

Lo gestured to the Ouija board.

"My mother," John said slowly. "She can travel in dreams. Maybe she can break their spell."

The planchette moved immediately to the *Yes.*

They all took a moment to absorb it. "I think it could work," John said at last.

Cat folded her arms over her chest. "I don't know..."

Felix put a hand on her shoulder. "Isn't this what we hoped for? That he would have a plan to save us?"

She put her hand over Felix's. "I hadn't considered the price. That was silly of me, wasn't it? There's always a price."

"It's only for one hundred days," Felix said again. "I have endured much worse than that, if you recall."

Cat didn't respond. Instead, she turned to Lo. "We should clean you up. If we are to do this, you swallow your pride and cease your provocations of my husband."

Lo looked grim at the thought, but she nodded. She and Cat disappeared into the bathroom, leaving Felix and John alone.

John sank down to the sofa. Felix sat beside him. John stared down at his fidgeting hands. Neither of them said anything for a long moment. At last, Felix took John's hands in his own to still them.

"Why do you look so nervous? We're all but saved! I knew you would think of something."

"I wish I could be as confident as you. I don't really know if this will work." He stroked Felix's hand with his thumb. "And what I'm about to put you through sounds pretty terrible."

"I would endure all the sorrows in the world for your sake," Felix said grandly. "And for my sister's."

John smiled at him sadly. "But you don't really know what it will mean. Hell, I don't know what it will mean. It's easy to say that you can handle pain before you feel it. I wonder if you'll change your mind when you're in the midst of it."

Felix shook his head. "I won't. I swear to you I will bear it gladly."

"Why?"

Felix cocked his head. "What do you mean, 'why'?"

"I mean, I can understand your devotion to your sister, but why me? Why do you love me?"

Felix didn't answer right away. Instead, he kissed John's hand, holding his cold lips to his skin for a long moment.

"I think," he said at last, "that you are very clever, and clever people such as yourself often think there are answers to all questions. But alas, I was not clever in life, and am even less clever in death. I have no answer that would satisfy you. I believe there are some questions, like the whys and hows of love, that are ineffably beautiful because they have no answer. I was empty once, and your companionship has made me whole. I cannot explain why. Can you accept that?"

John put his arms around Felix and drew him into an embrace. When he pulled back, there were tears in his eyes.

"I think you're a lot smarter than you give yourself credit for," he said. He leaned in for a kiss.

When they parted, the tears in John's eyes spilled onto his cheeks. He tried to look away, but Felix put a gentle hand on his face. "Why are you crying?"

"Because I'm afraid I'm going to hurt you when I'm heartless," he said.

"I forgive you already."

That only made John cry harder. All the horrible events of the past twenty-four hours caught up with him at last. Felix held him as he wept his heart out.

After a while, his sobs became weaker before stopping altogether. He stayed in Felix's embrace, his head resting on his shoulder. "Poor Lo. I hate that I dragged her into this."

"None of this is your fault—not the curse, not what's happened with Richard. I'm certain Lo knows that. And she's your friend; she wanted to help you. You didn't drag her into anything."

By reflex, John almost started to argue, but he was starting to realize how self-defeating that was. "Poor Mike. I can't really say the same for him. He was kind of a shit boss, but he didn't deserve to die like that."

"His death was indeed unfortunate."

He snuggled in a little closer. "Poor Vince."

Felix drew back. "Poor *Vince*? It didn't look as if he were helping you; quite the opposite, it seemed!"

That was an understatement, but John didn't feel like getting into it. "I know. It's just—I've always wondered about my dad. Was he going to be an abusive asshole no matter what, or did the curse make him that way? Vince's life was a mess, and maybe he wasn't a good person, but..." John trailed off, then shrugged. "I don't know. I feel bad that he ended up like that."

Felix scoffed. "And I suppose you feel sorry for the monster sent to destroy you?"

"I do, a little."

Felix gave him an incredulous look. "I find that quite bizarre."

John smiled and touched his face. "Maybe you'll understand when you have a heart." John touched their foreheads together. "Are you sure you're ready for this?"

"Yes."

"Promise me you'll make sure Lo is okay."

"I promise."

"And—I know our plan is that I'm not supposed to remember, but try not to let me lose myself too much?"

Felix took John's hand and put it over his own chest. "I will keep you safe in here. I'll not forget you, even when you forget yourself."

They came together for another long kiss, pulling apart only when they heard someone clearing her throat. It was Cat; Lo was beside her dressed in a fluffy robe. She was scrubbed clean, her wet hair shining. It was strange to see her without her usual makeup and full hair; she looked very young.

"We have female things to do," Cat said. "Leave us."

They both stood. "Don't you need help with your makeup?" Felix asked.

Cat waved her hand. "I've learned to manage. The web camera is not as difficult as I imagined it to be." She looked to Lo. "Besides, I'm not alone, am I?"

Lo smiled a little. Whatever interaction they'd had in the bathroom seemed to have brought them to some sort of understanding; at least John didn't have to worry about that.

Felix and John relocated to Felix's room. They both washed up in his bathroom. Afterward, they didn't bother to get dressed. They fell into bed together, wrapped in each other's arms as they kissed, again and again, improbably aroused. The whole situation was so terrible that John was a little ashamed of grabbing this small pleasure, but he took it. They stroked each other to orgasm.

Afterward, they were both silent. What else was there to say? They held each other as they waited for night to fall.

Sixteen: I Thee Dread

A SMALL MEAL for John was sent up to Felix's room at around noon, as well as a pack of cigarettes. The tuxedos arrived a little after six o'clock, accompanied by an envelope. John opened it, and scoffed.

"What does it say?" Felix asked.

"It's an invitation to our own wedding. It says we should arrive in the ballroom at our convenience."

"You know, I never dreamed I would get married," Felix said. "In my day, it was unthinkable for me to marry a man, and I had little incentive to enter a marriage with a woman to begin with."

John gave Felix a small, sad smile. "I never thought I'd get married, either. Seemed kind of pointless."

Felix sighed. "I think this is the most wretched engagement that has ever been."

That got a laugh out of John, at least. Felix got dressed while John lit a cigarette.

Felix gave a little twirl when he was finished. "How do I look?"

"Good," he said. He smiled a little. "I wish the circumstances were different."

"As do I." Felix sat down on the bed. He laid his head on John's shoulder while John smoked. Felix thought he could stay forever like this, with John naked and sated and tangled up in his sheets.

But John was an efficient smoker, and his cigarette was finished all too soon. "I guess I should get dressed," He stubbed out the butt in the ashtray. "Might as well get this over with."

After John was dressed, they made their way to Cat's room. Cat was resplendent in a dress of white—it wasn't a bridal gown, but it was still lovely. Lo wore pale blue and carried a white clutch. She was almost unrecognizable with her hair and makeup done up like a silent film starlet. As soon as they entered the room, Lo pulled out a piece of paper and a pen from her clutch and scribbled something on a piece of paper. She handed it to John. Felix read it over John's shoulder.

If you say I look nice, I'm going to deck you.

John snorted. "I wouldn't dream of it."

"Well, I wouldn't mind a compliment," Cat said.

John smiled. "You look beautiful."

"Thank you." She smoothed her hand over her dress. "I always feel more in character when I'm properly costumed. Be prepared for a virtuoso performance from me tonight." She smiled brightly and batted her eyelashes. "The formerly estranged wife, overjoyed at reconciliation with her not-at-all repulsive husband."

Lo laughed; or well, it seemed like she laughed, since she was still silenced.

"Are we ready?" Felix asked.

John shook his head. "Not quite. I have a spell to cast." John looked around the room, his gaze lighted on each of them. "I'm sorry in advance."

Lo scribbled out another note and handed it to John. Felix read it over his shoulder. *Forget about it. Literally.* She smiled a little.

John smiled back. He went over to the coffee table, where the Ouija board was still set up. He knelt before it. "I could use your help, Mom."

Slowly, the planchette began to move. The center of John's chest began to glow. The planchette stilled. John got back to his feet and headed back to Felix, linking their arms together.

"Let's go."

The four of them made their way to the ballroom; the grand doors opened as they arrived. Felix took half a step backward at the sight. It was like looking back in time. The ballroom was done up as it had been so many decades ago, when Richard and Cat were the toast of the town. He remembered Hollywood in its giddy, golden days—or rather, its nights, all the opulence, the decadence, the parties that lasted for days with the biggest stars, the most powerful producers, all swept up in a fever of a kind of success that had never existed in the world before. A new type of royalty, crowned by the millions of filmgoers all over the world.

Richard was standing in the middle of the dance floor, dressed in a slightly baggy tuxedo. He was snapping his fingers along with the jazz quartet that was playing in the corner of the room. He turned around when he heard them enter, a smile lighting up his face.

"My darling!" he said as he approached Cat. He took her hand and kissed it. "You look ravishing."

She dipped her head and smiled coyly. "Do you really think so?"

"Yes, of course! You are exactly as you were." He gestured to the room. "It will all be as it was." He turned to Lo. "And don't you look lovely as well. If it were eighty years ago, I would sign you to a contract just on your face alone."

Lo's face twitched, but she managed a smile. It was forced and quite unnerving, but a smile nonetheless.

Richard returned it. "Silence suits you." It was an obvious jab, as if he were gauging her reaction. Her smile remained in place.

Richard chuckled and turned to John. "You look good as well. Very dashing." He looked at last at Felix. "I trust I'll have no trouble from you tonight?" Richard's blue gaze was as sharp as a shard of glass.

Felix looked away, to John—his almost-husband. "Why would I give you trouble?" He took John's free hand in his own. "He is my witch. I do as he commands."

"What a charming answer!" He turned to John and winked. "It seems the domestication process is coming along splendidly."

John said nothing. His nonresponse did not seem to bother Richard, however, whose attention was back with Cat. He took her by the hand and pulled her toward the dance floor. "Come, my darling—let's dance. Do you remember how?"

"Of course I do. I had lessons from Ginger Rogers, if you recall." She twirled away from him. "The real question is if *you* can keep up, old man."

This was the old Cat—beautiful and flirtatious and a little bit mean. It had always driven the men wild for some reason. It still seemed to work on Richard, because instead of getting angry, he laughed and took her in his frail arms.

"Be gentle with me for now, my love, but within the hour, you will find no complaints with my stamina."

As they danced, the rest of them took a seat at one of the tables. Bizarrely, the whole room had been set as if they were expecting fifty guests. The couple of waiters Richard had conjured up showed no sign of thinking any of it was unusual. One brought over a tray of champagne; he and John each took one, but Lo downed two flutes in quick succession and grabbed a third before the waiter left.

Felix only sipped at his. He wanted to face this moment clearly. Despite Cat and John's fears for him, there was a part of him that was actually happy. He was certain they were overstating the danger. He dealt with great pain through Richard's punishments before. Surely having a heart was less intense than being continually burned to a crisp for weeks. After all, all mortals had hearts and they seemed fine to him. And why shouldn't he be happy on the night of his wedding?

He smiled at John, but John wasn't looking at him. He was watching Richard. Lo's attention was similarly taken by the dancing couple. They were an odd sight—Cat, so perfectly beautiful, and Richard, wretchedly old and deceptively frail-looking. The thought of Richard at full strength did give Felix pause; *that* was what worried him the most.

After the dance, Richard and Cat joined them at the table. Richard's chest was heaving. The waiter returned with the champagne. Cat took a flute, but Richard waved them off.

"Water," he wheezed. "And entrees."

The waiter left without a word. It took a few moments for Richard to catch his breath enough to speak. "I had considered a four-course meal, but alas, my appetite is not what it used to be. Besides, I am anxious to get to the heart of the matter." He smirked. "So to speak."

Their entrees arrived swiftly—only for the mortals at the table. It was steak. "Dear me—I hadn't thought to ask how you like your steak. I always have mine rare," Richard said. "I hope that's acceptable."

Lo pulled out a piece of paper from her clutch and wrote. She handed the paper to Richard.

"You're vegetarian?" Richard said after reading it. Felix tensed, expecting Richard to be displeased. From Lo's expression, it seemed like she was also expecting him to be displeased, but looked cheerful about it.

However, she was to be disappointed, because Richard took it in stride. "You know, Mary Pickford was a vegetarian. I always made sure I planned for that; my skills as a host are somewhat deteriorated." He waved the waiter over. "Have the chef make a pasta dish for the young lady."

Lo scowled and then jumped a little, as if someone had kicked her under the table. Cat was giving her a pointed look. Lo's face contorted into a blander expression.

When the mortals were finished eating, Richard stood. "Take five, boys," he called over to the band. The music stopped. Richard turned back to them. "If you would follow me to the courtyard, we can begin the ceremony."

They all trailed after him. The courtyard was filled with roses of every color and variety—pinks and yellows, but most of all red. There was a pulpit set up in the middle; in front of it were a few chairs.

"Ladies, if you will have a seat," Richard said, gesturing to the chairs. As they sat down, Richard turned to Felix and John. "I considered bringing someone in to officiate, but seeing as Felix has no legal identity, it would be rather pointless. I will serve as officiant for you." He turned to Cat. "I'm afraid that means we will have no one to preside over our vows."

Cat waved her hand dismissively. "Why would we need one? The vows are between you and I, and that's all that matters. In fact, why don't we exchange them now? I have something prepared."

"Do you, now?" He took her hands in his own. "By all means, proceed."

Cat cleared her throat and began. "'*Doubt thou the stars are fire; Doubt that the sun doth move; Doubt truth to be a liar; But never doubt I love.*'" She leaned in and gave him a kiss.

"That was beautiful," Richard said with a smile. "I recognize the Bard, but can't quite place the play."

"*Hamlet*," she said. "It's quoted from a letter from Hamlet to Ophelia. That's before he rebuffs her and she goes off to drown herself, naturally."

Richard's pleased expression flickered. "Not exactly a cheerful context."

"Oh, but Ophelia was the role I played after I had your heart in my breast. Don't you remember? You told me I would win an Oscar for it, once I was able to fully appreciate the mortal condition." She smiled and batted her eyelashes. "I so wanted an Oscar, and you were right. I did get one. As always, you kept your promise."

From the corner of Felix's vision, he could see Lo smirking.

But the explanation seemed to appease Richard. He turned to Felix and John. "Take your places in front of the pulpit, if you would."

They did so. Richard took his place as well. He cleared his throat. "Dearly beloved—" He shot a look at Cat. "And dearly newly acquainted," he added with a nod and a wink to Lo, who crossed her arms and looked away. "We are gathered here tonight to witness the joining of this man and this vampire in unending matrimony."

Felix and John locked gazes. This was it. They only had a few moments before everything changed. John looked nervous. In fact, he had gone nearly white. Felix reached out and took both of John's hands in his own.

"Do you, John, take Felix to be your symbolically wedded husband, to have and to hold, for better—but not worse, for richer—never poorer, in eternal life and health, for as long as you both shall live?" He smirked. "That is to say, forever?"

Cat laughed as if he'd made a wonderfully witty comment, but John's face remained deadly serious.

"I do," he said quietly.

Felix felt a little flutter, almost as if he had a heart already. "I do as well!"

"Eager, are we?" Richard said with a laugh. "Very well. I pronounce thee wed. You may now kiss."

Felix drew John close and kissed him, although John did not meet him enthusiastically. Cat clapped—alone at first and then joined reluctantly by Lo.

Richard waited until they parted. "And now, the more important ceremony. Place one hand on each other's chest."

They did as they were told. John was shaking.

Richard continued. "Now, John, repeat after me—"

"Wait," John said. His breath was shallow.

Richard raised an eyebrow. "Not changing your mind, are you?"

John shook his head. "No, no, I just—" He launched forward suddenly, taking Felix in his arms and kissing him again. "I love you," he said when he pulled away. His face was wet with tears. He drew him into another fierce embrace. "Remember," he whispered in Felix's ear. "Please, remember."

Richard cleared his throat. "Very touching. Can we continue?"

Reluctantly, John pulled away. He gave Richard a shaky nod before turning to Felix again. They looked into each other's eyes, not wavering for a moment.

"Repeat after me: *To mine own love, I give my heart/that which is joined will never part.*"

John said the words, his voice shaky. Felix felt a strange tingle inside his chest that grew stronger by the second. Soon, his whole breast felt abuzz.

"And now Felix, your turn. *Fill at last this empty space/which now will be your heart's true place.*"

As soon as the last word left Felix's lips, he felt a *thud* inside of him. For one brief moment, everything around them seemed to vanish, and it was just he and John, their essences twined together so tightly it was as if they were one. Felix could feel that John felt the same way, because their feelings were one and the same. Their gazes were still locked; Felix could see himself reflected in John's eyes, as blue and deep as a lake on a clear summer day.

But then John blinked. When he opened his eyes again, his gaze seemed much changed—as if that lake had evaporated into a puddle. A smile began to creep across his face.

At that moment, Felix felt another thud in his chest, this one strong enough to send him stumbling back a few steps. The thud in his chest continued. Every beat brought pain, like he was being stabbed.

Richard handed him a towel he'd produced from the pulpit. "You're going to need this. I'm afraid this will be a bit messy, although it should pass soon. You should probably sit down."

Felix tried to walk to the chairs, but he started to waver. He was caught by Lo and Cat, who were suddenly by his side, concern in their eyes. He tried to say something, but instead, he spit out a mouthful of blood.

"Be careful," Richard said to the girls. "He'll get your dresses dirty."

When Richard turned his attention away from them, Lo gave him the finger.

They got Felix to a chair and helped him wipe his face. Felix held the towel to his face as blood continued to stream out of his mouth. That thud inside him was relentless; he felt as if his bones would shatter. Felix looked to John, hoping for some comfort, but John had turned to Richard.

"Is he going to be all right?" John asked. He sounded more curious than concerned.

"Of course," Richard replied. "It's just his body getting accustomed to the heart. It will pass."

Cat ran her hand in soothing circles over his back. "Shhh, brother. The pain will pass."

But that wasn't true, was it? This was what Cat had been trying to warn him about.

John didn't notice. He and Richard were still talking about something, all smiles and chuckles, although Felix couldn't quite make out what they were saying.

After a moment, Richard spoke a little louder. "There's one more thing for us to do," he said. "Shouldn't take but a moment."

He put his hand on John's shoulder. A light flashed, so brightly Felix flinched. His vision was whited out for a few moments, but once it returned to him, he was greeted with a very strange sight. At first he thought Richard had vanished, leaving another man standing in his place. But no, it wasn't another man. It was Richard, his youth restored. John appeared unchanged.

John and Richard both laughed with delight.

"You *are* very dashing!" John said. And he was: his hair was black again, with just a little bit of wave. Felix understood now why he'd worn a baggy tux; with his youth restored, he'd gained at least two inches in height as his spine became straight and strong again. His shoulders had broadened, too: Richard had cut quite an imposing figure in his day, and he'd regained that strength now. His face was smooth, with his cheekbones sharp again, no longer concealed under excess skin. His thin mustache was as dark as his hair.

Richard strode over to Cat and pulled her into his arms for a kiss. "Not such an old man now, eh, my love?"

"N-no," Cat stammered. Her eyes were wide; she seemed taken aback by his transformation. Felix couldn't blame her. It was as if they'd traveled back in time to the first day they'd set eyes on the dangerously handsome movie producer who would change their fates forever.

"I feel like dancing again, don't you?"

Before she could answer, Richard put an arm under her knees and swept her off her feet, like a groom carrying his bride, which Felix supposed was accurate enough. He carried her through the courtyard and back into the ballroom, leaving the rest of them behind.

When they were gone, John at last approached Felix and Lo, who was still sitting beside Felix, one hand on his shoulder. The pain in his chest had still not abated. Every beat of his new heart felt like shards of glass were ripping him apart from the inside.

John cocked his head as he looked down at Felix. "Does it hurt a lot?"

Felix couldn't bring himself to speak, so he simply nodded. His body jerked again, and he spit out another mouthful of blood.

John's lip curled slightly in disgust. "Well, I'm sure it will get better soon." He patted Felix's shoulder. When John touched him, his expression shifted ever so slightly; he blinked rapidly, as though he were confused. "But it's for the best." His gaze darted over to Lo. "We *did* decide it was for the best, didn't we?"

Lo's body was tense beside him, but she managed a brief nod.

John smiled. "Good." He gave Felix's shoulder one last pat. "I'm going to the ballroom. Come join me when you've gotten yourself together." With that, he wandered off.

Lo put her arm around Felix, squeezing his shoulders. Some time passed, although Felix couldn't be sure how much. The pain did start to abate, becoming duller although not disappearing. He stopped coughing up blood. When he felt steady enough, he rose to his feet. With Lo's help, they made their way to the ballroom.

The band was in full swing again. John was sitting at a table, enjoying a martini as he watched Richard whisk Cat around the dance floor. The moment she caught sight of Felix, she stopped dancing.

"Whatever is the matter?" Richard asked her.

"I'm tired."

Richard laughed. "That can't be true, darling. We used to dance for hours. Do you remember?" He followed her gaze to Felix. "Ah, I see. You'd like to see your brother. Very well." He released her.

She crossed the room and embraced him. "We should get you to your room."

Richard laughed. "What, and end the night so early? This is, after all, his wedding!"

John picked up his drink and sauntered over to Felix. "Yeah." He was swaying a little, his words slightly slurred. "It's our wedding. Don't you want to dance? Richard says you're an excellent dancer."

"He's not up to it," Cat said sharply.

Richard crossed the room to join them. He looked to Cat. "I must say that your joy at my restoration seems somewhat subdued."

Cat managed a smile. "Of course I am delighted, but let me see to my brother. Please."

He sighed dramatically. "Very well, let's take a break." He gestured to a waiter. "More drinks!"

Richard and John sat down; both seemed completely oblivious to the unhappiness of their companions.

Richard reached into the inside of his jacket. "Actually, this is a good opportunity for me to give you your wedding present." He handed John a small box.

"Thanks," John said, accepting it. "Can I open it now?"

"By all means."

It was a silver cigarette case, as well as a fancy lighter, much nicer than the one that Felix had stolen from him.

"You'll find that it is filled with hand-rolled cigarettes made of the finest tobacco. No more cheap dime-store cigarettes for you."

John laughed a little. "They're a lot more expensive than a dime nowadays." He opened the case, took one out, and lit it. "Really nice. Smooth." He took another drag. "You know, I always wondered whether I'd get cancer before the curse got me. Like, maybe the guy who was going to kill me was one of those angel-of-death nurse serial killers who prey on their patients." He laughed. "I suppose neither will now."

Richard laughed as well. "Indeed! May I have one?"

John passed the case to Richard. He even lit his cigarette.

The two of them continued to smoke and talk and laugh, although Felix lost the thread of the conversation. The drumming of his new heart drowned out the sound around him. He put his hands over his ears, as if he could stop it.

He became aware of another argument between Cat and Richard. It ended with Cat pulling Felix to his feet. He dropped his hands from his ears.

"...be back after I put him to bed," Cat was saying. "He'll spoil the fun."

Richard waved his hand. "Very well. Hurry back."

Lo rose as well, but Richard put a hand on her shoulder. "You aren't going anywhere. Why don't you take a spin around the dance floor with me while Cat's away?"

Lo recoiled. Richard rolled his eyes. "Come, now, be a good sport. I'll give you your voice back. Surely that's worth a dance?"

"Oh, don't make me share you!" Cat said, her voice unnaturally boisterous again.

Richard smirked. "Jealous, are you?"

Cat put her arms around Richard's neck. "Hopelessly." She kissed him. "Lo can see to Felix," she said when they parted. "She's not in the mood to be much fun, either. I will dance all night with you." She dropped her voice. "Unless you want to take me to bed right now?"

Richard's hand moved over her body. "Mmmm, that does sound appealing." He looked briefly to John. "Do you mind?"

"Not at all," John said. He approached Felix, looking him up and down with his shallow, empty eyes. "I suppose he isn't up to enjoying a wedding night, is he?" John was looking at Felix but directing his conversation to Richard, as if Felix's thoughts on the matter were completely incidental.

"I don't imagine so."

"He is going to get better, isn't he?"

"Oh yes," Richard replied. "It will be a week or so. A month at the most."

John frowned. "A month? That long?"

"What is a month in the face of eternity?"

"Good point." He brushed a hand over Felix's cheek and then trailed it down his body until he reached his hip. "I suppose we'll have to delay our honeymoon," he said, addressing Felix directly at last.

Felix looked away; he couldn't bear those empty eyes.

They exited the ballroom with Felix leaning on Lo's slight frame. They mounted the stairs. When they got to the top, Richard turned to John. "I've had a couple rooms made up for you and Lo—they're down that hall. You'll find your cat there. Don't hesitate to ask the staff if there's anything you need."

"Will do," John said with a smile.

"Excellent." Richard turned back to Cat. "And now, if you don't mind, my bride and I will retire." They disappeared into Cat's room.

When they were gone, John lingered, sliding up to Felix. "Sure you aren't up for it?" he asked, one hand looping over Felix's waist.

Lo shoved John away. She got out her pad and scribbled something furiously and then thrust the paper into John's hand. His eyes narrowed as he read it. He crumpled it up and threw it on the floor.

"We all agreed to this," he said sharply. "No need to be so sensitive."

Lo crossed her arms and glared.

"Fine," John spat. "But I didn't sign up for an eternity of moping." He turned around and stomped off down the hall.

Felix was going to ask her what the note had said but found he lacked the energy. Lo helped him into his room, brought him over to the bed, and then helped him out of his jacket.

She went into the bathroom. A moment later, Felix heard water running. When she returned, she wrote another note and handed it to him. *Ran you a bath*, it said. *Anything else I can do?*

Felix shook his head. "No." He tried to smile. "Thank you. I will be fine."

She bit her lip and then wrote another note. Felix read it. *100 days* was all it said.

He tried to smile. "One hundred days," he agreed. But every beat of his heart felt like an eternity; he couldn't even begin to comprehend that long.

She gave him another hug before she left and shut the door gently behind her.

With effort, Felix stripped out of the rest of his clothes and dropped them on the floor on the way to the bathroom. He slid into the bath until he was completely submerged. The warm water soothed him somewhat, muting the world as it engulfed him. Felix closed his eyes and drifted under the water. As an undead creature, he didn't need to breathe, so he could stay under water as long as he liked.

His chest still hurt, but the physical pain he felt now was negligible compared with the sorrow that swamped him—all the guilt and regret of more than a century crowded into his newly acquired heart. And John, his true love, the man for whom he swore he would bear this pain, had no care for him. None at all.

He had gained a heart and had it broken all at the same time.

Seventeen: One Hundred Days

AFTER THE WEDDING, Felix drifted in and out of torpor. He seemed to slip in and out of consciousness, his life becoming one long, strange dream. There was guilt, yes—as great as Cat had warned him. The blood that sustained him was full of fear—of violation—of pain. Every moment he was awake, he felt those jolts of terror, just as his victims must have. He felt poisoned by it. He thought of all his nameless victims over the years—no, not only nameless. They were faceless as well. He remembered so few of them, no more than a person would remember the cow that made his steak. He didn't know if that was better or worse.

He would remember from here on out, he knew.

John's cat slept near his head often, purring softly. Felix was aware sometimes of Lo or Cat by his side. Other times, he found himself in some gray, rainy realm, with Adelaide standing over him with an umbrella in hand. She could never keep him completely dry, although she tried.

John never came.

He didn't see him until after he came back into the waking world. He couldn't place a clear pinpoint on exactly when it happened; it felt fuzzy, like everything else. No one was with him. He wanted to stay in bed forever, but his body ached with hunger—more deeply than he had felt it in a long time. He sat up; the world swirled. The beat in his chest unsteadied him. Looking down, he saw that he was dressed in silk pajamas.

When he'd gotten a hold of himself, he gingerly got out of bed and padded barefoot out of his room. A quick glance at the clock on the wall told him it was 8:30. The sun was down, but only just. He went to Cat's room, but astonishingly, she was not there. Neither did he see Lo. Confused, he continued down the hallway. Where could they be?

He heard laughter and male voices coming from downstairs. He hesitated; there was a part of him that yearned to see John. Every painful thump of his—no, *John's*—heart pushed Felix toward him, and yet he knew the creature downstairs was not his John. Not truly.

But the heart won out, as hearts tend to do. Summoning his courage, he descended the stairs and followed the sounds to the library. When he opened the door, he saw Richard and John standing in front of a giant canvas propped up on an easel. John wore a smock and held a pallet of paint in one hand. Paints and tools rested on a table beside him.

Richard saw him first. "Felix!" he said brightly. "You're up and around again!" He gestured. "Don't just lurk in the doorway—come in."

Felix obeyed.

"I like the pajamas," John said with a grin. "How are you feeling?"

Felix had no words for what he was feeling, so he didn't answer.

John frowned and turned to Richard. "Is this normal? Can't he talk?"

"Perfectly ordinary," Richard reassured him. "Cat did not speak for several weeks after our wedding."

"She spoke to me," Felix said, earning him startled looks from both men.

John laughed. "That solves that mystery!"

Felix looked at the canvas. "What are you doing?"

"Painting. It's what I dreamed I would do," John said. He paused. "Or, well—I never really let myself have dreams." He smiled again. "But now I can have as many of them as I want!"

"It should be easy," Richard said. "Just a little push on some influential critics—"

"I don't care how much magic you use," John said, interrupting him. "I'm going to have to put something on this canvas before we can start anything!"

John looked thoughtfully at the blank canvas for a few moments. He took it off the easel and put it on the ground. After taking a tube of red paint from the table, he squirted a large glob of it right in the center. He knelt beside the canvas and put his fist in it, pressing down. When he pulled his hand away, the shape he left looked almost like a heart.

He put the canvas back on the easel. The paint dripped, leaving red trails dribbling down the canvas.

"What is it supposed to be?" Felix asked.

John and Richard both laughed, as if he'd made a joke.

"Really, Felix," Richard said. "You're so literal."

That got another laugh out of John. He wiped the paint off his hand with a cloth, but it was still stained red. "I need a break. I am absolutely famished."

Richard and John headed over to the next room, where a luncheon spread had been set out. John wasn't kidding; he ate as though he was starved, devouring a sandwich in mere minutes before grabbing another and disposing of it just as quickly. He selected an orange and began to peel.

As Felix watched, he noticed something. "What's that ring?"

John paused. "Oh, this?" He held out his hand. It was a gold band with a large amber stone—just like Richard's. "It was a gift from Richard."

"He's going to need it," Richard said. "To store his power."

John went back to peeling the orange, sinking his fingers into the juicy flesh as he ripped it apart.

Richard gave Felix a look. "He's hungry, you know."

"I can see that."

Richard shook his head. "He needs more than this. You feel it, too. It's why you got up, isn't it?"

Felix didn't bother to deny it, but he didn't answer, either.

John finished his orange, licking the juice from his fingers. He moved toward Felix until they were face-to-face. Or well, face to chest—Felix still towered over him. Even so, Felix felt paradoxically small beside him.

John reached out and put a hand on the back of Felix's head, pulling him down into a kiss. The heart in Felix's chest beat more quickly, each thud sending a burst of pain through him.

"We'll follow Cat's rules," John said. "Only those who are already suicidal. Lo says she'll help find them."

Just the thought of it made Felix's stomach clench into knots. John must have sensed some hesitation in him, because his grip on Felix's head tightened. "It has to be done. Soon." He kissed him again, harder this time. "I'm so *hungry*—"

Felix broke away. "I know."

John frowned. "Where is Lo, by the way?"

"She and Cat were going shopping," Richard said. "She's been so much better lately. I knew bringing in another female would be good for her."

John snorted. "I didn't think Lo was really the type to appreciate retail therapy. But I hope they're enjoying themselves." John turned back to the table. "I need cake," he said. "And strawberries."

"Then brandy and cigars," Richard suggested.

"It's like you read my mind!" John turned to Felix. "I'll let Lo know you're up."

He'd been dismissed. John and Richard were talking again; John didn't even watch Felix leave. He returned to his bedroom. What else was there to do? He lay down on his bed and curled up into a ball, trying to stave off the hunger inside him.

Some time later, the door to his room opened. Both Cat and Lo entered. He couldn't bring himself to get up to greet them. One of them turned on the light; he winced and retreated under the covers.

Cat sat down on the bed beside him. "They said you were awake." Gently, she folded back the covers until he was exposed.

Felix snatched them back. "I don't want to be."

Cat smoothed a hand over his hair. "Brother, you have to get up."

Felix just shook his head.

Lo sat down on his other side. She took a hold of his arm and forced him into a sitting position. She was surprisingly strong, although in truth Felix wasn't putting up much of a fight.

"I know it sucks, but we need you."

"You got your voice back," Felix said. "How?"

Lo let out a dramatic sigh and rolled her eyes. "Don't ask. It involved a lot of bullshit."

"Has he hurt you?"

"Nah," Lo said. "Cat's got Richard wrapped around her finger. Gross for her, but good for us."

"I didn't mean Richard," Felix said quietly.

They were all silent for a moment. "That's not really him," Lo said. "We knew this was going to happen." Lo half smiled. "And hey, you slept through about ten days of it. So only ninety more to go."

"*Only* ninety more?" Felix said with sudden anger. "How can you say *only* when each moment feels like torture?"

Cat shushed and petted him. "I know, dear. I know."

Felix looked at her as if for the first time. She had been bearing this pain for decades. She *did* know—far better than him.

"I'm sorry." His voice was barely more than a whisper. "All these years you've borne this, and I was blind to it."

She brushed a strand of hair away from his face. "No need to be sorry. It was by design. My one comfort was that you were spared." She smiled a little. "You may not recall, but you were not without sympathy."

It was true. He had held her often in those weeks following her wedding, when she did nothing but sleep and weep. He was perplexed at her pain, but she was his sister. And when Richard had come to demand she fulfill her duty, he had stood up to him. That was when his own punishment had started—the weeks in the glass coffin, where he burned continuously. By the time he was released, Cat no longer wept. Instead, she withdrew from the world. They had never spoken of those times since then.

Felix wrapped his arms around her and tried very hard not to start crying. What miserable wretches they were.

Finally, Lo cleared her throat, causing the two of them to part. "Okay, now that we're done with that wallow, we need to get this over with."

"What do you mean?" Felix asked.

"You're going to have to feed. One a month—that's what Cat said."

Felix moaned and lay back on the bed. "I can't." He shook his head. "I can't!"

Lo hauled him up again. "I said wallowing time is over. You think that I want to do this, either?" She took a deep breath. "It's only for three months. Anyone we take is going to live through this. Once we have the cures for ourselves, we'll cure them, too. You need to be brave."

Felix looked back and forth between Lo and Cat, who both had more bravery in their little fingers than he had in his whole body. And he was behaving like a coward. "All right," he said, straightening himself up as best he could.

Lo patted him on the shoulder and then stood up and sighed. "Guess that means I'm up." She gritted her teeth. "I'm going to find someone for you. Don't know how long it will take, but I'll be back tonight." She thrust out her chin. "Ninety more days," Lo muttered, mostly to herself. She left the room, leaving Cat and Felix alone.

Felix put his head in his hands. Cat ran a hand in soothing circles over his back as he collected himself.

"He's so changed," Felix said after some time. "The way he spoke to me...the way he looked at me. Like I was a possession of his—a useful tool, or a plaything, but not as myself."

Cat cupped his face in her hands and pulled him upward to meet his eyes. "Lo has told me much of him. He is a good man, and he will be again. You must have faith." She smiled a little sadly. "At least you have that much. Richard was never a good man. I just didn't have the ability to see it, until it was too late."

"But perhaps he was, before he became heartless," Felix said. "As you said, we didn't have a moral sense. Perhaps he was better than we remembered."

Cat scoffed. "Not likely. He never had a moment's qualm about our predatory nature. In fact, he took pleasure in it. No, he was quite wicked, even before he lost his heart."

"But weren't we wicked in our lives as well? As you have said, we led lives of great selfishness." Felix frowned. "Come to think of it, why would Richard's heart put moral sense into you? It is not a particularly good heart."

Cat was quiet for a moment. "I don't really know. We were wicked, yes, but we weren't sadistic. Swindling fools out of their money is one thing. Taking active pleasure in their pain is another. Were we still human, I think we would have recoiled at what we've become. Having a heart again restored my own humanity—it was not imported from him."

"But we were still predators. Does it really matter whether or not we were capable of feeling remorse? In a way, didn't that make it worse? That we knew wrong but did it anyway?"

Cat sighed. "I'm afraid I am at the peak of my abilities to contemplate moral philosophy." She kissed him on the cheek. "We can only move forward, as Lo is fond of saying."

"You two have really taken a liking to each other, haven't you?"

Cat smiled a little shyly. "Well, she is a very admirable person. Quite forthright and brave. And it's nice to have a friend."

"I'm glad of it," he said. "Truly."

Cat smiled again, but then her expression grew more serious. "Do you want me to wait here with you?"

"No. I could use some time to collect myself."

"Very well." She stood. "Don't hesitate to come to me after it's done."

"I won't."

With that, she left.

Felix tried to motivate himself to get up, get changed into some real clothes, or brush his hair, which must surely seem a fright. But his ambition failed him, so he simply sat on his bed and waited.

THE MOMENT LO let the poor creature into the room, Felix pounced. It was over quickly. It helped that he really was hungry. He barely looked at the wan face of the man, choosing instead to huddle in his bed while Lo and Cat bore his comatose body away. He went straight to the bathroom to clean himself, standing in the shower with the water as scalding hot as he could stand. His body, newly infused with blood, went pink under the heat.

Cat came back later to comfort him, but he sent her away. The other cat had little use for Felix's orders and installed herself, purring, on the pillow again. The aches of Felix's body had left him, but the mental anguish had increased. Is this how Cat felt all the time? Another stab of self-loathing stabbed through him.

Later, around three in the morning, his door opened. He sat up in bed, expecting to see Cat and wondering what she wanted. But it wasn't Cat. It was John.

John stood for a moment, a dark silhouette in front of the light coming in from the hallway. Part of Felix hoped he would leave, but another part wanted him to stay. His heart—*their* heart—beat more quickly, as if it wished to leap out of his chest and back to its rightful home. He loathed what John had become, but he longed to have him close all the same.

As soon as John entered the room, the cat hissed and jumped off the bed. John scowled as she shot out of the room. "That cat would be dead without me. You'd think she'd show a little loyalty."

Felix said nothing.

John crossed the room and sat down on the edge of the bed. "How are you feeling?"

"Do you really want to know?"

"I suppose I know already. Richard said it would be hard for you at first. But it will get better with time." He sighed. "You're going to have to learn to use your head and ignore your heart. It's lying to you right now, like it used to lie to me. We aren't doing anything wrong, to end lives that want to be ended anyway—"

"*Stop!*" Felix cried, his voice so loud that it took both of them by surprise. "Just—stop. I do not wish to discuss it."

John was quiet for a moment. "All right," he said, but didn't get up from the bed. Instead, he reached out and touched Felix's hand. Felix wanted to push him away, or to pull him close. He couldn't decide so he did nothing. When Felix didn't rebuff him, John moved closer still. He put a hand over Felix's chest. Slowly, he undid the buttons on his shirt, one by one, until his hand lay over Felix's bare chest.

"I can still feel it beating, you know," he said quietly. "My heart, I mean. Like an echo in an empty cavern." His breath was coming heavier now; it had the same stink as Richard's, only not as strong. "Richard says that Cat hated him for a long time. Do you hate me?"

Remember. That had been the real John's last word to him. "Never," Felix said softly. "I could never hate you."

John smirked. "That's what I told Richard. He owes me five dollars."

Felix just stared at him for a moment, utterly appalled at this smirking, self-satisfied creature that had replaced his thoughtful, melancholy John. The pain in his heart, which had abated, now returned, hitting him like a spike into the very core of him with every beat.

John closed the last inch between them and kissed him. It was like something had broken loose in Felix; he pushed John back on the bed, covering his body with his own. John moaned and thrust upward, rolling their hips together. They were both hard already; desire flooded through Felix so thick and fast that he was made brainless by it, rutting against John like an animal. John ran his hands up Felix's back under the shirt, pushing the fabric down Felix's shoulders. Felix stripped it off the rest of the way and then wrapped his arms around John, his grip fierce as they kissed again, viciously. Felix's bared fangs slashed against John's lip and cheek, causing him to bleed.

John pushed him off with a shout. Felix released him. The cut was deep; blood streamed out of it. They stared at one another for a moment, John's chest heaving with the force of his breath. John wiped his mouth with the back of his hand, smearing the blood on his face. Briefly, Felix wondered if he was going to leave, but then he reached for Felix again. John kissed Felix's neck as he ran his hands over Felix's shoulders. The coppery scent of John's blood filled his nostrils, exciting him in spite of himself.

John pulled back just enough to remove his own shirt. They came together again, their bare chests pressed against each other as John continued to lavish attention on Felix's neck and shoulders, smearing him with his own blood. They parted to remove the rest of their clothing.

John had come prepared, a bottle of lube in his pocket. He pressed it into Felix's hand, and he accepted it. Felix wanted to be inside of him, the way the real John was inside of Felix. With shaky hands, he prepared John and himself. He lined himself up and pushed inside. John wailed, his back arching off the bed, his hands twisting in the sheets.

Their coupling was brutal; Felix held nothing back. John's moans grew louder with each thrust until he was nearly screaming. Felix bent forward and licked his tongue over John's mouth, lapping up the blood there. John's tongue met his own, tangling them together briefly before he drew back, his head hitting the bed, his moans growing more frantic. Felix could feel John's hand working his own cock as Felix fucked him, moving faster and faster, and then John screamed and spilled himself all over his stomach. His climax pulled Felix's own as he pushed in for one last thrust, emptying everything he had inside him.

Felix collapsed on top of John, his cock still inside him. John let out a grunt but did not push him away. Felix buried his head in the crook of John's neck; his chest hurt with the painful beating of their heart. The heaving of John's chest moved them both, heavily at first, then more gently as John caught his breath. Felix's heartbeat slowed, too.

Eventually, Felix found the strength to raise his head. When he looked down at John, he was surprised to see tears coursing down his cheeks.

"Did I hurt you?" he asked.

John shook his head. "No. I just—for a moment, I felt like I remembered—" He looked at Felix with some strange expression, his eyes wide as if in awe or shock or fear.

Abruptly, he pushed Felix away. As soon as Felix's cock slid out of him, it was like the spell had been broken. John looked a fright, his stomach smeared in white and his face in red. He used the sheets to hastily wipe himself down.

Felix reached out for him. "John—"

"Don't come looking for me tomorrow," John said, cutting him off. "Richard and I are going out tomorrow to forge me a new legal identity. It will take some effort, seeing how things have become a little more sophisticated since the last time he did it, but I think we'll manage." John beamed. "I'm going to be his son. So we're going out celebrating afterward."

The bleeding from his lip grew heavier; he cursed in annoyance, but then his expression shifted.

"Do you want to see a trick?" John didn't wait for Felix's response. He held his hand over his face; the ring on his finger glowed momentarily. When he pulled his hand away, his face was healed.

"Pretty amazing, huh?" He smiled. "And we've only got one life so far. Imagine what will happen when we have more." He picked up the sheet again and wiped his face. "You're going to need to be a little more careful with that next time." He gave Felix a pat on the ass. "It was good, though. Glad you're back to normal." He got up and left without a backward glance.

Felix pulled the blankets over himself, not bothering to dress himself again. He closed his eyes and tried to wish himself into unconsciousness, but it didn't work.

Shortly after, there was a knock at the door. He didn't have the energy to answer it. After a few more knocks, the door opened and someone entered. Felix uncurled himself enough to see who it was.

"Felix? Are you all right? I just saw John leave..."

When Felix didn't answer, Lo walked over to the bed. "Jesus Christ," she said as she pulled back the covers. "Whose blood is this?"

Felix still couldn't bring himself to answer. Lo's gaze skittered down to give him a quick look, then skittered right back up again. "Right, so, I think I can figure out what he came here for." She added, more quietly, "Did he force you?"

"No," Felix said, finally speaking up. "I wanted him, too. So badly it ached. Does it make me terrible that I would crave his touch still?"

"Of course it doesn't make you terrible!" Lo sucked in a breath and then let it out slowly. "I'm going to run you a bath. You're going to get cleaned up, and then we're moving you to Cat's room. No arguing." She added the last bit before Felix had a chance to say anything. "Do you need help?"

Felix shook his head, and Lo went to the bathroom and started the bath. While it was running, she re-entered the bedroom and picked out some clothes, which she laid out on the bed.

"I'm going to give you some privacy," she said. "Come to Cat's room when you're ready."

Felix did as he was told. When he entered Cat's room, he found Lo pacing back and forth, clearly having some witchly thoughts. Cat ushered him in, urging him to sit beside her on the sofa. They both watched the witch, waiting for her pronouncement.

"Okay," she said at last. "This is what we're doing. I'm going to make an image of Felix in bed. We're going to tell John you've gone back under. Meanwhile, you stay in here."

"Why?" Felix asked.

"Because one, you are clearly more than a little fucked up and not in the position to be having sex, and two, when John finally comes back to himself, he is not exactly going to cherish the memories of him taking advantage of you!"

Felix frowned. "Do you think he would be fooled by such a simple trick?"

"Yes," she said. "Because becoming heartless apparently also makes you a moron. He and Richard are too busy making plans to pay much attention to what I'm up to. Richard thinks he's got me tamed, especially since I performed my 'duties' so well tonight." She smiled grimly. "What a couple of dumbasses."

"And when it becomes time for us to perform our duties again?" Felix asked.

"Same deal. We'll 'wake' you up and then you'll appear to go right back under."

Cat still looked concerned. "Won't Richard find him here when he comes to see me?"

"No, because you'll go to him. No one but us will come in this room." She looked back and forth between the two of them. "We're going to get through this. Do you believe me?"

"Yes," they said simultaneously.

She nodded. "Good. Now if you'll excuse me, I'm going back to my room to throw up. This has been the worst fucking day of my entire life."

When she was gone, Cat squeezed Felix's shoulders. "There, you see? All will be well. I am sorry I ever doubted the existence of good witches. She has things well in hand." She turned on the television. "Now, let's have a rest from thinking about all this unpleasantness."

Felix couldn't pay much attention to it. He didn't want to discourage Cat, but there was no diverting his attention. He was reminded of his pain with every sharp beat of his heart.

THE NEXT MONTH went by exactly as Lo had said it would. John and Richard did not investigate Lo's claims that he was in torpor. That was good, obviously, but a part of Felix was hurt that John seemed to care so little. The mansion had come to life again, ebbing and flowing with fashionable guests as Richard remade himself into a man of importance once more. He heard the guests sometimes, laughing and carrying on.

Their end of the manor was very quiet. The torpor line wasn't even a total lie. Felix drifted in and out of consciousness, losing track of the days. When he was awake, he watched television, finding himself incapable of gathering up the energy to do much more.

Cat and Lo came and went; Cat often went to Richard's parties, playing the part of his beautiful wife and keeping him distracted. Lo was off doing witchly things. The two of them also went off together. They had the rose to make, after all, using Cat's blood, although they were often gone much longer than it would take to drop her blood on the rose. Felix didn't mind. He was not feeling particularly sociable.

Cat bought a calendar and marked each day off with a big X. At around day sixty-seven, they started to make plans.

"They are both going to have to be distracted," Lo was saying, speaking mostly to Cat. Felix had the television on, watching some news program while he munched on some pills. Cat had stopped taking them entirely.

"I don't think that will be a problem," Cat said. "Both of them are rather easily distracted as of late."

"Yeah, I noticed. They're so confident they've won." Lo scoffed. "I mean, I know that it's a good thing we've got the element of surprise, but I'm still a little insulted that they don't see either of us as a threat."

"So how do you suggest we proceed?"

Lo rubbed her chin. "We need you and Richard and Felix and John near each other. You'll have to be touching for me to transfer your hearts back to them."

"What happens when they have their hearts again?"

"Well, Richard's immortality will be gone, for one."

"And then what?"

Lo ran a hand through her hair. "I don't know. I mean, just getting rid of his immortality should kill him, right? Like, maybe he'll age all those years he's avoided."

"But you don't know that for certain?"

"No, I don't," Lo snapped. "I'm pretty fucking new at this, okay?" She let out a frustrated sound. "Shit. I'm sorry. I just wish I had the answers, but I don't."

"It's all right," Cat said gently. "We're all tense."

Lo rubbed her temples as she thought. "If just taking away his immortality doesn't work, then I guess I'll have to kill him."

"How?"

"I don't know, stab him? Shoot him?"

Cat was very quiet for a moment. "And you would be the one to do it?"

"Yeah." She paused. "Why are you looking at me like that?"

"To take a life is not so easy."

"I've already stabbed him once!"

"While in the heat of the moment, as you were trying to escape. It's different when it's planned."

"Trust me, I have zero qualms about putting this asshole in the ground."

Cat crossed her arms. "I don't know..."

"What, you think I'm going to chicken out?"

"Of course not. It's just that I prefer for you to remain a good witch."

"You think killing him will make me evil?" Lo sounded exasperated. "*Not* killing him would be the evil thing in this situation!"

"Are you certain?"

"Yes, I'm fucking certain. He deserves to die for what he's done! You of all people should know that."

"There, that's precisely my point," Cat said sharply. "I don't like it when witches start talking about who deserves to live and who deserves to die."

"So you're saying, what? That I should spare him?" She paused. When she spoke again, her voice wavered. "Do you still love him?"

"That's not it at all—it's *you* whom I'm concerned for! I don't wish for you to become wicked; I couldn't bear it!"

"For the last time, I'm not turning evil. Stop projecting your experiences with him all over me!"

Felix tuned out of their argument as the news program returned from commercial break. A picture of the Five Star Diner came onto the screen. The reporter started talking about what they were calling the Diner Massacre. Felix really ought to have changed the channel, but instead he found himself fascinated.

Apparently, it had become quite the story. It was easy to see why. The female reporter went over the details—the savageness of the slayings, the mysterious disappearance of the corpse of the murderer and the subsequent vanishing of his accomplices. And then there was the criminal connections of the victims, which is what the reporter was exploring tonight.

A picture of Vince lingered on the screen before cutting to the reporter again. "Tonight I'm speaking with the mother of one of the victims," the reporter was saying. "Marla Ricci, thank you for being with us. I'm so sorry for your loss."

Vince's mother nodded. She was a painfully thin woman with bleach-blonde hair and a careworn face.

"I realize that this must be difficult to talk about, but your son was convicted of gang-related crimes several years ago. Do you think his murder had anything to do with his criminal past?"

"All I can say is he left that life behind him." She jutted out her chin defiantly. "I know he had a past, but he didn't deserve this." She started to cry. "His life was wasted."

Felix watched her cry for a moment, her tears streaking her heavy mascara.

"What is a life for?" Felix wondered out loud.

Cat and Lo stopped their arguing to look at him. Lo looked at the screen to see what he was watching.

"Jesus, Felix. Why the fuck are you watching that?" She picked up the remote and turned the television off.

"If a life can be wasted, that must mean that it's for something," Felix continued. "So what is it for?"

Lo pinched the bridge of her nose. "I'm not really in the mood to be philosophical right now."

Felix's interruption seemed to have punctured Lo and Cat's argument. They all lapsed into silence.

Cat was the one who spoke first. "A film festival," she said. "We put on a film festival of all his old movies with only the five of us as the guests. That will flatter his vanity and keep his attention. John and Richard will be sitting beside one another. I can sit at Richard's other side, and Felix will sit beside John. You can slip behind us and do the transfer."

Lo nodded. "I think that could work. And then you and Felix can have like, wine or something—we'll put the cure in there. As soon as the transfer is complete, you can drink it."

"I'll be heartless again once you make the transfer," Cat said. "Do you think I can be trusted to take the cure?"

"It will be in the space of like five seconds," Lo said. "Is that long enough for you to turn all evil?"

"I don't know." Cat bit her lip. "I would rather die than be as I was before."

Lo sighed. "Tell you what. If I think that you've become a heartless monster, I'll kill you myself. And if you think that I've become totally evil, I give you permission to kill me. Does that make you feel better?"

The corners of Cat's lip quirked upward. "That is indeed comforting to hear."

Lo grinned back. "Oh yeah. And if things go really bad, we can do the full Hamlet ending. Just to be on the safe side."

Cat actually laughed. "How romantically tragic." Then something very extraordinary happened. She kissed Lo. And Lo kissed her back. Felix blinked. What was going on?

"I'm going to go talk to Adelaide," Lo said once they had parted. "Maybe she'll have some ideas." She put a hand on Cat's cheek. "We're going to get out of this, okay?" Lo kissed her one more time before leaving the room.

Felix stared at his sister. "Are you two together?"

"Yes." Cat smoothed a nonexistent wrinkle on her skirt. "Goodness, you *have* been out of it."

"I did not think you would risk pledging yourself to a witch again."

Cat gave him a small smile. "I didn't either."

Felix managed to return the smile. "I'm glad for you. She is a very good witch."

"Do you really think so?" Cat bit her thumbnail. "Are we being fools yet again?"

"If we are fools, then we are fools for love. That at least is something noble to be foolish about."

Cat sighed. She glanced over at the calendar, which depicted a kitten hanging from a tree, its two paws clutching the branch. "I suppose in thirty-three more days, we'll find out."

Cat picked up the remote and turned on the television. They watched a man who traveled the world to experience exotic cuisine.

"I will travel once I'm human," Cat decided. "All over the world. No matter what happens, I will not be imprisoned ever again."

Felix looked around the room. It *was* a prison, despite its finery. He had been so out of it he hadn't considered it, but now he felt as if the walls were contracting.

He stood up. "I'm going for a walk."

Cat looked up at him. "Do you think that's wise?"

"Perhaps not, but I think I'll go insane if I can't leave this room at all for the next month." He paused. "Well, *more* insane."

"What will you do if you see John?"

"Talk to him, I suppose."

"Lo won't like that."

"Will she punish me?"

"Of course not!"

"Then I will do as I please."

Cat let out an annoyed sigh. "Very well. Don't be long."

Felix left the room. He wasn't sure quite where he wanted to go. There was noise coming from the dining room, so he opted to jump out the window. He told himself the noise was good, since it meant John was distracted and unlikely to run into him. But in truth, there was a part of him that wished to see him again, however foolish that was.

He zipped over to the gardens, slowing to walk the winding paths. The paths burst into light; Richard must have activated the motion-sensored lights again. Felix wondered if the activation of the lights would draw attention. The artificial lights cast a harsh glow over the flowers, but he enjoyed the sight nonetheless. He wondered where Cat and Lo were growing the rose; probably not here, lest Richard or John discover it.

He'd been walking for about half an hour when he saw a figure coming toward him. Felix stopped in his tracks, his heart beating a little more quickly. It was John, dressed in a fine shirt and trousers—nothing like the old beat-up clothes he used to wear.

"Felix!" John said, smiling widely. "You're up!"

"I am."

John was at his side now, with that smile still on his face, as artificial as the lights around them. "You should have come to me. We're having a party with some friends. I'd love to introduce you—none of them believe I actually have a husband."

Felix shook his head. "Perhaps some other time."

John's smile flickered. "So you aren't better yet."

There was no good answer, so Felix said nothing.

"Well, you're walking around again," John said when it became apparent Felix wouldn't answer him. "That's something, I guess."

"I suppose it is."

John trotted out in front of him, blocking his way. "If you won't come to my party, I can always come to your room tonight." He ran a hand along his arm, his smile turning wicked. "Or you could come to mine. It's really great—I'd love to show you the bed."

Felix smiled back, but shook his head. "Not tonight."

John's expression soured. "So you're just going to freeze me out, like Cat did to Richard."

"I can't freeze you out." Felix put his hand over his chest. "You're inside me."

John put his hand over Felix's. "So then why won't you come with me?" He sounded plaintive now. "I'm happy! For the first time since I lost my mom, I have an actual *life*. Isn't that why we did this—so I could live?"

"Yes." And it was true—just not for the reasons John currently thought.

"Then come to my party. Meet my new friends. I'm having such a wonderful time, but I want you with me. I *ache*, Felix. I ache for you."

Felix wanted to draw John into his arms, but instead, he pulled away. He remembered his promise to John, to not let him become someone he was not. Playing along with his new life would break that promise.

"I'm sorry, but I cannot go with you. Please don't ask me again; my answer will not change."

John's expression hardened. "Why not? Is it because of Lo?" His lip curled into a sneer. "She still thinks she's better than me. Is this her vengeance—keeping you from me?"

"Why would she be trying to get revenge on you?"

"Because she doesn't approve! She thinks we're doing something wrong, but we aren't." John pointed in the direction of the Extras' cabin. "I have been at the same place in my life as the people we take, and trust me, we are doing them a favor. I wanted to die for years, but was too afraid to pull the trigger."

"But you've changed your mind," Felix said quietly. "Surely some of them may as well."

John laughed—an ugly sound. "And what do they have to live for? They're miserable junkies and runaways, whores and hobos—the only lives they had were physical—their stupid organs continuing to breathe and pump blood and piss and shit, and what is that worth? Nothing to them. But it's everything to us."

"They're people, John," Felix said quietly. "Living, breathing people."

John rubbed his face. "All right, fine. If Lo has a problem with putting people out of their misery, then maybe she'll feel better if we go after bad guys. That ought to appeal to her smug self-righteousness. The city is full of rapists and stalkers and murderers and thieves. That's got to be a good thing, right? Getting those people off the street?"

"You felt sorry for them, too, once."

"And I was a fucking idiot for it!" John exploded. "Christ, Vince harassed me—assaulted me, and I felt sorry for him? What was wrong with me? He deserved to pay." His face suddenly twisted from anger to thoughtfulness. "You know, it doesn't matter who we take. Either they're miserable and we're doing them a favor, or they're evil and deserve to die." He laughed a little. "There's no reason to feel bad about any of it."

Felix peered at him. He was so intent on justifying himself—was there perhaps a little of the real John still in there? "If everyone deserves to die, then what is a life for?"

John's brows furrowed. "What do you mean by that?"

"What is a life for?" Felix repeated. "You said you are happy to have a life, but just now you said that no one deserves to live. Are you the exception?"

John slapped him. It didn't really hurt—John wasn't strong enough—but it did surprise him. John's contorted expression was almost like a mask; Felix could barely recognize him.

"Fuck you for trying to ruin this for me!" he spat. "And don't look at me like that; it's not like I hurt you. If I really wanted to hurt you, believe me, you'd know!"

Suddenly, John let out a sharp cry and put his hand to his head, as if in pain. He stumbled; Felix caught him before he could fall.

"Are you all right?" Felix asked, still holding John in his arms.

John looked up at him. His face was so flushed it was as if he had a fever. "I don't know." He looked at Felix in confusion. "I feel like I've forgotten something important." John put his arms around Felix and laid his head on Felix's chest. "When you hold me like this, I forget. But

I don't remember what I forget." John's arms tightened around him. "I feel like I'm dreaming sometimes. I dreamed that I hurt you. Why would I do that?"

Felix kissed his temple. As much as he wanted John to remember, it was important that he stay ignorant for now. It was enough to know that his John was still in there. "You should go back to your party."

"My party?" John asked, still sounding confused. When Felix was sure John had his footing, he pulled away. John shook his head vigorously. "My party," he said again, more sure this time. "Yes. And you aren't coming?"

"No."

For a moment, Felix was afraid they would have the whole dreadful argument again, but John just shook his head. "All right, then." He turned and headed back toward the mansion.

Felix didn't leave right away. His heart was pounding again, a fresh stab with every beat. It didn't matter. He was strong enough to endure it.

FELIX DID NOT fall back into torpor again. Lo dropped the illusion in his room; after Felix and John's last fight, it seemed unlikely John would be looking for him any time soon. He still spent most of his nights with Cat—that is, when she was there. She and Lo were out quite often. He marked the days off the calendar diligently at each dawn, anxious for the day they would all be free.

Unfortunately, there was a downside to the passage of time. Felix had to take one more victim. Lo procured them as she had before, leading her latest find to Felix's room before disappearing. She never said anything when she brought a victim. He supposed he couldn't blame her—what was there to say?

Felix did not pounce right away, as he had done with the others. He stood facing the opposite wall until he heard the door close.

"So, uh, are we going to party, or what?" The voice was male and young. It sounded like he was trying to affect coolness, but he couldn't hide the waver in his voice. Besides, Felix could smell his fear—just a whiff of sweetness so far. He must be very brave indeed to only just now become alarmed. The last two had already been frightened out of their wits.

"Do you know what a life is for?" Felix asked.

The young man didn't respond at first. "Your friend said there was going to be a party." His voice wavered further. The smell grew stronger, coming off him in waves.

Felix turned around at last to look at him, his last victim. He was dressed in tattered jeans and an oversized flannel shirt. A knitted beanie sat on top of his long, dirty blond hair.

"What is a life for?" Felix asked again.

The boy stumbled backward until his back hit the door. He tried the handle, but it was locked, naturally. Felix wanted to tell him not to be afraid, but that would defeat the purpose.

The boy shut his eyes briefly and breathed. When he spoke again, his voice was steadier. "Listen, man, you want me to suck your dick? I'll do it. I'll let you fuck me. And then I'll just go, okay?"

Felix looked into his large, blue eyes—paler than John's, almost translucent. Felix held out his hand. "Come sit with me."

Felix thought that he would try the door again, but he didn't. The smell of him was overpowering now; he was *ripe*, his fear at that perfect level before it spoiled into outright terror. But instead of trying to escape, he put his trembling hand into Felix's and let himself be led to the bed.

Felix encouraged him to sit on the edge of the bed. Those eyes of his remained wide as saucers, but he did not blink or look away. To Felix's great shock, he felt a great tenderness toward this boy, despite that fact that he didn't even know his name. In fact, he loved him.

The heart inside him felt as if it were growing, bursting forth from him in painful expansion. He found he loved his victims, each and every one, although it pained him to love those whom he had hurt so terribly. He loved the dancers in the nightclubs he frequented, and the strangers he passed on the street every night. He loved people in his past—the stars and the starlets, the successful and the sycophants, and all those in between. He even loved the wicked, like poor, lost Vince; and the heartless, like Richard, who Felix could now see as a pitiful creature whose power was nothing in comparison to the sheer scope of all of humanity.

Most of all, he loved John. John, with his sarcasm that masked a deep and abiding compassion for all things. John, who had taken a chance by letting himself love Felix. John, whose heart was so good he could feel compassion even toward those who had wronged him. He had said Felix might understand once he had a heart of his own, but it hadn't hit him until just now. It amazed Felix, the abundance of his love. Strange, then, that he should feel so light, as if he had broken free of shackles he hadn't even been aware of.

He brushed a few strands of hair from the boy's face. "When people say a life has been wasted, I couldn't understand what it meant. If a life can be wasted, then it must have some purpose—some reason for being that has been squandered, yes?"

"I-I guess," the boy stammered.

Felix shook his head. "I don't think so, actually. A life is its own reason; the only purpose is to live it. And thus no life can be wasted."

"That's like, really deep," the boy said, his voice still trembling. "So can I go now?"

"Not yet, I'm afraid," Felix said as his fangs began to protrude.

The boy sucked in a breath to scream, but Felix took him before he had the chance. When he was finished, he laid the boy's limp form tenderly on the bed. A calm had settled over him, despite the terror and the distaste of that moment. This boy would find life again when this was all over. And so would Felix and John and Lo and Cat. They would all have lives—imperfect, filled with as many hardships as pleasures. But those hardships were what made the pleasures possible—it was impossible to feel true joy unless you were also capable of feeling real pain. There would be no one happy ending, no perfect miracle that would solve all their troubles. But they would get to *live*, and that in itself was miracle enough.

Eighteen: Curses, Foiled at Last

"HOW DO I look?" Cat asked, twirling in her blue dress. It was the sort of gown one would wear to a movie premiere—a slinky number that sparkled like the ocean, paired with elbow-length white gloves. A sapphire necklace adorned her neck.

"Beautiful, as always," Felix said. He himself was dressed in a tuxedo—the same one he had worn at his "wedding." He normally disliked dressing up, but the event called for it. This was the night they would become human. Or else, it was the night they would be damned for all time. Either way, it would be eventful.

Lo entered the room, carrying a bag of fast food and a large soda. She put her meal on the coffee table before going over to give Cat a quick kiss on the cheek. "Nice dress."

"I have one picked out for you as well." Cat took her hand and led her over to a yellow dress she'd hung on the armoire. "Isn't it lovely?" She took it off the hanger and held it up to Lo. "I had it made for me for the premiere of *The Girls in Their Dresses*, but ended up not wearing it. I never really could pull off yellow, but I think it will look beautiful on you."

Lo rolled her eyes in faux exasperation. "You do know that this is the last time you'll ever get me into a 'gown,' right?"

"We'll see about that." They kissed, for real this time. Felix couldn't help but smile. He even had the audacity to feel a tiny bit of hope.

"You'd better eat," Cat said when they parted. She hung the dress back up. "Richard and John are expecting us at eight o'clock. You need to be dressed."

"Yeah, yeah," Lo said. She wolfed down her burger but did not finish her enormous soda. Instead, she went into the bathroom. When she returned, she held the blue rose in her hand.

They all stared at it for a moment as it shimmered in the light, impossibly beautiful. It had bloomed the previous evening and then been hidden away. Felix's heart thumped madly at the sight of it. Lo held their entire future in her hand.

Cat broke the silence. "I thought we weren't going to use it until later."

"You two aren't," Lo said. "Unfortunately, we are going to have to wait until the last minute to avoid suspicion, since Richard and John would definitely feel your curses being lifted. But there's no reason we can't get rid of mine right now."

She plucked off a few petals and dropped them in her soda. She stirred it with her straw and then took a long drink. She finished with a loud slurp.

"Well?" Cat asked anxiously. "Do you feel any differently? Are you cured?"

She shrugged. "I should be. Adelaide said it would work."

"Seems a bit anticlimactic."

Lo laughed a little. "Don't worry. If everything goes as planned, you'll get your big cinematic climax tonight."

"What do you mean?"

"Me and Adelaide have a plan. I thought it would be better not to tell you the exact details so you don't accidentally give anything away. It's got to go down at midnight, though. I'll pour your wine ahead of time. Just be prepared to drink when I give you the signal."

"And what's the signal?"

"Trust me, you'll know." Lo touched Cat on the shoulder. "Hey," she said gently. "It's going to be all right. I'm not going to die."

Cat swept Lo into her arms, hugging her fiercely. "You better not." She pulled away, wiping her eyes with a finger. "Oh dear," she said, looking down at her bloodstained finger. "I'm going to have do my makeup again."

Felix stood up. "I'll help."

She smiled at him. "I'll go wash my face." She disappeared into the bathroom.

When she was gone, Lo turned to Felix. "How are you feeling?"

"Nervous."

"Don't be. The only thing you have to do is drink some wine. Me and Adelaide will handle the rest."

Felix looked down at his hands. "What if it doesn't work? Are you truly going to destroy us?"

"It's going to work," she said firmly. "I need you to believe me, okay?"

Felix nodded and tried his best to look confident.

Lo sighed and gave him a pat on the arm. "Guess I ought to get ready."

She fetched her dress and headed to the bathroom just as Cat emerged. Cat sat down at her vanity; Felix joined her.

"After tonight, you won't have much use for my makeup skills," he commented. He felt a strange pang in his heart at the thought. "Why does that make me sad? It's a good thing this ritual is coming to an end."

"I feel much the same way." Cat took his hands in hers and squeezed. "Hearts are peculiar things."

They shared a smile. Felix reached for her foundation and began.

The appointed hour arrived. Lo put the rest of the rose petals into a bottle of white wine, giving it a good shake. She said a quick spell to transport it to a bucket of ice she'd had set at the theater; it would join the refreshments Richard had commanded his staff to prepare. With that done, they all descended the stairs together. Richard and John were waiting for them, dressed to the nines.

"Such visions of beauty," Richard said, his hungry eyes dancing between Cat and Lo both. Richard offered both of his arms. "Shall we, ladies?"

Cat smiled and took her place at his side. Even with everything that was at stake, Lo couldn't manage the same level of feigned enjoyment, but Felix got the impression Richard took perverse pleasure at her obvious discomfort.

Felix turned to John, who was looking at him coolly. They had not spoken since their fight in the gardens. Felix looked deeply into his eyes, trying to search for the John he knew was still inside. But John's eyes had always been inscrutable to Felix, and tonight was no different.

"Are we going to have a nice night tonight, or am I going to have to put up with more of your moralizing?"

In place of an answer, Felix drew John into his arms and kissed him until his rigid muscles relaxed into his embrace.

Richard's raucous laughter pulled them apart. "Although I'm glad to see Felix has come around, there will be more than enough time for hanky-panky later on. Come now—I've been looking forward to this."

A limo waited for them at the front door, which was rather ridiculous since it was a mere ten-minute walk. But Richard was determined to make a night of it. Philip's replacement, neatly dressed in his uniform, held the door open. Felix tried not to look, but he still got a glimpse of the man's unnaturally still face, his complexion already turning gray.

As they all settled in their seats in the limo, Richard popped open a bottle of champagne, pouring them all a glass. "This was a splendid idea, my darling," he said to Cat. "A celebration of old triumphs as we move toward the new." He held up his glass. "To new beginnings!"

"To new beginnings!" Cat echoed gaily.

They all clinked glasses and drank, some of them more enthusiastically than others. Richard leveled his gaze at Lo. "I'm so pleased that you're joining us at last." He put a hand on Cat's thigh. "And don't think for a moment that I haven't seen the way you look at my wife. We would be more than happy to welcome you into our bed tonight."

"If you mean that, then you'll let her sit over here with me," Lo said evenly. Felix thought that her restraint was heroic.

When Richard gave the nod, Cat moved beside Lo. They clasped hands, which signaled more comfort than passion, but Richard seemed too pleased with his perceived conquest to see the difference.

"I knew you would come around eventually." He drank more champagne. "Everything will change tonight, I can feel it."

"Me too," Lo said, deadpan.

Within a few minutes, the limo stopped again, and they all climbed out. The theater was lit up, brighter than a thousand stars. There was even a red carpet leading to the front door.

John started laughing. "You really did go for the full fantasy, didn't you?" he said to Richard. He waved at the imaginary crowds.

Richard laughed as well and waved his hand. The sound of applause suddenly thundered into existence. They all jumped in surprise, but soon John was laughing again.

Richard turned to Cat. "Just like the old times, eh?"

Cat just smiled in response.

The interior of the theater had been done up as well, brought back to its earlier elegance. In the 1920s, all the theaters had been magnificent, having more in common with opera houses than the modern chain movie places. Richard's was small, given that it was private, but he had made sure that it possessed that same opulent feel.

There was a table set up with refreshments for the witches and wineglasses for all of them. Several wine bottles adorned the table or else rested in a bucket of ice. One of those bottles was the one that held their cure, but Felix couldn't be sure which.

"Let's start with a red," Richard said. He selected a bottle and poured each of them a glass. The witches made themselves little plates from the appetizers offered. With that done, they went to their seats. Lo subtly made sure they sat in the proper places: with Cat at the far end, Richard on her right, then John, Felix, and at last Lo herself, so she could move quickly out to the aisle. Once they were settled, Richard waved a hand. The lights went down, the organ began to play, and the projector switched on, streaming light on the screen. The show had begun.

They started with the *Hatshepsut: Queen of Egypt*. Felix remembered how difficult that shoot had been, since Cat couldn't be filmed in the sun. Her Hatshepsut held her court in throne rooms and temples. She simmered in the role, every inch a powerful queen.

After a brief break, they moved to *The Deathly Lover*. The film seemed to spark some in-joke between John and Richard, because they began laughing and chatting. Felix didn't pay them much heed, for he was fascinated by the image of himself playing across the scene. His only film appearance. Watching the silvery screen image made him feel as if he were being haunted by himself—that carefree, heartless creature he had been.

When *The Deathly Lover* was finished, Richard turned to Cat. "What next, do you think? *Mermaids of the Blue Lagoon*?"

"How about *Hamlet*?"

"I had thought we would end the evening with your greatest triumph, but I suppose it doesn't matter. *Hamlet* it is!" He waved his hand.

As the movie started, Lo stood up and went to the refreshment table. She entered the aisle behind them, holding two glasses of white wine. She gave one to Felix and one to Cat, which meant the time was near.

The reel began to play. But instead of the credits for *Hamlet* coming up, a scene of a beach appeared in black-and-white.

Richard frowned. "What's this?" He waved his hand again, but the movie didn't change.

Felix felt a tap on his shoulder. "Now," Lo whispered. Felix glanced over at Cat. They drained their glasses at the same time.

A parasol came in to view, as if someone was stepping in from behind the camera. The woman holding the parasol turned around to face the camera and smiled.

John gasped. "Mom?"

Felix heard Lo mumble something quickly under her breath as she put her hands on Richard and Cat's shoulders. As soon as she was finished, she did the same to John and Felix.

Richard got unsteadily to his feet. "What is this?" He sounded as confused as he was angry. "What the *fuck* is this?"

Richard stumbled out into the aisle, but he didn't get far. He clasped a hand over his chest and fell to his knees. Felix looked to John, who hadn't moved. He was breathing so fast he was hyperventilating. An enormous thud shook Felix's chest; from the way John jolted beside him, he could tell he felt the same. John turned to look at him, his eyes wide and wild.

"Felix?" He spoke as if he hadn't seen him in a long time. "What's happening?"

Relief poured over him. John sounded so much more like himself. Felix put an arm around him and drew him close. "It's all right."

The picture on the screen was slowly gaining color, the lapping waves and sunny sky turning blue, the sand glowing like gold. And behind her, there was a crowd of people, all dressed from different eras of the last seventy-five years. They looked joyous in the way people look when a great wrong is about to be righted.

Adelaide smiled at them from the screen. "It's time to go, Richard."

"No!" he snarled. He crawled down the aisle, trying to get away from the screen, but his progress was stopped by Astray, who looked disdainfully down at him.

The cat wasn't the real impediment, though. It was the fifteen people behind her. The Extras had woken up. They were silent and pale, but they were awake.

Now Richard began a desperate scramble backward, only to run into Lo. "What have you done?" he shrieked.

"I gave you back your heart," she said. "Don't you feel it? I bet it's beating like a motherfucker right now."

He snarled and tried to grab her, but then he spasmed in pain. John spasmed, too; Felix held him tight through it. Three wisps of white floated out from his mouth and into the crowd of Extras. Felix recognized his last three victims as a wisp returned to each of them. They breathed in deeply and began to look well again.

A larger number of wisps began to flow out of Richard—not only through his mouth, but through his ears, his nose, his eyes. The rest of the Extras were restored, but the wisps didn't stop. Richard clawed at his face, trying to stop it, but it kept going, on and on. They floated up to the screen.

The scene on the screen grew even more celebratory; they could hear cheers. Richard had ceased to move, lying curled in the fetal position on the floor. Cat stood up and went to him. Felix thought he must be dead, but he wasn't quite yet. He was, however, very old. Older than Felix thought a man was capable of appearing.

He looked up at her with milky white eyes. "Catherine? My Cat?" His voice was so frail. He put a hand on the hem of her skirt. "Is that you?"

Cat knelt beside him. "Yes, it's me," she said with surprising gentleness.

"What's happened?" he asked, his eyes darting around in confusion.

"You're dying."

Richard began to weep. "I don't want to die."

She ran a hand through his thin hair. "I know. But you must."

"I'm frightened—so frightened..." He wept so bitterly that it was hard not to feel sorry for him. "I've been wicked, so very wicked...what will become of me?"

Cat just shushed him, taking his hand in her own.

He clutched it one last time. "Your hands—they're so warm."

Those were his last words. He went limp in her arms. His body began to disintegrate, until all that was left was a pile of ash.

No one moved for a long moment. At last, Cat stood up and brushed herself off. As she did so, the ash vanished as if it had never been there, leaving her clean. Lo embraced her.

"You didn't owe him that kindness," Lo said.

Cat smiled. "I owed it to myself."

On the screen, the crowd had begun to disperse until only Adelaide was left. She smiled at them all, and then looked to John in particular.

"I love you," she said. Her voice was clear and beautiful.

John started weeping, so hard that his body shook with it. "I love you, too," he managed to say.

She smiled at them all again and then gave them a cheery wave. The color began to fade into black-and-white as she made her way toward the sparkling ocean, and then the screen went dark.

Lo waved her hand, turning the lights on. The Extras were all stumbling around, confused, but they were not Felix's concern at the moment. Lo and Cat could help them. Right now, John needed him.

"I'm sorry," John said, still racked with sobs. "Oh my God, Felix, I am *so sorry...*"

Felix stopped him with a kiss. "You have nothing to be sorry for," he said when they parted. "It was part of the plan." He smiled and took John's hand. "And it worked!" He brought John's hand to his chest, so that he could feel the heart that was beating there.

John's sobs stopped as his expression changed to one of wonder. "You're human?"

"It appears so." Felix moved their hands until they were over John's chest, over his own beating heart. "And all is right here as well."

John started crying again. Felix's own eyes began to water. When he blinked, tears rolled down his cheeks. Real tears. He touched his own face; his fingers came away wet, but clear. No more blood.

John noticed as well. He started to laugh with joy, which set Felix off laughing as well. They embraced, holding each other as their bodies roiled with the full gamut of human emotions—relief at what they'd escaped, grief at the pain they'd endured, regret at the wrongs they'd committed, but mostly with joy. They each had lives now—real, human lives, with a future as wide as the ocean. They were no longer cursed.

They were blessed.

Epilogue

THE FERRY TO Catalina was crowded and the weather was less than perfect. John had hoped for a clear day for his one-year anniversary, but the sky was a stubborn gray. It was the infamous southern Californian "June Gloom"; he still wasn't used to temperatures actually dropping when his Midwestern sensibilities said they ought to be rising. He shivered a little and wished he hadn't packed his jacket away.

Felix emerged from the interior of the ferry to join John on the deck. "I brought coffee." He held out a Styrofoam cup.

John accepted it. "Thanks." He took a sip and made a face; it was lukewarm at best. "You'd think they'd make sure that the coffee was hot on a day like this?"

"Are you cold?" Felix asked. "Here, you can have my jacket—"

"No, no—then you'll be cold!"

"I don't mind."

"But I do."

Felix looked thoughtful for a moment. "I have an idea." He set his coffee down and pulled out one arm of his jacket. "Put your arm in this sleeve."

"You want to share a jacket?"

"Why not?" Felix said with a grin.

John put down his coffee and worked his arm into the sleeve. Felix's jacket was large, but definitely not big enough for two grown men. Plus, the height difference made it even more awkward. By the time they'd wrestled themselves into it, they were both laughing. John supposed he could have done a spell to warm himself a little, but this was much more fun.

They maneuvered themselves enough to reach their coffee cups with their free hands. Somehow, the coffee tasted better to John now, even if it was lukewarm and stale. He nuzzled Felix's chin, enjoying the scrape of Felix's stubble against his skin. It turned out that Felix was able to grow a very impressive beard, although they both decided they liked him better without one.

"How much longer until we get there?" Felix asked.

"Probably another fifteen minutes or so. We should be able to see the island soon."

"Did you remember to call to confirm our reservation?"

"Yeah."

"Have you remembered your sunscreen?"

"It's a cloudy day," John protested.

"You're putting some on when we get to the island." When he had first become mortal, Felix had gotten a vicious sunburn and was now obsessed with sunscreen safety.

"And did you remember your Nicorette patches?"

"Yes, *Dad*." John had been trying to quit smoking, but it still remained a struggle.

"Why would you call me your dad? Is it like that movie we watched with all the spanking?" He lowered his voice. "That hardly seems appropriate in public, but you can call me 'Dad' later in the hotel, if it pleases you."

John couldn't help but laugh. A lot had changed in their lives—for example, they now both had one—but Felix was still reliably Felix. Which was a good thing, because he loved the hell out of Felix.

After Richard's death, John had inherited everything. He'd given a million dollars to each of the surviving Extras, who were under the impression that they'd won the lottery. He and Lo had muddled their memories enough that they would forget their time at Happy Endings. Money couldn't solve all the problems that had led them to despair before Richard took them, but it certainly didn't hurt.

John had sold Happy Endings, which gave them enough cash to do basically whatever they wanted with the rest of their lives. They both agreed they didn't want to live lavishly; they'd found a nice little house in Silver Lake. Since Richard had secured a new identity for him, the police weren't looking for him. John used what he had learned from Richard to forge a new identity for Lo as well. The Diner Massacre was still a subject of fascination for the public, but John used his magic to keep himself and Lo obscured enough that people didn't recognize either of them from the mug shots.

He'd told the neighbors he was an artist, which was true. He'd begun painting again, and had even managed to sell a few pieces, although certainly not enough to make a living. The neighbors all suspected it was Felix's inheritance that kept them living in style. Although Felix was much more sensible than he used to be, he was still not quite caught up with the times to pass himself off as anything but a lovable eccentric who hadn't worked a day in his life, so that was the story that they'd invented for him. He was famous for walking Astray on a leash around the neighborhood each day. People got a kick out of a cat on a leash. John couldn't understand why Astray put up with it, but he sometimes got the impression that she liked Felix better than him nowadays.

"Fuck, it's cold." Lo had emerged from the cabin as well and joined Felix and John, with Cat trailing not far behind her.

"You think this is cold?" John said. "Try winter in the Midwest. Now *that's* cold."

"Then why are you bundled up against your husband like you're in the middle of a snowstorm?"

John laughed. "Guess I've gone native."

"Well, I don't care if it's cloudy the whole week," Cat huffed. "I brought a bikini and I intend to use it."

Lo grinned. "I have no issue with that."

They kissed. Lo and Cat weren't married; Cat was understandably skittish about binding herself to someone so permanently. John had split his fortune with Lo, who bought a house in downtown LA. She and Cat lived together, although they hadn't spent much time in their new house. They'd just got back from Europe, and after their Catalina trip was done, they were going on a tour of Japan.

An elderly man approached them. "Excuse me, young lady," he said to Cat. "I hope you don't mind me saying so, but you bear the most remarkable resemblance to my favorite movie star."

Cat tossed her now waist-length hair over one shoulder. "Oh yeah?" she said in her best "modern" voice. She had been practicing.

"Yes. Her name was Catherine Neville." The old man's gaze went a little dreamy. "I was just a child when I saw her in *Mermaids of the Blue Lagoon*. They don't make stars like her anymore."

Cat smiled. "I'm sure she would be pleased to hear it," she said. Then she hastily added: "Dude."

Lo put her hand around Cat's waist. "Nice to meet you!" she said in a clear "go away" tone.

The man gave her a funny look and left.

When he was gone, they all set their gazes on the horizon. "There," John said after a few minutes. "I see it!"

Even in the gray weather, the island was beautiful. As they grew closer, they could make out the dozens of cheery sailboats anchored in the blue bay. The brightly colored buildings of the town of Avalon seemed to defy the gloomy weather.

"I can't wait to go snorkeling!" Cat said. "And hiking—there's an enormous botanical garden that sounds absolutely gorgeous."

"And the restaurants!" Felix said, equally enthusiastic. "I am going to eat so many crab legs." Felix nudged John. "And we'll get you some better coffee."

John smiled up at him. "Actually, I think I'm pretty happy with this coffee." Felix and the girls went back into the cabin to get their luggage together. John went to throw his coffee cup away before he joined them. He took a quick peek at his phone, looking up the ten-day forecast. It would take a couple of days, but looked like the future was going to be sunny.

About the Author

Sera Trevor is terminally curious and views the thirty-five book limit at her local library as a dare. She's a little bit interested in just about everything, which is probably why she can't pin herself to one subgenre. Her books are populated with dragons, vampire movie stars, shadow people, and internet trolls. (Not in the same book, obviously, although that would be interesting!) Her works have been nominated for several Goodreads M/M Romance Reader's Choice Awards, including Best Contemporary, Best Fantasy, and Best Debut, for which she won third prize in 2015 for her novella *Consorting with Dragons*.

She lives in California with her husband, two kids, and a cat the size of three cats. You can keep up with her new releases and gain access to bonus content by signing up for her newsletter.

Email: seratrevor@gmail.com

Facebook: www.facebook.com/SeraTrevorauthor

Twitter: www.twitter.com/SeraTrevor

Website: www.seratrevor.com

Newsletter: www.seratrevor.com/newsletter.html

Also Available from NineStar Press

Connect with NineStar Press

www.ninestarpress.com

www.facebook.com/ninestarpress

www.facebook.com/groups/NineStarNiche

www.twitter.com/ninestarpress

www.tumblr.com/blog/ninestarpress

CPSIA information can be obtained
at www.ICGtesting.com
Printed in the USA
BVOW06s0949060218
506816BV00009B/123/P